Richard A. (Richard Anthony) Proctor

Rough ways made smooth

a series of familiar essays on scientific subjects

Richard A. (Richard Anthony) Proctor

Rough ways made smooth
a series of familiar essays on scientific subjects

ISBN/EAN: 9783337414245

Printed in Europe, USA, Canada, Australia, Japan

Cover: Foto ©Andreas Hilbeck / pixelio.de

More available books at **www.hansebooks.com**

"KNOWLEDGE" LIBRARY

ROUGH WAYS MADE SMOOTH

A SERIES OF

Familiar Essays on Scientific Subjects

BY

RICHARD A. PROCTOR

AUTHOR OF

'MYTHS AND MARVELS OF ASTRONOMY' 'PLEASANT WAYS IN SCIENCE'
'SCIENCE BYWAYS' 'THE BORDERLAND OF SCIENCE' AND
'LIGHT SCIENCE FOR LEISURE HOURS'

NEW EDITION

LONDON
LONGMANS, GREEN, AND CO.
AND NEW YORK : 15 EAST 16th STREET
1888

PREFACE.

IT is scarcely necessary for me to explain the plan of the present work, because I have already—in introducing my 'Light Science for Leisure Hours,' my 'Science Byways,' and my 'Pleasant Ways in Science'—described the method on which, as I think, such treatises as the present should be written. This work deals with similar subjects in a similar way; but I think the experience I have acquired in writing other works on the same plan has enabled me to avoid some defects in the present work which I have recognised in the others.

The list of subjects indicates sufficiently the range over which the present volume extends. Some of them might be judged by their names to be in no way connected with science, but it will be found that none have been treated except in their scientific significance, though in familiar and untechnical terms.

RICHARD A. PROCTOR.

S.S. 'ARIZONA,' IRISH SEA
    October 18, 1879.

ROUGH WAYS MADE SMOOTH.

THE SUN'S CORONA AND
HIS SPOTS.

ONE of the most important results of observations made upon the eclipse of July 29, 1878, indicates the existence of a law of sympathy, so to speak, between the solar corona and the sun-spots. The inquiry into this relation seems to me likely to lead to a very interesting series of researches, from which may possibly result an interpretation not only of the relation itself, should it be found really to exist, but of the mystery of the sun-spot period. I speak of the sun-spot period as mysterious, because even if we admit (which I think we cannot do) that the sun-spots are produced in some way by the action of the planets upon the sun, it would still remain altogether a mystery how this action operated. When all the known facts respecting the sun-spots are carefully considered, no theory yet advanced respecting them seems at all satisfactory, while no approach even has been made to an explanation of their periodic increase and diminution in number. This seems to me one of the most interesting problems which astronomers have at present to deal with; nor do I despair of seeing it satisfactorily solved within no very long interval of time. Should the recognition of a sympathy between the corona and the sun-spots be satisfactorily established, an important step in advance will have been made,—possibly even the key to the enigma will be found to have been discovered.

I propose now to consider, first, whether the evidence we have on this subject is sufficient, and afterwards to discuss some of the ideas suggested by the relations which have been recognised as existing between the sun-spots, the sierra, the coloured prominences, and the zodiacal light.

The evidence from the recent eclipses indicates beyond all possibility of doubt or question, that during the years when sun-spots were numerous, in 1870 and 1871, the corona, at least on the days of the total solar eclipses in those years, presented an appearance entirely different from that of the corona seen on July 29, 1878, when the sun was almost free from spots. This will be more fully indicated further on. At present it is necessary to notice only (1) that whereas in 1870 and 1871 the inner corona extended at least 250,000 miles from the sun, it reached only to a height of some 70,000 miles in 1878; (2) in 1870 and 1871 it possessed a very complicated structure, whereas in 1878 the definite structure could be recognised only in two parts of the inner corona; (3) in 1871 the corona was pink, whereas in 1878 it was pearly white; (4) the corona was ten times brighter in 1871 than in 1878; lastly, in 1871 the light of the corona came in part from glowing gas, whereas in July, 1878, the light came chiefly, if not wholly, from glowing solid or liquid matter. I must here point out, that the evidence of change, however satisfactory in itself, would be quite insufficient to establish the general theory that the corona sympathises with the solar photosphere in the special manner suggested by the recent eclipse observations. There are few practices more unscientific, or more likely to lead to erroneous theorising, than that of basing a general theory on a small number of observations. In this case we have, in fact, but a single observed correspondence, though the observations establishing it form a series. It has been shown that so far as the special sun-spot period from the minimum of 1867 to the minimum of 1878 is concerned, there has been a certain correspondence between the aspect of the corona and the state of the sun's surface, with regard to spots. To assume from that single correspondence that the corona and the sun-spots are related in the same way, would be hazardous in the extreme. We may indeed find, when we consider other matters, that the probability of a general relation of this sort existing is so great antecedently, that but slight direct evidence would be required to establish the existence of the relation. But it must be remembered that before the eclipse of 1878 was observed, with the special result I have noticed, few were bold enough to assert the probable existence of any such relationship ; and certainly no one asserted that the probability was very strong. I believe, indeed, that no one spoke more definitely in favour of the theory that the corona probably sympathises with the sun-spots than I did myself before the recent eclipse ; but certainly I should not then have been willing to say that I considered the evidence very strong.

We must then look for evidence of a more satisfactory kind.

Now, although during the two centuries preceding the invention of the spectroscope and the initiation of the solar physical researches now in progress, observations of eclipses were not very carefully conducted, yet we have some records of the appearance of the corona on different occasions, which, combined with the known law of sun-spot periodicity, may enable us to generalise more safely than we could from observations during the present spot-period, though these observations have been far more exact than the older ones. I propose to examine some of these. Necessarily I must make some selection. I need hardly say that even if there were no such relation as that which seems to be indicated by recent observations, and if my purpose were simply to prove, either that such a relation exists or that it does not, I could very readily bring before the reader of these pages what would seem like the most satisfactory evidence that the relation is real. I must ask him to believe, however, that my purpose is to ascertain where the truth lies. I shall neither introduce any observation of the corona because it seems specially favourable to the theory that the corona sympathises with the photosphere, nor omit any, because it seems definitely opposed to that theory. To prevent any possibility of being unconsciously prejudiced, I shall take a series of coronal observations collected together by myself, on account of their intrinsic interest, several years ago, when I had not in my thoughts any theory respecting periodic changes in the corona—the series, namely, which is included in the sixth chapter of my treatise on the sun. Each of these observations I shall consider in connection with the known condition of the sun as to spots, and those results which seem to bear *clearly*, whether favourably or unfavourably, on the theory we are enquiring into, I shall bring before the reader.

Kepler, whose attention had been specially drawn to the subject of the light seen round the sun during total eclipse, by certain statements which Clavius had made respecting the eclipse of 1567, describes the eclipse of 1605 in the following terms :—' The whole body of the sun was completely covered for a short time, but around it there shone a brilliant light of a reddish hue and uniform breadth, which occupied a considerable portion of the heavens.' The corona thus seen may fairly be assumed to have resembled in extent that of 1871. A bright corona, reaching like that seen during the eclipse of July 1878 to a height of only about 70,000 miles from the sun's surface, would certainly not have been described by Kepler as occupying a considerable portion of the heavens, for a height of 70,000 miles would correspond only to about a twelfth of the sun's diameter ; and a ring so narrow would be described very differently. It seems, then, that in 1605 a corona was seen which corresponded with that observed when the sun has had many spots on his surface. Now we have no record of the condition of the sun with regard to spots in 1605; but we know that the year 1615 was one of many spots, and the year 1610 one of few spots; whence we may conclude safely that the year 1605 was one of many spots. This case then is in favour of the theory we are examining.

In passing we may ask whether the observation by Clavius which had perplexed Kepler, may not throw some light on our subject. Clavius says that the eclipse of 1567 which should have been total was annular. The usual explanation of this has been that the corona was intensely bright close to the sun. And though Kepler considered that his own observation of a broad reddish corona satisfactorily removed Clavius's difficulty, it seems tolerably clear that the corona seen by Clavius must have been very unlike the corona seen by Kepler. In fact the former must have been like the corona seen in July, 1878, much smaller than the average, but correspondingly increased in lustre. Now with regard to the sun-spot period we can go back to the year 1567, though not quite so securely as we could wish. Taking the average sun-spot period at eleven years, and calculating back from the minimum of spots in the year 1610, we get four years of minimum solar disturbance, 1599, 1588, 1577, and 1566. We should have obtained the same result if we had used the more exact period, eleven one-ninth years, and had taken 1610·8 for the epoch of least solar disturbance (1610·8 meaning about the middle of October, 1610). Thus the year 1567 was a year of few sun-spots, probably occupying almost exactly the same position in the sun-spot period as the year 1878. Clavius's observation, then, is in favour of our theory.

But another observation between Clavius's and Kepler's may here be noticed. Jensenius, who observed the eclipse of 1598 at Torgau in Germany, noticed that, at the time of mid-totality, a bright light shone round the moon. On this occasion, remarks Grant, the phenomenon was generally supposed to arise from a defect in the totality of the eclipse, though Kepler strenuously contended that such an explanation was at variance with the relation between the values of the apparent diameters of the sun and moon as computed for the time of the eclipse by aid of the solar and lunar tables. The corona, then, must have resembled that seen by Clavius, and since the year 1598 must have been very near the time of fewest spots, this observation accords with the theory we are examining.

The next observation is that made by Wyberd during the eclipse of 1652. Here there is a difficulty arising from the strange way in which the sun-spots behaved during the interval from 1645 to 1679. According to M. Wolf, whose investigation of the subject has been very close and searching, there was a maximum of sun-spots in 1639 followed by a minimum in 1645, the usual interval of about six years having elapsed ; but there came a maximum in 1655, ten years later, followed by a minimum in 1666, eleven years later, so that actually twenty-one years would seem to have elapsed between successive minima (1645 and 1666). Then came a maximum in 1675, nine years later, and a minimum in 1679, four years later. Between the maxima of 1639 and 1675, including two spot periods, an interval of thirty-six years elapsed. There is no other instance on record, so far as I know, of so long an interval as this for two spot-periods. In passing, I would notice how little this circumstance accords with the theory that the sun-spots follow an exact law, or that from observations of the sun, means can ever be found for forming a trustworthy system of weather prediction, even if we assumed (which has always seemed to me a very daring assumption), that terrestrial weather is directly dependent on the progress of the sun-spot period. But here the irregularity of the spot changes affects us only as preventing us from determining or even from guessing what may have been the condition of the sun's surface in the year 1652. This year followed by seven years a period of minimum disturbance, and preceded by three years a period of maximum disturbance ; but it would be unsafe to assume that the sun's condition in 1652 was nearer that of maximum than that of minimum disturbance. We must pass over Wyberd's observations of the corona in 1652, at least until some direct evidence as to the sun's condition shall have been obtained from the papers or writings of the observers of that year. I note only that Wyberd saw a corona of very limited extent, having indeed a height not half so great as that of many prominences which have been observed during recent eclipses. If the theory we are examining should be established beyond dispute, we should be led to infer that the year 1652 was in reality a year of minimum solar disturbance. Perhaps by throwing in such a minimum between 1645 and 1666, with of course a corresponding maximum, the wild irregularity of the sun-spot changes between 1645 and 1679 would be to some degree diminished.

We are now approaching times when more satisfactory observations were made upon the corona, and when also we have more complete records of the aspect of the sun's surface.

In 1706 Plantade and Capies saw a bright ring of white light extending round the eclipsed sun to a distance of about 85,000 miles, but merging into a fainter light, which extended no less than four degrees from the eclipsed sun, fading off insensibly until its light was lost in the obscure background of the sky. This corresponds unmistakably with such a corona as we should expect only to see at a time of many sun-spots, if the theory we are examining is sound. Turning to Wolf's list, we find that the year 1705 is marked as a year of maximum solar disturbance, and the year 1712 as that of the next minimum. Therefore 1706 was a year of many sun-spots—in fact, 1706 may have been the year of actual maximum disturbance, for it is within the limits of doubt indicated by Wolf. Certainly a corona extending so far as that which Plantade and Capies saw would imply an altogether exceptional degree of solar disturbance, if the theory we are considering is correct.

In 1715 Halley gave the following description of the

corona :—'A few seconds before the sun was all hid, there discovered itself round the moon a luminous ring about a digit' (a twelfth) ' or perhaps a tenth part of the moon's diameter in breadth.   It was of a pale whiteness or rather pearl colour, seeming to me a little tinged with the colours of the Iris, and to be concentric with the moon.'   He added that the ring appeared much whiter and brighter near the body of the moon than at a distance from it, and that its exterior boundary was very ill-defined, seeming to be determined only by the extreme rarity of the luminous matter.   The French astronomer Louville gave a similar account of the appearance of the ring.   He added, however, that 'there were interruptions in its brightness, causing it to resemble the radial glory with which painters encircle the heads of the saints.'   The smallness of the corona on this occasion corresponds with the description of the corona seen in July 1878 ; and though Louville's description of gaps is suggestive of a somewhat different aspect, yet, on the whole, the corona seen in 1715 more closely resembles one which would be seen at a time of minimum solar disturbance, if our theory can be trusted, than one which would be seen at a time of maximum disturbance.   Wolf's list puts the year 1712 as one of minimum disturbance, with one year of doubt either way, and the middle of the year 1817 as the epoch of maximum disturbance, with a similar range of uncertainty. The case, then, is doubtful, but on the whole inclines to being unfavourable.   I may remark that because of its un-favourable nature, I departed from the rule I had set myself, of taking only the cases included in my treatise on the sun.   For the corona of 1715 is not described in that treatise, as indeed affording no evidence respecting this solar appendage.   The evidence given in this case is probably affected in some degree by the unfavourable atmospheric conditions under which Halley certainly, and Louville probably, observed the eclipse.   In any case the evidence is not strong ; only I would call attention here to the circumstance that if, as we proceed, we *should* come to a case in which the evidence is plainly against the theory we are examining, we must give up the theory at once. For one case of d scordance does more to destroy a theory respecting association between such and such phenomena, than a hundred cases of agreement would do in the way of confirming it.

In 1724, Maraldi noticed that the corona was broadest first on the side towards which the moon was advancing, and afterwards on the side which the moon was leaving. From this we may infer that the corona was only a narrow ring on that occasion, since otherwise the slight difference of breadth due to the moon's eccentric position at the beginning and end of totality would not have been notice-able.   Now, the year 1723 was one of minimum disturbance, with one year of doubt either way.   Thus 1724 was certainly a year of few sun-spots, and may have been the actual year of minimum disturbance.   The corona then presented an appearance according with the theory we are considering.

Few eclipses have been better observed than that of the year 1733.   The Royal Society of Sweden invited all who could spare the time to assist, as far as their ability permitted, in recording the phenomena presented during totality. The pastor of Stona Malm states that at Catherines-holm, there was a ring around the sun about 70,000 miles in height.   (Of course these are not his exact words ; what he actually stated was that the ring was about a digit in breadth.)   This is the exact height assigned to the coronal ring by the observers of the eclipse of last year. The ring seemed to be of a reddish colour. Another clergyman, Vallerius, states also that the ring was of this colour, but adds that at a considerable distance from the sun it had a greenish hue. This suggests the idea that the outer corona was seen also by Vallerius, and that it had considerable breadth.   The reddish colour of the inner light portion would correspond to the colour it would have if it consisted in the main of glowing hydrogen.   If that really was its constitution, then the theory advanced by one observer of the last eclipse, that at the time of minimum solar disturbance the glowing hydrogen is withdrawn from the corona, would be shown to be incorrect. For 1733 was the actual year of minimum solar disturbance. The pastor of Smoland states that 'during the total obscuration the edge of the moon's disc resembled gilded brass, and the faint ring round it emitted rays in an upward as well as in a downward direction, similar to those seen beneath the sun when a shower of rain is impending.' The mathematical lecturer of the Academy of Charles-stadt, M. Edstrom, observed these rays with special attention : he says that 'they plainly maintained the same position, until they vanished along with the ring upon the re-appearance of the sun.' On the other hand, at Lincopia no rays were seen. On the whole it seems clear from the accounts of this eclipse that the inner corona was bright and narrow ; rays issued from the outer faint ring ; but they were very delicate phenomena, easily concealed by atmospheric haze, and thus were not everywhere observed. As rays were seen in July 1878, there is nothing in the evidence afforded by the eclipse of 1733, occurring at a time of few spots, which opposes itself definitely to the theory we are considering. But the reddish colour of the corona as already noticed is a doubtful feature : in July, 1878, the bright inner corona was of a pearl colour and lustre.

During the eclipse of February, 1766, the corona presented four luminous expansions, and seems to have presented a greater expansion than we should expect in a year of minimum solar disturbance. Such, however, the year 1766 certainly was. The evidence in this case is unfavourable to our theory—not quite decisively so, but strongly. For we should expect that in the year of actual minimum disturbance the corona would be even narrower than in the year 1878, which was the year following that of least disturbance. And again, a strongly distinctive feature in the corona of July, 1878, was the absence of wide expansions, such as were seen in 1870 and 1871. Now if this peculiarity should really be attributed to the relation existing between the corona and the sun-spots, we should infer that in 1766 the corona would have been still more markedly uniform in shape. The existence of four well marked expansions on that occasion forces us to assume that either the relation referred to has no real existence, or else that the corona may change from week to week as the condition of the sun's surface changes, and that in February, 1766, the sun was temporarily disturbed, though the year, as a whole, was one of minimum disturbance. But as the epoch of actual minimum was the middle of 1766, February 1766 should have been a time of very slight disturbance. I do not know of any observations of the sun recorded for the month of February, 1766. On the whole, the eclipse of 1766 must be regarded as throwing grave doubt on the relation assumed by our theory as existing between the corona and the sun-spots ; and as tending to suggest that some wider law must be in question than the one we have been considering—if any association really exists.

The account given by Don Antonio d'Ulloa of the appearance presented by the corona during the total eclipse of 1778, is rendered doubtful by his reference to an apparent rotatory motion of the normal rays. He says that about five or six seconds after totality had begun, a brilliant luminous ring was seen around the dark body of the moon. The ring became brighter as the middle of totality approached. 'About the middle of the eclipse, the breadth of the ring was equal to about a sixth of the moon's diameter. There seemed to issue from it a great number of rays of unequal length, which could be discerned to a distance equal to the moon's diameter.' Then comes the part of d'Ulloa's description which seems difficult to accept. He says that the corona ' seemed to be endued with a rapid rotatory motion, which caused it to resemble a firework turning round its centre.' The colour of the light, he proceeds, ' was not uniform throughout the whole breadth of the ring. Towards

the margin of the moon's disc it appeared of a reddish hue ;
then it changed to a pale yellow, and from the middle to the
outer border the yellow gradually became fainter, until at
length it seemed almost quite white.'   Setting aside the rays
and their rotation, d'Ulloa's account of the inner corona
may be accepted as satisfactory.   The height of this ring
was, it seems, about 140,000 miles, or twice that of the ring
seen in July 1878.   As the year 1779 was one of maximum
solar disturbance, there were doubtless many spots in 1778;
and the aspect of the corona accorded well with the theory
that the corona expands as the number of sun-spots
increases.

We come now to three eclipses which are especially
interesting as having been all carefully observed, some
observers having seen all three,—the eclipses, namely, of
1842, 1851, and 1860.   Unfortunately the eclipses of 1842
and 1851 occurred when the sun-spots were neither at their
greatest nor at their least degree of frequency.   For a
maximum of sun-spots occurred in 1837, and a minimum in
1844, so that 1842 was on what may be called the descending slope of a sun-spot wave, nearer the hollow than the
crest, but not very near either : again, a maximum occurred
in 1848, and a minimum in 1856, so that 1851 was also on
the descending slope of a sun-spot wave, rather nearer the
crest than the hollow, but one may fairly say about midway
between them.   Still it is essential in an inquiry of this sort
to consider intermediate cases.   We must not only apply the
comparentia ad intellectum instantiarum convenientium, but
also the *comparentia instantiarum secundum magis ac minus.*
If the existence of great solar disturbances causes the
corona to be greatly enlarged, as compared with the corona
seen when the sun shows no spots, we should expect to
find the corona moderately enlarged only when the sun
shows a considerable but not the maximum number of
spots.   And again, it is conceivable that we may find some
noteworthy difference between the aspect of the corona
when sun-spots are diminishing in number, and its aspect

when they are increasing. This point seems the more to need investigation when we note that the evidence derived from eclipses occurring near the time either of maximum or of minimum solar disturbance has not been altogether satisfactory. It may be that we may find an explanation of the discrepancies we have recognised, in some distinction between the state of the corona when spots are increasing and when they are diminishing in number.

It is noteworthy that several careful observers of the corona in 1842 believed that they could recognise motion in the coronal rays. Francis Baily compared the appearance of the corona to the flickering light of a gas illumination. O. Struve also was much struck by the appearance of violent agitation in the light of the ring. It seems probable that the appearance was due to movements in that part of our atmosphere through which the corona was observed. The extent of the corona was variously estimated by different observers. Petit, at Montpelier, assigned to it a breadth corresponding to a height of about 200,000 miles ; Baily a height of about 500,000 miles ; and O. Struve a height of more than 800,000 miles. The last-named observer also recognised luminous expansions extending fully four degrees (corresponding to nearly seven million miles) from the sun. Picozzi, at Milan, noticed two jets of light, which were seen also by observers in France. Rays also were seen by Mauvais at Perpignan, and by Baily at Paria. But Airy, observing the corona from the Superga, could see no radiation ; he says 'although a slight radiation might have been perceptible, it was not sufficiently intense to affect in a sensible degree the annular structure by which the luminous appearance was plainly distinguished.' These varieties in the aspect of the corona were doubtless due to varieties in the condition of the atmosphere through which the corona was seen. Now it cannot be questioned that, so far as extension is concerned, the corona seen in 1842 was one which, if the theory we are considering were sound, we should expect to see near the time of maximum rather than of minimum solar disturbance. On the other hand, in brightness the corona of 1842 resembled, if it did not surpass, that of July 1878.

'I had imagined,' says Baily, 'that the corona, as to its brilliant or luminous appearance, would not be greater than that faint crepuscular light which sometimes takes place (*sic*) in a summer evening, and that it would encircle the moon like a ring. I was therefore somewhat surprised and astonished at the splendid scene which now so suddenly burst upon my view.'

The light of the corona was so bright, O. Struve states, that the naked eye could scarcely endure it ; 'many could not believe, indeed, that the eclipse was total, so strongly did the corona's light resemble direct sunlight.' Thus while as to extent the corona in 1842 presented the appearance to be expected at the time of maximum solar disturbance, if our theory is sound, its brightness was that corresponding to a time of minimum disturbance. Its structure corresponded with the former condition. The light of the corona was not uniform, nor merely marked by radiations, but in several places interlacing lines of light could be seen. Arago, at Perpignan, observed with the unaided eye a region of the corona where the structure was as of intertwined jets giving an appearance resembling a hank of thread in disorder.

Certainly, for an eclipse occurring two years from the time of minimum, and five years from the time of maximum disturbance, that of July, 1842,[1] has not supplied evidence

---

[1] The actual condition of the sun in 1842 may be inferred from the following table, showing the number of spots observed in 1837 the preceding year of maximum disturbance in 1842, and in 1844 the following year of minimum disturbance ; the observer was Schwabe of Dessau :

	Days of observation	Days without spots	New groups observed
1837 . . .	168	0	333
1842 . . .	307	64	68
1844 . . .	321	111	52

Only it should be noticed that nearly all the spots seen in the year 1844

favouring the theory with which we started. Whether any other theory of association between the corona and the sun-spots will better accord with the evidence hitherto collected remains to be seen.

Turn we now to the eclipse of 1851, occurring nearly midway between the epochs of maximum solar disturbance (1848) and minimum solar disturbance (1856). I take the account given by Airy, our Government astronomer, as he was one of the observers of the eclipse of 1842.

'The corona was far broader,' he says, 'than that which I saw in 1842. Roughly speaking, the breadth was little less than the moon's diameter, but its outline was very irregular. I did not notice any beams projecting from it which deserved notice as much more conspicuous than the others; but the whole was beamy, radiated in structure, and termi-nated—though very indefinitely—in a way which reminded me of the ornament frequently placed round a mariner's compass. Its colour was white, or resembling that of Venus. I saw no flickering or unsteadiness of light. It was not separated from the moon by any interval, nor had it any annular structure. It looked like a radiated luminous cloud behind the moon.'

The corona thus described belongs to that which our theory associates with the period of maximum rather than of minimum solar disturbance. Definite peculiarities of structure seem to have been more numerous and better marked than in 1842. It accords with our theory that 1851 was a year of greater solar disturbance than was observed in 1842, as the following numbers show :—

	Days of observation	Days without spots	New groups observed
1842	307	64	68
1851	308	0	141
1860	332	0	211

I have included the year 1860, as we now proceed to con-sider the corona then seen by Airy. The year 1860 did not

belonged to the next period, the time of actual minimum occurring early in 1844.

differ very markedly, it will be observed, from 1851, as
regards the number of new groups of spots observed by
Schwabe, especially when account is taken of the number
of days in which the sun was observed in these two years.
But 1860 was a year of maximum solar disturbance, whereas
1851 was not.[1]

Airy remarks of the corona in 1860 :—'It gave a considerable body, but I did not remark either by eye-view or
by telescope-view anything annular in its structure; it
appeared to me to resemble, with some irregularities (as I
stated in 1851), the ornament round a compass-card.'

Bruhns of Leipsic noted that the corona shone with an
intense white light, so lustrous as to dim the protuberances.
He noticed that a ray shot out to a distance of about
one degree indicating a distance of at least 1,500,000 miles
from the sun's surface. This was unquestionably a coronal
appendage as neither the direction nor the length of the ray
varied for ten seconds, during which Bruhns directed his
attention to it. Its light was considerably feebler than that
of the corona, which was of a glowing white, and seemed to
coruscate or twinkle. Bruhns assigned to the inner corona
a height varying from about 40,000 to about 80,000 miles.
But this was unquestionably far short of the true height. In
fact, Secchi's photographs show the corona extending to a
distance of at least 175,000 miles from the surface of the

---

[1] The following table shows the position occupied by the years 1851
and 1860 in this report, as compared with the year 1848 (maximum
next preceding 1851), 1856 (minimum next following 1851) and 1867,
minimum next following 1860 :—

	Days of observation	Days without spots	New groups observed
1848	278	0	930
1851	308	0	141
1856	321	193	34
1860	332	0	211
1867	312	195	25

A comparison of the three tables given in these notes and the text will
afford some idea of the irregularities existing in the various waves of
sun-spots.

sun. Therefore probably what Bruhns calls the base of the corona was in reality only the prominence region, and the inner corona was that which he describes as varying in breadth or height from nearly one-half to a quarter of a degree—that is from about 800,000 to about 400,000 miles. De la Rue gives a somewhat similar general description of the corona seen in 1860. He remarks that it was extremely bright near the moon's body, and of a silvery whiteness. The picture of the corona by Feilitsch (given at p. 343 of my book on the Sun) accords with these descriptions.

On the whole, the eclipse of 1860 affords evidence according well with the theory we have been considering, except as regards the brightness and the colour of the corona, which correspond more closely with what was observed in July, 1878, with the lustre and colour of the corona in 1870 and 1871. In this respect, it is singular that the eclipse of 1867 which occurred (see preceding note) when the sun spots were fewer in number, presented a decided contrast to that of 1860,—the contrast being, however, precisely the reverse of that which our theory would require, if the colour and brightness of the corona be considered essential features of any law of association.

Herr Grosch, describing the corona of 1867, says, 'There appeared around the moon a reddish glimmering light similar to that of the aurora, and almost simultaneously with this (I mean very shortly after it) the corona.' It is clear, however, from what follows, that the reddish light was what is now commonly called the inner corona, which last July, when the sun was in almost exactly the same condition as regards the spots, was pearly white and intensely bright. 'This reddish glimmer,' he proceeds, 'which surrounded the moon with a border of the breadth of at most five minutes' (about 140,000 miles) 'was not sharply bounded in any part, but was extremely diffused and less distinct in the neighbourhood of the poles.' Of the outer corona he remarks that 'its apparent height amounted to about 280,000 miles opposite the solar poles, but opposite the polar equator to about 670,000 miles.   Its light was white. This white light was not in the least radiated itself, but it had the appearance of rays penetrating through it ; or rather as if rays ran over it, forming symmetrical pencils diverging outwards, and passing far beyond the boundary of the white light.   These rays had a more bluish appearance, and might best be compared to those produced by a great electro-magnetic light.   Their similarity to these, indeed, was so striking, that under other circumstances I should have taken them for such, shining at a great distance.   The view of the corona I have described is that seen with the naked eye. . . . In the white light of the corona, close upon the moon's edge, there appeared several dark curves. They were symmetrically arched towards the east and west, sharply drawn, and resembling in tint lines drawn with a lead pencil upon white paper. . . . Beginning at a distance of one minute (about 26,000 miles), they could be traced up to a distance of about nine minutes (some 236,coo miles from the moon's edge.'

Almost all the features observed in this case correspond closely with those noted and photographed during the eclipse of December, 1871.   In other words the corona seen in 1867, when the sun was passing through the period of least solar disturbance, closely resembled the corona seen in 1871, when the sun was nearly in its stage of greatest disturbance.   Even the spectroscopic evidence obtained in 1871 and July, 1878, may be so extended as to show with extreme probability what would have been seen in 1867 if spectroscopic analysis had then been applied.   We cannot doubt that the reddish inner corona, extending to a height of about 140,000 miles, would have been found under spectroscopic analysis to shine in part with the light of glowing hydrogen, as the reddish corona of 1871 did.   The white corona of July, 1878, on the contrary, shone only with such light as comes from glowing solid or liquid matter.   Here then, again, the evidence is unfavourable to our theory ;

for the corona in 1867 should have closely resembled the corona of 1878, if this theory were sound.

It would be idle, I think, to seek for farther evidence either in favour of the theory we originally proposed to discuss, or against it : for the evidence of the eclipse of 1867 disposes finally of the theory in that form. I may note in passing that the eclipse of 1868 gave evidence almost equally unfavourable to the theory, while the evidence given by the eclipse of 1869 was neutral. It will be desirable, however, to consider, before concluding our inquiry, the evidence obtained in 1871 and last July, in order that we may see what, after all, that evidence may be regarded as fairly proving with regard to coronal variations.

First, however, as I have considered two eclipses which occurred when the sun spots were decreasing in number—namely, those of 1842 and 1851, midway (roughly speaking) between the crest and hollow of the sun-spot wave on its descending slope, it may be well to consider an eclipse which was similarly situated with respect to the ascending slope of a sun-spot wave. I take, then, the eclipse of 1858, as seen in Brazil by Liais. The picture drawn by this ob-server is one of the most remarkable views of the corona ever obtained. It is given at p. 339 of my book on the Sun. Formerly it was the custom to deride this drawing, but since the eclipse of 1871, when the corona was photographed, it has been admitted that Liais's drawing may be·accepted as thoroughly trustworthy. It shows a wonderfully complex corona, like that of 1871, extending some 700,000 miles from the sun, and corresponding in all respects with such a corona as our theory (if established) would have associated with the stage of maximum solar disturbance. As in this respect the eclipse of 1858, when sun-spots were increasing, resembled those of 1842 and 1851, when sun-spots were diminishing in number, we find no trace of any law of association depending on the rate of increase or diminution of solar disturbance.

If we limited our attention to the eclipses of 1871 and

of July, 1878, we should unquestionably be led to adopt the belief that the corona during a year of many spots differs markedly from the corona when the sun shows few spots, or none. So far as the aspect of the corona is concerned, I take the description given by the same observer in both cases, as the comparison is thus freed as far as possible from the effect of personal differences.

Mr. Lockyer recognised in 1871 a corona resembling a star-like decoration, with its rays arranged almost symmetrically—three above and three below two dark spaces or rifts at the extremity of a horizontal diameter. The rays were built up of innumerable bright lines of different length, with more or less dark spaces between them. Near the sun this structure was lost in the brightness of the central ring, or inner corona. In the telescope he saw thousands of interlacing filaments, varying in intensity. The rays so definite to the eye were not seen in the telescope. The complex structure of interlacing filaments could be traced only to a height of some five or six minutes (from 135,000 to 165,000 miles) from the sun, there dying out suddenly. The spectroscope showed that the inner corona, to this height at least (but Respighi's spectroscopic observations prove the same for a much greater distance from the sun), was formed in part of glowing gas—hydrogen—and the vapour of some as yet undetermined substance, shining with light of a green tint, corresponding to 1474 of Kirchhoff's scale. But also a part of the coronal light came from matter which reflected sunlight; for its spectrum was the rainbow-tinted streak crossed by dark lines, which we obtain from any object illuminated by the sun's rays. It should be added that the photographs of the corona in 1871 show the three great rays above and three below, forming the appearance as of a star-like decoration, described by Mr. Lockyer; insomuch as it is rather strange to find Mr. Lockyer remarking that 'the difference between the photographic and the visible corona came out strongly, . . . and the non-solar origin of the radial structure was conclusively established.' The resemblance is, indeed, not indicated in the rough copy of the photographs which illustrates Mr. Lockyer's paper ; but it is clearly seen in the photographs themselves, and in the fine engraving which has been formed from them for the illustration of the volume which the Astronomical Society proposes to issue (some time in the present century, perhaps).

Now, in July, 1878, the corona presented an entirely different appearance. Mr. Lockyer, in a telegram sent to the *Daily News*, describes it as small, of pearly lustre, and having indications of definite structure in two places only. Several long rays were seen ; but the inner corona was estimated as extending to a height of about 70,000 miles from the sun's surface. The most remarkable change, however, was that which had taken place in the character of the corona's spectrum—or, in other words, in the physical structure of the corona. The bright lines or bright images of the inner corona (according as it was examined through a slit or without one) were not seen in July, 1878, showing that no part, or at least no appreciable part, of its light came from glowing gaseous matter. But also the dark lines seen by Janssen in 1871 were wanting on this occasion, showing that the corona did not shine appreciably by reflecting sunlight. The spectrum was, in fine, a continuous rainbow-tinted streak, such as that given by glowing solid or liquid matter.

The inference clearly is: 1. That in July, 1878, the gaseous matter which had been present in the corona in 1871 was either entirely absent or greatly reduced in quantity ; 2. The particles of solid or liquid (but probably solid) matter which, by reflecting sunlight, produced a considerable portion of the corona's light in 1871, were glowing with heat in July, 1878, and shone in the main with this inherent light; and 3. The entire corona was greatly reduced in size in July, 1878, as compared with that which formed the ' starlike decoration ' around the black body of the moon in December, 1871.

We cannot, however, accept the theory that such a corona as was seen in 1871 invariably surrounds the sun in years of great disturbance, while the corona of last month is the typical corona for years of small solar disturbance. The generalisation is flatly contradicted by the evidence which I have presented in the preceding pages. It may be that such a corona as was seen in 1871 is common in years of great disturbance, just as spots are then more common, though not always present ; while such a corona as was seen in July, 1878, is more common in years of small disturbance, just as days when the sun is wholly without spots are then more common, though from time to time several spots, and sometimes very large spots, are seen in such years. On the whole, I think the evidence I have collected favours ráther strongly the inference that an association of this sort really exists between the corona and the sun-spots. It would, however, be unsafe at present to generalise even to this extent ; while certainly the wide generalisation telegraphed to Europe from America as the great result of the eclipse observations in July, 1878, must unhesitatingly be rejected.

It remains to be considered how science may hope to obtain more trustworthy evidence than we yet have respect ing the corona and its changes of form, extent, lustre, and physical constitution. In the case of the prominences, we have the means of making systematic observations on every fine, clear day. It has been, indeed, through observations thus effected by the spectroscopic method that an association has been recognised between the number, size, and brilliancy of the prominences on the one hand, and the number, size, and activity of the sun-spots on the other. But in the case of the corona, we are as yet unable to make any observations except at the time of total solar eclipse. It seems almost impossible to hope that any means can be devised for seeing the corona at any other time. Of course, without the aid of the spectroscope the corona, as ordinarily seen during total eclipses, must be entirely invisible when the sun is shining in full splendour. No one acquainted with even the merest elements of optics could hope to see the corona with an ordinary telescope at such a time. The spectro- scope, again, would not help in the slightest degree to show such a corona as was shining in July, 1878. For the power of the spectroscope to show objects which under ordinary conditions are invisible, depends on the separation of rays of certain tints from the rays of all the colours of the rainbow, which make up solar light ; and as the corona in July, 1878, shone with all the colours of the rainbow, and not with certain special tints, the power of the spectroscope would be thrown away on a corona of that kind. All that we can ever hope to do is to discern the gaseous corona when, as in 1871, it is well developed, by spectroscopic appliances more effective for that purpose than any which have hitherto been adopted ; for all which have as yet been adopted have failed.

Now, the difficulty of the problem will be recognised when we remember that the strongest tints of the corona's light—the green tint classified as 1474 Kirchhoff—has been specially but ineffectually searched for in the sun's neighbourhood with the most powerful spectroscopic appliances yet employed in the study of the coloured prominences. In other words, when the light of our own air over the region occupied by the corona has been diluted as far as possible by spectroscopic contrivances, the strongest of the special coronal tints has yet failed to show through the diluted spectrum of the sky. Again, we have even stronger evidence of the difficulty of the task in the spectroscopic observations made by Respighi during the eclipse of 1871. The instrument, or I should rather, perhaps, say the arrangement, which during mid totality showed the green image of the corona to a height of about 280,000 miles, did not show any green ring at all at the beginning of totality. In other words, so faint is the light of the gaseous corona, even at its brightest part, close to the sun, that the faint residual atmospheric light which illuminates the sky over the eclipsed sun at the beginning of totality sufficed to obliterate this part of the coronal light.

Whether with any combination specially directed to meet the difficulties of this observation, the gaseous corona can be rendered discernible, remains to be seen. I must confess my own hopes that the problem will ever be successfully dealt with are very slight, though not absolutely evanescent. It seems to me barely possible that the problem might be successfully attacked in the following way. Using a telescope of small size, for the larger the telescope the fainter is the image (because of greater loss of light by absorption), let the image of the sun be received in a small, perfectly darkened camera attached to the eye-end of the telescope. Now if the image of the sun were received on a smooth white surface we know that the prominences and the corona would not be visible. And again, if the part of such a surface on which the image of the sun itself fell were exactly removed, we know (the experiment has been tried by Airy) that the prominences would not be seen on the ring of white surface left after such excision. Still less, then, would the much fainter image of the corona be seen. But if this ring of white surface, illuminated in reality by the sky, by the ring of prominences and sierra, and by the corona, were examined through a battery of prisms (used without a slit) adjusted to any one of the known prominence tints, the ring of prominences and sierra would be seen in that special tint. If the battery of prisms were sufficiently effective, and the tint were one of the hydrogen tints—preferably, perhaps, the red—we might possibly be able to trace the faint image of the corona in that tint. But we should have a better chance with the green tint corresponding to the spectral line 1474 Kirchhoff. If the ring of white surface were replaced by a ring of green surface, the tint being as nearly that of 1474 Kirchhoff as possible, the chance of seeing the coronal ring in that tint would be somewhat increased ; and, still further, perhaps, if the field of view were examined through green glass of the same tint. It seems just possible that if prisms of triple height were used, through which the rays were carried three times, by an obvious modification of the usual arrangement for altering the level of the rays, thus giving a power of eighteen flint glass prisms of sixty degrees each, evidence, though slight perhaps, might be obtained of the presence of the substance which produces the green line. Thus variations in the condition of the corona might be recognised, and any law affecting such variations might be detected. I must confess, however, that a consideration of the optical relations involved in the problem leads me to regard the attempt to recognise any traces of the corona when the sun is not eclipsed as almost hopeless.

It is clear that until some method for thus observing the corona has been devised, future eclipse observations will acquire a new interest from the light which they may throw on the coronal variations, and their possible association in some way, not as yet detected, with the sun-spot period. Even when a method has been devised for observing the gaseous corona, the corona whose light comes either directly or by reflection from solid or liquid matter will still remain undiscernible save only during total eclipses of the sun. Many years must doubtless pass, then, before the relation of the corona to the prominences and the sun-spots shall be fully recognised. But there can be no question that the solution of this problem will be well worth waiting for, even though it should not lead up (as it most probably will) to the solution of the mystery of the periodic changes which affect the surface of the sun.

SUN-SPOTS AND COMMERCIAL PANICS.

WE are not only, it would seem, to regard the sun as the ultimate source of all forms of terrestrial energy, existent or potential, but as regulating in a much more special manner the progress of mundane events.   Many years have passed since Sabine, Wolf, and Gauthier asserted that variations in the daily oscillations of the magnetic needle appear to synchronise with the changes taking place in the sun's condition, the oscillations attaining their *maximum* average range in years when the sun shows most spots, and their *minimum* range when there are fewest spots.   And although it is well known that the Astronomer Royal in England and the President of the Academy of Sciences in France reject this doctrine, it still remains in vogue.   True, the average magnetic period appears to be about 10.45 years, while Wolf obtains for the sun-spot period 11.11 years ; but believers in the connection between terrestrial magnetic disturbances and sun-spots consider that among the imperfect records of the past condition of the sun Wolf must have lost sight of one particular wave of sun-spots, so to speak.   If there have been 24 such waves between 1611 and 1877, when sun-spots were fewest, we get Wolf's period of 11.11 years ; if there have been 25 such waves then, taking an admissible estimate for the earliest epoch, we get 10 45 years, the period required to synchronise with the period of terrestrial magnetic changes.   The matter must be regarded as still *sub judice.* This, however, is only one relation out of many now suggested. Displays of the aurora, being unquestionably dependent on the magnetic condition of the earth, would of course be associated with the sun spot period, if the magnetic period is so ; and certainly the most remarkable displays of the aurora in recent times have occurred when the sun has shown many spots. Yet this of itself proves nothing more than had been already known— namely, that the last few magnetic periods have nearly synchronised with the last few sun-spot periods. It is rather strange, too, that no auroras are mentioned in the English records for 80 years preceding the aurora of 1716, and in the records of the Paris Academy of Sciences one only —that of 1666, which occurred when sun-spots were fewest. The great aurora of 1723, seen as far south as Bologna, also occurred at the time of *minimum* solar activity. Here we are not depending on either Wolf's period of 11 years or Brown's of 10½ years ; from records of actual observation it is known that in 1666 and 1713 there were no sun-spots. In fact it is worth mentioning that Cassini, writing in 1671, says, ' It is now about 20 years since astronomers have seen any considerable spots on the sun,' a circumstance which throws grave doubt on the law of sun-spot periodicity itself. It is at least certain that the interval from *maximum* spot-fre- quency to *maximum,* or from *minimum* to *minimum,* has sometimes fallen far short of 9 years, and has at others exceeded 18 years.

It appears again that certain meteorological phenomena show a tendency, more or less marked, to run through a ten-year cycle. Thus, from the records of rainfall kept at Oxford it appears that more rain fell under west and south- west winds when sun-spots were largest and most numerous than under south and south-east winds, these last being the more rainy winds when sun-spots were least in size and fewest in number. This is a somewhat recondite relation, and at least proves that earnest search has been made for such cyclic relations as we are considering. But this is not

all. When other records were examined, the striking circumstance was discovered that elsewhere, as at St. Petersburg, the state of things observed at Oxford was precisely
reversed. At some intermediate point between Oxford and
St. Petersburg, no doubt the rainfall under the winds named
was equally distributed throughout the spot period. Moreover, as the conditions thus d ffer at different places, we
may assume that they differ also at different times. Such
relations appear then to be not only recondite, but complicated.

When we learn that during nearly two entire sun-spot
periods cyclones have been somewhat more numerous in the
Indian Seas when spots are most numerous than when the
sun is without spots, and *vice versâ*, we recognise the possible
existence of cyclic relations better worth knowing than those
heretofore mentioned. The evidence is not absolutely
decisive ; some, indeed, regard it as scarcely trustworthy.
Yet there does seem to have been an excess of cyclonic
disturbance during the last two periods of great solar disturbance, precisely as there was also an excess of magnetic
disturbance during those periods. The excess was scarcely
sufficient, however, to justify the rather daring statement
made by one observer, that 'the whole question of cyclones
is merely a question of solar activity.' We had records of
some very remarkable cyclonic disturbances during the
years 1876 and 1877, when the sun showed very few spots,
the actual *minimum* of disturbance having probably been
reached late in 1877. A prediction that 1877 would be a
year of few and slight storms would have proved disastrous
if implicit reliance had been placed on it by seamen and
travellers.

Rainfall and atmospheric pressure in India have been
found to vary in a cyclic manner, of late years at any rate,
the periods being generally about 10 or 11 years. The
activity of the sun, as shown by the existence of many
spots, apparently makes more rainfall at Madras, Najpore,
and some other places ; while at Calcutta, Bombay, Mysore,

and elsewhere it produces a contrary effect. Yet these effects are produced in a somewhat capricious way ; for sometimes the year of actual *maximum* spot frequency is one in which rainfall is below the average (instead of above) at the former stations, and above the average (instead of below) at the latter. It is only by taking averages—and in a somewhat artificial manner—that the relation seems to be indicated on which stress has been laid.

Since Indian famines are directly dependent on defective rainfall, it is natural that during the years over which observation has hitherto extended the connection apparently existing between sun-spots and Indian rainfall should seem also to extend itself to Indian famines. It was equally to be expected that since cyclones have been rather more numerous, for some time past, in years when sun-spots have been most numerous, shipwrecks should also have been somewhat more frequent in such years. Two years ago Mr. Jeula gave some evidence which, in his opinion, indicated such a connection between sun-spots and ship-wrecks. He showed that in the four years of fewest spots the mean percentage of losses was 8.64 ; in four intermediate years the mean percentage was 9.21 ; in three remaining years of the eleven-year cycle—that is, in three years of greatest spot frequency the mean percentage was 9.53. Some suggested that possibly such events as the American war, which included two of the three years of greatest spot frequency, may have had more effect than sun-spots in increasing the percentage of ships lost ; while perhaps, the depression following the commercial panic of 1866 (at a time of fewest sun-spots) may have been almost as effective in reducing the percentage of losses as the diminished area of solar maculation. But others consider that we ought rather to regard the American war as yet another product of the sun's increased activity in 1860-61, and the great commercial panic of 1866 as directly resulting from diminished sun-spots at that time, thus obtaining fresh evidence of the sun's specific influence on terrestrial phenomena instead of explaining away the evidence derived from Lloyd's list of losses.

This leads us to the last, and, in some respects, the most singular suggestion respecting solar influence on mundane events—the idea, namely, that commercial crises synchronise with the sun-spot period, occurring near the time when spots are least in size and fewest in number ; or, as Professor Jevons (to whom the definite enunciation of this theory is due) poetically presents the matter, that from 'the sun, which is truly "of this great world both eye and soul," we derive our strength and our weakness, our success and our failure, our elation in commercial mania, and our despondency and ruin in commercial collapse.' We have better opportunities of dealing with this theory than with the others, for we have records of commercial matters extending as far back as the beginning of the eighteenth century. In fact, we have better evidence than Professor Jevons seems to have supposed, for whereas in his discussion of the matter he considers only the probable average of the sun-spot period, we know approximately the epochs themselves at which the *maxima* and *minima* of sun spots have occurred since the year 1700. The evidence as presented by Professor Jevons is very striking, though when examined in detail it is rather disappointing. He presents the whole series of decennial crises as follows :—1701 ? (such query marks are his own), 1711, 1721, 1731-32, 1742 (?), 1752 (?), 1763, 1772–73, 1783, 1793, 1804-5 (?), 1815, 1825, 1836–9 (1837 in the United States), 1847, 1857, 1866 and 1878. The average interval comes out 10.466 years, showing, as Jevons points out, 'almost perfect coincidence with Brown's estimate of the average sun-spot period.' Let us see, however, whether these dates correspond so closely with the years of *minimum* spot-frequency as to remove all doubt. Taking 5¼ years as the average interval between *maximum* and *minimum* sun-spot frequency, we should like to find every crisis occurring within a year or so on either side of the *minimum* though we should prefer perhaps to find the crisis always following the time of fewest sun-spots, as this would more directly show the depressing effect of a spotless sun. No crisis ought to occur within a year or so of *maximum* solar disturbance; for that, it should seem, would be fatal to the suggested theory. Taking the commercial crises in order, and comparing them with the known (or approximately known) epochs of *maximum* and *minimum* spot frequency, we obtain the following results (we italicize numbers or results unfavourable to the theory) :—The doubtful crisis of 1701 followed a spot *minimum* by *three* years; the crisis of 1711 preceded a *minimum* by one year; that of 1721 preceded a *minimum* by *two* years; 1731–32, preceded a *minimum* by one year; 1742 preceded a *minimum* by *three* years; 1752 followed a *maximum* by *two years*; 1763 followed a *maximum* by *a year and a half*; 1772–73 came *midway* between a *maximum* and a *minimum*; 1783 preceded a *minimum* by *nearly two* years; 1793 came *nearly midway* between a *maximum* and a *minimum*; 1804–5 coincided with a *maximum*; 1815 preceded a *maximum* by *two years*; 1825 followed a *minimum* by *two* years; 1836-39 *included* the year 1837 of *maximum* solar activity (that year being the time also when a commercial crisis occurred in the United States); 1847 preceded a *maximum* by a *year and a half*; 1866 preceded a *minimum* by a year; and 1878 followed a *minimum* by a year. Four favourable cases out of 17 can hardly be considered convincing. If we include cases lying within two years of a *minimum*, the favourable cases mount up to seven, leaving ten unfavourable ones. It must be remembered, too, that a single decidedly unfavourable case (as 1804, 1815, 1837) does more to disprove such a theory than 20 favourable cases would do towards establishing it. The American panic of 1873, by the way, which occurred when spots were very numerous, decidedly impairs the evidence derived from the crises of 1866 and 1878.

NEW PLANETS NEAR THE SUN.

PERHAPS no scientific achievement during the present century has been deemed more marvellous than the discovery of the outermost member (so far as is known) of the sun's family of planets. In many respects, apart from the great difficulty of the mathematical problem involved, the discovery appealed strongly to the imagination. A planet seventeen hundred millions of miles from the sun had been discovered in March, 1781, by a mere accident, though the accident was not one likely to occur to any one but an astronomer constantly studying the star-depths. Engaged in such observation, but with no idea of enlarging the known domain of the sun, Sir W. Herschel perceived the distant planet Uranus. His experienced eye at once recognised the fact that the stranger was not a fixed star. He judged it to be a comet. It was not until several weeks had elapsed that the newly discovered body was proved to be a planet, travelling nearly twice as far away from the sun as Saturn, the remotest planet before known. A century only had elapsed since the theory of gravitation had been established. Yet it was at once perceived how greatly this theory had increased the power of the astronomer to deal with planetary motions. Before a year had passed more was known about the motions of Uranus than had been learned about the motion of any of the old planets during the two thousand years preceding the time of Copernicus. It was possible to calculate in advance the position of the newly discovered planet, to calculate retrogressively the path along which it had been travelling, unseen and unsuspected, during the century preceding its discovery. And now observations which many might have judged to be of little value, came in most usefully. Astronomers since the discovery of the telescope had formed catalogues of the places of many hundreds of stars invisible to the naked eye. Search among the observations by which such catalogues had been formed, revealed the fact that Uranus had been seen and catalogued as a fixed star twenty-one several times ! Flamsteed had seen it five times, each time recording it as a star of the sixth magnitude, so that five of Flamsteed's stars had to be cancelled from his lists. Lemonnier had actually seen Uranus twelve times, and only escaped the honour of discovering the planet (as such) through the most marvellous carelessness, his astronomical papers being, as Arago said, ' a very picture of chaos.' Bradley saw Uranus three times.[1] Mayer saw the planet once only.

It was from the study of the movements of Uranus as thus seen, combined with the planet's progress after its discovery, that mathematicians first began to suspect the existence of some unknown disturbing body. The observations preceding the discovery of the planet range over an interval of ninety years and a few months, the earliest observation used being one made by Flamsteed on December 23, 1690. There is something very strange in the thought that science was able thus to deal with the motions of a planet for nearly a century before the planet was known. Astronomy calculated in the first place where the planet had been during that time ; and then, from records made by departed observers, who had had no suspicion of the real nature of the body they were observing, Astronomy corrected her calculations, and deduced more rigorously the true nature of the new planet's motions.

[1] Two observations of Uranus, by Bradley. were discovered by the late Mr. Breen, and published in No. 1463 of the *Astronomitche Nach-richten.*

But still stranger and more impressive is the thought that from researches such as these, Astronomy should be able to infer the existence of a planet a thousand million miles further away than Uranus itself. How amazing it would have seemed to Flamsteed, for example, if on that winter evening in 1693, when he first observed Uranus, he had been told that the orb which he was entering in his lists as a star of the sixth magnitude was not a star at all, and that the observation he was then making would help astronomers a century and a half later to discover an orb a hundred times larger than the earth, and travelling thirty times farther away from the sun.

Even more surprising, however, than any of the incidents which preceded the discovery of Neptune was this achievement itself. That a planet so remote as to be quite invisible to the naked eye, never approaching our own earth within less than twenty-six hundred millions of miles, never even approaching Uranus within less than nine hundred and fifty millions of miles, should be detected by means of those particular perturbations (among many others) which it produced upon a planet not yet known for three-quarters of a century, seemed indeed surprising. Yet even this was not all. As if to turn a wonderful achievement into a miracle of combined skill and good fortune, came the announcement that, after all, the planet discovered in the spot to which Adams and Leverrier pointed was not the planet of their calculations, but travelled in an orbit four or five hundred millions of miles nearer to the sun than the orbit which had been assigned to the unknown body. Many were led to suppose that nothing but a most marvellous accident had rewarded with such singular success the calculations of Adams and Leverrier. Others were even more surprised to learn that the new planet departed strangely from the law of distances which all the other planets of the solar system seemed to obey. For according to that law (called Bode's law) the distance of Neptune, instead of being about thirty times, should have been thirty-nine times the earth's distance from the sun.

In some respects the discovery of a planet nearer to the sun than Mercury may seem to many far inferior in interest to the detection of the remote giant Neptune. Between Mercury and the sun there intervenes a mean distance of only thirty-six millions of miles, a distance seeming quite insignificant beside those which have been dealt with in describing the discovery of Uranus and Neptune. Again it is quite certain that any planet between Mercury and the sun must be far inferior to our own earth in size and mass, whereas Neptune exceeds the earth 105 times in size and 17 times in mass. Thus a much smaller region has to be searched over for a much smaller body. Moreover, while mathematical calculation cannot deal nearly so exactly with an intra-Mercurial planet as with Neptune, for there are no perturbations of Mercury which give the slightest information as to the orbital position of his disturber, the part of the heavens occupied by the intra-Mercurial planet is known without calculation, seeing that the planet must always lie within six or seven degrees or so of the sun, and can never be very far from the ecliptic.

Yet in reality the detection of an intra-Mercurial planet is a problem of far greater difficulty than that of such a planet as Neptune, while even now when most astronomers consider that an intra-Mercurial planet has been detected, the determination of its orbit is a problem which seems to present almost insuperable difficulties.

I may remark, indeed, with regard to Neptune, that he might have been successfully searched for without a hundredth part of the labour and thought actually devoted to his detection. It may sound rather daring to assert that any fairly good geometrician could have pointed after less than an hour's calculation, based on the facts known respecting Uranus in 1842, to a region within which the disturbing planet must certainly lie,—a region larger considerably no doubt than that to which Adams and Leverrier pointed, yet a region which a single observer could have swept over adequately in half-a-dozen favourable evenings, two such surveys sufficing to discover the disturbing planet. I believe, however, that no one who examines the evidence will deny the accuracy of this statement. It was manifest, from the nature of the perturbations experienced by Uranus, that between 1820 and 1825 Uranus and the unknown body had been in conjunction. From this it followed that the disturber must be behind Uranus in 1840–1845 by about one-eighth of a revolution round the sun. With the assumptions made by Adams and Leverrier, indeed, the position of the stranger in this respect could have been more closely determined. There could be little doubt that the disturbing planet must be near the ecliptic. It followed that the planet must lie somewhere on a strip of the heavens, certainly not more than ten degrees long and about three degrees broad, but the probable position of the planet would be indicated as within a strip four degrees long and two broad.[1] Such a strip could be searched over effectually in the time I have named above, and the planet would have been found in it. The larger region (ten degrees long and three broad) could have been searched over in the same time by two observers. If indeed the single observer used a telescope powerful enough to

[1] Let the student make the following construction if he entertains any doubt as to the statements made above. Having traced the orbits of the earth and Uranus from my chart illustrating the article 'Astronomy' in the *Encyc. Brit.*, let him describe a circle nearly twice as large to represent the orbit of Neptune as Bode's law would give it. Let him first suppose Neptune in conjunction with Uranus in 1820, mark the place of the earth on any given day in 1842, and the place of the fictitious Neptune ; a line joining these points will indicate the direction of Neptune on the assumptions made. Let him next make a similar construction on the assumption that conjunction took place in 1825. (From the way in which the perturbation of Uranus reached a maximum between 1820 and 1825, it was practically certain that the disturber was in conjunction with Uranus between those years.) These two constructions will give limiting directions for Neptune as viewed from the earth, on the assumption that his orbit has the dimensions named. He will find that the lines include an angle of a few degrees only, and that the direction line of the true Neptune is included between them.

detect the difference of aspect between the disc of Neptune and the point-like image of a star (the feature by which Galle, it will be remembered, recognised Neptune), a single night would have sufficed for the search over the smaller of the above-mentioned regions, and two nights for the search over the larger. The search over the smaller, as already stated, would have revealed the disturbing planet.

On the other hand, the astronomer could not determine the direction of an intra-Mercurial planet within a considerably larger space on the heavens, while the search over the space within which such a planet was to be looked for was attended by far more serious difficulties than the search for Neptune. In fact, it seems as though, even when astronomers have learned where to look for such a planet, they cannot expect to see it under ordinary atmospheric conditions when the sun is not eclipsed.

Let us consider the history of the search for an intra-Mercurial planet from the time when first the idea was suggested that such a planet exists until the time of its actual discovery—for so it seems we must regard the observations made during the total eclipse of July, ·1878.

On January 2, 1860, M. Leverrier announced, in a paper addressed to the Academy of Sciences, that the observations of Mercury could not be reconciled with the received elements of the planet. According to those elements, the point of Mercury's orbit which lies nearest to the sun undergoes a certain motion which would carry it entirely round in about 230,000 years. But to account for the observed motions of Mercury as determined from twenty-one transits over the sun between the years 1697 and 1848, a slight increase in this motion of the perihelion was required, an increase, in fact, from 581 seconds of arc in a century to nearly 585. The result would involve, he showed, an increase in our estimate of the mass of Venus by a full tenth. But such a change would necessarily lead to difficulties in other directions ; for the mass of Venus had been determined from observations of changes in the position of the earth's path, and these changes had been too carefully determined to be readily regarded as erroneous. 'This result naturally filled me with inquietude,' said Leverrier later. 'Had I not allowed some error in the theory to escape me? New researches, in which every circumstance was taken into account by different methods, ended only in the conclusion that the theory was correct, but that it did not agree with the observations.' At last, after long and careful investigation of the matter, he found that a certain slight change would bring observation and theory into agreement. All that was necessary was to assume that matter as yet undiscovered exists in the sun's neighbourhood. 'Does it consist,' he asked, 'of one or more planets, or other more minute asteroids, or only of cosmical dust? The theory tells us nothing on this point.'

Leverrier pointed out that a planet half the size of Mercury between Mercury and the sun would account for the discrepancy between observation and theory. But a planet of that size would be a very conspicuous object at certain times, even when the sun was not eclipsed; and when favourably placed during eclipses would be a resplendent orb which would attract the notice of even the most careless observer. For we must remember that the brightness of a planet depends in part on its size and its distance from the earth, and in part on its distance from the sun. A planet half as large as Mercury would have a diameter about four-fifths of Mercury's, and at equal distance would present a disc about two-thirds of Mercury's in apparent size. But supposing the planet to be half as far from the sun as Mercury (and theory required that the planet should be rather nearer the sun), its surface would be illuminated four times as brightly as that of Mercury. Hence, with a disc two-thirds as large as Mercury's, but illuminated four times as brightly, the planet would shine nearly three times as brilliantly when seen under equally favourable conditions during eclipse. In such an inquiry, the mean distance of the two bodies need not be specially considered.

Each planet would be seen most favourably when in the part of its path remotest from the earth, so that the planet nearest to the sun would on the whole have the advantage of any difference due to that cause. For, of course, while Mercury, being farther from the sun, approaches the earth nearer when between the earth and sun, he recedes farther from the sun for the same reason when on the part of his path beyond the sun.

It was perfectly clear that no such planet as Leverrier considered necessary to reconcile theory and observation exists between the sun and Mercury's orbit. It appeared necessary, therefore, to assume that either there must be several smaller planets, or else that a cloud of cosmical dust surrounds the sun. Now it is to be noticed that in either case the entire mass of matter between Mercury and the sun must be greater to produce the observed disturbance than the mass of a single planet travelling at the outside of the region supposed to be occupied either by a group of planets or a cloud of meteorites.

Leverrier considered the existence of a ring of small planets afforded the most probable explanation. He recommended astronomers to search for such bodies. It is noteworthy that it was in reference to this suggestion that M. Faye (following a suggestion of Sir J. Herschel's) proposed that at several observatories, suitably selected, the sun should be photographed several times every day with a powerful telescope. 'I have myself,' he says, 'shown how to give these photographs the value of an astronomical observation by taking two impressions on the same plate after an interval of two minutes. It will be sufficient to superpose the transparent negatives of this size taken at a quarter of an hour's interval, to distinguish immediately the movable projection of a small planet in the middle of the most complex groups of small spots.'

It was while Leverrier and Faye were discussing this matter, that news came of the recognition of an intra-Mercurial planet by Lescarbault, a doctor residing at Orgères, in the department of Eure et Loire. The story has been so often told that I am loth to occupy space with it here. An account is given of the leading incidents in an article called 'The Planets put in Leverrier's Balance,' in my 'Science Byways,' and a somewhat more detailed narrative in my 'Myths and Marvels of Astronomy.' Here, it will suffice to give a very slight sketch of this interesting episode in the history of astronomy.

On January 2, 1860, news reached Leverrier that Lescarbault had on March 26, 1859, seen a round black spot on the sun's face, and had watched it travelling across like a planet in transit. It had remained in view for one hour and a quarter. Leverrier could not understand why three-quarters of a year had been allowed to elapse before so important an observation had been published. He went to Orgères with the idea of exposing a pretender. The interview was a strange one. Leverrier was stern and, to say the truth, exceedingly rude in his demeanour, Lescarbault singularly lamb-like. If our chief official astronomer called uninvited upon some country gentleman who had announced an astronomical discovery, and behaved as Leverrier did to Lescarbault, there would most certainly have been trouble ; but Lescarbault seems to have been rather pleased than otherwise. 'So you are the man,' said Leverrier, looking fiercely at the doctor, 'who pretend to have seen an intra-Mercurial planet. You have committed a grave offence in hiding your observation, supposing you really have made it, for nine months. You are either dishonest or deceived. Tell me at once and without equivocation what you have seen.' Lescarbault described his observation. Leverrier asked for his chronometer, and, hearing that the doctor used only his watch, the companion of his professional journeys, asked how he could pretend to estimate seconds with an old watch. Lescarbault showed a silk pendulum 'beating seconds,'—though it would have been more correct to say 'swinging seconds.' Leverrier then examined the doctor's telescope, and presently asked for the record of the observations. Lescarbault produced it, written on a piece of laudanum-stained paper which at the moment was doing service as a marker in the *Connaissance des Temps.* Leverrier asked Lescarbault what distance he had deduced for the new planet. The doctor replied that he had been unable to deduce any, not being a mathematician : he had made many attempts, however.[1] Hearing this, Leverrier asked for the rough draft of these ineffective calculations. 'My rough draft?' said the doctor. 'Paper is rather scarce with us here. I am a joiner as well as an astronomer' (we can imagine the expression of Leverrier's face at this moment) ; 'I calculate in my workshop, and I write upon the boards ; and when I wish to use them in new calculations, I remove the old ones by planing.' On adjourning to the carpenter's shop, however, they found the board with its lines and its numbers in chalk still unobliterated.

This last piece of evidence, though convincing Leverrier that Lescarbault was no mathematician, and therefore probably in his eyes no astronomer, yet satisfied him as to the good faith of the doctor of Orgères. With a grace and dignity full of kindness, which must have afforded a singular contrast to his previous manner, he congratulated Lescarbault on his important discovery. He made some inquiry also at Orgères, concerning the private character of Lescarbault, and learning from the village *curé*, the *juge de paix*, and other functionaries, that he was a skilful physician, he determined to secure some reward for his labours. At Leverrier's request M. Rouland, the Minister of Public Instruction, communicated to Napoleon III. the result of Leverrier's visit, and on January 25 the Emperor bestowed on the village doctor the decoration of the Legion of Honour.

To return to astronomical facts.

It appears from Lescarbault's observation, that on March

---

[1] The problem is in reality, at least in the form in which Lescarbault attacked it, an exceedingly simple one. A solution of the general problem is given at p. 181 of my treatise on the *Geometry of Cycloids.* It is, in fact, almost identical with the problem of determining the distance of a planet from observations made during a single night.

26, 1859, at about four in the afternoon, a round black spot entered on the sun's disc. It had a diameter less than one-fourth that of Mercury (which he had seen in transit with the same telescope and the same magnifying power on May 8, 1845). The time occupied in the transit of this spot was about one hour seventeen minutes, and, the chord of transit being somewhat more than a quarter of the sun's diameter in length, Lescarbault calculated that the time necessary to describe the sun's diameter would have been nearly four and a half hours. The inclination of the body's path to the ecliptic seemed to be rather more than 6 degrees, and was probably comprised between $5\frac{1}{3}$ and $7\frac{1}{3}$ degrees.

From Leverrier's calculations, it appeared that the time of revolution of the new planet would be 19 days 17 hours, its distance from the sun about 147, the earth's being taken as 1,000 ; giving for Mars, the earth, Venus, Mercury, and Vulcan (as the new planet was named), the respective distances 1, 524, 1,000, 723, 387, and 147. Leverrier assigned $12\frac{1}{8}$ degrees as Vulcan's inclination, and the places where it crosses the ecliptic he considered to be in line with those occupied by the earth on or about April 3 and October 6. Judging from Lescarbault's statement respecting the apparent size of the dark spot, Leverrier concluded that the volume of the stranger must be about one-seventeenth of Mercury's, the masses being presumably in the same proportion. Hence he inferred that the new planet would be quite incompetent to produce the observed change in the orbit of Mercury.

Leverrier further found that the brilliancy of Vulcan when the planet was furthest from the sun on the sky (about eight degrees) would be less than that of Mercury when similarly placed in his orbit, and he hence inferred that Vulcan might readily remain unseen, even during total eclipse. Here, as it seems to me, Leverrier's reasoning was erroneous. If Vulcan really has a volume equal to one-seventeenth of Mercury's, the diameter of Vulcan would be rather less than two-fifths of Mercury's and the disc of

Vulcan at the same distance about two-thirteenths of Mercury's. But Vulcan, being nearer the sun than Mercury in the ratio of 147 to 387, or say 15 to 39, would be more brightly illuminated in the ratio of 39 times 39 to 15 times 15, or nearly as 20 to 3. Hence if we first diminish Mercury's lustre when at his greatest apparent distance from the sun in the ratio of 2 to 13, and increase the result in the ratio of 20 to 3, we get Vulcan's lustre when he is at his greatest apparent distance from the sun. The result is that his lustre should exceed Mercury's in the same degree that 40 exceeds 39. Or practically, for all the numbers used have been mere approximations, the inference is that Vulcan and Mercury, if both seen when at their greatest distance from the sun during eclipse, would probably shine with equal lustre. But in that case Vulcan would be a very conspicuous object indeed, at such a time ; for Mercury when at his greatest distance from the sun, or greatest elongation, is a bright star even on a strongly illuminated twilight sky ; moreover, Vulcan, when at either of his greatest elongations, ought to be visible in full daylight in a suitably adjusted telescope. For Mercury is well seen when similarly placed, and even when much nearer to the sun and on the nearer part of his path where he turns much more of his darkened than of his illuminated hemisphere towards us. Venus has been seen when so near the sun that the illuminated portion of her disc is a mere thread-like sickle of light. Nay, Professor Lyman, of Yale College, in America, has seen her when so near the sun that she appeared to be a mere circular thread of light, the completion of the circle being the best possible proof how exceedingly fine the thread must have been, and also how small its intrinsic lustre.

This is indeed the chief difficulty in Lescarbault's supposed observation. If he really saw a body in transit across the sun, moving at the observed rate, and having anything like the observed diameter, that body ought to have been seen repeatedly during total eclipses of the sun, and ought not to have escaped the search which has been made over and over again near the sun for intra-Mercurial planets. Either we must reject Lescarbault's narrative absolutely, or we must suppose that he greatly over-estimated the size of the body he observed.

Another difficulty almost equally important is found to exist when we consider the circumstances of Lescarbault's supposed discovery.   Suppose the path of Vulcan to be inclined about twelve degrees or thereabouts to the ecliptic or to the plane in which the earth travels.   Then, as seen from the earth on April 3, and October 6, this path, if it were a material ring, would appear as a straight line across the sun's centre, and extending on either side of the sun to a distance of about 16 sun-breadths.   As seen on January 3 and July 5, when it would have its greatest opening, Vulcan's path would appear as an oval whose longest axis would be about 32 sun-breadths, while its shortest would be little more than 6 sun-breadths, the sun of course occupying the centre of the ellipse, which, where closest to him, would lie but about $2\frac{1}{2}$ sun-breadths only from the outline of his disc.   Now it is easily seen that the path of Vulcan, changing in this way from apparent straightness to a long oval (whose breadth is about one-fifth its length), back to straightness but differently inclined, then to the same oval as before but opened out the other way, and so back to its original straightness and inclination, must, for no inconsiderable portion of the year on either side of April 3 and October 6, intersect the outline of the sun's disc.   From a rough but sufficiently accurate calculation which I have made, I find that the interval would last about 36 days at each season, that is, from about March 16 to April 21 in spring, and from about September 18 to about October 24 in autumn.   But during a period of 36 days there would generally be two passages of Vulcan between the earth and sun, and there would always be one (in any long period of time two such passages would be five times as common an event during one of these intervals as a single passage). Consequently there would be at least two transits of Vulcan every year, and there would generally be four transits ; the average number of transits would be about eleven in three years. With a wider orbit and a greater inclination transits would be fewer ; but even with the widest orbit and the greatest inclination that can possibly be allowed, there would be at least one transit a year on the average.

Now when we remember that, so far as the northern hemisphere is concerned, the sun is observed on every fine day in almost every country in Europe and in half the States of the American Union, to say nothing of observations in Asia, where England and Russia have several observatories, while in the southern hemisphere there are many observatories, in Australia, South Africa, and South America (on both side of the Andes), we see how exceedingly small must be the chance that Vulcan could escape detection even for a single year. Far less could Vulcan have escaped all the years which have elapsed since Lescarbault announced his discovery, to say nothing of all the observations made by Carrington, Schwabe, and many others, before the year 1860. If Vulcan really exists, and really has the dimensions and motions described by Lescarbault, the planet must long ere this have been repeatedly seen upon the sun's disc by experienced observers.

As a matter of fact, Wolf has collected nineteen observations of dark bodies unlike spots on the sun, during the interval between 1761 and 1865. But as Professor Newcomb justly points out, with two or three exceptions, the observers are almost unknown as astronomers. In one case at least the object seen was certainly not a planet, since it was described as a cloud-like appearance. ' On the other hand,' says Newcomb, ' for fifty years past the sun has been constantly and assiduously observed by such men as Schwabe, Carrington, Secchi, and Spörer, none of whom have ever recorded anything of the sort. That planets in such numbers should pass over the solar disc, and be seen by amateur astronomers, and yet escape all these skilled astronomers, is beyond all moral probability.'

It must be remembered that an inexperienced observer of the sun might readily mistake a spot of unusual roundness and darkness for a planet's disc. The practised observer would perceive peculiarities at once indicating the object as a spot on the sun ; but these peculiarities would escape the notice of a beginner, or of one using a telescope of small power. Again, an inexperienced observer is apt to mistake the change of position which a spot on the sun undergoes on account of the diurnal motion, for a change of place on the sun's disc. At noon, for instance, the uppermost point of the sun's disc is the north point ; but in the afternoon the uppermost point is east of the true north point. Thus a spot which at noon was a short distance below the highest point of the sun's disc would at two or three be considerably to the west of the highest point, though it had undergone in the interval no appreciable change of position on the solar disc. Suppose now that at two or three in the afternoon clouds come over the sun's face, and he is not seen again that day. On the morrow the spot may have disappeared, as solar spots are apt enough to do. The observer, then (assuming him to be inexperienced like most of those who have described such spots), would say, I saw at noon a small round spot which in the course of the next three hours moved over an appreciable arc towards the west (the right direction, be it remembered, for a planet to cross the sun's face). An experienced observer would not make such a mistake. But let one point be carefully noted. An experienced astronomer would be very apt to forget that such a mistake could be made. He would take it for granted that the observer who described such a change in a spot's position meant a real change, not a change due to the diurnal motion.

Therefore, although Leverrier, Moigno, Hind, and other men of science, have adopted Lescarbault's account, I hold it to be absolutely certain that that account is in some respect or other erroneous. Newcomb goes even farther. He says, it is very certain that if the disturbance of Mercury is due to a group of planets, ' they are each so small as to be invisible in transits across the sun. They must also,' he proceeds, 'be so small as to be invisible during total eclipses of the sun, because they have always failed to show themselves then.' This remark relates, of course, to naked-eye vision. As no intra-Mercurial planet had ever been searched for systematically with the telescope, before the recent eclipse, there was nothing to prevent astronomers from believing that a group of planets, visible in the telescope during total eclipse, may travel between the sun and the path of Mercury.

I proceed at once to consider the evidence afforded during the eclipse of July, 1878, not discussing further the question of Lescarbault's Vulcan, because it appears to me so clear that there must have been some mistake, and because later observations seem to throw clearer evidence on the matter than any which had been before obtained. Yet it must be admitted that even now the evidence is not all that could be desired.

Professor Watson, of Ann Arbor, the discoverer of more than a score of the small planets which travel between the paths of Mars and Jupiter, had been searching for an *extra-Neptunian* planet, when the approach of the eclipse of July, 1878, suggested the idea that he should return for a while from those dismal depths which lie beyond the path of Neptune to seek for a new planet within the glowing region between the sun and the path of Mercury. The occasion was exceptionally favourable because of the great height above the sea-level from which the eclipse could be observed. Accordingly he betook himself to Rawlins, Wyoming, and prepared for the search by providing his telescope with card circles in such sort that the place of any observed star could be recorded by a pencil-mark on these circles, instead of being read off (with the possibility of error) in the usual way. It is unnecessary to explain further, because every one who has ever used an equatorial telescope, or is acquainted with the nature of the instrument, will at once understand Professor Watson's plan, whereas those unfamiliar with the instrument, would not gain any insight into the nature of his plan without much more explanatory matter than could be conveniently given here, even if any explanation without illustrations could make the matter clear. Let it suffice to note that, having brought any star centrally into the telescopic field of view, Professor Watson marked in pencil where the ends of certain pointers came ; and that these marks served to indicate, after the eclipse was over, the position of the observed star.

Thus provided, Professor Watson, so soon as totality began, searched on the eastern side of the sun, and there saw certain stars belonging to the constellation Cancer, where the sun was situate at the time. He then examined the western side of the sun, and having swept out to a star which he took to be Zeta Cancri (though he was rather surprised at its brightness,—but of that more anon) he returned towards the sun, encountering on his way a star of the fourth magnitude or rather less, about two degrees to the west of the sun. Close by was the star Theta Cancri ; but Theta was much fainter, and was seen at the same time a little further west. It is not easy to understand why Watson did not make comparison between the position of the new star and Theta, instead of making comparison between the new star, the sun, and the star which he took to be Zeta. For a comparison with a known object so close as Theta would have given more satisfactory evidence than a comparison with objects farther away. However, as he distinctly states in a letter to Sir G. Airy that the new star was very much brighter than Theta Cancri, which was seen a little farther to the west, we cannot doubt that he had sufficient evidence to prove the new star and Theta Cancri to be distinct orbs.

He adds that there was no appearance of elongation, as might be expected if the new object were a comet. It had a perceptible disc, though the magnifying power was only forty-five.

The accompanying figure will serve to give a fair idea of the position of the stranger.

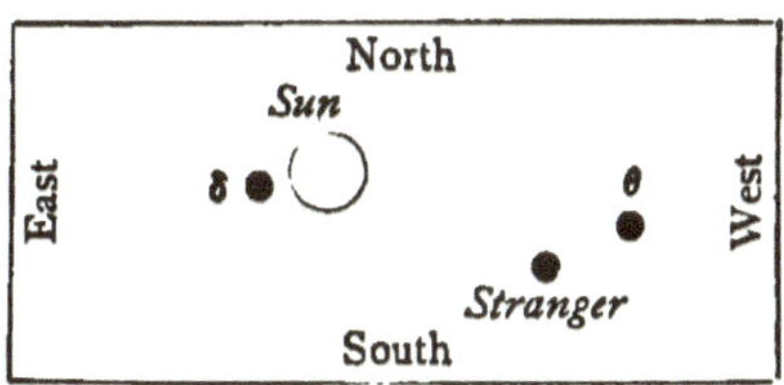

Fig. 1.—Watson's new Planet.

Now comes the evidence which was at first supposed to be strongly corroborative of Watson's observation,—the recognition of a star of about the fourth magnitude, near Theta Cancri, by Professor Louis Swift, who observed the eclipse from Pike's Peak, in Colorado.

Professor Swift also made some rather unusual arrangements with his telescope, but they were not altogether so well adapted to advance his purpose as were Professor Watson's. To prevent the instrument from swaying he tied what he calls a pole (but what in England I imagine would be called a stick), ten feet long, about a foot from the eye-end of the telescope, leaving the other end of this singular appendage to trail on the ground. (The telescope was set low, Professor Swift judging, it would seem, that the most comfortable way to observe was to lie on his back.) As a natural consequence, while he could move his telescope very readily one way, trailing the stick along, he could not move it the other way, because the stick's end immediately stuck into the ground. As the stick was on the west of the telescope, Professor Swift could move the eye-end eastwards, following the sun's westwardly motion. Of course the telescope was to have been released from the stick when totality began, but unfortunately Professor Swift omitted to do this, so that he had to work during totality with a hampered telescope.

The following is his account of what he saw :—

'My hampered telescope behaved badly, and no regularity in the sweeps could be maintained. Almost at once my eye caught two red stars about three degrees south-west of the sun, with large round and equally bright discs which I estimated as of the fifth magnitude, appearing (this was my thought at the time) about as bright in the telescope as the pole-star does to the naked eye. I then carefully noted their distance from the sun and from each other, and the direction in which they pointed, &c., and recorded them in my memory, where, to my mind's eye, they are still distinctly visible. I then swept southward, not daring to venture far to the west, for fear I should be unable to get back again, and soon came upon two stars resembling in every particular the former two I had found, and, sighting along the outside of the tube, was surprised to find I was viewing the same objects. Again I observed them with the utmost care, and then recommenced my sweeps in another direction ; but I soon had them again, and for the third time, in the field. This was also the last, as a small cloud hindered a final leave-taking just before the end of totality, as I had intended. I saw no other star besides these two, not even Delta, so close to the eastern edge of the sun.'

He adds that the apparent distance between the two bodies was about one-fourth the sun's diameter. (These are not his words, but convey the same meaning.)

Again, he adds that, from three careful estimates, he found the two stars pointed exactly to the sun's centre. He knew one of the two bodies was Theta ; but unfortunately he could not tell which was Theta and which the new star or planet. 'But,' he says, 'Professor Watson happily comes to the rescue, and with his means of measuring finds the planet nearest to the sun.'

Unhappily, however, Professor Watson does not come absolutely to the rescue here. On the contrary, to use Professor Swift's words in another part of his letter (and speaking of another matter), 'it is just here where the trouble begins.' If we construct a little map illustrating what Professor Swift describes, we get the accompanying arrangement (fig. 2). It is clearly quite impossible to reconcile this view of the supposed new planet with Professor Watson's. If three careful estimates showed

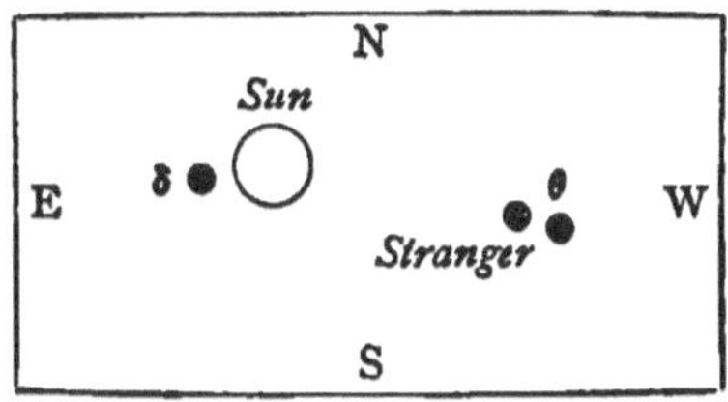

Fig. 2.—Swift's new Planet?

Swift the stranger and Theta situated as in fig. 2, it is absolutely certain that either Watson's observation was very far from the truth, or else the strange orb he saw was not the same that Swift saw. On the o her hand, if Watson's observation was trustworthy, it is certain that either Swift's three estimates were inexact or he saw a different new body. Again, their accounts of the relative brightness of Theta and the stranger could not possibly be reconciled if we supposed they were observing the same new planet, for Watson says distinctly that the stranger was *very much brighter* than Theta ; while Swift says, with equal distinctness, that the two stars were *equally bright.*

If we accept both observations, we must consider that the strange orb seen by Swift was not the nearer to the sun, but the other, for Watson, in his letter to Sir G. Airy, says that he saw both Theta and his own new planet, and he could not have overlooked Swift's new planet, if placed as in fig. 2, whereas if the star there marked as the stranger were really Theta, Watson might readily enough have overlooked the other star, as farther away from his newly-discovered planet. According to this view, the actual arrangement at the time of the eclipse was as shown in fig. 3.

But this is not quite all. Professor Watson saw another body, which in his opinion was a planet. I have already mentioned that he thought Zeta remarkably bright. It seemed to him a star of nearly the third magnitude, whereas Zeta Cancri is only of the fifth. Nay, speaking of the planet near Theta, and of this star which he took for Zeta, he says, 'they were probably really brighter [than the $4\frac{1}{2}$

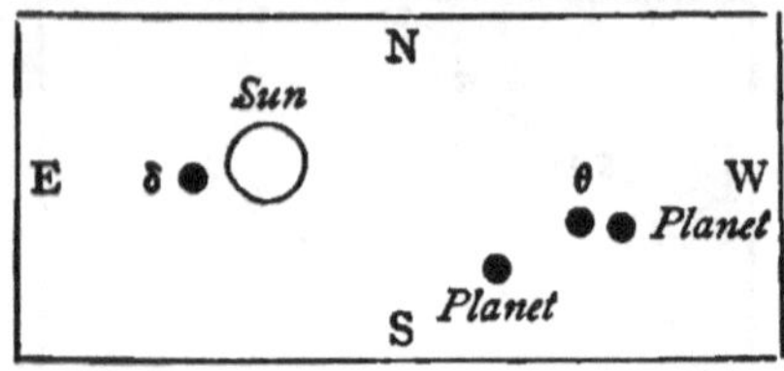

Fig. 3.—Suggested explanation of Watson's
and Swift's observations.

and $3\frac{1}{2}$ magnitude respectively], because the illumination of the sky was not considered in the estimates.' Before he had thoroughly examined the pencil marks on his card circles, and made the necessary calculations, he supposed the brighter star to be Zeta, because he did not see the latter star. But when he examined his result carefully, he found that the bright star was set (according to his pencil marks) more than one degree east of Zeta. Writing on August 22, he says, 'The more I consider the case the more improbable it seems to me that the second star which I observed, and thought it might be Zeta, was that known star. I was not certain, in this case, whether the wind had disturbed the telescope or not. As it had not done so in the case of any other of six pointings which I recorded, it seems almost

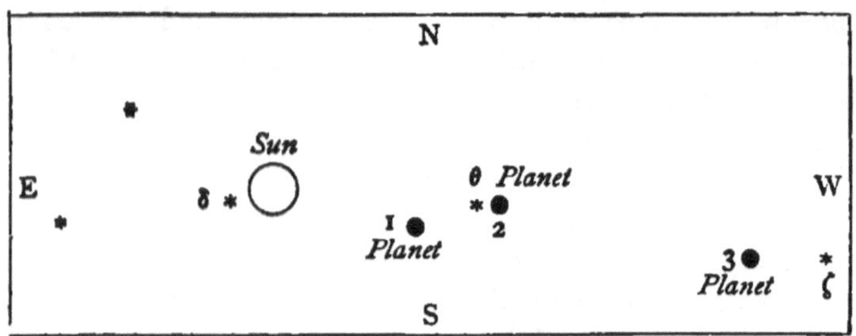

Fig. 4.—Showing all the stars observed by Watson and Swift.

certain that the second was a new star.' It would be easy to understand why Professor Watson had not seen Zeta, for he only swept as far as the star he mistook for Zeta, and, as the accompanying figure shows, Zeta was beyond that star on the west.[1]

Fig. 4 represents the apparent result of the observations made by Professors Watson and Swift, if all the observations are regarded as trustworthy. The six stars shown in the figure were probably the six referred to in the preceding paragraph. The two unnamed ones are well-known red stars.

Let it be noticed, that we cannot reject planet 1, without rejecting all Watson's observations. We cannot reject planet 2, without rejecting all Swift's observations. We cannot set this planet to the left of Theta without throwing doubt on Watson's observations. If Watson swept over Theta westward without seeing 2, Swift must have made some mistake as yet unexplained. As for planet 3, if we admit the possibility that this object really was Zeta, we must admit also the possibility that the object marked as planet 1 was really Theta, or rather we should have to do so, were it not that Watson saw Theta also, and (I suppose) in the same field of view, since he speaks confidently of the inferiority of Theta in brightness.

It should further be noticed, that though Swift's and Watson's observations by no means agree in details, they do in reality support each other (unless Watson should definitely assert that no star as bright as Theta existed either to the west or to the east of that star, at the distance indicated by Swift.) For they agree in indicating the existence of small planets near the sun, such as can only be seen with the telescope.

On the other hand, it is to be noted that other observers failed to see any of these bodies, though they looked

[1] It may be necessary, perhaps, to explain to some why the western side is on the right in the little maps illustrating this paper, and not, as usual with maps, on the left. We are supposed to look down towards the earth in the case of a terrestrial map, and to look up from the earth in the case of a celestial map, and naturally right and left for the former attitude become respectively left and right for the latter.

specially for intra-Mercurial planets. Thus Professor Hall, of the Washington Observatory, searched over a larger space than is included in fig. 4, without seeing any unknown body. But as he also failed to see many known bodies which should have been seen, it is probable that the search was too hurried to be trustworthy.

It would be satisfactory to be able to say that any of the supposed planets might have been Lescarbault's Vulcan. But in reality, I fear, this cannot have been the case. In the *Times*, I expressed, in an article dated August 14, 1878, the opinion that the evidence obtained establishes the existence of the planet which had so long been regarded as a myth. That opinion was based on a very careful investigation of the evidence available at the time. But it does not accord with what has since been learned respecting Watson's observations.

We may dismiss planet 3 at once. If Watson is right about this body being distinct from Zeta (a point about which, I must confess, I feel grave doubts), then this must be a planet travelling in an orbit much wider than we can possibly assign to Vulcan. For even at the distance of some seven degrees from the sun it showed no sign of gibbosity. If it had then been at its greatest elongation it would have appeared only half-full. But with the power Watson was using, which enabled him to pronounce that the smaller body near Theta showed no elongation, he would at once have noticed any such peculiarity of shape. He could not have failed to observe any gibbosity approaching to that of the moon when three-quarters full. Moreover on July 29 a planet which has its points of crossing the ecliptic opposite the earth's place on April 3 and October 6, could not appear where Watson saw this body (fully two degrees from the ecliptic) unless either its orbit were far wider than that which Leverrier assigned to Vulcan, or else its inclination far greater. Neither supposition can be reconciled with Lescarbault's observation.

With regard to planets 1 and 2, the case is equally

strong against the theory that Vulcan was observed. The same reasoning applies to both these bodies. When I speak therefore of planet 1, it will be understood that planet 2 also is dealt with. First, as this planet appeared with a disc appreciably round, it is clear that it must have been near the point of its orbit farthest from the earth, that is, the point directly beyond the sun. It was then nearly at its brightest. Yet it appeared as a fourth-magnitude star only. We have seen that Lescarbault's Vulcan, even when only half-full, would appear as bright as Mercury at his brightest, if Lescarbault's account can be accepted in all its details. Situated as planet 1 was, Vulcan would have shown much more brightly than an average first-magnitude star. At a very moderate computation it would have been twice as bright as such a star. But planet 1 appeared fainter than a fourth-magnitude star. Assume, however, that in reality it was shining as brightly as an average third-magnitude star. Then it shone with much less than a twentieth of the lustre Vulcan should have had, if Lescarbault's estimate were correct. Its diameter then cannot be greater than a quarter of that which Leverrier assigned to Vulcan on the strength of Lescarbault's observation. In fact, the apparent diameter of planet 1, when in transit over the sun's face, could not be more than a sixteenth of Mercury's in transit, or about two-fifths of a second,—roughly, about a 5000th part of the sun's apparent diameter. It is certain that Lescarbault could not have made so considerable a mistake as this. Nay, it is certain, that with the telescope he used he could not have seen a spot of this size at all on the sun's face.

It will be seen that Lescarbault's observation still remains unconfirmed, or rather, to speak more correctly, the doubts which have been raised respecting Lescarbault's Vulcan are now more than ever justified. If such a body as he supposed he saw really travels round the sun within the orbit of Mercury, it is certain that the observations made last July by those who were specially engaged in seeking for Vulcan must have been rewarded by a view of that planet.   In July, Lescarbault's Vulcan could not have been invisible, no matter in what part of his orbit it might be, and the chances would have been greatly in favour of its appearing as a very bright star, without telescopic aid.

But on the other hand it seems extremely probable,—in fact, unless any one be disposed to question the veracity of the observers, it is certain,—that within the orbit of Mercury there are several small planets, of which certainly two, and probably three, were seen during the eclipse of July 29, 1878. All these bodies must be beyond the range of any except the most powerful telescopes, whether sought for as bright bodies outside the sun (not eclipsed) or as dark bodies in transit across the sun's face. The search for such bodies in transit would in fact be hopeless with any telescope which would not easily separate double stars one second of arc apart. It is with large telescopes, then, and under favourable conditions of atmosphere, locality, and so forth, that the search for intra-Mercurial planets in transit must in future be conducted. As the observed disturbance of Mercury's perihelion, and the absence of any corresponding disturbance of his nodes (the points where he crosses the plane of the earth's motion) show that the disturbing bodies must form a ring or disc whose central plane must nearly coincide with the plane of Mercury's path, the most favourable time for seeing these bodies in transit would be the first fortnights in May and November ; for the earth crosses the plane of Mercury's orbit on or about May 8 and November 10. I believe that a search carried out in April, May, and June, and in October, November, and December, with the express object of discovering *very* small planets in transit, could not fail to be quickly rewarded,—unless the observations made by Watson and Swift are to be wholly rejected.

[Since this was written, Professor Swift has expressed the opinion that his planet cannot possibly have been the one seen near Theta Cancri by Professor Watson,—who it seems saw Theta in the centre of a large field of view, and must therefore have seen Swift's planet had that object been placed either as shown in fig. 2 or fig. 3. Hence Professor Swift considers that both the stars he himself saw were planets, and that he did not see Theta at all. The reasoning in the last five paragraphs of the above essay would not be in the least affected if we adopted Professor Swift's conclusion, that four and not three intra-Mercurial planets were detected during the eclipse of July last. Yet later Professor Peters of Clinton has indicated reasons for believing that while Watson simply mistook for planets the two fixed stars, Theta and Zeta Cancri, Professor Swift saw no planets at all. This interpretation would account fully, though not very satisfactorily, for all that is mysterious in the two narratives.]

RESULTS OF THE BRITISH TRANSIT EXPEDITIONS.

ANOTHER noteworthy attempt has been made to estimate the distance which separates our earth from the mighty central orb round which she travels with her fellow-worlds the planets. In other words, the solar system itself has been remeasured ; for the measurement of any part of the system is in fact the measurement of the entire system, the proportions of which, as distinguished from its actual dimensions, have long been accurately known.

I propose briefly to describe the results which have been obtained (after some three years of careful examination) from the observations made by the British parties sent north, south, east, and west to observe the transit of Venus on December 9, 1874 ; and then to consider how these results compare with those which had before been obtained. First, however, it may be well to remind the reader of the unfavourable conditions under which the task of measuring our distance from the remote sun must of necessity be attacked.

Not unfrequently we hear the measurement of the sun's distance, and the various errors which astronomers have had to correct during the progress of their efforts to deal with the problem, referred to in terms which would imply that astronomy had some reason to be ashamed of labours which are in reality among the most noteworthy achievements of their science. Because, some twenty years ago, the estimate of 95 million miles, which had for half a century held its ground in our books of astronomy as the true distance of the sun, was replaced for a while by an estimate of about $91\frac{1}{2}$ million miles, which has in turn been displaced for an estimate of about $92\frac{1}{3}$ million miles, it has been said that astronomy has very little claim to be called the exact science. It is even supposed by some that astronomy is altogether at sea respecting the sun's distance—which, if the estimates of astronomers thus vary in the course of three-quarters of a century, may in reality, it is thought, be very different from any of the values hitherto assigned. Others suppose that possibly the sun's distance may vary, and that the diminution of three or four million miles in the estimates adopted by astronomers may correspond to an approach of the earth towards the sun by that amount, an approach which, if continued at the same rate, would, before many centuries, bring the earth upon the surface of the sun, to be consumed as fuel perhaps for the warming of the outer planets, Mars, Jupiter, and the rest.

All these imaginings are mistaken, however. The exactness of astronomy, as a science, does not depend on the measurement of the sun's distance or size, any more than the accuracy of a clock as a timekeeper depends on the exactness with which the hands of the clock are limited to certain definite lengths. The skill with which astronomy has dealt with this particular problem of celestial surveying has been great indeed ; and the results, when considered with due reference to the conditions of the problem, are excellent : but in reality, if astronomers had failed utterly to form any ideas whatever as to the sun's distance, if for aught they knew the sun might be less than one million, or more than a million millions of miles from us, the exactness of astronomy as a science would be no whit impaired. And, in the second place, no doubts whatever need be entertained as to the general inference from astronomical observations that the sun's distance is between 92 and 93 millions of miles. All the measurements made during the last quarter of a century lie between 90 and 95 millions of miles, and by far the greater number of those made by the best methods, and under the most favourable conditions, lie between 91 and 94 millions of miles. All the very best cluster closely around a distance of $92\frac{1}{3}$ millions of miles. We are not for the moment, however, concerned with the question of the exact distance, but with the question whether astronomy has obtained satisfactory evidence that the sun's distance lies in the neighbourhood of the distances deduced by the various methods lately employed. Putting the matter as one of probabilities, as all scientific statements must be, it may be said as confidently that the sun's distance lies between 85 millions and 100 millions of miles as that the sun will rise to-morrow; and the probability that the sun's distance is less than 90 millions, or greater than 95 millions of miles, is so small that it may in effect be counted almost as nothing. Thirdly, the possibility that the earth may be drawing nearer to the sun by three or four millions of miles in a century may be dismissed entirely from consideration. For, one of the inevitable consequences of such a change of distance would be a change in the length of the year by about three weeks; and so far from the year diminishing by twenty days or so in length during a century, it has not diminished ten seconds in length during the last two thousand years. If there has been any change year by year in the earth's distance from the sun, it is one to be measured by yards rather than by miles. Astronomers would be well content if their 'probable error' in estimating the sun's distance could be measured by thousands of miles; so that any possible approach of the earth towards the sun would go but a very little way towards accounting for the discrepancies between the different estimates of the distance, even if these estimates grew always smaller as time passed, which is assuredly not the case.

But in truth, if we consider the nature of the task undertaken by astronomers in this case, we can only too readily understand that their measurements should differ somewhat widely from each other, Let us picture to ourselves for a moment the central sun, the earth, and the earth's path, not as they really are, for the mind refuses altogether to picture the dimensions even of the earth, which is but an atom compared with the sun, whose own proportions, in turn, mighty though they are, sink into utter insignificance compared with the enormous scale of the orbit in which the earth travels around him. Let us reduce the scale of the entire system to one 500-millionth part of its real value : even then we have a tolerably large orbit to imagine. We must picture to ourselves a fiery globe 3 yards in diameter to represent the sun, and the earth as a one-inch ball circling round that globe at a distance of about 325 yards, or about 350 paces. The diameter of the earth's orbit would on this scale, therefore, be somewhat more than a third of a mile. If we imagine the one-inch ball moving round the fiery globe once in a year, while turning on its axis once in a day, we find ourselves under a difficulty arising from the slowness of the resulting motions. We should have found ourselves under a difficulty arising from the rapidity of the actual motions if we had considered them instead. The only resource is to reduce our time-scale, in the same way that we have reduced our space-scale : but not in the same degree ; for if we did we should have the one-inch ball circling round its orbit, a third of a mile in diameter, sixteen times in a second, and turning on its axis five thousand times in a second. Say, instead, that for convenience we suppose days reduced to seconds. Then we have to picture a one-inch globe circling once in rather more than six minutes about a globe of fire 3 yards in diameter, one-sixth of a mile from it, and turning on its axis once in a second. We must further picture the one-inch globe as inhabited by some 1,500 millions of creatures far too small to be seen with the most powerful microscope—in fact, so small that the tallest would be in height but about the seven-millionth of an inch—and we must imagine that a few of these creatures undertake the task of determining from their tiny home swiftly rotating as it rushes in its orbit around a large globe of fire, 325 yards from them

—the number of yards really intervening between that globe and their home. If we rightly picture these conditions, which fairly represent those under which the astronomer has to determine the distance of the sun from the earth, we shall perceive that the wonder rather is that any idea of the sun's distance should be obtained at all, than that the estimates obtained should differ from each other, and that the best of them should err in measurable degree from the true distance.

Anything like a full explanation of the way in which transits of Venus across the sun's face are utilised in the solution of the problem of determining the sun's distance would be out of place in these pages. But perhaps the following illustration may serve sufficiently, yet simply, to indicate the qualities of the two leading methods of using a transit. Imagine a bird flying in a circle round a distant globe in such a way that, as seen from a certain window (a circular window suppose), the bird will seem to cross the face of the globe once in each circuit. Suppose that though the distance of the globe is not known, the window is known to be exactly half as far again from the globe as the bird's path is, and that the window is exactly a yard in diameter. Now in the first place, suppose two observers watch the bird, one (A) from the extreme right side, and the other (B) from the extreme left side of the window, the bird flying across from right to left. A sees the bird begin to cross the face of the globe before B does,—say they find that A sees this exactly one second before B does. But A's eye and B's being 3 feet apart, and the bird two-thirds as far from the globe as the window is, the line traversed by the bird in this interval is of course only 2 feet in length. The bird then flies 2 feet in a second (this is rather slow for a bird, but the principle of the explanation is not affected on that account). Say it is further observed that he completes a circuit in exactly ten minutes or six hundred seconds. Thus the entire length of a circuit is 1,200 feet,—whence by the well-known relation between the circumference and the diameter of a circle, it follows that the diameter of the bird's path is about 382 feet, and his distance from the centre of the globe 191 feet. So that the distance of the globe from the window, known to be half as great again, is about 286½ feet.

If we regard the globe as representing the sun; the window of known size as representing our earth of known dimensions; the bird travelling round in a known period and at a distance whose proportion to the window's distance is known, as representing Venus travelling in a known period round the sun and at a distance bearing a known proportion to the earth's; this way of determining the distance of a remote globe illustrates what is called Delisle's method of determining the sun's distance. It requires that the two observers, A and B, should each make exact note of the moment when the bird seemed to begin to cross the disc of the remote globe; and in like manner Delisle's method requires that two observers, widely separated on the earth in a direction nearly parallel to that in which Venus is travelling, should make the most exact note of the moment when Venus begins to cross the sun's face. Also, as all I have said about the bird's beginning to cross the face of the distant globe would apply equally well if said about the end of his seeming passage across that disc, so two observers, widely separated on the earth, can determine the sun's distance by noting the end of her transit instead of the beginning, if they are suitably placed for the purpose. The window of our illustration remains unchanged during the bird's imagined flight, but as the face of the earth turned sunwards (which corresponds to that window) is all the time changing with the earth's rotation, a different pair of stations would have to be selected for observing the end of transit, than would be suitable for observing the beginning.   ·

So much for the method called Delisle's. The other is in principle equally simple. In the imaginary experiment just described we supposed the two observers at the right and left sides of the circular window. Imagine them now to watch the bird from the top and bottom of the window, 3 feet apart. Suppose they note that the two tracks along which, as seen from these two points, the bird seems to cross the face of the distant globe, lie at a distance from each other equal to one-third of the globe's apparent diameter. Now, the bird being twice as far from the globe as from the window, the two tracks on the globe necessarily lie twice as far apart as the two points from which they are seen—or they lie 6 feet apart. The globe's diameter therefore is 18 feet. Knowing thus how large it is, and knowing also how large it looks, the observers know how far from them it lies. So, in the Halleyan method of determining the sun's distance by observing Venus in transit, astronomers are stationed far north and far south on the sunlit half of the earth, corresponding to the window of the imaginary experiment. Venus corresponds to the bird. The observers note along what track she travels across the sun's face. (That they partially determine this by noting how long she is in crossing, in no sense affects the principle of the method.) They thus learn that such and such a portion of the sun's diameter equals the distance separating them,—some six or seven thousand miles perhaps,—whence the sun's diameter is known. And as we know how large he looks, his distance from the earth is determined.

A peculiarity distinguishing this method from the former is that the observers must have a station whence the whole transit can be seen ; for practically the place of Venus's track can only be ascertained satisfactorily by timing her passage across the sun's disc, so that the beginning and end must be observed and very carefully timed. This is to some degree a disadvantage ; for during a transit lasting several hours the earth turns considerably on her axis, and the face turned sunwards at the beginning is thus very different from the face turned sunwards at the end of transit. It is often exceedingly difficult to find suitable northern and southern stations belonging to both these faces of the earth. On the other hand, the other method has its peculiar disadvantage. To apply it effectively, the observer must know the exact Greenwich time (or any other selected standard time) at his station,—or in other words he must know exactly how far east or west his station is from Greenwich (or some other standard observatory). For all the observations made by this method must be compared together by some absolute time standard. In the Halleyan method the duration of transit only is wanted, and this can be as readily determined by a clock showing local time (or indeed by a clock set going a few minutes before transit began and showing wrong time altogether, so only that it goes at the right rate) as by a clock showing Greenwich, Paris, or Washington time. The clock must not gain or lose in the interval. But a clock which would gain or lose appreciably in four or five hours, would be worthless to the astronomer ; and any clock employed for scientific observation might safely be trusted for an interval of that length ; whereas a clock which could be trusted to retain true time for several days, is not so readily to be obtained.

We need not consider here the origin of the misapprehension (under which our principal Government astronomer lay for some time), that the Delislean method was alone available during the transit of 1874, the Halleyan method, to use his words, 'failing totally.' The British stations were selected while this misapprehension remained as yet uncorrected. Fortunately the southern stations were suitable for both methods. The northern were not : for this reason, simply, that one set were so situated that night began soon after the beginning of transit, which alone could be observed; while the other set were so situated that night only came to an end a short time before the transit ended, so that the end of transit only could be observed. No doubt when the mistake just mentioned had been clearly recognised,—as it was early in 1873,— measures would have been taken to rectify its effect by occupying some suitable northern stations for observing the whole transit, if Great Britain had been the only nation taking part in the work. Fortunately, however, other nations might be trusted to occupy the northern region, which had so long been overlooked. England simply strengthened the southern observing corps : this could be done without any change by which the Government astronomers would have seemed to admit that 'some one had blundered.' Thus the matter was arranged—America, Russia, and Germany occupying a large number of stations admirably suited for applying the method which had been supposed to 'fail totally.' The British Official astronomers, on whom of course responsibility for adequately observing the transit (or at least for properly applying money granted by the nation for the purpose) alone rested, did in reality all, or nearly all, that was necessary in doubling some of the southern observing parties, and strengthening all of them ; for unquestionably other nations occupied suitable northern stations in sufficiently strong force.

It is to be remembered, however, in estimating the probable value of the result which has been deduced from the British observations, that as yet only a portion of these observations has been effectively dealt with. The British observations of the beginning of transit at northern and southern stations give, when combined together, a value of the sun's distance. The British observations of the end of transit at other northern and southern stations give also, when combined together, a value of the sun's distance. And both sets combined give of course a mean value of the sun's distance, more likely on the whole to be correct than either value taken separately. But the British observations of the duration of transit as observed from southern stations do not of themselves give any means of determining the sun's distance. They must be combined with observations of the duration of transit as observed from northern stations ; and no British party was stationed where such observations could be obtained. The value, then, of these particular British southern observations can only be educed when comparison is made between them and the northern observations by American, German, and Russian astronomers.

We must not, then, be disheartened if the results of the

British operations *alone* should not seem to be altogether satisfactory. For it may still happen that that portion of the British operations which only has value when combined with the work of other countries may be found to possess extreme value. We had good reason for doubting beforehand whether results of any great value could be obtained by Delisle's method. It was only because Halley's was supposed to fail totally that the Government astronomers ever thought of employing that method, which the experience of former transits had taught us to regard as of very little value.

It may be asked, however, how we are to form an opinion from the result of calculations based on the Delislean operations during the last transit, whether the method is satisfactory or not. If as yet the sun's distance is not exactly determined, a result differing from former results may be better than any of them, many will think; and therefore the method employed to obtain it may be more satisfactory than others. If, they may reason, we place reliance on a certain method to measure for us a certain unknown distance, how can we possibly tell from the distance so determined whether the method is trustworthy or not?

Perhaps the readiest way of removing this difficulty, and also of illustrating generally the principles on which the determination of the most probable mean value of many different estimates depends, is by considering a familiar experience of many, a case in which the point to be determined is the most probable time of day. Suppose that we are walking along a route where there are several clocks, the time shown by our own watch being, for whatever reason, open to question. We find, say, that as compared with our watch time, one clock is two minutes fast, the next three minutes fast, the next one minute slow, and so on, two or three perhaps being as much as six or seven minutes fast, and two or three being as much as three or four minutes slow as compared with the watch. We note, however, that these wider ranges of difference occur only in the case of clocks presumably inferior—cheap clocks in small shops, old clocks in buildings where manifestly the flight of time is not much noted, and so forth. Rejecting these from consideration, we find other clocks ranging from one minute or so before our watch time to four minutes or so after it. Before striking a rough average, however, we consider that some among these clocks are placed where it is on the whole better to be a minute or two before the time than a second late,—as, for instance, at banks, where there may be occasion to send out clerks so as to make sure of reaching certain places (Clearing-House, General Post-office, and so forth) within specified time limits. On the other hand, we note that others of these clocks are placed where it is better to be a minute or two after time than a second before it,—as at railway stations, post-offices, and so on, where it is essential that the public should be allowed time fully up to a specified hour, for some particular service. Taking fair account of such considerations, we might find that most probably the true time lay between half a minute *before* and two minutes and a half *after* our watch time. And thus we might infer that in reality the true time was one minute or so later than that shown by our watch. But if we were well acquainted with the characteristics of different clocks along our route, we might infer the time (nay, we might to all intents and purposes *know* the time) far more accurately than this. We might, for instance, pass six or seven shop-windows where first-class specimens of horological work were shown,—in each window, perhaps, several excellent clocks, with compensated pendulums and other contrivances for securing perfect working. We might find at one of these shops all such clocks showing the same time within two or three seconds ; at the next all such clocks also agreeing *inter se* within two or three seconds, but perhaps their mean differing from the mean at the last shop of the kind by seven or eight seconds ; and all six or seven shops, while showing similar agreement as regards the clocks severally displayed at each, agreeing also with each other so closely that ten or twelve seconds would cover the entire range between their several mean times. If this were observed, we should not hesitate to place entire reliance on these special sets of clocks ; and we should feel certain that if we took the mean of all their means as the true time (perhaps slightly modifying this mean in order to give due weight to the known superiority of one or other of these clock-shops), we should not be in error by more than five or six seconds, while most probably we should have the time true within two or three seconds.

So far the illustration corresponds well with what had been done during a quarter of a century or so before the last transit of Venus. Several different methods of determining the sun's distance had been applied to correct a value which for many reasons had come to be looked upon with suspicion. This value—95,365,000 miles—was known to be certainly too large. The methods used to test it gave results varying between about 90 million miles and about 96 million miles. But all the methods worthy of any real reliance gave results lying between 91 million miles and 94 million miles. Not to enter more fully into details than would here be suitable, we may pass on at once to say that those most experienced in the matter recognised seven methods of determining the distance, on which chief reliance must be placed. Of these seven methods, six—each applied, of course, by many different observers—were dealt with exhaustively by Professor Newcomb, of the Washington Observatory, a mathematician who has undoubtedly given closer attention to the general problem of determining the sun's distance than any living astronomer. The six methods give six several results ranging from about 92,250,000 miles to about 92,850,000 miles ; but when due weight is given to those of the six methods which are undoubtedly the best, the most probable mean value is found to be about 92,350,000 miles. The seventh method, conceived by Leverrier, the astronomer to whom, with our own Adams, the discovery of Neptune was due, and applied by him as he only could have applied it (he alone possessing at once the necessary material and the necessary skill), gives the value, 92,250,000 miles. From this it may fairly be concluded that Newcomb's mean value, which has in fact been accepted by all American and Continental astronomers, is certainly within 600,000 miles, and most probably within 300,000 miles of the true mean distance of the sun.

But now, to revert to our illustrative case, let us suppose that after passing the windows of six or seven horologists, from whose clocks we have obtained such satisfactory evidence as to the probable hour, we bethought ourselves of a place where, from what we had heard, a still more exact determination of the hour might be obtained. While still on the way, however, we learn from a friend certain circumstances suggesting the possibility that the clocks at the place in question may not be so correct as we had supposed. Persisting, however, in our purpose, we arrive at the place, and carefully compare the indicati ns of the various clocks there with the time indicated by our watch, corrected (be it supposed) in accordance with the results of our former observations. Suppose now that the hour indicated by the various clocks at this place, instead of agreeing closely with that which we had thus inferred, differs from it by fully half a minute. Is it not clear that instead of being led by this result to correct our former estimate of the probable hour, we should at once infer that the doubts which had been suggested as to the correctness of the various clocks at this place were fully justified? The evidence of the other sets of clocks would certainly not be invalidated by the evidence given by the set last visited, even if the accuracy of these had not been called in question. But if, as supposed, some good reason had been given for doubt on this point,—as for instance, that of late the supervision of the clocks had been interrupted,—we should not hesitate for a moment to reject the evidence given by these clocks, or at least to regard it as only tending to demonstrate what before we had been led to surmise, namely, that these clocks could not be relied upon to show true time. If however, furthermore, we found, not only that the mean of the various times indicated by the clocks at this last-visited place differed thus widely from the time which we had every reason to consider very nearly exact, but that the different clocks here differed as widely from each other, it would be absurd to rely upon their evidence. The circumstance that there was a range of difference of fully half a minute in their indications would of itself suffice to show how untrustworthy they were, at least for the use of any one who wished to obtain the time with great accuracy. Combined with the observed difference between their mean time and that before obtained, this circumstance would prove the inaccuracy of the clocks beyond all possibility of doubt or question.

Now the case here imagined corresponds very closely with the circumstances of the recent attempt to correct our estimate of the sun's distance by Delisle's method. Our Government astronomers bethought themselves of this method as likely to give the best possible means for correcting, by observations of Venus in transit, the estimate of the sun's distance which had been deduced by Newcomb, and confirmed by Leverrier. While as yet their plans were not finally decided upon, reasons for questioning this conclusion were indicated to those officials by unofficial astronomers entertaining very friendly feelings towards them. Retaining, however, their reliance on the method thus called in question, they carried out their purpose, though fortunately making provision, very nearly sufficient, for the use of another method. Now, instead of the estimate of the sun's distance obtained from the observations by Delisle's method agreeing closely with Newcomb's mean value,—about 92,350,000 miles,—it exceeds this value by about a million miles. (See, however, note on the last page of this article.) According to various ways of considering the results sent in by his observers, the chief official astronomer obtains a mean value ranging from about 93,300,000 miles to about 93,375,000 miles. The last named estimate seems preferred on the whole ; but if we take 93,350,000 miles, we shall probably give about the fairest final mean value. We have seen, however, that the results of observations by seven distinct methods give values ranging only between 92,250,000 miles and 92,850,000 miles,—the six best methods giving values ranging only between 92,250,000 miles and about 92,480,000 miles. The new value thus lies 500,000 miles above the largest and admittedly the least trustworthy of the seven results, 870,000 miles above the next largest, a million miles above the mean value, and 1,100,000 miles above the least value. It certainly ranges 500,000 miles above the largest admissible value from those seven trusted methods, dealt with most skilfully, cautiously, and laboriously, by such mathematicians as Newcomb and Leverrier.

Can we hesitate as to the inference we should deduce from this result? We need not for a moment call in question the skill or care with which the British observing parties carried out their operations. Nor need we doubt that the results obtained have been most skilfully and cautiously investigated by those to whom the work of supervision and of reduction has been entrusted. We need not even question the policy of devoting so large a share of labour and expense to the employment of a method held in little favour by most experienced Continental and American astronomers, and objected to by many in England, including some even among official astronomers. It was perhaps well that the method should have one fair and full trial. And it is certain that all who have taken part in the work have done their duty zealously and skilfully. Captain Tupman, to whom Sir George Airy, our chief official astronomer, entrusted the management of the calculations, has received, and justly, from his official superior, the highest commendation for his energy and discrimination. But beyond all manner of doubt the method employed has failed under the test thus applied to it. I do not say that hereafter the method may not succeed. Some of the conditions which at present render it untrustworthy are such as may be expected to be modified with the progress of improvement in the construction of scientific instruments. But as yet the method is certainly not trustworthy.

This might be safely concluded from the wide discrepancy between the new result and the mean of those before obtained. Yet if all the various observations made by the British observing parties agreed closely together, the circumstance, though it could hardly shake our inference on this point, would yet cause some degree of perplexity, since, of itself, it would seem to imply that the method was trustworthy. Fortunately we are not thus troubled by conflicting evidence. The indications of the untrustworthy nature of the method, derived from the discordance between the results obtained by it and those before inferred, are not a whit clearer, clear and convincing though they are, than are the indications afforded by their discordance *inter se.* The distance derived from northern and southern observations of the beginning of transit ought of course to be the same as that derived from northern and southern observations of the end of transit. If both sets of observations were exactly correct, the agreement between the results would be exact. The discordance between them could only be wide as a consequence of some serious imperfection in this method of observing a transit. But the discordance is *very* wide. The observations of the beginning of transit by the British parties give a distance of the sun exceeding by rather more than a million miles that deduced from the observations of the end of transit.

I am well assured that neither Continental nor American astronomers will accept the new estimate of the sun's distance, unless—which I venture to predict will not be the case—the entire series of transit observations should seem to point to the same value as the most probable mean. Even then most astronomers will, I believe, think rather that transits of Venus do not afford such satisfactory means of determining the sun's distance as had been supposed. This opinion, it is well known, was held by Leverrier, insomuch that he declined to support with the weight of his influence the proposals for heavy expenditure by France upon expeditions for observing the recent transit and the approaching transit of the year 1882.

I doubt whether many, even among British astronomers, will accept the new value. Already the Superintendent of the *Nautical Almanac* has given his opinion upon it in terms which cannot be regarded as favourable. ' It is well known,' he says (I quote at least from an article which has been attributed to him without contradiction on his part), ' that some astronomers have not expected our knowledge of the sun's distance to be greatly improved from the observations of the transit of Venus. Many, we can imagine, will regard with some suspicion ' so great a value as 93,300,000 miles (I substitute these words for technical expressions identical in real meaning). ' Nevertheless, whatever degree of doubt might be entertained by competent authorities, it appears to have been felt by those immediately responsible for action, in different civilised nations where science is encouraged, that so rare a phenomenon as a transit of Venus could not be allowed to pass without every exertion being made to utilise it.'

Sir George Airy, very naturally, attaches more value to the result of the British expeditions, or at least of that part of the operations for which he was responsible, than others are disposed to do. In an address to the Astronomical Society, he expressed the opinion that ' the results now presented are well worthy of very great confidence. . . . Considering that the number of observers was eighteen, and that they made fifty-four observations, and considering also the degree of training they had, and their zeal, and the extreme care that was taken in the choice of stations, I think,' he said, ' that there will not be anything to compete with the value which has been deduced.' This is, as I have said, very naturally his opinion ; and although ordinarily it is rather for the employers than for the employed to estimate the value of the results sent in, yet at least we cannot object to his just and generous praise of those who have worked under his orders.

Nevertheless, it must not be forgotten that on a former occasion when equal satisfaction was expressed with the result of a rather less costly but still a laborious and difficult experiment, the scientific world did not accept (and has since definitely rejected) the conclusion thus confidently advanced. I refer to the famous Harton Colliery experiment for determining the mass of the earth. The case is so closely analogous to that we are dealing with, that it will be instructive briefly to describe its leading features. Maskelyne, formerly the chief Government astronomer of this country, from observations of the effect of the mass of Mount Schehallien in deflecting a plumb-line, had inferred that the density of the earth is five times that of water. Bouguer from observations in Chimborazo, and Colonel James from observations on Arthur's Seat, had deduced very similar results. From pendulum observations on high mountains, Carlini and Plana made the earth's density very nearly the same. Cavendish, Reich, and our own Francis Baily, weighed the earth against two great globes of lead, by a method commonly known as the Cavendish experiment, but really invented by Michell. These experiments agreed closely together, making the earth's density about $5\frac{1}{2}$ times that of water, or giving to the earth a mass equivalent to that which would be contained in 6,000 millions of millions of millions of tons. Now, from the Harton Colliery experiments, in 1854, in which the earth's weight was estimated by comparing the vibrations of a pendulum at the mouth of the mine with those of a similar pendulum at a depth of about 1,260 feet, it appeared that the earth's density is rather more than $6\frac{1}{2}$ times that of water, corresponding to an increase in our estimate of the earth's mass by nearly 1,100 millions of millions of millions of tons, or by more than a sixth of the entire mass resulting from the most trustworthy former measurements. Sir G. Airy considered that 'this result will compete on at least equal terms with those obtained by other methods;' but nearly a quarter of a century has passed during which no competent astronomer has adopted this opin on, or even suggested any modification of the former mean estimate of the earth's mass on account of the unexpectedly large value deduced from the Harton experiment.

It appears to me probable that a similar fortune will attend the latest measurement of the sun's distance. But fortunately the matter will not rest merely on measurements already made. Many fresh measurements will be made during the next few years by methods already tried and *not* (like Delisle's transit method) found wanting. The recent close approach of the planet Mars was not allowed to pass without a series of observations specially directed to the determination of the sun's distance ; and we know that observations of Mars are among the most advantageous means available for the solution of this difficult problem. It was indeed from such observations that the first really trustworthy measures of the sun's distance were obtained two centuries ago. The small planets which travel in hundreds between the paths of Mars and Jupiter have also been pressed into the service. And now so many of these are known that scarcely a month passes without one or other of them being favourably placed for the purpose of distance measurements. For this too their star-like discs make these bodies specially suitable.

The most probable inference respecting the results obtained by the British expedition is that their chief value resides in the evidence which they afford respecting the Delislean method of observation. They seem to demonstrate what had before been only surmised (though with considerable confidence by some astronomers), that this method cannot be relied upon to correct our estimate of the sun's distance. In the transit of 1882, which by the way will be visible in this country, we may be certain that other and more satisfactory methods of observation will be employed.

Before concluding, it may be well to make a few remarks upon some misapprehensions which seem to exist as to the propriety in the first place, and the desirability in the second, of comments upon the arrangements adopted by Government astronomers to utilize particular astronomical phenomena, and upon the value of the results which may be obtained by means of such arrangements. Many seem to suppose that astronomical matters are in some sense like military or naval (warlike) manœuvres, to be discussed effectively only by those who 'are under authority, having (also) soldiers under them,' in other words by Government astronomers. It would be very unfortunate for science were this so, seeing that in that case those chiefly responsible for the selection of methods and the supervision of operations would be perfectly free from all possibility of criticism. No one under their authority would be very likely to speak unfavourably of their plans. And no one possessing higher general authority would be likely to have any adequate knowledge of astronomy to form an opinion, either as to the efficiency of the arrangements adopted in any case, or as to the significance of the results obtained. In warlike matters, to some degree, the wisdom of the strategy employed is tested by results which all can appreciate, seeing that they affect directly the well-being of the nation. Moreover, there are special reasons in these cases why in the first place there should be a complete system of subordination, and why in the second few should undertake the study of the science unless they proposed to take their part in its practical application and therefore to submit to its disciplinary system. But it is quite otherwise with the science of astronomy. The nation requires, chiefly for the regulation of its commerce, a certain number of trained astronomers, to carry out systematically observations of a certain class,—observations having in the main scarcely any closer relation to the real living science of astronomy than land surveying has to such geology as Lyell taught, or the bone-trade to the science of anatomy. The stars by their diurnal motion form the most perfect time-measurers, therefore they must be constantly timed by trained observers. The sun and moon are the most effective time-indicators for seamen, and therefore their movements must be most carefully noted. Our *Nautical Almanac* in fact embodies the kind of astronomical materials which Government astronomers are employed to collect and arrange. Such work may rather be called celestial surveying than astronomy. But from the days of Flamsteed, the first of our Astronomers Royal (as the chief Government astronomer is technically called) whose contemporary, Newton, discovered the great law of the universe, to those of Maskelyne and Sir G. Airy, whose contemporaries, the elder and the younger Herschel, disclosed the structure of the universe, there have always been astronomers outside the ranks of official astronomy, in no way desirous of entering those ranks, and in fact so taking their course from the beginning of their study of the science as to preclude themselves from all possibility of undertaking any official duties in astronomy. ' Non sua se voluntas,' necessarily, 'sed suæ vitæ rationes, hoc aditu laudis, qui semper optimo cuique maxime patuit, prohibuerunt :' though, indeed, it may not untruly be said that to one who apprehends the true sublimity of astronomy as a science the routine of official astronomy is by no means inviting, and probably personal tastes have had very much to do with the choice, by such men, of the more attractive departments of astronomy. Be this as it may, it is certain that the astronomers who thus keep outside the official ranks are not only free, and may not only be fully competent, to express an opinion on the arrangements made by Government astronomers, or on the results obtained by them, but as the only members of the community who are at once free and able so to do, their right to speak may often involve, in some degree, the duty of speaking. If through some mistake wrong arrangements were proposed for instance,—and all men, even officials (Herbert Spencer says, *especially* officials), are apt to make mistakes,—then, unless non-official astronomers, who had carefully examined the subject, expressed their doubts, it is certain that there would be no means whatever of correcting the error, or even of detecting its consequence, until many years had elapsed. The leading official astronomers would in such a case be apt, in fact they are apt enough as it is, to stand by each other,—a chief in one department commending the zeal and energy of the chief in another department, this chief in turn commending the industry and ability of the other, and so forth,—while subordinates of all ranks might be apt either to maintain a judicious silence, or else at least to avoid any utterance which would endanger their position. It may, on the one hand, be to some degree questioned whether it would be fitting that discipline should be so far neglected in such a case that a subordinate should have eyes to see, or ears to hear, or thoughts to note, any error on the part of his superior in office. And on the other hand, those who know little or nothing of astronomy can of course form no opinion on astronomical matters, however high they may be in authority outside matters scientific. To assert, then, that it is either improper or undesirable for unofficial astronomers to comment on the plans or results of astronomers employed and paid by the nation is practically equivalent to asserting that it is improper or undesirable for the work of these paid astronomers to be examined at all,— a conclusion manifestly absurd.[1]

[1] The following lines are from a letter of mine, which appeared in the *Times* of April 13, some time after the present article was written :—

' A few months ago I said in these columns that the determination of the sun's distance, then recently communicated to Parliament— namely, 93,375,000 miles—was probably some 800,000 miles too great ; and I spoke of the method on which the determination was based as to some degree discredited by the wide range of difference both between that result and the mean of the best former measurements, and between the several results of which that one was itself the mean. Captain Tupman, as straightforward as he is skilful and zealous, announces as the result of a re-examination of the British observations a distance about 600,000 miles less than the above, or, more exactly, about 92,790,000 miles, as the sun's mean distance. But while he obtains from the ingress observations a mean distance of only 92,300,000 miles, he obtains from the egress observations a mean distance of about 93,040,000 miles ; and the value, 92,790,000 miles, is only obtained as the mean of these two values duly weighted, the egress observations being more satisfactory than the ingress observations.

' It appears to me that the doubts which I formerly expressed as to the trustworthiness of the method employed, are to some degree justified.

' To the general public it will be more interesting to inquire what probably is the true mean distance of the sun. To this it may be replied that in all probability the sun's mean distance does not lie so much as 600,000 miles on either side of the value 92,300,000 miles' (it should be 92,400,000).

THE PAST HISTORY OF OUR MOON.

THE moon, commonly regarded as a mere satellite of the earth, is in truth a planet, the least member of that family of five bodies circling within the asteroidal zone, to which astronomers have given the name of the terrestrial planets. There can be no question that this is the true position of the moon in the solar system. In fact, the fashion of regarding her as a mere attendant of our earth may be looked upon as the last relic of the old astronomy in which our earth figured as the fixed centre of the universe, and the body for whose sake all the celestial orbs were fashioned. In this aspect, also, the moon is a far more interesting object of research than when viewed as belonging to another and an inferior order. We are able to recognise, in her, appearances probably resulting from the relative smallness of her dimensions, and hence to derive probable information as to the condition of other orbs in the solar system which fall below the earth in point of size. Precisely as the study of the giant planets, Jupiter and Saturn, has led astronomers to infer that certain peculiarities must result from vastness of dimensions, so the study of the dwarf planets, Mars, our moon, and Mercury, may indicate the relations we are to associate with inferiority of size.

This thought immediately introduces us to another conception, which causes us to regard with even greater interest the evidence afforded by the moon's present condition. It can scarcely be questioned that the size of any member of the solar system, or rather the quantity of matter in its orb, assigns, so to speak, the duration of that orb's existence, or rather of the various stages of that existence. The smaller body must cool more rapidly than the larger, and hence the various periods during which the former is fit for this or that purpose of planetary life (I speak with purposed vagueness here) are shorter than the corresponding periods in the life of the latter. Thus the sun, viewed in this way, is the youngest member of the solar system, while the tiniest members of the asteroid famiiy, if not the oldest in reality, are the oldest to which the telescope has introduced us. Jupiter and Saturn come next to the sun in youth ; they are still passing through the earliest stages of planetary existence, even if we ought not rather to adopt that theory of their condition which regards them as subordinate suns, helping the central sun to support life on the satellites which circle around them. Uranus and Neptune are in a later stage, and perchance when telescopes have been constructed large enough to study these planets with advantage, we may learn something of that stage, interesting as being intermediate to the stages through which our earth and Venus on the one hand, and the giant brothers Jupiter and Saturn on the other, are at present passing. After our earth and Venus, which are probably at about the same stage of planetary development (though owing to the difference in their position they may not be equally adapted for the support of life), we come to Mars and Mercury, both of which must be regarded as in all probability much more advanced and in a sense more aged than the earth on which we live. In a similar sense,—even as an ephemeron is more aged after a few hours of existence than a man after as many years,—the small planet which we call 'our moon' may be described as in the very decrepitude of planetary existence, nay (some prefer to think), as even absolutely dead, though its lifeless body still continues to advance upon its accustomed orbit, and to obey the law of universal attraction.

Considerations such as these give singular interest to the discussion of the past history of our moon, though they add to the difficulty of interpreting the problems she presents to us. For we have manifestly to differentiate between the effects due to the moon's relative smallness on the one hand, and those due to her great age on the other. If we could believe the moon to be an orb which simply represents the condition to which our earth will one day attain, we could study her peculiarities of appearance with some hope of understanding how they had been brought about, as well as of learning from such study the future history of our own earth. But clearly the moon has had another history than our earth. Her relative smallness has led to relations such as the earth never has presented and never will present. If our earth is, as astronomers and physicists believe, to grow dead and cold, all life perishing from her surface, it is tolerably clear, from what we already know of her history, that the appearance she will present in her decrepitude will be utterly unlike that presented by the moon. Grant that after the lapse of enormous time-intervals the oceans now existing on the earth will be withdrawn beneath her solid crust, and even (which seems incredible) that at a more distant future the atmosphere now surrounding her will have become greatly reduced in quantity, either by similar withdrawal or in any other manner, yet the surface of the earth would present few features of resemblance to that of the moon. Viewed from the distance at which we view the moon, there would be few crateriform mountains indeed compared with those on the moon ; those visible would be small by comparison with lunar craters even of medium dimensions ; and the radiated regions seen on the moon's surface would have no discernible counterpart on the surface of the earth. The only features of resemblance, under the imagined conditions, would be probably the partially flat sea bottoms (though these would bear a different proportion to the more elevated regions) and the mountain ranges, the only terrestrial features of volcanic disturbance which would be relatively more important than their lunar counterparts.

I do not purpose, however, to discuss the probable future

of the earth, having only indicated the differences just touched upon in order to remind the reader at the outset that we have not in 'the moon' a representation of the earth at any stage of her history. Other and different relations are presented for our consideration, although it may well be that by carefully discussing them we may learn somewhat respecting our earth, as also respecting the past history and future development of the solar system.

It appears reasonable to regard the moon, after her first formation as a distinct orb, as presenting the same general characteristics that we ascribe to our earth in its primary stage as a planet. In one respect the moon, even at that early stage, may have differed from the earth. I refer to its rotation, the correspondence between which and its revolution may probably have existed from the moon's first formation. But this would not materially have affected the relations with which we have to deal at present. We may apply, then, to the moon the arguments which have been applied to the discussion of the first stages of our earth's history.

Adopting this view, we see that at the first stage of its existence as an independent planet, the moon must have been an intensely heated gaseous globe, glowing with in-herent light, and undergoing a process of condensation, 'going on at first at the surface only, until by cooling it must have reached the point where the gaseous centre was exchanged for one of combined and liquefied matter.' To apply now to the moon at this stage the description which Dr. Sterry Hunt gives of the earth. 'Here commences the chemistry of the moon. So long as the gaseous con-dition of the moon lasted, we may suppose the whole mass to have been homogeneous ; but when the temperature became so reduced that the existence of chemical com-pounds at the centre became possible, those which were most stable at the elevated temperature then prevailing would be first formed. Thus, for example, while compounds of oxygen with mercury, or even with hydrogen, could not exist, oxides of silicon, aluminium, calcium, magnesium, and iron, might be formed and condensed in a liquid form at the centre of the globe. By progressive cooling still other elements would be removed from the gaseous mass, which would form the atmosphere of the non-gaseous nucleus.' 'The processes of condensation and cooling having gone on until those elements which are not volatile in the heat of our ordinary furnaces were condensed into a liquid form, we may here inquire what would be the result on the mass of a further reduction of temperature. It is generally assumed that in the cooling of a liquid globe of mineral matter congelation would commence at the surface, as in the case of water ; but water offers an exception to most other liquids, inasmuch as it is denser in the liquid than in the solid form. Hence, ice floats on water, and freezing water becomes covered with a layer of ice which protects the liquid below. Some metals and alloys resemble water in this respect. With regard to most other earthy substances, and notably the various minerals and earthy compounds like those which may be supposed to have made up the mass of the molten globe, the case is entirely different. The numerous and detailed experiments of Charles Deville and those of Delesse, besides the earlier ones of Bischoff, unite in showing that the density of fused rocks is much less than that of the crystalline products resulting from their slow cooling, these being, according to Deville, from one-seventh to one-sixteenth heavier than the fused mass, so that if formed at the surface they would, in obedience to the laws of gravity, tend to sink as soon as formed.'

Here it has to be noted that possibly there existed a period (for our earth as well as for the moon) during which, notwithstanding the relations indicated by Dr. Hunt, the exterior portions of the moon were solid, while the interior remained liquid. A state of things corresponding to what we recognise as possible in the sun may have existed. For although undoubtedly any liquid matter forming in the sun sinks in obedience to the laws of gravity towards the centre, yet the greater heat which it encounters as it sinks must vapourise it, notwithstanding increasing pressure, so that it can only remain liquid near the region where rapid radiation allows of sufficient cooling to produce liquefaction. And in the same way we may conceive that the solidification taking place at any portion of the surface of the moon's or the earth's liquid globe, owing to rapid radiation of heat thence, although it might be followed immediately by the sinking of the solidified matter, would yet result in the continuance (rather than the existence) of a partially solid crust. For the sinking solid matter, though subjected to an increase of pressure (which, in the case of matter expanding on lique-faction, would favour solidification), would nevertheless, owing to the great increase of heat, become liquefied, and, expanding, would no longer be so much denser [1] than the liquid through which it was sinking as to continue to sink rapidly.

Nevertheless, it is clear that after a time the heat of the interior parts of the liquid mass would no longer suffice to liquefy the solid matter descending from the surface, and then would commence the process of aggregation at the centre described by Dr. Hunt. The matter forming the solid centre of the earth consists probably of metallic and metalloidal compounds of elements denser than those form-ing the known portions of the earth's crust.[2] In the case of the moon, whose mean density is very little greater than the mean density of the matter forming the earth's crust, we

---

[1] It would still be somewhat denser, because under the circumstances it would be somewhat cooler.

[2] It is thus, and not by the effects due to increasing pressure (effects which probably do not increase beyond a certain point), that we are to explain the fact that the earth's density as a whole is about twice the mean density of the matters which form its solid surface. It may be that this con-sideration, supported by the results of recent experimental researches, may give a significance hitherto not .noted to the relatively small mean density of the moon.

must assume that the matter forming the solid nucleus at that early stage was relatively less in amount, or else that we may attribute part of the difference to the comparatively small force with which lunar gravity operated during various , stages of contraction and solidification.

In the case of the moon, as in that of the earth, before the last portions became solidified, there would exist a condition of imperfect liquidity, as conceived by Hopkins, 'preventing the sinking of the cooled and heavier particles, and giving rise to a superficial crust, from which solidification would proceed downwards. There would thus be enclosed between the inner and outer solid parts a portion of uncongealed matter,' which may be supposed to have retained its liquid condition to a late period, and to have been the principal seat of volcanic action, whether existing in isolated reservoirs or subterranean lakes, or whether, as suggested by Scrope, forming a continuous sheet surrounding the solid nucleus.

Thus far we have had to deal with relations more or less involved in doubt. We have few means of forming a satisfactory opinion as to the order of the various changes to which, in the first stages of her existence as a planet, our moon was subject. Nor can we clearly define the nature of those changes. In these matters, as with the corresponding processes in our earth's case, there is much room for variety of opinion.

But few can doubt that, by whatever processes such condition may have been attained, the moon, when her surface began to form itself into its present appearance, consisted of a globe partially molten surrounded by a crust at least partially solidified. Some portions of the actual surface may have remained liquid or viscous later than others but at length the time must have arrived when the radiating surface was almost wholly solid. It is from this stage that we have to trace the changes which have led to the present condition of the moon's surface.

It can scarcely be questioned that those seismologists are

in the right who have maintained in recent times the theory that in the case of a cooling globe, such as the earth or moon at the stage just described, the crust would in the first place contract more quickly than the nucleus, while later the nucleus would contract more quickly than the crust. This amounts, in fact, to little more than the assertion that the process of heat radiation from the surface would be more rapid, and so last a shorter time than the process of conduction by which in the main the nucleus would part with its heat. The crust would part rapidly with its heat, contracting upon the nucleus ; but the very rapidity (relative) of the process, by completing at an early stage the radiation of the greater portion of the heat originally belonging to the crust, would cau-e the subsequent radiation to be comparatively slow, while the conduction of heat from the nucleus to the crust would take place more rapidly, not only relatively but actually.

Now it is clear that the results accruing during the two stages into which we thus divide the cooling of the lunar globe would be markedly different. During the first stage forces of tension (tangential) would be called to play in the lunar crust ; during the later stage the forces would be those of pressure.

Taking the earlier stage, during which the forces would be tensional, let us consider in what way these forces would operate.

At the beginning, when the crust would be comparatively thin, I conceive that the more general result of the rapid contraction of the crust would be the division of the crust into segments, by the formation of numerous fissures due to the lateral contraction of the thin crust. The molten matter in these fissures would film over rapidly, however, and all the time the crust would be growing thicker and thicker, until at length the formation of distinct segments would no longer be possible. The thickening crust, plastic in its lower strata, would now resist more effecively the tangential tensions, and when yielding would yield in a different manner.

It was at this stage, in all probability, that processes such as those illustrated by Nasmyth's globe experiments took place, and that from time to time the crust yielded at particular points, which became the centres of systems of radiating fissures. Before proceeding, however, to consider the results of such processes, let it be noted that we have seen reason to believe that among the very earliest lunar formations would be rifts breaking the *ancient* surface of the lunar crust. I distinguish in this way the ancient surface from portions of surface whereof I shall presently have to speak as formed at a later time.

Now let us conceive the somewhat thickened crust contracting upon the partially fluid nucleus. If the crust were tolerably uniform in strength and thickness we should expect to find it yielding (when forced to yield) at many points, distributed somewhat uniformly over its extent. But this would not be the case if—as we might for many reasons expect—the crust were wanting in uniformity. There would be regions where the crust would be more plastic, and so readier to yield to the tangential tensions. Towards such portions of the crust the liquid matter within would tend, because there alone would room exist for it. The down-drawing, or rather in-drawing, crust elsewhere would force away the liquid matter beneath, towards such regions of less resistance, which would thus remain at (and be partly forced to) a higher level. At length, however, the increasing tensions thus resulting would have their natural effect ; the crust would break open at the middle of the raised region, and in radiating rifts, and the molten matter would find vent through the rifts as well as at the central opening. The matter so extruded, being liquid, would spread, so that—though the radiating nature of the rifts would still be indicated by the position of the extruded matter—there would be no abrupt changes of level. It is clear, also, that so soon as the outlet had been formed the long and slowly sloping sides of the region of elevation would gradually sink, pressing the liquid matter below towards the centre of outlet, whence it would continue to pour out so long as this process of contraction continued. All round the borders of the aperture the crust would be melted, and would continue plastic long after the matter which had filled the fissures and flowed out through them had solidified. Thus there would be formed a wide circular orifice, which would from the beginning be considerably above the mean level of the moon's surface, because of the manner in which the liquid matter within had been gathered there by the pressure of the surrounding slopes.[1]   Moreover, around the orifice, the matter

[1] I have occasion to make some remarks at this stage to avoid possible and (my experience has shown me) not altogether improbable misconception, or even misrepresentation. The theory enunciated above will be regarded by some, who may have read a certain review of my Treatise on the Moon, as totally different from what I have advocated in that work, and, furthermore, as a theory which I have borrowed from the aforesaid review. I should not be particularly concerned if I had occasion to modify views I had formerly expressed, since I apprehend that every active student of science should hope, rather than dread, that as his work proceeds he would form new opinions. But I must point out that earlier in my book I had advocated the theory urged above. After describing the radiations from Tycho and other craters, I proceed as follows in chapter iv.—'It appears to me impossible to refer these phenomena to any general cause but the reaction of the moon's interior overcoming the tension of the crust, and to this degree Nasmyth's theory seems correct ; but it appears manifest, also, that the crust cannot have been fractured in the ordinary sense of the word. Since, however, it results from Mallet's investigations that the tension of the crust is called into play in the earlier stages of contraction, and its power to resist contraction in the later stages,—in other words, since the crust at first contracts faster than the nucleus, and afterwards not so fast as the nucleus,—we may assume that the radiating systems were formed in so early an era that the crust was plastic. And it seems reasonable to conclude that the outflowing matter would retain its liquid condition long enough (the crust itself being intensely hot) to spread widely,—a circumstance which would account at once for the breadth of many of the rays, and for the restoration of level to such a degree that no shadows are thrown. It appears probable, also, that not only (which is manifest) were the craters formed later which are seen around and upon the radiations, but that the central crater itself acquired its actual form long after the epoch when the rays were formed.'

outflowing as the crust continued to contract would form a raised wall, Until the time came when the liquid nucleus began to contract more rapidly than the crust, the large crateriform orifice would be full to the brim (or nearly so), at all times, with occasional overflows : and as a writer who has recently adopted this theory has remarked, 'We should ultimately have a large central lake of lava surrounded by a range of hills, terraced on the outside,—the lake filling up the space they enclosed.'

The crust might burst in the manner here considered, at several places at the same—or nearly the same—time, the range of the radiating fissures, depending on the extent of the underlying lakes of molten matter thus finding their outlet ; or there might be a series of outbursts at widely separated intervals of time and at different regions, gradually diminishing in extent as the crust gradually thickened and the molten matter beneath gradually became reduced in relative amount. Probably the latter view should be accepted, since, if we consider the three systems of radiations from Copernicus, Aristarchus, and Kepler, which were manifestly not formed contemporaneously, but in the order in which their central craters have just been named, we see that their dimensions diminished as their date of formation was later. According to this view we should regard the radiating system from Tycho as the oldest of all these formations.

At this very early stage of the moon's history, then, we regard the moon as a somewhat deformed spheroid, the regions whence the radiations extended being the highest parts, and the regions farthest removed from the ray centres being the lowest.[1] To these lower regions whatever was

---

[1] Where several ray centres are near together, a region directly between two ray centres would be at a level intermediate between that of the ray centres and that of a region centrally placed within a triangle or quadrangle of ray centres; but the latter region might be at a higher level than another very far removed from the part where the ray centres were near together. For instance, the space in the middle

liquid on the moon's surface would find its way. The down-flowing lava would not be included in this description, as being rather viscous than liquid ; but if any water existed at that time it would occupy the depressed regions which at the present time are called Maria or Seas.

It is a question of some interest, and one on which different opinions have been entertained, whether the moon at any stage of its existence had oceans and an atmosphere corresponding in relative extent to those of the earth.   It appears to me that, apart from all the other considerations which have been suggested in support of the view that the moon formerly had oceans and an atmosphere, it is exceedingly difficult to imagine how, under any circumstances, a globe so large as the moon could have been formed under conditions not altogether unlike, as we suppose, those under which the earth was formed (having a similar origin, and presumably constructed of the same elements), without having oceans and an atmosphere of considerable extent.   The atmosphere would not consist of oxygen and nitrogen only or chiefly, any more than, in all probability, the primeval atmosphere of our own earth was so constituted. We may adopt some such view of the moon's atmosphere—*mutatis mutandis*—as Dr. Sterry Hunt has adopted respecting the ancient atmosphere of the earth. Hunt, it will be remembered, bases his opinion on the former condition of the earth by conceiving an intense heat applied to the earth as now existing, and inferring the chemical results. 'To the chemist,' he remarks, 'it is evident that from such a process applied to our globe would result the oxidation of all carbonaceous matter ; the conversion of all carbonates, chlorides, and sulphates into silicates ; and the separation of the carbon, chlorine, and

of the triangle having Copernicus, Aristarchus, and Kepler at its angles (or more exactly between Milichius and Bessarion) is lower than the surface around Hortensius (between Copernicus and Kepler), but not so low as the Mare Imbrium, far away from the region of ray centres of which Copernicus, Aristarchus, and Kepler are the principal.

sulphur in the form of acid gases ; which, with nitrogen, watery vapour, and an excess of oxygen, would form an exceedingly dense atmosphere, The resulting fused mass would contain all the bases as silicates, and would probably nearly resemble in composition certain furnace-slags or basic volcanic glasses. Such we may conceive to have been the nature of the primitive igneous rock, and such the composition of the primeval atmosphere, *which must have been one of very great density.'* All this, with the single exception of the italicised remark, may be applied to the case of the moon. The lunar atmosphere would not probably be dense at that primeval time, even though constituted like the terrestrial atmosphere just described. It would perhaps have been as dense, or nearly so, as our present atmosphere. Accordingly condensation would take place at a temperature not far from the present boiling-point, and the lower levels of the half-cooled crust would be drenched with a heated solution of hydrochloric acid, whose decomposing action would be rapid, though not aided—as in the case of our primeval earth—by an excessively high temperature. 'The formation of the chlorides of the various bases and the separation of silica would go on until the affinities of the acid were satisfied.' 'At a later period the gradual combination of oxygen with sulphurous acid would eliminate this from the atmosphere in the form of sulphuric acid.' 'Carbonic acid would still be a large constituent of the atmosphere, but thenceforward (that is, after the separation of the compounds of sulphur and chlorine from the air) there would follow the conversion of the complex aluminous silicates, under the influence of carbonic acid and moisture, into a hydrated silicate of alumina or clay, while the separated lime, magnesia, and alkalies would be changed into bicarbonates, and conveyed to the sea in a state of solution.'

It seems to me that it is necessary to adopt some such theory as to the former existence of lunar oceans in order to explain some of the appearances presented by the so-called lunar seas.   As regards the present absence of water we may adopt the theory of Frankland, that the lunar oceans have withdrawn beneath the crust as room was provided for them by the contraction of the nucleus.   I think, indeed, that there are good grounds for looking with favour on the theory of Stanislas Meunier, according to which the oceans surrounding any planet—our own earth or Mars, for example—are gradually withdrawn from the surface to the interior. And in view of the enormous length of the time-intervals required for such a process, we must consider that while the process was going on the lunar atmosphere would not only part completely with the compounds of sulphur, chlorine, and carbon, but would be even still further reduced by chemical processes acting with exceeding slowness, yet effectively in periods so enormous.   But without insisting on this consideration, it is manifest that—with very reasonable assumptions as to the density of the lunar atmosphere in its original complex condition—what would remain after the removal of the chief portion by chemical processes, and after the withdrawal of another considerable portion along with the seas beneath the lunar crust, would be so inconsiderable in quantity as to accord satisfactorily with the evidence which demonstrates the exceeding tenuity of any lunar atmosphere at present existing.

These considerations introduce us to the second part of the moon's history,—that corresponding to the period when the nucleus was contracting more rapidly than the crust.

One of the first and most obvious effects of this more rapid nuclear contraction would be the lowering of the level of the molten matter, which up to this period had been kept up to, or nearly up to, the lips of the great ringed craters. If the subsidence took place intermittently there would result a terracing of the interior of the ringed elevation, such as we see in many lunar craters.   Nor would there be any uniformity of level in the several crater floors thus formed, since the fluid lava would not form parts of a single fluid mass (in which case, of course, the level of the fluid surface would be everywhere the same), but would belong to independent fluid masses. Indeed it may be noticed that the very nature of the case requires us to adopt this view, since no other will acount for the variety of level observed in the different lunar crater-floors. If these ceased to be liquid at different times, the independence of the fluid masses is by that very fact established ; and if they ceased to be liquid at the same time, they must have been independent, since, if communication had existed between them, they would have shown the uniformity of surface which the laws of hydrostatics require.[1]

The next effect which would follow from the gradual retreat of the nucleus from the crust (setting aside the withdrawal of·lunar seas) would be the formation of corrugations, —in other words, of mountàin-ranges. Mallet describes the formation of mountain-chains as belonging to the period when 'the continually increasing thickness of the crust remained such that it was still as a whole flexible enough, or opposed sufficient resistance of crushing to admit of the uprise of mountain-chains by resolved tangential pressures.' Applying this to the case of the moon, I think it is clear that —with her much smaller orb and comparatively rapid rate of cooling—the era of the formation of mountain-chains would be a short one, and that these would therefore form a less important characteristic of her surface than of the earth's. On the other hand, the period of volcanic activity which would follow that of chain-formation would be *relatively* long continued ; for regarding this period as beginning when the thickness of the moon's crust had become too great to admit of adjustment by corrugation, the comparatively small pressure to which the whole mass of the moon had been subjected by lunar gravity, while it would on the one hand cause the period to have an earlier commencement (relatively), would on the other leave greater play to the

---

[1] It is important to notice that we may derive from these considerations an argument as to the condition of the fluid matter now existing beneath the solid crust of the earth.

effects of contraction. Thus we can understand why the signs of volcanic action, as distinguished from the action to which mountain-ranges are due, should be far more numerous and important on the moon than on the earth.

I do not, however, in this place enter specially into the consideration of the moon's stage of volcanic activity, because already, in the pages of my Treatise on the Moon (Chapter VI.), I have given a full account of that portion of my present subject. I may make a few remarks, however, on the theory respecting lunar craters touched on in my work on 'The Moon.' I have mentioned the possibility that some among the enormous number of ring-shaped depressions which are seen on the moon's surface may have been the result of meteoric downfalls in long past ages of the moon's history. One or two critics have spoken of this view as though it were too fantastic for serious consideration. Now, though I threw out the opinion merely as a suggestion, distinctly stating that I should not care to maintain it as a theory, and although my own opinion is unfavourable to the supposition that any of the more considerable lunar markings can be explained in the suggested way, yet it is necessary to notice that on the general question whether the moon's surface has been marked or not by meteoric downfalls scarcely any reasonable doubts can be entertained. For, first, we can scarcely question that the moon's surface was for long ages plastic, and though we may not assign to this period nearly so great a length (350 millions of years) as Tyndall—following Bischoff—assigns to the period when our earth's surface was cooling from a temperature of 2000° C. to 200°, yet still it must have lasted millions of years ; and, secondly, we cannot doubt that the process of meteoric downfall now going on is not a new thing, but, on the contrary, is rather the final stage of a process which once took place far more actively. Now Prof. Newton has estimated, by a fair estimate of observed facts, that each day on the average 400 millions of meteors fall, of all sizes down to the minutest discernible in a telescope, upon the earth's atmosphere, so that on the moon's unprotected globe —with its surface one thirteenth of the earth's—about 30 millions fall each day, even at the present time.   Of large meteoric masses only a few hundreds fall each year on the earth, and perhaps about a hundred on the moon ; but still, even at the present rate of downfall, millions of large masses *must* have fallen on the moon during the time when her surface was plastic, while *probably* a much larger number—including many much larger masses—must have fallen during that period.   Thus, not only without straining probabilities, but by taking only the most probable assumptions as to the past, we have arrived at a result which compels us to believe that the moon's surface has been very much marked by meteoric downfall, while it renders it by no means unlikely that a large proportion of the markings so left would be discernible under telescopic scrutiny.

I would, in conclusion, invite those who have the requisite leisure to a careful study of the distribution of various orders of lunar marking.   It would be well if the moon's surface were isographically charted, and the distribution of the seas, mountain-ranges, and craters of different dimensions and character, of rills, radiating streaks, bright and dark regions, and so on, carefully compared *inter se*, with the object of determining whether the different parts of the moon's surface were probably brought to their present condition during earlier or later periods, and of interpreting also the significance of the moon's characteristic peculiarities.   In this department of astronomy, as in some others, the effectiveness of well-devised processes of charting has been hitherto overlooked.

A NEW CRATER IN THE MOON.

DR. KLEIN, a German astronomer, has recently called the attention of astronomers to a lunar crater some three miles wide, which had not before been observed, and which, he feels sure, was not in existence two years ago. Astronomers have long since given up all hope of tracing either the signs of actual life upon the moon or traces of the past existence of living creatures there. But there are still among them those who believe that by sedulous and careful scrutiny processes of material change may be recognised in that seemingly inert mass. In reality, perhaps, the wonder rather is that signs of change should not be often recognised, than that from time to time a new crater should appear or the walls of old craters fall in. The moon's surface is exposed to variations of temperature compared with which those affecting the surface of our earth are altogether trifling. It is true there is no summer or winter in the moon. Sir W. Herschel has spoken of the lunar seasons as though they resembled our own, but in reality they are very different. The sun's midday height at any lunar station is only about three degrees greater in summer than in winter ; whereas our summer sun is 47° higher in the sky at noon than our winter sun. In fact, a midsummer's day on the moon does not differ more from a midwinter's day, as far as the sun's actual path on the sky is concerned, than with us the 17th of March differs from the 25th, or the 19th of September from the 27th. It is the change from day to night which chiefly affects the moon's surface. In the lunar year of seasons, lasting 346⅔ of our days, there are only 11¾ lunar days, each lasting 29¾ of ours. Thus day lasts more than a fortnight, and is followed by a night of equal length. Nor is this all. There is neither air nor moisture to produce such effects as a.e produced by our air' and the moisture it contains in mitigating the heat of day and the cold of night. Under the sun's rays the moon's surface becomes hotter and hotter as the long lunar day proceeds, until at last its heat exceeds that of boiling water. But so soon as the sun has set the heat thus received is rapidly radiated away into space (no screen of moisture-laden air checking its escape), and long before lunar midnight a cold exists compared with which the bitterest weather ever experienced by Arctic voyagers would be oppressively hot. These are not merely theoretical conclusions, though even as such they could be thoroughly relied upon. The moon's heat has been measured by the present Lord Rosse (using his father's splendid six-feet mirror). He separated the heat which the moon simply reflects to us from that which her heated surface itself gives out (or, technically, he separated the reflected from the radiated heat), by using a glass screen which allowed the former heat to pass while it intercepted the latter. He thus found that about six-sevenths of the heat we receive from the moon is due to the heating of her own substance. From the entire series of observations it appeared that the change of temperature during the entire lunar day—that is, from near midnight to near midday on the moon—amounts to fully 500° Fahrenheit. If we assume that the cold at lunar midnight corresponds with about 250° below zero (the greatest cold experienced in Arctic travelling has never exceeded 140° below zero), it would follow that the midday heat is considerably greater than that of boiling water on the earth at the sea-level. But the range of change is not a matter of speculation. It certainly amounts to about 500°, and in whatever way we distribute it, we must admit, first, that no such life as we are familiar with could possibly exist on the moon ; and, secondly, that the moon's crust must possess a life of its own, so to speak, expanding and contracting unceasingly and energetically. Professor Newcomb, by the way, in his fine work on Popular Astronomy, rejects the idea that the expansions and contractions due to these great changes of temperature can cause any disintegration at the present time. There might, he says, be bodies so friable that they would crumble, 'but whatever crumbling might thus be caused would soon be done with, and then no further change would occur.' For my own part, I cannot consider that such a surface as the moon at present possesses can undergo these continual expansions and contractions without slow disintegration. It seems to me also extremely probable that from time to time the overthrow of great masses, the breaking up of arched crater-floors, and other sudden changes discernible from the earth, might be expected to occur. Professor Newcomb has, I conceive, omitted to consider the enormous volumetric expansion as distinguished from mere lateral extension, resulting from the heating of the moon's crust to considerable depths. On a very moderate computation, the surface of the central region of the full moon must at that time rise above its mean position to such a degree that hundreds, if not thousands, of cubic miles of the moon's volume lie above the mean position of the surface there. At new moon—that is, at lunar midnight for the same region—the same enormous quantity of matter is correspondingly depressed. And though the actual range in vertical height at any given point may be small, we cannot doubt that the total effect produced by these constant oscillations is considerable. Years or centuries may pass without any great or sudden change, but from time to time such catastrophes must surely occur. I believe that all the cases of supposed change in the moon, if all were regarded as proved, could be thus fully accounted for without any occasion to assume the action of volcanic forces properly so called.

Before considering the evidence for the new lunar

volcano to which Dr. Klein has recently called the attention of astronomers, it may be well briefly to describe the condition of the moon's surface.

This surface, which is equal in extent to about that of the American Continent, or to Europe and Africa together (without their islands), is divided into two chief portions—the higher levels, which are in the main of lighter tint; and the lower levels, which are, almost without exception, dark. It may be remarked in passing that very erroneous ideas are commonly entertained respecting the moon's general colour. The moon is very far from being white, as many suppose. On the contrary, she is far more nearly black than white. It has been well remarked by Tyndall that if the moon were covered with black velvet (14,600,000 square miles of that material would be required for the purpose), she would still appear white to us, for we should see her disc projected on the blackness of star-strewn space. The actual tint of the moon as a whole is nearly the same as that of gray weathered sandstone. The brightest parts, however, are much whiter ; Zöllner infers from his photometric experiments that they can be compared with the whitest of terrestrial substances. On the other hand, the darkest parts of the moon are probably far darker than porphyry, even if they are not so dark that on earth we should call them black. The fact that the low-lying parts of the moon are much darker than the higher regions is full of meaning, though hitherto its significance does not seem to have been much noticed. Either we must assume that these lower regions, the so-called seas (certainly now dry), are old sea bottoms, and owe their darkness to the quality of the matter deposited there in remote ages, or else we must suppose that the matter which last remained fluid when the moon's surface was consolidating was of darker material than the rest. For such matter would occupy the lowest lunar regions. There is here room for a very profitable study of the moon's aspect by geologists. I doubt not that, however different the general past history of our earth may have have been from the moon's, terrestrial regions exist where the characteristic features of the moon's surface are more or less closely illustrated. On the American continent, for example, there are peculiarities of geological formation which seem to correspond closely with some of the features of the lunar globe, presently to be noticed; and it seems to me not improbable that geologists might find in the study of certain regions in North America the means of interpreting the difference of tint between higher and lower levels on the moon. If so, light would probably be thrown on very difficult questions relating to the remote past, not only of the moon, but of our own earth.

The lunar feature which comes next in importance to the difference of tint between the so-called 'seas' and the higher lands is the existence of remarkable series of radiating streaks extending from certain important craters— centres probably of past disturbance. It is impossible to contemplate the disc of the full moon, as seen with a powerful telescope, without feeling that these systems of rays must have resulted from the operation of forces of the most stupendous nature, though as yet their true meaning is hid from us. They would be marvellous phenomena, even if they were not so mysterious—marvellous in their enormous extension, their singular brightness, and their manner of traversing 'seas,' craters, and mountain-ranges indifferently. But their chief marvel resides in the mysterious manner of their appearance as the moon approaches her full illumination. Other lunar features are most clearly recognised when the moon is not full, for then the shadows which afford our only means of estimating the height of lunar irregularities are clearly seen along the border between the bright and dark parts of her face, and we have only to wait until this border passes over any object we wish to study to obtain satisfactory evidence of its nature. It is quite otherwise with the rays. The regions occupied by these radiating streaks are neither raised nor depressed in such sort as either to throw shadows or to lie in shadow when surrounding regions are in sunlight. But when the moon approaches her full illumination, the radiating regions come into view, as bright streaks—bright even on the light-tinted lunar uplands. A mighty system of rays can be seen extending from the great crater Tycho in all directions. Other systems, scarcely less wonderful, extend from the battlemented crater, Copernicus, the brilliant Aristarchus, and the solitary Kepler. One ray from Tycho can be traced round nearly an entire hemisphere of the moon's surface. It is specially noteworthy of this great ray that, where it crosses the lunar Sea of Serenity, that great plain seems to be divided as by a sort of ridge line, the slope of the plain from either side of the ray's track being clearly discernible when the moon is near her first quarter.

What are these mysterious ray systems? How are we to explain the circumstance that though only the most tremendous forces seem competent to account for bands such as these, many miles broad and many hundreds of miles in length, there are yet none of the usual signs of the action of volcanic forces? If mighty rifts had been formed in the moon's crust by the outbursting action of a hot nucleus, or through the contraction of the crust on an unyielding nucleus (for the effect would be the same in either case), we should scarcely expect to find that after such rifts had formed no signs of any difference of level would appear. If lava flowed out all along the rift, one would imagine that it would form a long dyke which would throw an obvious shadow, except under full solar illumination. If the rift were not filled with lava, the bottom of the rift would certainly remain in shadow long after the surrounding region was illuminated. That lava should exactly fill the rift along its entire length seems incredible. This might happen by a strange chance in the case of a single rift, but not with all the rifts of a radiating system, still less with all the rifts of all the radiating systems. Yet I believe that neither astronomers nor geologists can form any other opinion respecting these.

mysterious ray-systems than that they were caused by what Humboldt (speaking of the earth) calls the reaction of the interior on the crust. Nasmyth has admirably indicated their appearance, or rather their radiating form, by filling a globular glass shell with water, hermetically closed, and then freezing the water. The expansion of the water bursts the glass shell, and the lines of fracture are found to extend in a series of rays from the part of the shell which first gave way. But this experiment of itself does not explain the mystery of the lunar rays. Accepting the theory that the moon's crust yielded in some such way, we have still to explain how the rifts which were thus formed came to be covered over with matter lying nearly at the same level as the surrounding surface. It appears to me that the only available way of explaining this is somewhat as follows. First, from the way in which the streaks are covered like the surrounding region with craters, we may conclude that the streaks are older than any except the largest craters; from the great extension of many of them, we may safely infer that the lunar crust possessed a large measure of plasticity when they were formed (for otherwise it would have yielded over a smaller area). It was, therefore, probably still hot during the era (which may have lasted millions of years) to which the formation of the rifts belonged : accordingly the· lava which flowed out through the rifts remained liquid for a considerable time, and was thus able to spread widely on either side of the rift, forming a broad band of lava-covered surface, instead of a steep and narrow dyke. This seems not only to account for the most striking peculiarity of the bands, but to accord well with all that is known about them, and even to suggest explanations of some other lunar features which had appeared perplexing. I understand that in certain regions of North America there are lava-covered rifts large enough to form geographical features, and, therefore, fairly comparable with the lunar radiating streaks. But as yet American geologists have not presented in an accessible form a description of the peculiar features of the American continent ; in fact, it may be doubted whether as yet the materials for such a description exist.

The mountain-ranges of the moon do not differ to any marked degree from those of our own earth. They are few in number; in fact, mountain-ranges form a less important feature of lunar than of terrestrial geography. On the other hand, the lunar ring-mountains and craters far exceed those of our earth in size and importance. The large craters may, in fact, be regarded as characteristic features of lunar scenery. There are several craters exceeding 100 miles in diameter. It is strange to consider that though the ringed wall surrounding some of these larger craters exceeds 10,000 feet in height, no trace of the highest peaks of such a wall would be visible from the middle of the enclosed plain. Conversely, an observer standing on one of the highest peaks beside one of these great craters, would not see half the floor of the crater, while more than half the horizon line around him would belong to the enclosed plain, and would appear as level as the horizon seen from a height overlooking a great prairie. These ringed plains and larger craters seem to belong to the third great era of the moon's history. The bright high regions and dark low levels called seas must have been formed while the greater part of the crust was intensely hot. The contraction of the cooling crust on the nucleus, which cooled far less slowly, led to the formation of the great ray systems. But though such systems extend from great craters, these craters themselves probably attained their present form far later. The crust having in great part cooled, the nucleus began in turn to shrink more quickly than the crust, having more heat to part with. Thus the crust, closing in upon the shrinking nucleus, formed the corrugations and wrinkles which can be seen under telescopic scrutiny in nearly every part of the visible lunar surface. The process was accompanied necessarily by the development of great heat—the thermal equivalent of the mechanical process of contraction. Mallet has shown that the process of contraction at present occurring in the earth's crust gives rise to the greater part of the heat to which volcanic phenomena are due. If this is so in the earth's case at present, how tremendous must have been the heat evolved by the far more rapid contraction of the moon's mass in the remote era we are considering, when probably her heat passed into space unchecked by the action of a dense moisture-laden atmosphere! We can well understand that enormous volumes of heated gas would be formed—including steam, for there is good reason to believe that water is present in large quantities in the moon's interior. The imprisoned gas would find an outlet at points of least resistance, the centres, namely, of the great radiating systems of streaks. These centres would certainly be regions of outlet. But they would not be sufficient. We can understand then why every ray system extends from a great crater, though that crater was really formed after the system of radiating streaks ; and we can equally understand why these central craters are not the only or even the chief of the great craters in the moon. Here again I would suggest that possibly the careful study of American geology might disclose features illustrating the great lunar craters.

When we pass to the smaller craters, ranging in diameter from seven or eight miles to less than a quarter of a mile, even if there be not some far smaller and beyond the range of the most powerful telescopes man can construct, we find ourselves among objects resembling those with which the study of our own earth has rendered us familiar. When Sartorius's map of Etna and the surrounding region was first seen at the Geological Society's rooms, many supposed that it represented lunar features. The Vesuvian volcanic region, again, is presented side by side with a lunar region of similar extent in Nasmyth's fine treatise on the moon, and the resemblance is very close. Considering the part which water plays in producing terrestrial volcanic phenomena, it may reasonably be doubted whether there is in reality so close a resemblance as a superficial comparison (and we can make no other) would suggest. There are those, indeed, who believe that some of the multitudinous small craters of the moon have had their origin in the downfall of meteoric masses on her once plastic surface ; and strange though the thought may seem, there would be considerable difficulty in showing how the surface of the moon could have remained without traces of the meteoric downfall to which during myriads of centuries she was exposed undefended by that atmospheric shield which protects our earth from millions of meteors yearly falling upon her. We could only attribute the smallest lunar craters, however, to this cause. It may be noticed in passing that Professor Newcomb, apparently referring to this sugges- tion, which some had thought too fanciful to be seriously advanced, says that 'the figures of these inequalities (the small craters) can be closely imitated by throwing pebbles upon the surface of some smooth plastic mass, as mud or mortar.' Craters, however, larger than a mile or so in diameter, and many also of smaller dimensions, must be re- garded as due to the same process of contraction which pro- duced the great craters, but as belonging to an era when this process went on less actively. In like manner another feature of the moon's surface, the existence of narrow furrows called *rilles*, which sometimes extend to a considerable dis- tance, passing across levels, intersecting crater walls, and reappearing beyond mountain-ranges as though carried under like tunnels, must be regarded as due to the cracking of the crust thus slowly shrinking.

It is noteworthy that the signs of change which have been suspected during recent years belong to these smaller and probably more recent lunar formations. In November, 1866, Dr. Schmidt, chief of the Athens Observatory, an- nounced that the crater Linné in the lunar. Sea of Serenity was missing. To understand the importance of this an- nouncement, let it simply be noted that the quantity of matter necessary to fill that crater up would be at least equal to that which would be required to form a mountain covering the whole area of London to a height of two miles ! The crater was described by former lunar

observers as at least five miles in diameter and very deep.
It is not now actually missing, as Schmidt supposed,
but it is certainly no longer deep.   It is, in fact, exceedingly
shallow.   Sir J. Herschel's opinion was that the crater had
been filled up from beneath by an effusion of viscous lava,
which, overflowing the rim on all sides, poured down the
outer slope so as to efface its ruggedness and convert it into
a gradual declivity casting no stray shadows.   But the
stupendous nature of the disturbing forces necessary to
produce such an overflow of molten matter has led most
astronomers to adopt in preference the theory that the wall
surrounding the crater has been overthrown, either in consequence solely of the processes of contraction and expansion described above, or from the reinforcement of their
action by the effects due to sublunarian energies.   Some
consider that the descriptions of the crater by Mädler and
Lohrmann (which slightly differ) were erroneous, and that
there has been no real change.   Others deny that any
change has occurred, on the ground that Linné varies in
aspect according to the manner of its illumination.   This I
perceive is Professor Newcomb's explanation, who considers
such variations 'sufficient to account for the supposed
change.'   But since the time of Schmidt's announcement
Linné has several times been observed under nearly the
same conditions as by Mädler and Lohrmann, as the great
shadows formerly seen in its interior have not reappeared.
There seems to be great reason for believing that a change
has really occurred there.

The discovery announced by Dr. Klein is of a different nature.   Near the middle of the visible half of the
moon there is a well-known though small crater called
Hyginus, the neighbourhood of which has been often and
carefully examined.   While examining this part of the
moon's surface with an excellent $5\frac{1}{2}$in. telescope, in May,
1877, Dr. Klein observed a small crater full of shadow, and
apparently nearly three miles in diameter,   It formed a conspicuous object on the Sea of Vapours.   Having frequently

observed this region during the last few years, he felt certain that no such crater existed there in 1876. He communicated his discovery to Dr. Schmidt, who stated, in reply, that in all the numerous drawings he had made of this lunar region no such crater was indicated. It is not shown in the great chart by Beer and Mädler, or in Lohrmann's map. Further observation showed that the crater is a deep, conical opening in the moon's surface. Soon after the sun has risen at that part of the moon, and, as later observations confirm, shortly before sunset there, the opening is entirely in shadow, and appears black. But when the sun is rather higher it appears grey, and with a yet higher sun it can no longer be distinguished. It can, however, be seen when the sun is very high on that part of the moon, appearing then somewhat brighter than the surrounding region, a circumstance which does not hitherto seem to have been noticed by either Klein or Schmidt.

The moon's surface has been so long and so carefully studied, that it is almost impossible to understand how such a crater as now certainly exists in the Sea of Vapours near Hyginus could have escaped detection. Craters of the kind exist, indeed, in hundreds on the moon's surface. But many astronomers have given years of their life to the study of such objects; and the centre of the moon's disc, for reasons which astronomers will understand, has been studied with exceptional care. It seems so unlikely that a deep crater three miles in diameter could escape recognition, that some astronomers have not hesitated to regard the newly-detected crater as certainly a new formation. For my own part, though it seems almost impossible to explain how such a crater could have remained so long unnoticed, I can regard the evidence of change as amounting only to extreme probability so far as it depends on the result of past telescopic scrutiny of the moon.

Admitting that a change had occurred, it would not follow that it had been produced by volcanic forces. It seems far more likely that a floor originally cover-

ing the conical hole now existing in the Sea of Vapours
has given way at last under the effect of long-continued processes of expansion and contraction, which would operate
with special energy over a region, like the Sea of Vapours,
near the moon's equator.

But there remains to be mentioned a form of evidence
respecting lunar features which could not be effectively
applied to the case of the crater Linné, because the moon
had only been subject to the necessary method of examination during a few years before that crater was missed. I
refer to lunar photography. Many objects less than two
miles in diameter are shown in the best photographs of our
satellite by Rutherfurd, De la Rue, Ellery, and Draper; and
as the moon has been photographed in every phase, some
among the views might fairly be expected to show Klein's
crater if it really existed before 1877. I do not find that
in any lunar photographs the crater is shown as a black or
dark gray spot. But in Rutherfurd's splendid photograph of
the moon on March 6, 1865 (when the moon was about nine
days five hours old), the place of Klein's crater is occupied
by a small spot lighter than the surrounding 'sea.' This is
the usual appearance of a small crater under a high sun ;
and though it may indicate only the existence of a flat crater
floor in 1865 where now a great conical hole exists, it throws
some degree of doubt on the occurrence of any change at all
there. The case strongly suggests the necessity for continuing the work of lunar photography, which seems of late years
to have flagged. Photographs of the moon should be taken
in every aspect and in every stage of her librational swayings.
Possessing such a series, we should be able to decide at once
whether any newly-recognised crater was in reality a new
formation or not.

DURING November 13 and 14 the earth is passing through the region along which lies the course of the family of meteors called the Leonides, sometimes familiarly known as the November meteors. When at this time of the year the meteor region thus traversed by the earth is densely strewn with meteors, there occurs a display of falling stars, one of the most beautiful, and, rightly understood, one of the most remarkable of all celestial phenomena. Of old, indeed, when it was supposed that these meteors were purely meteorological phenomena, they were not thought specially interesting objects. They were held by some as mere weather-portents. It was only when a storm of wind was approaching, *vento impendente*, according to Virgil, that a shower of meteors was to be seen. Gross ignorance, indeed, has given to showers of falling stars an interest surpassing even that which has become attached to them through the discoveries of modern science, for they have been regarded as portending the end of the world. The shower of November 13, 1833, which was seen in great splendour in America, frightened the negroes of the Southern States nearly out of their wits. A planter of South Carolina relates that he was awakened by shrieks of horror and cries for mercy from 600 or 700 negroes. When he went out to see what was the matter, he found the negroes prostrate on the ground, 'some speechless, some with bitterest cries imploring God to spare the world and them.'

There is, however, a grandeur in the interpretation placed by modern science upon these beautiful displays which dwarfs into littleness even such ideas as have been suggested by the terrors of superstition. We perceive that meteors are not mere terrestrial phenomena, nor of brief existence. They speak to us of domains in space compared with which the volume of our earth—nay, even the volume of the sun himself—is a mere point ; of time-intervals compared with which the millions of years spoken of by geologists appear but as mere seconds.

The special meteor family whose track the earth crosses on November 13–14 forms a mighty ellipse round the sun, extending more than 19 times farther from him than the track of our earth, which yet, as we know, lies more than 92,000,000 miles from the sun. Along this tremendous orbit the meteors speed with planetary but varying velocity, crossing the track of our earth with a velocity exceeding by more than a third her own swift motion of about 19 miles in every second of time. Coming down somewhat aslant, but otherwise meeting the earth almost full tilt, the meteors rush into our air at the rate of more than 40 miles per second. They are so intensely heated as they rush through it that they are turned into the form of vapour, insomuch that we never make acquaintance with the members of this particular meteoric family in the solid form. In this respect they resemble the greater number of our meteoric visitants. It is, indeed, a somewhat fortunate circumstance for us that this is so, for if Professor Newton, of Yale College (United States), is right in estimating the total number of meteors, large and small, which the earth encounters per annum at 400,000,000, it would be rather a serious matter if all or most of these bodies were not warded off. The least of them, even though a mere grain perhaps in weight, would yet, arriving with planetary velocity exceeding a hundredfold or more the velocity of a cannon-ball, prove an awkward missile if it struck man or animal. But the air effectually saves us from all save a few fire-balls which are large enough to remain in great part solid until they actually strike the earth itself.

The importance of the meteors in the planetary system will be recognised when we remember that the November group alone extends along its oval course in one complete system of meteors for a length of more than 1,700 millions of miles, with an average thickness of about a million miles (determined by noting the average time occupied by the earth in passing through the system on November 13–14), and an unknown cross breadth which probably does not fall short of three or four millions of miles. Other systems are, no doubt, far more important, for it has been found that meteors follow in the track of comets. Now the November meteors follow in the track of a comet (Tempel's comet of 1866), which was so small when last favourably placed for observation that it escaped detection by the naked eye. If so small a comet as this is followed by so large a meteoric system, in which also meteors are strewn so richly that during the passage of the earth through it, tens of thousands of meteors have been counted, how vast must be the numbers and how large probably the individual bodies following in the track of such splendid comets as Newton's, Donati's (1858), the comets of 1811, 1847, 1861, and others! For it should be remembered that we become cognisant of the existence of a meteoric system only when the earth threads its way through one, when those which she encounters may become visible as falling stars if it so chances that she encounters them on the dark or night half of her surface. But the earth is far smaller compared with a system like the November meteor-flight than a rifle-ball compared with the largest flight of birds ever yet seen. Such a ball fired into a very dense and widely extending flock of birds might encounter here and there along its course some five or six birds—not one in 10,000, perhaps, of the entire flight; and if the flock continued flying with unchanging course, a hundred rifle balls might be fired through it without seemingly reducing its numbers. Our earth has passed hundreds of times through the November meteor system, yet its meteoric wealth has scarcely been reduced at all, so exceedingly minute is the track of the earth through the meteor system compared with the extension of the system itself. The region through which the earth has passed is less than a billionth part of the entire region occupied by the system. But the November system is but one among several hundreds through which the earth passes —in other words, the systems which chance to be traversed by that mere thread-like ring in space traversed each year by the earth, are not a millionth, not a billionth, of the total number of such systems. It will be conceived, therefore, that the total amount of meteoric matter, travelling on orbits of all degrees of eccentricity and extension from the sun and inclined at all angles to the general plane of the solar system, must be enormously great. The idea once advanced by an eminent astronomer that the total quantity of unattached matter, so to speak, existing within the solar domain must be estimated rather by pounds than by tons is now altogether exploded. It would be truer to say that the totality of matter thus freely travelling around the sun must be estimated by billions of tons rather than by millions.

Whether it is likely that there will be a display of meteors to-night (or, rather, to-morrow morning), is a question to which most astronomers would be disposed, we believe, to reply definitely in the negative. The display of November 13–14, 1866, was very brilliant ; that of 1867 (best seen in the United States) was almost equally so ; but successive showers steadily diminished. In other words, the part of the system crossed by the earth in 1866 and 1867 was very rich, but the part which she crossed afterwards (the rich part having passed far on towards the remote aphelion of the system outside the orbit of Uranus) was less rich. For the last few years very few November meteors have been seen, though the few stragglers which have been seen, and have been identified as belonging to the family by their paths athwart the star-depths, have been almost as interesting to astronomers as the showers of such bodies seen in 1799, 1833, 1866, and 1867. But it is not altogether impossible that in the small hours 'ayont the twal' to-morrow morning a shower of meteors may be seen. For Schiaparelli (the Italian astronomer who first started the ideas which led when properly followed up to the discovery of the relations existing between meteors and comets) asserts that it has happened before now that the November meteors have appeared in great numbers in years lying midway between the times of *maximum* display. These times are separated on the average by about 33¼ years. Thus, in 1799, there was a great display of November meteors, a shower rendered specially celebrated by Humboldt's description. In 1833 there was another, the display which so terrified the negroes of South Carolina, but more interesting scientifically as described by Arago. In 1866 the shower again attained its *maximum* splendour, though the display of 1867 was little inferior. It will not be till 1899 that another great shower of November meteors may be confidently looked for. But if Schiaparelli be right, it is quite possible that there may be a shower this year, due to some scattered flight of the November meteors which, delayed accidentally (through some special perturbation) many hundreds of years ago, has come in the course of ages to travel nearly half a circuit behind the richest part of the system, the 'gem of the meteor-ring,' as it has been poetically called. Even, however, though no display of November meteors should be seen, yet the recognition of even a few scattered stragglers would be exceedingly interesting to astronomers. A single meteor seen to-night which could be regarded as certainly belonging to the November system would suffice to show the possibility that a whole flight of the November meteors might travel at a similar distance behind the main body. It would be more easy, however, to identify two such meteors than one, six than two, and a score than half-a-dozen. The only way in which a meteor can be questioned, so to speak, respecting the family it belongs to, is by noting its path across the sky. If this path tends directly from the constellation Leo (however remote Leo may be from the part of the heavens traversed by the meteor), the chances are that the meteor is a Leonid, or one of the November family. If the path tends from that particular part of the constellation Leo (near the end of the curved blade of the so-called Sickle in Leo), the probability of the meteor being a Leonid is increased. If two or more meteors are seen to-morrow morning (after 12.30) which both tend from the Sickle in Leo, even though they seem to tend in opposite directions, the chances are yet greater that they are travelling in parallel paths along the track of the November meteors, but some 2,000 million miles behind the main body. Should the number mount up to a score or so, the conclusion would be, to all intents and purposes, certain ; and the possible occurrence of even a shower of Leonids at a time midway between the customary *maxima* of the meteoric displays would be placed beyond question.

We must, however, admit that it seems less likely there will be anything like a display of Leonids to-night than that patient observers may be able to identify a few of these bodies, and thus—though by observations of a less attractive kind—to advance our knowledge of this interesting system. Far more likely is it that towards the end of the month there will be a display of meteors belonging to another and an entirely distinct family, a family scarcely less worthy to be called November meteors *par excellence*, but actually rejoicing in the classically unsatisfactory name of Andromeds.

EXPECTED METEOR SHOWER.

(From the *Times* of November 25, 1878.)

IT is probable that during the next three nights some light may be thrown on one of the most perplexing yet most interesting of all the problems recently suggested to the study of astronomers. It is confidently expected that many of those November meteors called Andromeds will be seen on one or other of those nights, if not on all three. No meteor systems, not even the famous systems of August and November, are more remarkable than this singular family. To explain why astronomers regard the Andromeds with so much interest, it will be necessary to speak of an object which at first sight seems in no way connected with them—an object, in fact, which, so long as it was actually known to astronomers, was never supposed to be connected with any family of meteors—the celebrated lost comet called Biela's (or, by Frenchmen, Gambart's comet). In February, 1826, Biela discovered in the constellation Aries a comet which was found to be travelling in an oval path round the sun, in a period of about six years seven and a half months. Tracing its course backwards, astronomers found that it had been seen in 1772 by Montaigne, and observed for two or three weeks in that year by Messier, the great. comet hunter. Nothing very remarkable was recognised regarding this comet in 1826, except the fact that its path nearly intersects that of our own earth ; so that if ever the earth is to encounter a comet, here seemed to be the comet she had to fear. Great terror was, indeed, excited by the announcement that in 1832 the comet would cross the earth's track only four or five weeks before the earth came to the place of danger. But no harm happened. In that year, and again in 1839, the comet returned quietly enough, though in 1839 it was not observed, being so placed that it was lost in the splendour of the solar rays. In February, 1846, the comet was again seen, this being the third return since its discovery in 1826, or rather, since its recognition as a member of the solar system, the eleventh since it was first seen by Montaigne. At this time everything seemed to suggest that this comet, unless our earth at some future time should absorb it, would remain for a long time a steady member of the sun's comet family. But only a few days after its detection in February, 1846, the comet was found to have divided into two, which travelled side by side until both vanished from view with increasing distance. In 1852 the companion comets reappeared, and again both continued in view till their motion carried them beyond telescopic range. As the distance between the coupled comets had increased from about 160,000 miles in 1846 to about 1,250,000 miles in 1852, astronomers anticipated a most interesting series of observations at the successive returns of the double comet to the earth's neighbourhood. Unfortunately, in 1859 the comet's course carried it athwart a part of the sky illuminated by the sun's rays, so that astronomers could not then expect to see it. But in 1866 it was looked for hopefully. Its orbit had now been most carefully computed, and many observers, armed with excellent telescopes, were on the watch for it, with very accurate knowledge of the course along which it might be expected to travel, and even of its position from day to day and from hour to hour. But it was not seen. Nor, again, was it seen in 1872, when fresh computations had been made, and observations were extended over a wider range, to make sure, as was hopefully thought, that this time it should not escape recognition. Could it have come, asked Herschel in 1866—and in 1872 the same question might still more pertinently be asked—into contact or exceedingly close approach to some asteroid as yet undiscovered? or, peradventure, had it plunged into and got bewildered among the rings of meteorolites, which astronomers more than suspected?

Between 1866, when Sir John Herschel thus wrote, and 1872, when again Biela's comet was sought in vain, a series of strange discoveries had been made respecting meteors, which led astronomers to believe that, even though the missing comet might never again be seen as a comet, we might still learn something respecting its present condition. It had been noticed that the remarkable comet of 1862 (comet 11 of that year) crossed the earth's track near the place where she is on August 10–11, the time of the August meteors, called the Tears of St. Lawrence in old times, but now known as the Perseids, because they seem to radiate from the constellation Perseus. Later the idea occurred to Schiaparelli, an Italian astronomer, that the August meteors may travel along the path of that comet. He could not prove this, but he advanced very strong evidence in favour of the opinion, for he found that bodies travelling along the path of the comet of 1862 would seem to radiate from Perseus as they traversed the earth's atmosphere. It was as if a person suspected that a steam-cloud seen on a distant railway track belonged to a particular train, and, though unable actually to prove this, was yet able to show that, with the wind and weather then prevailing, that train, travelling at its customary rate, would leave a steam-cloud behind it precisely of the apparent length and position of the observed steam-cloud. This cloud might have the observed position though otherwise produced, yet the evidence would be thought strongly to favour the supposition that it came from the train in question. In like manner the August meteors might be travelling on any one of a great number of tracks intersecting the earth's orbit in the place occupied by the earth on August 10–11 ; yet it was at least a striking coincidence that a flight of meteors travelling in the orbit of the chief comet of 1862 would seem to radiate from the constellation Perseus, precisely as the August meteors do.

While astronomers were still discussing the ideas of Schiaparelli, Professor Newton of Yale College, in America, called their attention to the great display of November meteors which might be expected on November 13-14, 1866. The fine shower of that year was well observed, and the part—we may almost say the point—of the constellation Leo from which the meteors radiated was correctly determined. And now a strange thing happened. Those who believed in Schiaparelli's account of the August meteors supposed of necessity that the bodies forming that system travel in an orbit of enormous extent, for the comet of 1862 travels on a path extending much further from the sun than the path of Neptune. There was, therefore, nothing to prevent them from believing that the Leonides travel in a track carrying them far away from the sun. The recurrence of great displays of these meteors at intervals of about 33 years might be readily explained on such an assumption, for if the Leonides have a period of about 33 years, their path must extend far beyond the path of Uranus. But hitherto astronomers had not been ready to admit such an explanation of the periodic recurrence of great displays of the November meteors. They preferred theories (for several were available) which accounted for the 33-year period, while assigning to the Leonides paths of much less extent. Now that the idea of vast meteoric orbits had been fairly broached, some astronomers thought it might at least be worth while to calculate the path of the November meteors on the assumption that their true period is about $33\frac{1}{4}$ years. This was perfectly easy, because the period of a body travelling round the sun determines the velocity at any given distance from the sun, and knowing thus (at least, on this assumption) the true velocity of the Leonides as they rush into our air, while their apparent path is known, their true course is as readily determined as the true course of the wind can be determined by a seaman from the apparent direction and velocity with which it reaches his ship. When the path of the November meteors had been determined (on the assumption mentioned), it was found to be identical with the path of a comet which had only been discovered a few months before—the comet called Tempel's. That a comet which is invisible to the naked eye should have been discovered in the very year when first astronomers made exact observations of the meteors which travel in its track—for it will presently be seen that the assumption above mentioned was a just one—cannot but be regarded as a very singular coincidence. It was a most fortunate coincidence for astronomers, since there can be but little doubt that but for it Schiaparelli's theory would very soon have been forgotten. As that theory was itself suggested by the fortuitous recognition of another comet (only visible at intervals of more than a century) at a time when attention had been specially directed to the August meteors, it may fairly be said that the theory which now associates meteors and comets in the most unmistakable manner was suggested by one accident and confirmed by another. Albeit such accidents happen only to the zealous student of nature's secrets. We shall presently see that the fortunate detection of Tempel's comet in 1866 was not the last of the series of coincidences by which the theory of meteors was established.

Although the evidence favouring Schiaparelli's theory was now strong, yet it was well that at this stage still more convincing evidence was forthcoming. The date of the November display has changed since the Leonides were first recognised, in such sort as to show that the position of their path has changed. The change is due to the disturbing attractions of the planets. It occurred to our great astronomer Adams, discoverer with Leverrier of distant Neptune, to inquire whether the observed change accorded with the calculated effects of planetary attraction, if the Leonides are supposed to travel in any of the smaller paths suggested by astronomers, or could be explained only by the assumption that the meteors travel on the widely-extending path corresponding to the $33\frac{1}{4}$-years period. The problem was worthy of his powers—in other words, it was a problem of exceeding difficulty. By solving it, Adams made that certain which Schiaparelli and his followers had merely assumed. He showed beyond all possibility of doubt or question that of all the paths by which the periodic meteoric displays could be accounted for, the wide path carrying the November meteors far beyond the track of Uranus was the only one which accorded with the observed effects of planetary perturbation.

It was in the confidence resulting from this masterly achievement that in 1872 some astronomers (among them Professor Alex. Herschel, one of Sir J. Herschel's sons) announced the probable occurrence of a display of meteors when the earth crossed the track of Biela's missing comet. An occurrence of this sort was alone wanting to complete the evidence for the meteoric theory. It had been found that the August Perseids move as if they followed in the track of a known comet; the path of the November Leonides had been shown to be identical with that of another comet; if astronomers could predict the appearance of meteors at the time when the earth should pass through the track of a known comet, even those who could not appreciate the force of the mathematical evidence for the new theory would be convinced by the meteoric display. Possibly such observers would have been satisfied with a meteor shower which would not have contented astronomers. The display must have special characteristics to satisfy scientific observers. The path of a body following Biela's comet being known, and its exact rate of motion, the direction in which it must enter our earth's atmosphere (if at all) is determined. Calculation showed this direction to be such that every meteor would appear to travel directly from the constellation Andromeda,—from a point near the feet of the Chained Lady. A meteor might appear in any part of the sky, but its course must be directed from that point, otherwise it could not possibly be travelling in the track of Biela's comet.

The event corresponded exactly with the anticipations of astronomers. On the evening of November 27, 1872, many thousands of small meteors were seen. In England between 40,000 and 50,000 were counted. In Italy the meteors were so numerous that at one time there seemed to be a cloud of light around the region near the feet of Andromeda whence all the meteor-tracks seemed to radiate. The meteors were unmistakably travelling on the track of Biela's comet. They overtook the earth on a path slanting downwards somewhat from the north—precisely in the direction in which Biela's comet would itself have descended upon the earth if at any time the earth had chanced to reach the part of her path crossed by the comet's when the comet was passing that way.

Strangely enough, a German astronomer, Klinkerfues, seems to have regarded the meteoric display of November 27, 1872, as an actual visit from Biela's comet. He telegraphed to Pogson, Government Astronomer at Madras, ' Biela touched earth on November 27, look out for it near Theta Centauri ; ' which, being interpreted, means, Biela's comet then grazed the earth, coming from the feet of Andromeda, look for it where it is travelling onwards in the opposite direction—that is towards the shoulder of the Centaur. As Biela's comet had in reality passed that way twelve weeks earlier, the instructions of Klinkerfues were somewhat wide of the mark. However, Pogson followed them, and near the spot indicated he saw two faint cloudlike objects, slowly moving athwart the heavens. These he supposed to be the two comets into which the missing comet had divided. It so happens, strangely enough, that these objects, though moving parallel to the track of the missing comets, were neither those comets themselves, nor the meteor flight through which the earth ·had passed a few hours before. They were probably somewhat richer meteor clouds, fragments (like the cloud through which our earth had passed) of this most mysterious of all known comets.

To-night, or perhaps to-morrow or next night (for the position of the meteor flights is not certainly known) we shall probably see meteors travelling in advance of the main body.

For the earth passes during the next three days across the orbit of Biela's comet, about as far in front of the head as she passed behind the head in 1872. Now, there is no known reason for supposing (on *à priori* grounds) that meteors get strewn behind a comet's nucleus more readily than in front of it. The disturbing forces which would tend to delay some meteoric attendants would be balanced by forces which would tend to hasten others. As a matter of fact it would seem that the meteor flights which follow a comet's nucleus are commonly denser than those which precede the nucleus. Yet in 1865 many thousands of Leonides were seen which were in advance of the main body forming the comet of 1866. In 1859, 1860, and 1861, many Perseids were seen, which were in advance of the comet of 1862. So that we might fairly expect to see a great number of Andromeds to-night (or on the following nights) even if we had none but the probabilities thus suggested to guide us. But since many were seen on November 27 last, when the head of the comet, now some four months' journey from us, was a whole year's journey further away, it seems probable that on the present occasion a display well worth observing will be seen should fine weather prevail. It will be specially interesting to astronomers, as showing how meteors are strewn in front of a comet. How meteors are strewn behind a comet we already know tolerably well from observations made on the Perseids since 1862 and on the Leonides since 1865.

COLD WINTERS.

DURING the cold weather of last December (1878) we heard much about old-fashioned winters. It was generally assumed that some thirty or forty years ago the winters were colder than they now are. Some began to speculate on the probability that we may be about to have a cycle of cold winters, continuing perhaps for thirty or forty years, as the cycle of mild winters is commonly supposed to have done. If any doubts were expressed as to the greater severity of winter weather thirty or forty years ago, evidence was forthcoming to show that at that time our smaller rivers were commonly frozen over during the winter, and the larger rivers always encumbered with masses of ice, and not unfrequently frozen from source to estuary. Skating was spoken of as a half-forgotten pastime in these days, as compared with what it was when the seniors of our time were lads. Nor were dismal stories wanting of villages snowed up for months, of men and women who had been lost amid snowdrifts, and of other troubles such as we now associate rather with Siberian than with British winters.

Turning over recently the volume of the 'Penny Magazine' for the year 1837, I came across a passage which shows that these ideas about winter weather forty years ago were entertained forty years ago about winter weather eighty or ninety years ago. It occurs in an article on the 'Peculiarities of the Climate of Canada and the United States.' Discussing the theory whether the clearing away of forests has any influence in mitigating the severity of winter weather, the

writer of the article says, ' Many persons assert, and I believe
with some degree of accuracy, that the seasons in Europe,
and in our own island particularly, have undergone a
remarkable change within the memory of many persons now
living ; and if such really be the case, how few attempts
have been made to account for this change, since no great
natural phenomenon, like that of clearing away millions of
acres of forest timber, and thereby exposing the cold and
moist soil to the action of the sun's rays, has recently taken
place here ; so that if the climate of Great Britain has
actually undergone a change, the cause, whatever that may
be, must be of a different nature from that generally
supposed to affect the climate of North America.'   It must
be explained that, though in this passage the writer does not
speak of a diminution in the severity of the winters, it is a
change of that sort that he is really referring to.   He had
said, a few lines before, that ' some of the older inhabitants
of North America will declare to you that the winters are
much less severe "now" than they were forty or fifty years
ago,' and in the passage quoted he is discussing the possibility of a similar change in Europe, where, however, as he
points out, the cause assigned to the supposed change in
America has certainly no existence.   Since 1830, by the way,
the theory has been advanced that the supposed mildness of
recent winters may have been caused by the large increase
in the consumption of coal, owing to the use of steam machinery, gas for lighting purposes, and so forth.

I believe it will be found on careful inquiry that the
change for which forty years ago men sought a cause in
vain, and for which at present they assign a perfectly in-
adequate cause, has had no real existence.   The study of
meteorological records gives no valid support to the theory
of change.   Nor is it difficult to understand how the idea
that there has been a change has arisen from the changed
conditions under which men in middle life, as compared with
children, observe or feel the effects of milder weather.   A
child gives no heed to mild winters. They pass. like ordinary

spring or autumn days, unnoted and unremembered. But a bitter winter, or even a spell of bitter weather such as is felt almost every year, is remembered. Even though it lasts but for a short time, it produces as much effect on the childish imagination as a long and bitter winter produces on the minds of grown folk. Looking back at the days of child-hood, the middle-aged man or woman recalls what seems like a series of bitter winters, because recalling many occa-sions when, during what seemed a long time, the snow lay deep, the waters were frozen, and the outdoor air was shrewd and biting.

Before considering some of the remarkable winters which during the last century have been experienced in Great Britain and in Europe generally, I would discuss briefly the evidence on which I base the belief that the winter weather of Europe, and of Great Britain especially, has undergone no noteworthy change during the last century.

If there is any validity in the theory at present in vogue that our winters are milder now than they were forty or fifty years ago, and the theory in vogue as we have seen forty years ago that the winters then were milder than they had been forty or fifty years earlier, it is manifest that there ought to be a very remarkable contrast between our present winter weather and that which was commonly experienced eighty or ninety years since. Now, it so chances that we possess a record of the weather from 1768 to 1792, by a very competent observer —Gilbert White of Selborne—which serves to show what weather prevailed generally during that interval; while the same writer has described at length, in his own happy and effective manner, some of the winters which were specially remarkable for severity. Let us see whether the winters during the last third of the eighteenth century were so much more bitter or long-lasting than those now experienced as common ideas on the subject would suggest.

In 1768, the year began with a fortnight's frost and snow. The cold was very severe, as will presently be more particu-larly noted. Thereafter wet and rainy weather prevailed to

the end of February.   The winter of 1768-69 was marked
throughout by alternations of rain and frost ; thus from the
middle of November to the end of 1768 there were 'alternate rains and frosts ; ' in January and February, 1769, the
weather was 'frosty and rainy, with gleams of fine weather
in the intervals ; then to the middle of March, wind and rain.'
The last half of November, 1769, was dry and frosty,
December windy, with rain and intervals of frost, and the
first fortnight very foggy ; the first fortnight of January, 1770,
frosty, but on the 14th and 15th all the snow melted and to
the end of February mild hazy weather prevailed ; March
was frosty and bright.   From the middle of October, 1770,
to the end of the year, there were almost incessant rains ;
then severe frosts till the last week of January, 1771, after
which rain and snow prevailed for a fortnight, followed by
spring weather till the end of February.   March and April
were frosty.   The spring of 1771 was so exceptionally
severe in the Isle of Skye that it was called the Black
Spring ; in the south also it was severe.   November, 1771,
frost with intervals of fog and rain ; December, mild and
bright weather with hoar frosts ; January and the first week
of February, 1772, frost and snow ; thence to the end of the
first fortnight in March, frost, sleet, rain, and snow.

The winter of 1772-73 would fairly compare with the
mildest in recent years, except for one fortnight of hard frost
in February, 1773.   For from the end of September to
December 22 there were rain and mild weather—the first ice
on December 23—but thence to the end of the month foggy
weather.   The first week in January, frost, but the rest of the
month dark rainy weather ; and after the fortnight of hard
frost in February, misty showery weather to the end of the
first week in March, and bright spring days till April.

There were four weeks of frost after the end of the first
fortnight in November, 1773, then rain to the end of the
year, and rain and frost alternately to the middle of March,
1774.

In 1774-1775 there seems to have been no winter at all

worth mentioning. From August 24 to the end of the third week in November there was rain, with frequent intervals of sunny weather. Then to the end of December, dark dripping fogs. January, February, and the first half of March, 1775, rain almost every day ; and to the end of the first week in April, cold winds, with showers of rain and snow.

The end of the year 1775 was rainy, with intervals of hoar frost and sunshine. Dark frosty weather prevailed during the first three weeks of January, 1776, with much snow. Afterwards foggy weather and hoar frost. The cold of January. 1776, was remarkable, and will presently be more fully described.

November and December, 1776, were dry and frosty, with some days of hard rain. Then to January 10, 1777, hard frost ; to the 20th foggy with frequent showers ; and to February 18, hard dry frost with snow, followed by heavy rains, with intervals of warm dry spring weather to the end of May.

The winter of 1777–78 was another which resembled closely enough those winters which many suppose to be peculiar to recent years. The autumn weather to October 12 had been remarkably fine and warm. From then to the end of the year, grey mild weather prevailed, with but little rain and still less frost. During the first thirteen days of January there was frost with a little snow ; then rain to January 24, followed by six days of hard frost. After this, harsh foggy weather with rain prevailed till February 23 ; then five days of frost ; a fortnight of dark harsh weather ; and spring weather to the end of the first fortnight in April. The second fortnight of April, however, was cold, with snow and frost.

Similarly varied in character was the winter of 1778–79. From the end of September, 1778, to the end of the year the weather was wet, with considerable intervals of sunshine. January, 1779, was characterised by alternations of frost and showers. After this, to April 21, warm dry weather prevailed.

The winter of 1779–80 was rather more severe. During October and November the weather was fine with intervals of rain. December rainy, with frost and snow occasionally. January 1780, frosty. During February dark harsh weather prevailed, with frequent intervals of frost. March was characterised by warm, showery, spring weather.

November and December, 1781, were warm and rainy · and the same mild open weather prevailed till February 4. Then followed eighteen days of hard frost, after which to the end of March the weather was cold and windy, with frost, snow, and rain. Thus the first two-thirds of the winter of 1781–82 were exceptionally mild, while the last third was cold and bleak.

In November, 1782, we find for the first time in these records an instance of early and long-continued cold. ' November began with a hard frost, and continued throughout, with alternate frost and thaw. The first part of December frosty.' The latter half of December, however, and the first sixteen days of January were mild, with much rain and wind. Then came a week of hard frost, followed by stormy dripping weather to the end of February. Thence to May 9, cold harsh winds prevailed. On May 5 there was thick ice.

The next two winters were, on the whole, the severest of the entire series recorded by Gilbert White, though at no time in the winter of 1783-84 was the cold greater than has often been experienced in this country. White's record runs thus : From September 23 to November 12, dry mild weather. To December 18, grey soft weather with a few showers. Thence to February 19, 1784, hard frost, with two thaws, one on January 14, the other on February 5. To February 28, mild wet fogs. To March 3, frost with ice. To March 10, sleet and snow. To April 2, snow with hard frost.

The winter of 1784-85 was remarkable for the exceedingly severe cold of December, 1784, which will presently be referred to more particularly. From November 6 to the end of the year 1784, fog, rain, and hard frost alternated, the frost continuing longest and being severest in December. On January 2 a thaw began, and rainy weather with wind continued to January 28. Thence to March 15 hard frost; to March 21 mild weather with sprinkling showers; to April 7 hard frost.

After rainy weather till December 23, 1786, came frost and snow till January 7, 1787. Then a week of mild and very rainy weather, followed by a week of heavy snow. From January 21 to February 11, mild weather with frequent rains; to February 21 dry weather with high winds; and to March 10, hard frost. Then alternate rains and frosts to April 13.

Early in November, 1786, there was frost, but thence to December 16 rain with only 'a few detached days of frost.' After a fortnight of frost and snow, came 24 days of dark, moist, mild weather. Then four days (from January 24 to January 28, 1787) of frost and snow; after which mild showery weather to February 16, dry cool weather to February 28, stormy and rainy weather to March 10. The next fortnight bright and frosty; then mild rainy weather to the end of April.

November, 1787, was mild till the 23rd, the last week frosty. The first three weeks of December still and mild, with rain, the last week frosty. The first thirteen days of January mild and wet; then five days of frost, followed by dry, windy weather. February frosty, but with frequent showers. The first half of March hard frost, the rest dark harsh weather with much rain.

The winter of 1788–89 was very severe, hard frost continuing from November 22, 1788, to January 13, 1789. The rest of January was mild with showers. February rainy, with snow showers and heavy gales of wind. The first thirteen days of March hard frost, with snow; and then till April 18, heavy rain, with frost, snow, and sleet. This winter was very severe also on the Continent.

The winter of 1789-90 was as mild as that of 1788-89 had been severe. The record runs thus :—' November to 17th, heavy rains with violent gales of wind. To December 18, mild dry weather with a few showers. To the end of the year rain and wind. To January 16, 1790, mild foggy weather, with occasional rains. To January 21 ' (five days only) ' frost. To January 28, dark, with driving rains. To February 14, mild dry weather. To February 22 ' (eight days) ' hard frost.' To April 5 bright cold weather with a few showers.

In November, 1790, mild autumnal weather prevailed till the 26th, after which there were five days of hard frost. Thence to the end of the year, rain and snow, with a few days of frost. The whole of January, 1791, was mild with heavy rains; February windy, with much rain and snow. Then to the end of April dry, but ' rather cold and frosty.'

November, 1791, was very wet and stormy, December frosty. There was some hard frost in January, 1792, but the weather mostly wet and mild. In February also there was some hard frost and a little snow. March was wet and cold.

The record ends with the year 1792, the last three months of which are thus described : ' October showery and mild. November dry and fine. December mild.'

Certainly the account of the 23 years between 1768 and 1792 does not suggest that there is any material difference between the winter weather now common and the average winter weather a century ago. Still it may be necessary to show, that when men spoke of mild weather in old times, they meant what we should understand by the same expression. A reference to rain or showery weather shows sufficiently that a temperature above the freezing point existed while such weather prevailed. But it might be that what White speaks of as mild weather, is such as we should consider severe. In order to show that this is not the case, it will suffice to examine his statement respecting the actual temperature in particular winters, considering them always with due reference to what he says as to their exceptional character.

Take for instance his account of the frost in January, 1768. He says that, for the short time it lasted, this frost 'was the most severe that we had then known for many years, and was remarkably injurious to evergreens.' 'The coincidents attending this short but intense frost,' he proceeds, after describing his vegetable losses, 'were, that the horses fell sick with an epidemic distemper, which injured the winds of many and killed some; that colds and coughs were general among the human species; that it froze under people's beds for several nights; that meat was so hard frozen that it could not be spitted, and could not be secured but in cellars, &c.' On the 3rd of January a thermometer within doors, in a close parlour, where there was no fire, fell in the night to 20; on the 4th to 18; and on the 7th to $17\frac{1}{2}$ degrees, 'a degree of cold which the owner never since saw in the same situation.' The evidence from the thermometer is unsatisfactory, because we do not know how the parlour was situated. But there is reason for supposing that in the bitterest winters known during the last thirty or forty years, a greater degree of cold than that of January, 1768, has been experienced in England.

The frost of January, 1776, was also regarded as remarkable, and an account of it will therefore enable us to judge what was the ordinary winter weather of the last century.

In the first place, White notices that 'the first week of January, 1776, was very wet, and drowned with vast rains from every quarter; from whence may be inferred, as there is great reason to believe is the case, that intense frosts seldom take place till the earth is perfectly glutted and chilled with water; and hence dry autumns are seldom followed by rigorous winters.' On the 14th, after a week of frost, sleet, and snow, which after the 12th 'overwhelmed all the works of men, drifting over the tops of gates, and filling the hollow lanes,' White had occasion to be much abroad.   He thought he had never before or since encountered such rugged Siberian weather.   'Many of the narrow roads were now filled above the tops of the hedges, through which the snow was driven into most romantic and grotesque shapes, so striking to the imagination as not to be seen without wonder and pleasure.   The poultry dared not to stir out of their roosting places : for cocks and hens are so dazzled and confounded by the glare of snow, that they would soon perish without assistance.   The hares also lay sullenly in their seats, and would not move till compelled by hunger : being conscious, poor animals, that the drifts and heaps treacherously betray their footsteps and prove fatal to many of them.'   From the 14th the snow continued to increase, and began to stop the road-wagons and coaches, which could no longer keep their regular stages; and especially on the Western roads.   'The company at Bath that wanted to attend the Queen's birthday were strangely incommoded ; many carriages of persons who got on their way to town from Bath, as far as Marlborough, after strange embarrassments, here met with a *ne plus ultra*.   The ladies fretted, and offered large rewards to labourers, if they would shovel them a road to London ; but the relentless heaps of snow were too bulky to be removed ; and so the 18th passed over, leaving the company in very uncomfortable circumstances, at the Castle and other inns.'

Yet all this time and till the 21st the cold was not so intense as it was in December 1878.   On the 21st the thermometer showed 20 degrees, and had it not been for the deep snows, the winter would not have been very severely felt.   On the 22nd, the author had occasion to go to London 'through a sort of Laplandian scene, very wild and grotesque indeed.' But London exhibited an even stranger appearance than the country.   ' Being bedded deep in snow, the pavement of the streets could not be touched by the wheels or the horses' feet, so that the carriages ran almost without the least noise.' 'Such an exemption from din and clatter,' says White, ' was

strange but not pleasant ; it seemed to convey an uncomfortable idea of desolation :

Ipsa silentia terrent.

'The worst had not yet, however, been reached. On the
27th much snow fell all day, and in the evening the frost
became very intense. At South Lambeth, for the four following nights, the thermometer fell to eleven, seven, six, six ;
and at Selborne to seven, six, ten; and on the 31st, just
before sunrise, with rime on the trees and on the tube of the
glass, the quicksilver sank exactly to zero—*a most unusual
degree of cold this for the South of England.*' During these
four nights, the cold was so penetrating that ice formed
under beds; and in the day the wind was so keen, that persons of robust constitutions could hardly endure to face it.
'The Thames was at once frozen over, both above and
below bridge, that crowds ran about on the ice. The streets
were now strangely encumbered with snow, which crumbled
and trod dusty ; and turning gray, resembled bay salt ; what
had fallen on the roofs was so perfectly dry that from first
to last it lay twenty-six days on the houses in the city ; *a
longer time than had been remembered by the oldest housekeepers
living.*'

According to all appearances rigorous weather might now
have been expected for weeks to come, since every night increased in severity. 'But behold,' says White, 'without any
apparent cause, on February 1, a thaw took place, and some
rain followed before night, making good the observation that
frosts often go off as it were at once without any gradual de-
clension of cold. On February 2 the thaw persisted, and on
the 3rd swarms of little insects were frisking and sporting in
a court-yard at South Lambeth, as if they had felt no frost.
Why the juices in the small bodies and smaller limbs of
such minute beings are not frozen, is a matter of curious
inquiry.'

Although it is manifest that the weather of January, 1776,
was severe, yet the remarks italicised show that such weather

was regarded a century ago as altogether exceptional.
Again, the cold lasted only about three weeks.   And it may
be doubted whether in actual intensity it even equalled that
which was experienced in London and the south of England
generally during the first week of 1855.   Certainly the
evidence afforded by such remarks as I have italicised in
the above-quoted passage tends more to prove that winter
weather in England a hundred years hence was on the
average much like winter at present, than the unusual
severity of the weather during about twenty-four days in
January, 1776, tends to suggest that a marked change has
taken place.

Similar evidence is afforded by White's remarks respecting the severe cold of December, 1784.

As in January, 1776, so in December, 1784—a week of
very wet weather heralded the approach of severe cold.
'The first week of December,' says White, 'was very wet,
with the barometer very low.   On the 7th, with the barometer at 28.5, came on a vast snow, which continued all
that day and the next, and most part of the following night :
so that by the morning of the 9th the works of men were
quite overwhelmed' (there is something quite Homeric in
White's use of this favourite expression), 'the lanes filled so
as to be impassable, and the ground covered twelve or
fifteen inches without any drifting.   In the evening of the
9th the air began to be so very sharp that we thought it
would be curious to attend to the motions of a thermometer ;
we therefore hung out two, one made by Martin and one by
Dolland' (probably Dollond), 'which soon began to show us
what we were to expect ; for by ten o'clock they fell to
twenty-one, and at eleven to four, when we went to bed.
On the 10th in the morning the quicksilver of Dolland's
glass was down to half a degree below zero and that of
Martin's, which was absurdly graduated only to four degrees
above zero, sunk quite into the brass guard of the ball, so
that, when the weather became most interesting, this was
useless.   On the 10th, at eleven at night, though the air was

perfectly still, Dolland's glass went down to one degree below zero ! This strange severity of the weather made me very desirous to know what degree of cold there might be in such an exalted and near situation as Newton. We had, therefore, on the morning of the 10th, written to Mr. ——, and entreated him to hang out his thermometer, made by Adams, and to pay some attention to it, morning and evening, expecting wonderful phenomena in so elevated a region, at two hundred feet or more above my house. But, behold ! on the 10th, at eleven at night, it was down only to seventeen, and the next morning at twenty-two, when mine was at ten ! We were so disturbed at this unexpected reverse of comparative cold that we sent one of my glasses up, thinking that of Mr. —— must somehow be wrongly con-structed. But when the instruments came to be confronted they went exactly together, so that for one night at least the cold at Newton was eighteen degrees less than at Selborne, and through the whole frost ten or twelve degrees ; and indeed, when we came to observe consequences, we could readily credit this, for all my laurustines, bays, ilexes, arbutuses, cypresses, and even my Portugal laurels—and, which occasions more regret, my fine sloping laurel hedge— were scorched up, while at Newton the same trees have not lost a leaf . . . .' One circumstance noted by White, though not bearing specially on the degree of cold which prevailed on this occasion, is very interesting. ' I must not omit to tell you,' says White, ' that during those two Siberian days my parlour cat was so electric that had a person stroked her and been properly insulated, the shock might have been given to a whole circle of people.'

White's account of this severe frost bears very significantly on the theory that our winter weather has undergone a great change. It is obvious, in the first place, that the situation of his thermometers was such that they were likely to show a low temperature as compared with the indications in other places. It is also clear that the thermometer he used was trustworthy. If it were one of

Dollond's it would presumably be a good one, and I do not think that in White's time the trick of marking inferior instruments with the name Dolland had come into vogue. But in any case Adams's scientific instruments were excellent ; and, as the account shows, the thermometer used by White indicated the same temperature as Adams's. Now, the lowest temperature recorded was only one degree below zero ; and that this was altogether exceptional is shown not only by what White says in the passage I have quoted, but also by his remarking a little later that this frost 'may be allowed, from its effects, to have exceeded any since 1739–40.' Even this is not all. It would certainly prove beyond dispute that our winters were not milder than those of a century ago ; for a greater degree of cold than that recorded by White in December, 1784, has been more than once experienced in the same part of England during the last forty years. But it seems from a statement in Miller's 'Gardener's Dictionary,' that the Portugal laurels were untouched in the great frost of 1739–40, which would show that the frost of 1784 was more severe and destructive than that of 1739–40. If this were really so, the frost of 1784 was the severest (though owing to its short duration it did not produce the most remarkable effects in the country at large) of any during the periods noted between the years 1709 and 1788. On the Continent, the frost of December, 1788, was more severe in some places, though rather less severe at Paris, than that of 1709 ; but I do not know of any records which would enable us to make a direct comparison between the cold in 1709, 1784, and 1788, at any given place in Great Britain.

It will be well now to take a wider survey and consider some of the most severe winters experienced in Europe generally.

The winter of 1544 was remarkably severe all over Europe. In Flanders, according to Mézerai, wine froze in casks, and was sold in blocks by the pound weight. The winter of 1608 was also very severe. In the winter of 1709 the thermometer at the Paris Observatory recorded a cold of nearly ten degrees below zero.

Passing over the winter of 1776, of whose effects in England we have learned enough to enable us to judge how severely it must have been felt in those continental countries where the winter is always more severe than with us, we come to the severe winter of 1788-89.

We have seen that in England hard frost began on November 22 and continued till January 13. In France (or rather at Paris) the frost began three days later, but the thaw began on the same day, January 13. There was no intermission except on Christmas Day, when it did not freeze. In the great canal at Versailles the ice was two feet thick. 'The water also froze,' says Flammarion, ' in several very deep wells, and wine became congealed in cellars. The Seine began to freeze as early as November 26, and for several days its course was impeded, the breaking up of the ice not taking place until January 20 (1789). The lowest temperature observed at Paris was seven degrees below zero, on December 31. The frost was equally severe in other parts of France and throughout Europe. The Rhone was quite frozen over at Lyons, the Garonne at Toulouse, and at Marseilles the sides of the docks were covered with ice. Upon the shores of the Atlantic the sea was frozen to a distance of several leagues. The ice upon the Rhine was so thick that loaded wagons were able to cross it. The Elbe was covered with ice, and also bore up heavy carts. The harbour at Ostend was frozen so hard that people could cross it on horseback; the sea was congealed to a distance of four leagues from the exterior fortifications, and no vessel could approach the harbour.'

It was during the frost of 1788–89 that a fair was held on the Thames. The river was frozen as low as Gravesend; but it was only in London that booths were set up. The Thames fair lasted during the Christmas holidays and the first twelve days of January.

At Strasburg, on December 31, a temperature of fifteen

degrees below zero was shown.   At Berlin on the 20th, and
St. Petersburg on the 12th, temperatures of twenty and
twenty-three degrees below zero respectively were noted.
But in Poland and parts of Germany an even greater degree
of cold was recorded.   For instance, at Warsaw, $26\frac{1}{2}$
degrees below zero ; and at Bremen thirty-two degrees.   At
Basle, on December 18, the thermometer indicated nearly
thirty-six degrees below zero.   In the district around
Toulouse bread was frozen so hard that it could not be cut
till it had been laid before the fire.   Many travellers perished
in the snow.   At Lemburg, in Galicia, thirty-seven persons
were found dead in three days towards the end of December.
The ice froze so thick in ponds that in most of them all the
fish were killed.

The winter of 1794–95 was remarkable in this country
as giving the lowest average temperature for a month ever
recorded in England.   The mean temperature for January,
1795, was only 26.5 degrees ; or more than three degrees
lower than that of last January.   January 25, 1795, is
commonly supposed to have been the coldest day ever
known.   The thermometer in London stood at eight degrees
below zero during part of that bitter day ; and in Paris,
where also there were six consecutive weeks of frost, at $10\frac{3}{4}$
degrees below zero.   The Thames was frozen over at White-
hall in the beginning of January.   The Marne, the Scheldt, the
Rhine, and the Seine were so frozen over that army corps
and heavy carriages crossed over them.   Perhaps the
strangest of all the recorded results of cold weather occurred
during the same month.   The French General Pichegru,
who was then operating in the North of Holland, sent
detachments of cavalry and infantry about January 20, with
orders to the former to cross the Texel and to capture the
enemy's vessels, which were 'imprisoned by the ice.'   'The
French horsemen crossed the plains of ice at full gallop,' we
are told, 'approached the vessels, called on them to sur-
render, captured them without a struggle, and took the crews
prisoners :'   probably the only occasion in history when

effective use could have been made of a corps of horse-
marines.

The winter of 1798–99 was very cold, but not so exceptionally cold in England as on the Continent.   The Seine
was completely frozen over from the 29th of December to
the 19th of January, from the Pont de la Tournelle to the
Pont Royal.   Farther east the cold was much greater.   The
Meuse was frozen over so thickly that carriages could cross
it, and at the Hague and at Rotterdam fairs were held on
the river.   A regiment of dragoons starting from Mayence,
crossed the Rhine upon the ice.

The winter of 1812–13 was exceeding cold in November,
December and January.   It was this unusually early and
bitter winter which occasioned the destruction of Napoleon's army in Russia, and the eventual overthrow of his
power.   (For no one who considers his achievements during
the campaigns of 1813 and 1814 can doubt that, had the
army with which he invaded Russia been at his command,
he would have foiled all the efforts of combined Europe
against him.)   The cold became very intense in Russia after
the 7th of November.   On the 17th the thermometer fell
to 15 degrees below zero, according to Larrey, who carried
a thermometer suspended from his button hole.   The retreat from Moscow began on the 18th, Napoleon leaving the
still burning city on the 19th, and the evacuation being complete on the 23rd.   Everything seemed to conspire against
Napoleon and his army.   During the march to Smolensk
snow fell almost incessantly.   Even the only intermission of
the cold during the retreat caused additional disaster.   On
the 18th of November, Russian troops had crossed the
frozen Dwina with their artillery.   A thaw begun on the
24th, but continued only for a short time ; 'so that from the
26th to the 29th the Beresina contained numerous blocks of
ice, but yet was not so frozen over as to afford a passage to
the French troops.'   It was to this circumstance that the
terribly disastrous nature of the passage of the Beresina must
mainly be attributed.

The winter of 1813–14 was colder in England than on the Continent—I mean, the winter here was colder for England than the winter in any region of continental Europe was for that region. The frost lasted from December 26 to March 21, and the mean temperature of January was only 26.8 degrees. The Thames was frozen over very thickly, and a fair was held on the frozen river.

The winter of 1819–20 was bitter throughout Europe. Mr. Thomas Plant, in an interesting letter to the *Times* of February 4, says that this winter was one long spell of intense frost from November to March, and was almost as severe as that of 1813–14. In Paris there were forty-seven days of frost, nineteen of which were consecutive, from December 30, 1818, to January 17. 'In France,' says Flammarion, ' the intensity of the cold was heralded by the passage along the coast of the Pas de Calais of a great number of birds coming from the farthest regions of the north by wild swans and ducks of variegated plumage. Several travellers perished of cold ; amongst others a farmer near Arras, a gamekeeper near Nogent (Haute Marne) a man and woman in the Côte d'Or, two travellers at Breuil, on the Meuse, a woman and a child on the road from Etain to Verdun, six persons near Château Salins (Meurthe), and two little Savoyards on the road from Clermont to Chalons-sur-Saône. In the experiments made at the Metz School of Artillery, on the 10th of January, to ascertain how iron resisted low temperatures, several soldiers had their hands or their ears frozen.' During this winter the Thames, the Seine, the Rhône, the Rhine, the Danube, the Garonne, the lagoons of Venice, and the Sound, were so far frozen that it was possible to walk across them on the ice.

The winter of 1829–30 was remarkable as the longest winter of the first half of the present century. The cold was not exceptionally intense, but the long continuance of bitter weather occasioned more mischief in the long run than has attended short spells of severer cold. The river Seine was frozen at Paris first for twenty-nine days, from December 28th to January 26th, and then for five days from February 5th to February 10th. The river had not been so many days frost-bound in any winter since 1763. Even at Havre the Seine was frozen over ; and at Rouen a fair was held upon the river on January 18th. On January 25, after a thaw of six days, the ice from Corbeil and Melun blocked up the bridge at Choisy, forming a wall 16½ feet high.

The winter of 1837–38 was remarkable for the long frost of January and February, 1838. It lasted eight weeks. Mr. Plant mentions that 'the lowest point of the thermometer during this long and severe frost occurred on January 20, when the readings were from 5 degrees below zero, in this district' (Moseley, near Birmingham), 'to 8 and 10 degrees below zero in more exposed aspects.' 'On the 13th of January, the old Royal Exchange, London, was destroyed by fire ; and the frost was so great that, when the fire brigade had ceased playing on one portion of the burning pile, the water in a short time became icicles of such large dimensions, that the effect has been described as grand in the extreme.'

The winter of 1837–38 is not usually included as one among the exceptionally cold winters on the Continent, and the winter of 1840–41, though certainly cold in the British Isles, is not included by Mr. Plant in his list of the coldest winters since 1795. But this winter was exceedingly cold on the Continent. At Paris there were fifty-nine days' frost, twenty-seven of them consecutive—viz. from December 5th, when the cold began, to January 1st. The intermission which began on January 1, lasted only till January 3, when there was another week of frost. There was frost again from January 30 to February 10. One of the most remarkable stories connected with the cold of this winter is thus told by Flammarion :—'On the 15th of December, the ashes of Napoleon, brought back from St. Helena, entered Paris by the Arc de Triomphe. The thermometer in places exposed to nocturnal radiation, had that day marked 6.8 degrees above zero. An immense crowd, the National Guard of

Paris and its suburbs, and numerous regiments lined the Champs Elysées, from the early morning until two in the afternoon. Every one suffered severely from the cold. Soldiers and workmen, hoping to obtain warmth by drink-,ing brandy' (the most chilling process they could have thought of), 'were seized by the cold, and dropped down dead of congestion. Several persons perished, victims of their curiosity : having climbed up into the trees to see the procession, their extremities, benumbed by the cold, failed to support them, and they were killed by the fall.'

The winter of 1844–45 was remarkable for the long duration of cold weather. The whole of December was very cold, January not so severe, but still cold, February singularly cold, and the frost so severe in March that on Good Friday (March 21st) the boats, which had been frost-bound for weeks in the canals, were still locked tightly in ice.

Mr. Plant omits to notice in the letter above-mentioned the long winter of 1853–54, which was indeed less severe (relatively as well as absolutely) in England than on the Continent. Still, he is hardly right in saying, that after 1845 there was no winter of long and intense character until January and February 1855. On the Continent the winter of 1853–54 was not only protracted but severe, especially towards the end of December. Several rivers were frozen over. The cold lasted from March till November, with scarcely any intermission.

The winter of 1854–55 was still more severe than its predecessor. The frosts commenced in the east of France in October and lasted till the 28th of April. The mean temperatures for January and February, in England, were 31 degrees and 29 degrees respectively. This year will be remembered as that during which our army suffered so terribly from cold in the Crimea. But our brave fellows would have resisted Generals January and February (in whom the Czar Nicholas expressed such strong reliance), as well as the Russians themselves did, or maybe a trifle better (if we can judge from the way in which Englishmen have borne Arctic winters), had it not been for the gross negligence of the Red Tapists.

The winter of 1857–58 was rather severer than the average, but not much. The Danube and Russian ports in the Black Sea were frozen over in January, 1858.

The frost of December, 1860, and January, 1861, was remarkable. The coldest recorded mean temperature for a month in time (not the coldest month), was that for the thirty days ending January 16, 1861,—namely, 26 degrees. Mr. Plant remarks that 'the intense cold on Christmas-eve, 1860, finds no equal in his records, since January 20, 1838. The thermometer registered 34 degrees of frost, and in the valley of the Rea, five to seven degrees below zero. Strangely enough, Flammarion makes no mention of this bitter winter in his list of exceptionally cold winters.

The winter of 1864–65 lasted from December to the end of March, all of which four months, Mr. Plant notes, were of the true winter type. The Seine was frozen over at Paris, and people crossed the ice near the Pont des Arts.

The winter of 1870–71 will always be remembered as that during which the siege of Paris was carried on, and the last scenes of the Franco-Prussian war took place. As Flammarion justly remarks, this winter will be classed among severe winters, because of the extreme cold in December and January (notwithstanding the mild weather of February), and also because of the fatal influence which the cold exercised upon the public health at the close of the war with Germany. 'The great equatorial current,' he proceeds (meaning, no doubt, the winds which blow over the prolongation of the Gulf Stream), 'which genérally extends to Norway, stopped this year at Spain and Portugal, the prevailing wind being from the north. On the 5th of December there was a temperature of 5 degrees, and on the 8th, at Montpellier, the thermometer stood at 17.6 degrees. A second period of cold set in on the 22nd of December, lasting until the 5th of January. In Paris the Seine was blocked with ice, and seemed likely to become frozen over. On the 24th there were 21.6 degrees of frost, and at Montpellier, on the 31st, 28.8 degrees. It is well known that many of the outposts around Paris, and several of the wounded who had been lying for fifteen hours upon the field, were found frozen to death. From the 9th to the 15th of January a third period of cold set in, the thermometer marking 17.6 degrees' (14.4 degrees of frost) 'at Paris, and 8.6 degrees at Montpellier. The most curious fact was that the cold was greater in the south than in the north of France. At Brussels the lowest temperatures were 11.1 degree in December and 8.2 degrees in January. There were forty days' frost at Montpellier, forty-two at Paris, and forty-seven at Brussels during these two months. Finally, the winter average (December, January, and February) was 35.2 degrees in Paris, whereas the general average is 37.9 degrees.' In the north of Europe this was also a very hard winter, though the cold set in at a different time than that noted for France. There were forty degrees of frost at Copenhagen on February 12—that is, the temperature was 5 degrees below zero. By the documents which M. Renou furnished Flammarion with for France, 'I discover,' says the latter, 'a minimum of 9.4 degrees below zero at Périgueux, and of 13 degrees below zero at Moulins! I find by the documents supplied me by Mr. Glaisher,' he proceeds, 'that he also considers the winter of 1870–71 as appertaining to the class of winters memorable for their severity.'

.   Lastly, in the winter which as I write (February 10, 1879) seems to be nearly over, we have had for December a mean temperature of only 31 degrees in the midlands—the coldest December known there, followed by a January so cold that the mean temperature for the midlands was only 29.8 degrees. Mr. G. J. Symons, the well-known meteorologist, says of the past winter, that January was the coldest for at least twenty-one, and he believes for forty-one years, following a December which was also, with one exception, the coldest for twenty-one years.' He gives an abstract of the temperatures (both maximum and minimum) for

November, December, and January during the last twenty-one years, from which it appears :—

1. That the average *maximum* temperature of November was the lowest during the period with two exceptions, that of December the lowest with one exception, and that of January the lowest of the whole period.

2. That the average *minimum* of November was the lowest during the period with four exceptions, that of December the lowest with one exception, and that of January the lowest.

3. That the mean temperature of the three months was not only five degrees below the average, but also lower than in any previous year out of the twenty-one.

On the whole, the winter of 1878–79 must be regarded as the coldest we have had during at least the last score of years, and probably during twice that time. It was not characterised by exceptionally severe short periods of intense cold, like those which occurred during the winters of 1854–55, 1855–56, and 1860–61 ; but it has been surpassed by few winters during the last two centuries for constant low temperature and long-continued moderate frost. During the last ninety years there have been only four winters matching that of 1878–79 in these respects.

Since the preceding pages were written the weather record for February 1879 has been completed. Like the three preceding months, February showed a mean temperature below the average, though the deficit was not quite so great as in those months. The following table, drawn out by Mr. Plant, shows the mean temperature at Moseley for four winter months of 1878–79, and the average temperature for those months at Moseley during the last twenty years :—

1878-79	Deg.	Average of 20 years	Deg.
November . . .	37.0	November . . .	41.5
December . . .	31.0	December . . .	39.0
January	29.8	January	35.5
February . . .	35.8	February . . .	39.0
Mean of the four months in	33.4	Average of four months in 20 years' observations .	38.8

OXFORD AND CAMBRIDGE ROWING.

THE records of the last eighteen boat-races between Cambridge and Oxford indicate clearly enough the existence of a difference of style in the rowing of the two universities, a circumstance quite as plainly suggested by the five successive victories of Cambridge in the years 1870–74, as by the nine successive victories of Oxford which preceded them. For it is, or should be, known that the victories of Cambridge only began when Morrison, one of the finest Oxford oarsmen, had taught the Cambridge men the Oxford style, so far as it could be imparted to rowers accustomed, for the most part, in intercollegiate struggles, to a different system. With regard to the long succession of Oxford victories which began in 1861, and which, be it noticed, followed on Cambridge successes obtained when the light-blue stroke rowed in the Oxford style, I may remark that, viewing the matter as a question of probabilities, it may safely be said that the nine successive victories of Oxford could not reasonably be regarded as accidental. The loss of three or four successive races would not have sufficed to show that there was any assignable difference in the conditions under which the rival universities encountered each other on the Thames. In cases where the chance of one or other of two events happening is exactly equal, there will repeatedly be observed recurrences of th:s sort. But when the same event recurs so often as nine successive times, it is justifiable to infer that the chances are *not* precisely—or perhaps even nearly—equal. I believe I shall be able to indicate the existence of a cause quite sufficient to account for the series of defeats sustained in the years 1861–69 by Cambridge, and for the change of fortune experienced when for a while the Cambridge oarsmen adopted the style of rowing which has prevailed for many years at the sister university.

I may premise that Cambridge has an important advantage over Oxford in the fact that she has a far larger number of men to choose from in selecting a university crew. It may seem to many, at first sight, that as good a crew might well be selected from three hundred as from five hundred boating-men ; because it is not to be supposed that either number would supply many more than eight first-rate oarsmen. But it must be remembered that there are first-rate oarsmen *and* first-rate oarsmen. The unpractised eye may detect very little difference between the best and the worst oarsmen in such crews as Oxford and Cambridge yearly send to contend for the blue-riband of the river. But differences exist ; and if the best man of the crew were replaced by one equal in rowing ability to the worst, or *vice versâ*, an important difference wou'd be observed in the time of rowing over the racing course, under similar conditions of wind, tide, and so forth. Accordingly, a large field for the selection of the men is a most important advantage. Taking, for instance, the five hundred rowing men of Cambridge and dividing them into two sets —one of three hundred men, corresponding to the three hundred rowing men of Oxford, and the other of two hundred men—we see that the first set ought to supply a crew strong enough to meet Oxford, and the second a crew nearly as strong. Now, if the best men of the two Cambridge crews thus supposed to be formed are combined— say five taken from the first and three from the second, all the inferior men being struck out—a far stronger crew than either of the others would undoubtedly be formed.

So that if Cambridge were generally the winner in these contests, the Oxonians would be able to account for their want of success in a sufficiently satisfactory manner. The successive defeats sustained by the Cambridge crews in 1861–69 are therefore so much the less readily explained as due to mere accident, by which of course I mean simply such an accidental circumstance as that better oarsmen chanced to be at Oxford than at Cambridge in these years, not to accident occurring in the race itself.

Several reasons were assigned from time to time for the repeated victories of Oxford. Some of these may conveniently be examined here, before discussing what I take to be the true explanation.

Some writers in the papers advanced the general proposition that Oxford men are as a rule stronger and more enduring than Cambridge men. They did not tell us why this should be the case—to what peculiar influences it was due that the more powerful and energetic of our English youth should go to one university rather than the other. No evidence of this peculiarity could be found in the university athletic sports, in which success was, as it has since been, very equally divided. And what made the theory the less satisfactory was the circumstance that it afforded no explanation of the early triumphs of the Cantabs, who won seven of the nine races they rowed against Oxford. Of these races five were rowed from Westminster to Putney, a course two miles longer than the present course from Putney to Mortlake. A race over such a course and in the heavier old-fashioned racing-boats was a sufficient test of strength and endurance; yet the Cambridge men managed to win four out of these five events, and that not by a few seconds, but in three instances by upwards of a minute. If there were any reason for conceiving that Oxonians were as a rule stronger than Cantabs in the years 1861–69, there is at least no reason for conceiving that any change can have taken place in the time between the earlier races and that during which Oxford won so persistently. And as the earlier races show no traces of any difference such as was insisted upon by many journalists in the latter part of the period of the Oxford successes, we may reasonably con-clude that the difference had no real existence.

Another theory resembling the preceding was also often urged. It was said repeatedly in the papers that Cambridge traditions encouraged a light flashy stroke, pretty to look at but not effective; that again, Cambridge rowed the first part of the course well but exhausted themselves before the conclusion of the race, through their over-anxiety to get the advantage of their opponents in the beginning of the contest. Critics undertook to say that the Oxford men 'rowed within themselves' at first, reserving their strength for the last mile or two of the course. Now, it will presently appear that there does exist in a certain peculiarity of what may justly be called the Cambridge style, a true cause for want of success, and even for such a repeated series of defeats as the light-blue flag sustained in 1861–69. But the Cambridge style rowed during these years was very far from being a flashy style. On the contrary, the old Cam-bridge style, which is still too often seen in College contests, and has within the last four years been seen on the Thames, involves the rowing of a longer stroke than *seems* to be rowed in the true Oxford style. Oxford rowing is pre-eminently lively. Anyone who had been at the pains to time the strokes of the Oxford and Cambridge crews during the years 1861–69, would have been able at once to dispose of the notion that Cambridge men row the more rapid stroke. In these nine races, as in the practice preceding them, the Oxford crew often took forty-four strokes per minute. Especially did they rise to this swift stroke in some of those grand spurts which so often carried the dark-blue flag in front. I do not remember that the Cambridge crews ever went beyond forty-two strokes per minute. Then again as to starting early and being quickly spent, a good deal of nonsense was written. In some of the later con-tests of the series 1861–69, indeed, the Cambridge crews, urged by the thought of numerous past defeats, made unduly exhausting efforts in the earlier part of the race.

But nothing was done in this way which would have caused the loss of the race if the Cambridge crew had really had it in them to win. If the better of two crews puts on rather too much steam at first, they draw so quickly ahead that they soon begin to feel that they have the race in hand, and so proceed to take matters more steadily. In such powerful and well-trained crews as both universities usually send to the contest, very little harm is done by varying the order of the work a little—rowing hard at first and steadily afterwards, or *vice versâ*. It is easy for lookers-on, most of whom have never taken part in a boat-race, to theorise on these matters. But those who know what boat racing is (as distinguished, be it noticed, from most contests of speed) know that the better boat is almost sure to win in whatever way the stroke may set them their work. A good crew, unlike a good horse, requires no jockeying.

The difference of the rivers Cam and Isis has been urged as a sufficient reason for inferiority on the part of the Cambridge crews. That the difference used to tell unfavourably upon the chances of the light blue flag before the river had been widened and the railway bridge modified, and that even now the Cambridge crews would not be all the better for a better river to practice on, cannot be denied. But I question whether even before the widening of the river, this particular cause sufficed to counterbalance the advantage of the Cantabs in point of numbers. Nor do I think that those who urged the inferiority of the Cambridge river have recognised the principal disadvantage which it entailed upon the light-blue oarsmen.

The first circumstance to be noticed, in this connection, is the difference in the conditions under which racing-boats were and are steered along the two rivers. A Cambridge coxswain has in some respects an easier, in others a more difficult task than the Oxonian. In the first place, he has very little choice as to the course along which he shall take his boat. All he has to do is to steer as closely round each corner as possible ; and the narrowness of the river renders it difficult for him to fall into any error in running a straight line from corner to corner. The Oxonian coxswain, on the other hand, requires to be more carefully on the watch lest he should suffer his boat to diverge from the just course, which is far less obvious on the wider Isis than on the Cam. But although the Cambridge coxswain has the shores of the river close to him on either hand, and can thus never be at a loss as to his just course, yet to maintain this obvious course he has to be continually moving the rudder-lines. In fact, there are some 'eights' which steer so ill that it is no easy matter to keep them from the shores when the crew are sending them along at racing speed. In rounding the three great corners which have to be passed in the ordinary racing-course at Cambridge—viz., First Post Corner, Grassy Corner, and Ditton Corner—the rudder has to be made use of in a much more decided manner than in the straighter course along which the Oxford racing eights have to travel. I have seen the water bubbling over the rudder of a racing eight, as she rounded Grassy Corner, in a manner which showed clearly enough how her 'way' must have been checked ; yet, probably, if the rudder-lines had been relaxed for a moment, the ill-steering craft would have gone irretrievably out of her course, and been presently stranded on the farther bank. And even eights which steer well had to be very carefully handled along the narrow and winding ditch which we Cantabs used to call ' the river.'

A more serious disadvantage, so far as the prospects of University Boats were concerned, lay in the circumstance that there was no part of the Cam (within easy reach, at least, of Cambridge) along which the crew could row without a break, for four or five miles, as they had to do in the actual encounter with the Oxford boat. The whole range of the river between the locks next below Cambridge and Bait's Bite Locks, is somewhat under four miles and a half. But about a mile and a quarter from Bait's Bite sluice, the railway-bridge crosses the river, and until a few years ago, the supports of this bridge divided the river into three parts.

There was in my time a vague tradition that the University Eight had once or twice been steered through the widest of these passages without stopping; but I doubt much whether there could have been any truth in the story. Certainly no coxswain in my time at Cambridge ever achieved the feat, nor could it be safely attempted even by the most skilful steersman. The consequence was that there was a break in the long course which took away all its value as a preparation for the actual race. It may seem to the uninitiated a trifling matter that a crew should get a few seconds of rest in so long a pull. But those who know what racing is, are aware that the slightest break—one stroke even, shirked—is an immense relief to the tugging oarsman.

Beyond Bait's Bite Locks there is a three-and-a-half-miles course, liable to be broken by the manœuvres of a floating bridge or ferry boat opposite Clayhithe. Next comes another short course extending to Upware. And lastly from Upware to Ely there is a fine five-and-a-half-miles course, considerably wider than the Cam, and presenting several splendid reaches. To this course the Cambridge men used to betake themselves four or five times in the course of their preparation for the great race. But a course so far removed from the university itself was clearly far less advantageous than the convenient Oxford long course, extending from the ferry at Christ Church meadows to Newnham. Still, annoying as the want of a convenient long-course must be considered, I cannot attribute the long succession of Cambridge defeats in 1861–69 to such a cause as this. It is true that before the railway-bridge was built, the Cambridge crew used generally to win, and that since it has been so far modified as not to interfere with the passage of a racing eight, they have again been successful, whereas, while the supports of the bridge checked them midway on their course, they were less fortunate. But to connect these circumstances as cause and effect, would be as unsafe as the theory of the Margate fishermen who

ascribed the Goodwin Sands to the building of the Re-
culvers.

It has been said that the shallowness of the Cam affects
the style of Cambridge oarsmen. This seems to me a
fanciful theory. Occasionally in the course of a race close
steering round one or other of the sharper corners might
permit the oarsmen to 'feel the bottom,' for two or three
strokes ; but during all the rest of the course the oars find
plenty of water to take good hold of. The Cam was
undoubtedly growing shallower for some time after 1860 ;
and the change gave some degree of support to the theory
that the peculiarities of the Cambridge style were due to the
peculiarities of the Cambridge river. But I believe the
notion was a wholly mistaken one ; and I am confirmed in
this belief by noticing that the Cambridge style from 1860 to
1869 was in all essential respects, and especially in that feature
which I shall presently describe as its radical and fatal
defect, the same precisely as it had been in earlier times
when Cambridge was oftener successful than defeated.

I have heard Cambridge men say, indeed, that after
rowing on the Cam they feel quite strange on Thames water.
They feel, they say, as if the boat were running away with
them. I have experienced the feeling myself, when rowing
on the Thames anywhere below Teddington ; but most
markedly below Kew. It is not due, however, to the mere
difference in the depth of the two streams, but mainly. if not
wholly, to the circumstance that the lower part of the
Thames is a tidal river. It is not noticeable above Teddington, save (in a somewhat modified form) in those
portions of the river called 'races,' where the stream runs
with unusual rapidity. I should suppose that Oxonians
felt the influence of this peculiarity fully as much as Cambridge oarsmen do ; in fact, I know that this is the experience of some Oxonians, for they have told me as much.

I believe that the principal disadvantage which the
narrowness of the Cam entailed upon boating-men at Cambridge, lay in the circumstance that Cambridge men never,

had an opportunity of rowing a level race. They had 'bumpirg races' for the college eights—as the Oxonians had—and time-races to decide between the merits of two or three boats, whereas at Oxford two boats could contend side by side. Thus it was to many Cambridge men a novel and somewhat disturbing experience to find themselves rowing close alongside of their opponents. It may seem fanciful to notice any disadvantage in such a matter as this ; yet I believe that the matter was not a trifle. The excitement which men feel just before a race begins, and during the first half-mile or so of its progress, is so intense that a small difference of this sort is apt to produce much more effect than might be expected. I think the somewhat flurried style in which the Cantabs were often observed to row the first half-mile of the great race might be partly ascribed to this cause. Of course, I am far from saying that if a Cambridge crew had been decidedly better than their opponents, the race could have been lost or even endangered from such a cause as this.

And now it remains that I should point out that peculiarity in what may be called the Cambridge style of rowing—though it is not now systematically adopted by Cambridge crews—to which the defeats of the light-blue flag in the years 1861–69 were I believe to be chiefly attributed.

It should be remembered that before we can recognise a peculiarity of style as the cause of a long series of defeats, it must be shown that the peculiarity is neither trifling nor accidental. There are peculiarities in rowing which have a very slight effect upon the speed with which the boat is propelled by the crew. Amongst these may be fairly included such points as the following :—the habit of throwing out the elbows just before feathering, feathering high or low, rowing short or long (a technical expression now commonly, though incorrectly, applied tc the length of the stroke, but properly relating to the distance at which the stretcher or foot-board is placed from the seat), sitting high or low, and so on. All these peculiarities—of course within reasonable limits—are unimportant, save in so far as they indicate that the style of the stroke itself is faulty. Then again there are accidental peculiarities, which may be exceedingly important in themselves, but which yet produce only a transient influence, because they are personal peculiarities of such and such a stroke, and when he has left his university they remain no longer in vogue. As an illustration of this sort of peculiarity, I may notice the remarkably effective stroke rowed by Hall of Magdalen in the year 1858-60. There the radical defect of the Cambridge style was almost obliterated, and all the good points of that style were fully brought out. The result was that, out of three races rowed with Oxford, Cambridge won two, and though they lost the third, yet they lost it in such a manner as to obtain more credit than any winning race could have brought them. I refer to the memorable race of 1859, in which the Cambridge boat was, at starting, half full of water, and gradually filling as the race proceeded, sank about half-a-mile from the winning-post, being at the moment of sinking only four lengths behind Oxford, notwithstanding the tremendous difficulties under which the crew had all along been rowing.[1] Mr. Hall also rowed stroke in the great race with the famous London crew—Casamajor, Playford, the two Paynes, &c.—when Cambridge won by half a boat's length. We have, however, to inquire whether there is any point held to be essential by Cambridge oarsmen, which is sufficiently important and sufficiently faulty to account for the marked want of success which attended the light-blue flag in the years 1861-69. The following peculiarity appears to me to be precisely of such a character.

---

[1] 'Wat Bradwood,' in an article on 'Water Derbies,' afterwards referred to, says that Cambridge was fairly beaten when the boat sank. He might with equal justice have said that they were fairly beaten when they started. They never had a chance of winning from the start, having then half a boat-full, and for some time before they sank a whole boat-full, of water to take along with them.

It was formerly held by nearly all the Cambridge oarsmen that 'the instant the oar touches the water' (I am
quoting from a pamphlet called ' Principles of Rowing,'
much read by rowing-men at Cambridge) 'the arms and
body should begin to fall backwards, the former continuing
at their full stretch till the back is perpendicular ; they are
then bent, the elbows being brought close past the sides,' etc.
If a Cambridge oarsman broke this rule, so that his arms
began to bend before his back was upright, he would be
told that he was jerking. 'This is caused,' says our authority, ' by pulling the first part of the stroke with violence
and not falling gradually backwards to finish it. The most
muscular men are more than others guilty of it, because
they trust too much to their arms, instead of making each
part of the body do its proportionate quantity of work. It
is most annoying to the rest of the crew, injures the uniform
swing throughout the boat, and soon tires out the man
himself, however strong he may be, because he is virtually
rowing unsupported, and he has nearly the whole weight of
the boat on his arms alone.'

I was myself trained to row the Cambridge style, and
when I became captain of a boat-club, I was careful to in-
culcate this style on my crew, and on other crews which
came more or less directly under my supervision. But I am
convinced that the peculiarity so carefully enjoined in past
time by the Cambridge club-captains, and still retained, is
altogether erroneous for boats of the modern build. I first
became aware that the Cambridge style is not the waterman's—and, therefore, presumably not the most effective—
through practising in a racing-four with three of our most
noted Thames watermen—the two Mackinnys, and Chitty
of Richmond. They were then preparing for the Thames
National Regatta, though not as a set crew. Accordingly
the coxswain would frequently call upon us for a good lifting spurt of a quarter of a mile or so. During these spurts
the coxswain was continually telling me that I was not
keeping stroke, and I was sensible myself that something

was going wrong. One who has taken part in boat-races very soon detects any irregularity in the rowing—by which I do not of course refer to so gross a defect as not keeping time. All the men of a crew may be keeping most perfect time, and may even present the appearance of keeping stroke together, and yet may not be feeling their work simultaneously. I was aware that something was going wrong, but I found it impossible, without abandoning the style of rowing in which I had been so carefully trained, to keep stroke with the rest of the crew. It seemed to me that they were doubling over their work, because while I was still swaying backwards they had reached the limit of their swing. Then they did not seem to me to feather with that lightning flash which the Cambridge style enjoins. Altogether, I left them after three or four long pulls with the impression that, though they might be very effective watermen, they had but a poor style.

Soon after, however, I had occasion to watch Oxford oarsmen at their work, and I found that they row in a style which, without being actually identical with that of the London waterman, resembles it in all essential respects. The moment the oar catches the water, the body is thrown back as in the Cambridge style, but the arms, instead of being kept straight, immediately begin to do their share of the work. The result is that when the body is upright the arms are already bent, and the stroke is finished when the body is very little beyond the perpendicular position.

Now let us compare the two strokes theoretically. In each stroke the body does a share of the work, and in the Cambridge stroke the body even seems to do more work than in the Oxford stroke, since it is swayed farther back. In each stroke, again, the arms do a share of the work, but in the Oxford stroke the work of the arms is distributed equally as a help to that of the body, whereas in the Cambridge stroke the work of the arms is all thrown upon the finish of the stroke. At first sight it seems to matter very little in what order the work is done, so long as the same amount of work is done in the same space of time. But here an important consideration has to be attended to.

There are two things which the oarsman does in whatever style he rows. He propels the boat along, by pressing the blade of his oar against the water as a fulcrum ; but he also propels his oar more or less through the water. If instead of the actual state of things, the boat were to slide along an oiled groove in some solid substance, whose surface was so ridged that the oar could bear upon the ridges without any flexure, then indeed it would matter very little in what way the oar was pulled, so long as it was pulled through a good range in a short space of time. But the actual state of things being different, we have to inquire whether it is not possible that one style of rowing may serve more than another to make the slip of the oar through the water (a dead loss, be it remarked, so far as the propulsion of the boat is concerned) bear too large a proportion to the actual work done by the rower.

Let us make a simple illustration. Suppose a person standing on the edge of a sheet of water seeks to propel across the sheet a heavy log lying near the bank. If he gives the log a violent kick, it will scarcely move at all through the water, but after a few vibrations will be seen to lie a few inches from its former position. The force expended has not been thrown away, however, but has resulted in a violent shock to the kicker. But if instead of kicking the log the person apply the same amount of force gently at first and then with gradually increasing intensity, the log will receive a much more effective impetus, and its motion will continue long after the force has ceased to be exerted. The same amount of force which before produced a motion of a few inches will now project the log several yards.

And now to apply this illustration. If the object of the rower were to move his oar through the water—the boat being supposed for the moment to be a fixture—he could not do better than to adopt the Cambridge style of pulling. For this style gives a steady pressure on the oar at the beginning of the stroke, followed by a gradual increase, and ending by a sharp lift through the water. On the contrary, the Oxford style, in which arms and body apply all their strength at once to the oar, would probably, as in the case of our imaginary *fixed boats*, result in the fracture of the oar. If the boat were not fixed, but very heavy and clumsy, conclusions very different from the above would be arrived at. The Oxford style would be unsuitable to the propulsion of a heavy boat, because, although the oar would have very little slip through the water, yet the boat itself could not be moved in so sudden a manner as to make the applied force available. On the other hand, the Cambridge style would be very suitable; because, although there would be considerable 'slip,' this would in any case be inevitable, and the force would be applied to the boat (as well as to the oar) in the gradual increasing manner best suited to produce motion through the water. Hence we can understand the long series of victories gained by the light-blue oarsmen in the old fashioned racing eights. But when we come to consider the case of a boat like the present wager-boat—a boat which answers immediately to the slightest propelling force—we see that that mode of rowing must be the most effective which permits the oar to have the least possible motion *through* the water, which lifts the boat along from the water *as from an almost stable fulcrum.* Hence it is that that sharp grip of the water which is taken by London watermen, and by rowers at Oxford, Eton, Radley, and Westminster, is so much more effective than the heavy drag followed by a rapid and almost jerking finish which marks the Cambridge style.

The mention of public-school rowing leads me to urge another consideration. There are public-school oarsmen at Cambridge, and they hold, as might be supposed, a high position amongst university rowing-men. In general they form so small a minority of college racing-men, that they have to give up their own workmanlike style, and adopt the style of those they row with. But there is one club—the Third Trinity Club—which consists exclusively of Eton and Westminster men, and although it is a small club, it has been repeatedly at the head of the river, holding its own successfully against clubs which have sent in far heavier and better-trained crews. But even more remarkable is the fact that powerful college crews were sent from Cambridge to Henley between the years 1860-69 *which have actually been unable to maintain their own against Eton lads !* This of itself suffices to show that there was something radically wrong in the style then prevalent at Cambridge ; for in such races age, weight, strength, and length of practice were all in favour of the Cambridge crews.

When I first expressed these views about the Oxford and Cambridge style in the ' Daily News ' in April 1869, several Oxford and Cambridge men denied that the difference between the two styles was that which I have indicated, asserting that neither Oxford nor Cambridge oarsmen advocated working with the arms in the beginning of the stroke. It was so great a novelty to myself to learn, in 1858, that London watermen row in the manner I have described, and I found the very watermen who rowed in that way so confidently denying that they did so, that I was not greatly surprised to find many University men, and not a few of the first University oarsmen, persisting that the rules laid down in ' Principles of Rowing ' before the modern racing-boats were used are still valid and are still followed at Oxford as well as Cambridge. It was denounced as a special heresy to teach that work should be done by the arms at the beginning of the stroke, instead of the old rule being followed according to which the arms were to remain straight till the body was upright in the backward swing, the work being done entirely by the body and legs up to that moment, and then finished by the arms. But before I ventured to enunciate a theory on the subject I had been careful to apply a number of tests not only while watching Oxford and Cambridge eights, but in actual practice. I had inquired diligently also of those who are not merely able to adopt a good rowing style but to analyse it, so as to learn precisely where and

how they do their work.   In some cases, I found first-rate
oarsmen had given very little thought to the matter ; but on
the question being put to them, they quickly recognised the
essential principles on which the most effective and the
least tiring style for the modern racing-boat depends.   One
such oarsman said to me, after giving a few days' trial as
well as thought to the matter—' You are quite right ; arms,
legs, and body must work together from the very beginning ;
the work is done when the body comes upright ; and not
only must this be so for the work to be done in the most
effective way, but it is essential also if the hands are to be
quickly disengaged, the recovery quick, and a good reach
forward obtained.'

I found, however, that the essential distinction between
a good style in the modern racing eight, and a good style in
the old-fashioned boats, had been recognised (at least, so
far as the modern boats are concerned) a year before my
article in the 'Daily News' appeared.   In an article on
'Water Derbies,' 'Wat Bradwood,' describing the University
race of 1868, draws the following distinctions between the
two crews, which precisely accord with my own observations
on that occasion ; only it is to be noticed that, whereas he
is describing the beginning of the race, the whole of which
he witnessed from the Umpire's boat, my observations were
made from the shore not far from the finish, when Oxford
was so far ahead that there was ample time to note separately and closely the style of each boat :—' The styles of
progress of the two boats themselves are palpably distinct,'
he says ; ' Cambridge take a shorter time to come through
the air than to row through the water ; they go much
farther backward than Oxford, and are very slow in getting
the hands off the chest ; their boat is drawn through the
water at each stroke, but has hardly any perceptible " lift."
Oxford, on the other hand, swing just the reverse of Cambridge, a long time in getting forward' (he means of course,
a *relatively longer* time, for no good oarsman would ever
take a long time in getting forward), 'and very fast through

the water, driving the oars through with a hit like sledge-
hammers, while the boat jumps out of the water several
inches at each stroke.'   These last words again relate rather
to contrast between the boats than to the actual lift.   The
'drag at the end' in the Cambridge style used always to dip
the nose of the eight, whereas the quick disengagement of
the hands in the Oxford style prevents any dipping, so that
by contrast the Oxford boat seen beside the Cambridge
seemed lifted at the end of each stroke.   In reality there
was very little if any lifting, though the sharp grip of the
water at the beginning of the stroke caused the boat to dip
a little as compared with her position at the end.   Theoretically, the less change of level throughout the stroke (from
feather to finish) the better ; but if there is any such change,
it is far better it should be of the nature of a lift above the
flotation-level than of the nature of a dip below that level.

Again, towards the close of the same article 'Wat Bradwood' made the following pertinent remarks respecting the
Oxford style in 1868 and generally: 'The general style of
Oxford has not deteriorated ; though many outsiders fancied
that Oxford rowed a short stroke, it was more that the time
occupied by them in slashing the oar through the water was
short than the reach itself ; this deceived inexperienced eyes,
especially when compared to the slow 'draw through'
(query 'drag') of Cambridge, which often appeared for
similar reasons a longer stroke than it really was.[1]   He at-

---

[1] This agrees closely with my own description written later, but
independently, and flatly contradicted by more than one Oxford oarsman
at the time : 'In the case of Oxford,' I said, after describing the
lightning feather following the long sweeping stroke of Cambridge, 'we
observe a style which at first sight seems less excellent.   As soon as
the oars are dashed down and catch their first hold of the water, the
arms as well as the shoulders of each oarsman are at work.   The result
is that when the back has reached an upright position the hands have
already reached the chest, and the stroke is finished.   Thus the Oxford
stroke takes a perceptibly shorter time than the Cambridge stroke ; it
is also necessarily somewhat shorter in the water.   One would therefore
say it must be less effective.   Especially would an unpractised ob-

tributed the defeat of the Cantabs, who were a stronger set of men than the Oxonians, to the teaching of their 'coach,' who had been (though this he does not mention) as good a 'coach' as ever existed for rowing in the old fashioned style of boats, but whose 'experience availed nothing to teach the modern style of light-boat rowing.'

In another article by the same writer, in the 'Pall Mall Gazette,' (1868), a noteworthy illustration is given of the value of a good style. 'Among the college boats in the first division at Cambridge this year, the strongest were perhaps First Trinity, Trinity Hall, and notably Emmanuel ; the weakest in the division was the Lady Margaret crew,'— the crew representing St. John's College. 'But notwithstanding this, Lady Margaret went up one place, and pressed Trinity very hotly. There must, of course, be some special reason to account for eight weak men proving superior to eight strong ones.' There is a little (unintentional) exaggeration here ; the stroke of the Lady Margaret crew was a strong as well as an elegant oarsman, and two others of the crew could certainly not be called weak ; nevertheless the crew as a whole was undoubtedly weak compared with most of the other crews of the first division, 'That reason,' proceeds our author, 'is to be found in *style*. Every day of practice on the Cam you hear the "coaches" of the different racing-boats giving their crews certain directions, some absurd, and nearly all, from some accidental reason, useless. The chief of these is to "keep it long," and if you object to the results of this teaching, you are told that "length" is the great requisite of good rowing, and

server form this opinion, because the Oxford stroke seems to be much shorter in range than it is in reality. *There* we have the secret of its efficiency. It is actually as long as the Cambridge stroke, but is taken in a perceptibly shorter time. What does this mean but that the oar is taken more sharply, and therefore much more effectively, through the water? Much more effectively,' I proceeded, 'so far as the actual conditions of the contest are concerned,' going on to consider the difference between the modern and the old fashioned racing boats.—*Light Science for Leisure Hours :* Essay on Oxford and Cambridge Rowing Styles.

that " Oxford, sir, always beat us, because they are longer than we are."   Now, this is true and yet untrue.   At Cambridge "length" is acquired by making the men "finish the stroke," that is, by making them "swing well back" beyond the perpendicular.   Of course the oar remains longer in the water, but we maintain that the extra time it is kept there by the backward motion of the body is time lost. The "swinging back" throws a tremendous strain on the abdominal muscles, the weakest rowing muscles in the body ; very soon the men feel this strain, become exhausted, and unable to "get forward," and finally lose time and swing and "go all to pieces."   Length obtained by going backwards is of no possible use.   A crew ought to be "coached" to get as far *forward* as they can, to finish the stroke by bringing their elbows past their sides, and their hands well into their bodies, and then complaints about "wind" and "last" will be fewer.   This was abundantly proved in the late May races.   First Trinity, it is true, kept "head," but only because of their great strength, and because they had a stroke who understood the duties of his position.   Before the races every sporting newspaper, every supposed judge of rowing in the University, was certain about only one thing, and that was that Lady Margaret must go down ; the only question was where they would stop.   They, however, not only kept away from Trinity Hall, but finished above Emmanuel and Third Trinity, infinitely stronger ' (which no doubt must be understood as meaning ' far stronger ') ' boats. The reason was that they were the only boat on the river which rowed in anything like a good style.   They had the reach forward, the quick recovery, and the equally quick disengagement of the hands, which marked the Oxford crew of 1868. Consequently although a very weak lot of men, they were able to vindicate style against strength.   We hope' (added Wat Bradwood) 'that Cambridge generally will appreciate the lesson ; it is one that has not been taught them for years, and results on their own river ought to show its value.'   Less than a year after this was written, the Cambridge boat, with Goldie, the Lady Margaret stroke, at the aft thwart, were just beaten by Oxford in one of the best races ever rowed, and the year after, with the same stroke, they won for the first time in ten years. The subsequent successes of the Jesus boat on the Cam afforded further illustrations of the superiority of style over strength. For the Jesus boat has remained for years at the head of the river, though the crew as a whole has often been far surpassed in strength by the crews of Trinity, John's, and other colleges.

There is, as the writer from whom I have quoted above correctly says, ' no opposition between theory and practice in this matter, any more than there is in metaphysics or moral philosophy.' The ill-success of Cambridge in past years was in the main due to a want of appreciation of theory, and the absence of due recognition of the entire change which the introduction of the light outrigged racing-boat had produced in the art of effective rowing. The Cambridge 'finish to the stroke,' the 'lug at the end,' as sailors call it, was excellent with the old fashioned boats. It was indeed essential to success in a race, as was the lightning feather. But now the essential conditions are a sharp grasp of the water at the beginning of the stroke, the intensest possible action then and throughout the time the oar is in the water, so that the oar may be as short a time as possible in the water, but *in the time* may have the largest possible range. This result must not merely be obtained from each individual member of the crew, but from all together in precisely the same time. It is necessary that the stroke should mark the time in the most distinct and emphatic manner. In the Cambridge style, or what at least used so to be called, perfect time, though of course always desirable, was not so absolutely essential as in the Oxford style. The oars being a long time in the water, it mattered less if any oarsman was for a small fraction of a second behind or in advance of his fellows. But with the sharp dash upon the water and the quick tear through the

water of the better style, perfect simultaneity is all-important. The stroke must not only have first a good style himself, and secondly a keen sense of time, but he must have
that power of making his crew know and feel what he is
doing, and what he wants them to do, which constitutes the
essential distinction between the merely steady stroke and
such a stroke as every man of the crew feels to be made for
the place. When one of these 'born strokes' occupies the
aft thwart, there is no occasion for the coxswain to tell the
crew when to quicken or when to row steadily at their
hardest ; for the whole crew knows and feels the purpose
of the stroke as distinctly as he knows and feels it himself.

*The following paragraph, written a few days before the
race* (1879) *is left unaltered. I may note that Marriott, the
successful Oxford stroke of* 1878, *so far succeeded in improving
the style of the Oxford boat when he took the aft thwart in* '79
(*far too late by the way*), *that Cambridge did not win by anything like the expected distance.*

[Since the above was written I have seen both the crews
for the present year's race at work.   It is too early to venture
a prediction as to the result of the race, though the odds
offered on Cambridge would seem to imply that nothing
short of an accident can save Oxford from a crushing defeat.
It is manifest that Cambridge has the stronger crew, and the
style of the Oxford crew at present is not such as to indicate
that this year the Oxford style will defeat superior strength.
In fact, at present, Oxford shows defects which have been
wont to characterise Cambridge crews, and which unmistakably do characterise the present Cambridge crew,
fine though it undoubtedly is.   But if, as has before now
happened, the Oxford crew fall into the true Oxford style
during the fortnight before the race, the odds will not be
2 to 1 as at present, nor even 3 to 2, on Cambridge.]

PROFESSOR MARCY has recently discussed, in a lecture on Living Locomotors (*Moteurs Animés*), the principles of propulsion. Had he been an Englishman he would probably have found some of his most striking illustrations among different cases of propulsion through water. But, although he limited his discussion of animated motors to those which work on land, he yet laid down the fundamental principle of all propulsion, which is that as little as possible—and therefore, if possible, none at all—of the energy employed to produce propulsion should be expended in injurious work. Even with the best carriages, he pointed out, there remain vibrations and shocks which must be attacked and destroyed to render the conditions of traction more perfect ; they are veritable shocks, which use up part of the work of the horse in giving only hurtful effects, bruising the animal's breast, injuring his muscles, and, in spite of the padding of the collar, sometimes wounding him. Then he showed a simple experiment suggested by the able dynamician, Poncelet. To a weight of five kilos. (about 11lb.) a string is attached by which the weight can be lifted, but not much more. Then the experimenter tries to lift the weight rapidly with the string, which breaks without moving the weight, while the fingers are more or less hurt by the sudden shock. If now, a cord of equal strength, but slightly elastic, is substituted, the experiment ends differently. The sudden effort of elevation is transformed into a more prolonged action, and the weight is raised without bruising the fingers or breaking the cord. Yet a still more sudden movement would break the cord in this case, though a yet more extensible cord would resist even a yet more sudden jerk. According to the strength of the cord, its extensibility, and the weight to be lifted, must be the nature of the upward pull in order that the greatest possible velocity may be communicated without injury to the cord or to the lifter's hand. This simple series of experiments involves the essential principles of effective propulsion, where, at least, great velocity is among the results to be attained.

Although, perhaps, at present, the public are disposed to consider the University race from a sporting rather than from a scientific point of view, yet it has long been admitted, even by the most ardent lovers of rowing as a sport, that it has its scientific side. In a pamphlet on the 'Principles of Rowing,' by 'Oarsmen,' written somewhere about the year 1847,—it bears no date, but speaks of rowing as having first appeared as a public amusement 11 years ago, and the first University race on the Thames was rowed in 1836,—the writers urge that rowing surely deserves to be called a scientific pursuit, and proceed to trace out the 'main principles in virtue of which it claims a scientific character.' These principles, which were generally considered sound when they were originally enunciated, though even then they were beginning to be to some degree questionable, have been quoted over and over again since, or, if not verbally quoted, have been, in effect, adopted by writers on rowing. The justice of some of them has caused the entire set to be received without question, even by oarsmen who in practice depart from several of them in a very marked degree. The assumption has been that there is but one good rowing style, and that, therefore, a style adopted and proved by practice to be the best in the years 1836-1846 should be adopted as the best now. 'There is but one style,' says one authority, 'and one alone,' he adds with some redundancy. Now, in so far as river racing is almost always carried on in boats of the same kind for each class—eight oars, four oars, pairs, and sculls—it is in a sense true that there is but one racing style. But even in river rowing, as distinguished from river racing, there are more styles than one,—by which we mean more correct styles, for, of course, there are multitudinous bad styles in every kind of rowing. The style suitable for a racing boat moving at full speed would not be suitable even for the same boat at starting, and would be utterly unsuitable for a pleasure boat. We may remark, in passing, that, however suitable tubbing practice may be several weeks before a race, it is open to objection after a crew has settled into its racing stroke. No one who understands rowing will assert that even the two strongest members of either University crew *can* row in the same style in tub practice as in their eight at her full speed, or, seeing them, will fail to perceive that they row entirely different strokes in the tub and in the eight. Again, the style of rowing proved by practical experience to be best in seaside racing is entirely different from the style successful in river racing. Yet another style is essential to success in races rowed in the heavier boats used by men-of-war's men. And it will be admitted, we think, though no experiments have yet, to our knowledge, been made in this direction, that if matches were arranged among our best bargemen and lightermen we should see a mode of pulling which would differ as markedly from the man-of-war's man's strokes as that does from the stroke which O'Leary, of Folkestone, rows, and this in turn from the style of the best London or University oarsmen. So far as these last two styles are concerned, it should be remembered that they have been put to the test in the most decisive manner. The best London oarsmen have been repeatedly defeated in seaside rowing (even in still weather), and the best seaside oarsmen have been beaten in river rowing. It would be absurd to attribute this to awkwardness in unfamiliar boats, for any good oarsman can very soon row without awkwardness in any kind of boat. It was the style which made the difference—the style only. On *a priori* grounds, then, we should expect to find the question whether the style approved by 'Oarsmen' 30 years ago should be, as it is, the style constantly recommended now-a-days depending simply on the question whether the racing boat of our time is similar, so far as the requirements of propulsion are concerned, to the old-fashioned racing boats, however different in appearance the two kinds of boat may be. To assert this, however, would be almost equivalent to asserting that there has been no real improvement in the qualities of racing boats—nay, when one considers the great advantages possessed, in some respects, by the old fashioned boats and their much superior durability, we should have to acknowledge that racing boats had deteriorated. No one will for a moment assert this. We know that the racing boat of our time is not only much lighter, but travels with much less resistance through the water, maintains its velocity far better between the strokes, and can be made with equal effort to go at least one-fifth faster than the old fashioned racing boat. The antecedent probability is, then, that the modern racing boat requires a mode of propulsion unlike that which was approved in 1840 or thereabouts—requires, in fact, a style which in those days would have been justly regarded as radically bad.

There is direct evidence from the results of many years of racing to show that this difference really exists, as might be expected, though the evidence may probably be questioned by those who maintain that there is but one good rowing style. It is well known that the style approved by 'Oarsmen' in the work above mentioned was first definitely inculcated by Cambridge oarsmen. There is internal evidence in the pamphlet itself (as where the miseries of the Lent races at Cambridge are described) to show that some, and, therefore, probably all, who took part in preparing the work were Cambridge men. Again, it is well known that certainly until 1868, and perhaps later, the University crew at Cambridge was 'coached' by an 'ancient mariner,' who, if not one of the 'Oarsmen' and, as was generally reported, the actual

writer of the 'Principles of Rowing,' was unquestionably imbued with the old fashioned doctrines. Now, of the six
races rowed on the Thames in the old fashioned racing boats,
Cambridge won no less than five. The Oxford crews, who
rowed in a style more nearly resembling that now rowed by
the most successful crews (though scarcely ever inculcated in
verbal instructions), were not only beaten in every race save
one, but in three cases were beaten out of all reason. Half
a minute was the amount by which Cambridge won in 1845;
but in 1836 (certainly over a longer course) they won by one
minute, in 1841 by one minute and a quarter, and in 1839
by nearly two minutes. No wonder that when outrigged
boats came in Cambridge oarsmen were loth to modify a
style which had gained them so many and such striking successes. Nor did it greatly matter, when this happened in
1846, whether the style of rowing was modified or not. The
first specimens of outrigged racing boats occupied a sort of
half-way position between the old-fashioned inrigged craft
and the exceedingly light, keelless boats now used. Thus,
during the seven races rowed in the earlier form of outrigged
boats, success was pretty equally divided between Oxford
and Cambridge. In one race Oxford won on a foul; of the
other six Cambridge won three, and Oxford also won three.
But since the present form of racing boat was adopted (in
1857) Oxford has been almost as successful as Cambridge
had been in the first nine or ten races. In 1857 Oxford won
easily; in 1858 Cambridge won, but the stroke of the
Oxford boat could use but half his strength, the forward or
working thole of his rowlocks having been bent outwards by
a wave which caught his oar before the race began. (The
outriggers and rowlocks were shown to me at Searle's boat-
house a few days after the race, and there could be no question that the chances of the Oxford boat must have been
seriously impaired by the accident.) In 1859 Cambridge sank, and, though she was four lengths behind when
this happened, there can be little doubt she would have won
but for the original cause of the disaster—a wave which had

half filled the Cambridge boat as she was turning to take her place at the starting-point. In 1860 Cambridge won by one length only. Then, as everyone remembers, there followed nine successive Oxford victories, some of which were of the most hollow kind. Cambridge then gave up the style to which she had so long been faithful. One of the ablest of the Oxford oarsmen, who was, however, connected in some degree with Cambridge, trained and coached the Cambridge crew of 1870, the stroke of which, it should be mentioned, was proficient in the correct style before he went to Cambridge. That year and for the four next years Cambridge won, though never in the hollow fashion in which Oxford had won the victories of 1861, 1862, 1863, 1864, and 1868. The lead of Oxford at the finish of these five races averaged over nine lengths, while the lead of Cambridge in the five races of 1870–74 averaged little over two lengths. In 1875 Oxford won by ten lengths, Cambridge in 1876 by five. In 1877 occurred the celebrated dead heat ; but before bow's oar broke Oxford had won 'bar accidents.' In 1878 Oxford won, and again by ten lengths. Of the 25 races actually rowed to a finish (excluding the dead heat) since outriggers were introduced, Oxford has won 14, Cambridge 11 ; of the 19 so rowed out since the true modern racing boat was used, Oxford has won 11 and Cambridge 8. The difference is sufficient in either case to show (the numbers being considerable) that there is a true difference of style, the style of Oxford being the better. But when we consider how the victories have been won this comes out still more clearly. Making due estimate of the number of lengths corresponding to so many seconds of time difference (where the result of a race is so indicated in the list), for which purpose it is sufficient to note that as many seconds as the race itself has occupied minutes are equivalent to about $6\frac{1}{2}$ lengths, we find for the 11 victories of Cambridge since 1846 about $30\frac{1}{4}$ lengths, and for the 14 rowed-out victories of Oxford about $106\frac{1}{2}$ lengths—the Cambridge average lead being thus found to be less than three lengths, while the

Oxford average lead at the finish has been close on eight lengths.

The difference cannot reasonably be assigned to any cause which was in operation when Cambridge had the larger share of victories. Nearly every cause which has been commonly assigned, including the unquestionably inferior arrangements for college racing at Cambridge, falls into this category. There can be very little doubt that the true explanation, as well of Cambridge success before 1850 as of Oxford success since then, resides in the circumstance that the two Universities have in the main adopted throughout the whole series of contests two different styles—each style excellent in itself, but the Cambridge as unquestionably superior to the Oxford for the heavier kinds of river boats as the Oxford style is superior to the Cambridge for the boats now actually used in river races. What the difference in the two styles is I shall now briefly indicate.

I am satisfied that the essential excellence of the old fashioned racing style as used in the old fashioned boats becomes an inherent defect in the same style as used in modern racing boats. I refer to the principle involved in the words italicised (by myself) in the following quotation from ' Principles of Rowing ' :—' The instant the oar touches the water the arms and body begin to fall backwards, the *former continuing at their full stretch till the back is perpendicular.* They are then bent, the elbows being brought close past the sides, till the hands, which are now brought home sharply, strike the body above the lowest ribs.' Such was the stroke that brave old Coombes used to teach, and such was the stroke by which, time and again, races were won before 1850. But in proportion as the racing boat has been improved, both by diminution of weight and resistance and by change of leverage, the necessity has increased for a more energetic application of the oarsman's power. A stroke which resulted in mere jerking, injurious to the rower and not adding to speed, in the old racing boats, is absolutely essential to the effective propulsion of the modern racing boat, when once at least full speed has been attained, for before this the old fashioned long drag with lightning feather is as useful now as ever. Now, no one who has watched a really good Oxford crew at full speed can fail to observe the way in which the oars literally smite the water at the beginning of each stroke. No one who considers the velocity with which they must move to give this sledge-hammer stroke at the beginning can fail to perceive that the body alone cannot give this velocity of impulse in the first part of the stroke. There is only one way in which it can be attained, and that is by making the arms work from the beginning, not merely in the sense in which they may be said to work when continuing at their full stretch, but by actual and energetic contraction. In the Cambridge style arms and body only work together after the back is perpendicular ; in the Oxford style they work together from the beginning. The result is that by the time the Oxford oars man has brought his back perpendicular his stroke is finished ; whereas the Cambridge oarsman has still to give that drag at the end which used to be so much esteemed, and still is justly esteemed, by sailors for sea-racing. The oar of the Oxford rower is a much shorter time in the water, simply because it is propelled through the water with far greater, or rather with much more concentrated energy. The Oxford stroke, again, is necessarily a few inches shorter. For as Cambridge men go as far forward and swing further backward, it stands to reason that they get a little more length. But they get this additional length at the cost of a great strain on the abdominal muscles, and with no proportional effect. A very strong crew which can maintain the long, dragging stroke with the lightning feather from beginning to end may win, as Cambridge men have won, but only because of their superior strength, not by virtue of that lift at the end, which wearies the most stalwart, causes sluggish disengagement of the hands, and in a long race has often caused a powerful crew to be beaten by weaker men rowing in a more scientific manner. It is not impossible, now that the Oxford crew have had set them the true Oxford stroke that we may have an opportunity of witnessing something of this kind on Saturday, though the manifest superiority of the Cambridge crew in strength and the lateness of the change in the Oxford boat are unfavourable to the chances of the dark blue. To return to the point from which we started. The just style of propulsion for each class of boat is a matter to be determined on scientific principles. There is no real conflict between theory and practice in this matter. Every change which has tended to increase the speed of racing boats has (like the changes in Poncelet's experiment) rendered necessary an increased energy, or, as one may say, an increased intensity of propulsion.

ARTIFICIAL SOMNAMBULISM.

RATHER more than a quarter of a century ago two Ameri-
cans visited London, who called themselves professors of
Electro-Biology, and claimed the power of 'subjugating
the most determined wills, paralysing the strongest muscles,
preventing the evidence of the senses, destroying the
memory of the most familiar events or of the most recent
occurrences, inducing obedience to any command, and
making an individual believe himself transformed into any
one else.'   All this and more was to be effected, they said,
by the action of a small disc of zinc and copper held in the
hand of the 'subject,' and steadily gazed at by him, 'so as
to concentrate the electro-magnetic action.'   The preten-
sions of these professors received before long a shock as
decisive as that which overthrew the credit of the professors
of animal magnetism when Haygarth and Falconer successfully substituted wooden tractors for the metallic tractors
which had been supposed to convey the magnetic fluid.   In
1851, Mr. Braid, a Scotch surgeon, who had witnessed some
of the exhibitions of the electro-biologists, conceived the
idea that the phenomena were not due to any special qualities possessed by the discs of zinc and copper, but simply to
the fixed look of the 'subject' and the entire abstraction of
his attention.   The same explanation applied to the so-
called 'magnetic passes' of the mesmerists.   The monoto-
nous manipulation of the operator produced the same effect
as the fixed stare of the 'subject.'   He showed by his ex-

periments that no magnetiser, with his imaginary secret agents or fluids, is in the least wanted ; but that the subjects can place themselves in the same condition as the supposed subjects of electro-biological influences by simply gazing fixedly at some object for a long time with fixed attention.

The condition thus superinduced is not hypnotism, or artificial somnambulism, properly so called. 'The electro-biological' condition may be regarded as simply a kind of reverie or abstraction artificially produced. But Braid discovered that a more perfect control might be obtained over 'subjects,' and a condition resembling that of the sleep-walker artificially induced, by modifying the method of fixing the attention. Instead of directing the subject's gaze upon a bright object placed at a considerable distance from the eyes, so that no effect was required to concentrate vision upon it, he placed a bright object somewhat above and in front of the eyes at so short a distance that the convergence of their axes upon it was accompanied with sufficient effect to produce even a slight amount of pain. The condition to which the 'subjects' of this new method were reduced was markedly different from the ordinary 'electro-biological' state. Thus on one occasion, in the presence of 800 persons, fourteen men were experimented upon. 'All began the experiment at the same time ; the former with their eyes fixed upon a projecting cork, placed securely on their foreheads ; the others at their own will gazed steadily at certain points in the direction of the audience. In the course of ten minutes the eyelids of these ten persons had involuntarily closed. With some, consciousness remained ; others were in catalepsy, and entirely insensible to being stuck with needles ; and others on awakening knew absolutely nothing of what had taken place during their sleep.' The other four simply passed into the ordinary condition of electro-biologised 'subjects,' retaining the recollection of all that happened to them while in the state of artificial abstraction or reverie.

Dr. Carpenter, in that most interesting work of his, 'Mental Physiology,' thus describes the state of hypnotism :

—' The process is of the same kind as that employed for the induction of the "biological" state ; the only difference lying in the *greater intensity* of the gaze, and in the more complete concentration of will upon the direction of the eyes, which the nearer approximation of the object .requires for the maintenance of the convergence.   In hypnotism, as in ordinary somnambulism, no remembrance whatever is preserved in the waking state of anything that may have occurred during its continuance ; although the previous train of thought may be taken up and continued uninterruptedly on the next occasion that the hypnotism is induced. And when the mind is not excited to activity by the stimulus of external impressions, the hypnotised subject appears to be profoundly asleep ; a state of complete torpor, in fact, being usually the first result of the process, and any subsequent manifestation of activity being procurable only by the prompting of the operator.   The hypnotised subject, too, rarely opens his eyes ; his bodily movements are usually slow ; his mental operations require a considerable time in their performance ; and there is altogether an appearance of heaviness about him, which contrasts strongly with the comparatively wide-awake air of him who has not passed beyond the ordinary "biological" state.'

We must note, however, in passing, that the condition of complete hypnotism had been obtained in several instances by some of the earlier experimenters in animal magnetism. One remarkable instance was communicated to the surgical section of the French Academy on April 16, 1829, by Jules Cloquet.   Two meetings were entirely devoted to its investigation.   The following account presents all the chief points of the case, surgical details being entirely omitted, however, as not necessary for our present purpose :—A lady, aged sixty-four, consulted M. Cloquet on April 8, 1829, on account of an ulcerated cancer of the right breast which had continued, gradually growing worse, during several years. M. Chapelain, the physician attending the lady, had ' magnetised ' her for some months, producing no remedial effects, but only a very profound sleep or torpor, during which all sensibility seemed to be annihilated, while the ideas retained all their clearness. He proposed to M. Cloquet to operate upon her while she was in this state of torpor, and, the latter, considering the operation the only means of saving her life, consented. The two doctors do not appear to have been troubled by any scruples as to their right thus to conduct an operation to which, when in her normal condition, the patient strenuously objected. It sufficed for them that when they had put her to sleep artificially, she could be persuaded to submit to it. On the appointed day M. Cloquet found the patient ready 'dressed and seated in an elbow-chair, in the attitude of a person enjoying a quiet natural sleep.' In reality, however, she was in the somnambulistic state, and talked calmly of the operation. During the whole time that the operation lasted—from ten to twelve minutes—she continued to converse quietly with M. Cloquet, 'and did not exhibit the slightest sign of sensibility. There was no motion of the limbs or of the features, no change in the respiration nor in the voice; no motions even in the pulse. The patient continued in the same state of automatic indifference and impassibility in which she had been some minutes before the operation.' For forty-eight hours after this, the patient remained in the somnambulistic state, showing no sign of pain during the subsequent dressing of the wound. When awakened from this prolonged sleep she had no recollection of what had passed in the interval ; 'but on being informed of the operation, and seeing her children around her, she experienced a very lively emotion which the " magnetiser " checked by immediately setting her asleep.' Certainly none of the hypnotised 'subjects' of Mr. Braid's experiments showed more complete abstraction from their normal condition than this lady ; and other cases cited in Bertrand's work, 'Le Magnétisme Animal en France' (1826), are almost equally remarkable. As it does not appear that in any of these cases Braid's method of producing hypnotism by causing the eyes, or rather their optical axes, to be converged upon a point, was adopted, we must conclude that this part of the method is not absolutely essential to success. Indeed, the circumstance that in some of Braid's public experiments numbers of the audience became hypnotised without his knowledge, shows that the more susceptible 'subjects' do not require to contemplate a point near and slightly above the eyes, but may be put into the true hypnotic state by methods which, with the less susceptible, produce only the electro-biological condition.

It will be well, however, to inquire somewhat carefully into this point. My present object, I would note, is not merely to indicate the remarkable nature of the phenomena of hypnotism, but to consider these phenomena with direct reference to their probable cause. It may not be possible to obtain a satisfactory explanation of them. But it is better to view them as phenomena to be accounted for than merely as surprising but utterly inexplicable circumstances.

Now we have fortunately the means of determining the effect of the physical relations involved in these experiments, apart from those which are chiefly due to imagination. For animals can be hypnotised, and the conditions necessary for this effect to be fully produced have been ascertained.

The most familiar experiment of this sort is sometimes known as Kircher's. Let the feet of a hen be tied together (though this is not necessary in all cases), and the hen placed on a level surface. Then if the body of the hen is gently pressed down, the head extended with the beak pointing downwards, touching the surface on which the hen stands, and a chalk mark is drawn slowly along the surface, from the tip of the beak in a line extending directly from the bird's eye, it is found that the hen will remain for a considerable time perfectly still, though left quite free to move. She is, in fact, hypnotised.

We have now to inquire what parts of the process just

described are effective in producing the hypnotic condition, or whether all are essential to success in the experiment.

In the first place, the fastening of the feet may be dispensed with. But it has its influence, and makes the experiment easier. An explanation, or rather an illustration, of its effect is afforded by a singular and interesting experiment devised by Lewissohn of Berlin :—If a frog is placed on its back, it immediately, when the hand which had held it is removed, turns over and escapes. But if the two forelegs are tied with a string, the frog, when placed on its back, breathes heavily but is otherwise quite motionless, and does not make the least attempt to escape, even when the experimenter tries to move it. ' It is as though,' say Czermak, describing the experiment as performed by himself, 'its small amount of reasoning power had been charmed away, or else that it slept with open eyes. Now I press upon the cutaneous nerves of the frog, while I loosen and remove the threads on the fore-legs. Still the animal remains motionless upon its back, in consequence of some remaining after-effect ; at last, however, it returns to itself, turns over, and quickly escapes.'

Thus far the idea suggested is that the animal is so affected by the cutaneous pressure as to suppose itself tied and therefore unable to move. In other words, this experiment suggests that imagination acts on animals as on men, only in a different degree. I may cite here a curious case which I once noticed and have never been able to understand, though it seems to suggest the influence of imagination on an animal one would hardly suspect of being at all under the influence of any but purely physical influences. Hearing a noise as of a cat leaping down from a pantry window which looked out on an enclosed yard, I went directly into the yard, and there saw a strange cat running off with a fish she had stolen. She was at the moment leaping on to a bin, from the top of which, by another very easy leap, she could get on to the wall enclosing the yard, and so escape. With the idea rather of frightening her than of hurting her (does one missile out of a hundred flung at cats ever hit them?) I threw at the thief a small piece of wood which I had in my hand at the moment. It struck the wall above her just as she was going to leap to the top of the wall, and it fell, without touching her, between her and the wall. To my surprise, she stood perfectly still looking at the piece of wood; her mouth, from which the fish had fallen, remaining open, and her whole attitude expressing stupid wonder. I make no doubt I could have taken her prisoner, or struck her heavily, if I had wished, for she made no effort to escape, until, with a parlour broom which stood by, I pushed her along the top of the bin towards the wall, when she seemed suddenly to arouse herself, and leaping to the top of the wall she made off. My wife witnessed the last scene of this curious little comedy. In fact, it was chiefly, perhaps, because she pleaded for mercy on 'the poor thing' that the soft end of the broom alone came into operation; for, though not altogether agreeing with the Count of Rousillon that anything can be endured before a cat, I did not at the moment regard that particular cat with special favour.

The extension of the neck and depression of the head, in the experiment with the hen, have no special significance, for Czermak has been able to produce the same phenomena of hypnotism without them, and has failed to produce the hypnotic effect on pigeons when attending to this point, and in other respects proceeding as nearly as possible in the same way as with hens. 'With the hens,' he says, 'I often hung a piece of twine, or a small piece of wood, directly over their crests, so that the end fell before their eyes. The hens not only remained perfectly motionless, but closed their eyes, and slept with their heads sinking until they came in contact with the table. Before falling asleep, the hens' heads can be either pressed down or raised up, and they will remain in this position as if they were pieces of wax. That is, however, a symptom of a cataleptic condition, such as is seen in human beings, under certain pathological conditions of the nervous system.'

On the other hand, repeated experiments convinced Czermak that the pressure on the animal as it is held is of primary importance. It is frequently the case, he says, that a hen, which for a minute has been in a motionless state, caused by simply extending the neck and depressing the head, awakes and flies away, but on being caught again immediately, she can be placed once more in the condition of lethargy, if we place the animal in a squatting position, and overcome with gentle force the resistance of the muscles, by firmly placing the hand upon its back. During the slow and measured suppression, one often perceives an extremely remarkable position of the head and neck, which are left entirely free. The head remains as if held by an invisible hand in its proper place, the neck being stretched out of proportion, while the body by degrees is pushed downwards. If the animal is thus left entirely free, it remains for a minute or so in this peculiar condition with wide-open staring eyes. 'Here,' as Czermak remarks, 'the actual circumstances are only the effect of the emotion which the nerves of the skin excite, and the gentle force which overcomes the animal's resistance. Certainly the creature a short time before had been in a condition of immobility, and might have retained some special inclination to fall back into the same, although the awakening, flight, and recapture, together with the refreshment given to the nervous system, are intermediate circumstances.' Similar experiments are best made upon small birds. Now, it is well known to bird fanciers that goldfinches, canary-birds, &c. can be made to remain motionless for some time by simply holding them firmly for a moment and then letting them go. 'Here, in my hand,' said Czermak, in his lecture, 'is a timid bird, just brought from market. If I place it on its back, and hold its head with my left hand, keeping it still for a few seconds, it will lie perfectly motionless after I have removed my hands, as if charmed, breathing heavily, and without making any attempt to change its position or to fly away.' ('Two of the birds,' says the report, 'were treated in this manner without effect; but the third, a siskin, fell into a sleeping condition, and remained completely immovable on its back, until pushed with a glass tube, when it awoke and flew actively around the room.')

Also when a bird is in a sitting position, and the head is pressed slightly back, the bird falls into a sleeping condition, even though the eyes had been open. 'I have often noticed,' says Czermak, 'that the birds under these circumstances close their eyes for a few minutes or even a quarter of an hour, and are more or less fast asleep.'

Lastly, as to the chalk-line in Kircher's experiment. Czermak found, as already said, that pigeons do not become motionless, as happens to hens, if merely held firmly in the hand, and their heads and necks pressed gently on the table. Nor can they be hypnotised like small birds in the experiment last mentioned. 'That is,' he says, 'I held them with a thumb placed on each side of the head, which I bent over a little, while the other hand held the body gently pressed down upon the table; but even this treatment, which has such an effect on little birds, did not seem to succeed at first with the pigeons : almost always they flew away as soon as I liberated them and entirely removed my hands.' But he presently noticed that the short time during which the pigeons remained quiet lengthened considerably when the finger only of the hand which held the head was removed. Removing the hand holding the body made no difference, but retaining the other hand near the bird's head, the hand made all the difference in the world. Pursuing the line of research thus indicated, Czermak found to his astonishment that the fixing of the pigeon's look on the finger placed before its eyes was the secret of the matter. In order to determine the question still more clearly, he tried the experiment on a pigeon which he had clasped firmly by the body in his left hand, but whose neck and head were perfectly free. 'I held one finger of my right hand steadily before the top of its beak,—and what did I see? The first pigeon with which I made this attempt remained rigid and motionless, as if bound, for several minutes, before the outstretched forefinger of my right hand ! Yes, I could take my left hand, with which I had held the bird, and again touch the pigeon without waking it up ; the animal remained in the same position while I held my outstretched finger still pointing towards the beak.' 'The lecturer,' says the report, 'demonstrated this experiment in the most successful manner with a pigeon which was brought to him.'

Yet it is to be noticed that among animals as among men, different degrees of subjectivity exist. 'Individual inward relations,' says Czermak, 'as well as outward conditions, must necessarily exercise some disturbing influence, whether the animal will give itself up to the requisite exertions of certain parts of its brain with more or less inclination or otherwise. We often see, for example, that a pigeon endeavours to escape from confinement by a quick turning of its head from side to side. In following these singular and characteristic movements of the head and neck, with the finger held before the bird, one either gains his point, or else makes the pigeon so perplexed and excited that it at last becomes quiet, so that, if it is held firmly by the body and head, it can be forced gently down upon the table. As Schopenhauer says of sleeping, "The brain must bite." I will also mention here, by the way, that a tame parrot, which I have in my house, can be placed in this sleepy condition by simply holding the finger steadily before the top of its beak.'

I may cite here a singular illustration of the effect of perplexity in the case of a creature in all other respects much more naturally circumstanced than the. hens, pigeons, and small birds of Czermak's experiments. In the spring of 1859, when I was an undergraduate at Cambridge, I and a friend of mine were in canoes on the part of the Cam which flows through the College grounds. Here there are many ducks and a few swans. It occurred to us, not, I fear, from any special scientific spirit, but as a matter of curiosity, to inquire whether it was possible to pass over a duck in a canoe. Of course on the approach of either canoe a duck would try to get out of the way on one side or the other ; but on the course of the canoe being rapidly changed, the duck would have to change his course. Then the canoe's course would again be changed, so as to compel the duck to try the other side. The canoe drawing all the time nearer, and her changes of course being made very lightly and in quicker and quicker alternation as she approached, the duck would generally get bewildered, and finally would allow the canoe to pass over him, gently pressing him under water in its course. The process, in fact, was a sort of mild keel-hauling. The absolute rigidity of body and the dull stupid stare with which some of the ducks met their fate seems to me (*now* : I was not in 1859 familiar with the phenomena of hypnotism) to suggest that the effect was to be explained as Czermak explains the hypnotism of the pigeons on which he experimented.

We shall be better able now to understand the phenomena of artificial somnambulism in the case of human beings. If the circumstances observed by Kircher, Czermak, Lewissohn, and others, suggest, as I think they do, that animal hypnotism is a form of the phenomenon sometimes called fascination, we may be led to regard the possibility of artificial somnam-bulism in men as a survival of a property playing in all pro-bability an important and valuable part in the economy of animal life. It is in this direction, at present, that the evidence seems to tend.

The most remarkable circumstance about the completely hypnotised subject is the seemingly complete control of the will of the 'subject' and even of his opinions. Even the mere suggestions of the operator, not expressed verbally or by signs, but by movements imparted to the body of the subject, are at once responded to, as though, to use Dr. Garth Wilkinson's expression, the *whole man* were given to each perception. Thus, 'if the hand be placed,' says Dr. Carpenter, 'upon the top of the head, the somnambulist will frequently, of his own accord, draw up his body to its fullest height, and throw his head slightly back; his countenance then assumes an expression of the most lofty pride, and his whole mind is obviously possessed by that feeling. When the first action does not of itself call forth the rest, it is sufficient for the operator to straighten the legs and spine, and to throw the head somewhat back, to arouse that feeling and the corresponding expression to its fullest intensity. During the most complete domination of this emotion, let the head be bent forward, and the body and limbs gently flexed ; and the most profound humility then instantaneously takes its place.' Of course in some cases we may well believe that the expressions thus described by Dr. Carpenter have been simulated by the subject. But there can be no reason to doubt the reality of the operator's control in many cases. Dr. Carpenter says that he has not only been an eye-witness of them on various occasions, but that he places full reliance on the testimony of an intelligent friend, who submitted himself to Mr. Braid's manipulations, but retained sufficient self-consciousness and voluntary power to endeavour to exercise some resistance to their influence at the time, and subsequently to retrace his course of thought and feeling. 'This gentleman declares,' says Dr. Carpenter, 'that, although accustomed to the study of character and to self-observation, he could not have conceived that the whole mental state should have undergone so instantaneous and complete a metamorphosis, as he remembers it to have done, when his head and body were bent forward in the attitude of humility, after having been drawn to their full height in that of self-esteem.'

A most graphic description of the phenomena of hypnotism is given by Dr. Garth Wilkinson :—'The preliminary state is that of abstraction, produced by fixed gaze upon some unexciting and empty thing (for poverty of object engenders abstraction), and this abstraction is the logical premiss of what follows. Abstraction tends to become more and more abstract, narrower and narrower ; it tends to unity and afterwards to nullity. There, then, the patient is, at the summit of attention, with no object left, a mere statue of attention, a listening, expectant life ; a perfectly undistracted faculty, dreaming of a lessening and lessening mathematical point : the end of his mind sharpened away to nothing. What happens? Any sensation that appeals is met by this brilliant attention, and receives its diamond glare ; being perceived with a force of leisure of which our distracted life affords only the rudiments. External influences are sensated, sympathised with, to an extraordinary degree ; harmonious music sways the body into graces the most affecting ; discords jars it, as though they would tear it limb from limb. Cold and heat are perceived with similar exaltation ; so also smells and touches. In short, *the whole man appears to be given to each perception.* The body trembles like down with the wafts of the atmosphere ; the world plays upon it as upon a spiritual instrument finely attuned.'

This state, which may be called the natural hypnotic state, may be artificially modified. 'The power of suggestion over the patient,' says Dr. Garth Wilkinson, 'is excessive. If you say, "What animal is it ?" the patient will tell you it is a lamb, or a rabbit, or any other. "Does he see it?" "Yes." "What animal is it *now* ?" putting depth and gloom into the tone of *now*, and thereby suggesting a difference. "Oh !" with a shudder, "it is a wolf !" " What colour is it ?" still glooming the phrase. "Black." "What colour is it now?" giving the *now* a cheerful air. "Oh ! a beautiful blue !" (rather an unusual colour for a wolf, I would suggest), spoken with the utmost delight (and no wonder ! especially if the hypnotic subject were a naturalist). And so you lead the subject through any dreams you please, by variations of questions and of inflections of the voice ! and *he sees and feels all as real.*'

We have seen how the patient's mind can be influenced by changing the posture of his body. Dr. Wilkinson gives very remarkable evidence on this point. 'Double his fist and pull up his arm, if you dare,' he says, of the subject, ' for you will have the strength of your ribs rudely tested.

Put him on his knees and clasp his hands, and the saints and devotees of the artists will pale before the trueness of his devout actings. Raise his head while in prayer, and his lips pour forth exulting glorifications, as he sees heaven opened, and the majesty of God raising him to his place ; then in a moment depress the head, and he is in dust and ashes, an unworthy sinner, with the pit of hell yawning at his feet. Or compress the forehead, so as to wrinkle it vertically, and thorny-toothed clouds contract in from the very horizon ' (in the subject's imagination, it will be understood) ; 'and what is remarkable, the smallest pinch and wrinkle, such as will lie between your nipping nails, is sufficient nucleus to crystallise the man into that shape, and to make him all foreboding, as, again, the smallest expansion in a moment brings the opposite state, with a full breathing of delight.'

Some will perhaps think the next instance the most remarkable of all, perfectly natural though one half of the performance may have been. The subject being a young lady, the operator asks whether she or another is the prettier, raising her head as he puts the question. 'Observe,' says Dr. Wilkinson, 'the inexpressible hauteur, and the puff sneers let off from the lips' (see Darwin's treatise on the 'Expression of the Emotions,' plate IV. 1, and plate V. 1) 'which indicate a conclusion too certain to need utterance. Depress the head, and repeat the question, and mark the self-abasement with which she now says "*She is,*" as hardly worthy to make the comparison.'

In this state, in fact, 'whatever posture of any passion is induced, the passion comes into it at once, and dramatises the body accordingly.'

It might seem that there must of necessity be some degree of exaggeration in this description, simply because the power of adequately expressing any given emotion is not possessed by all. Some can in a moment bring any expression into the face, or even simulate at once the expression and the aspect of another person, while many persons, probably most, possess scarcely any power of the sort, and fail ridiculously even in attempting to reproduce the expressions corresponding to the commonest emotions. But it is abundantly clear that the hypnotised subject possesses for the time being abnormal powers. No doubt this is due to the circumstance that for the time being 'the whole man is given to each perception.' The stories illustrative of this peculiarity of the hypnotised state are so remarkable that they have been rejected as utterly incredible by many who are not acquainted with the amount of evidence we have upon this point.

The instances above cited by Dr. Garth Wilkinson, remarkable though they may be, are surpassed altogether in interest by a case which Dr. Carpenter mentions,—of a factory girl, whose musical powers had received little cultivation, and who could scarcely speak her own language correctly, who nevertheless exactly imitated both the words and the music of vocal performances by Jenny Lind. Dr. Carpenter was assured by witnesses in whom he could place implicit reliance, that this girl, in the hypnotised state, followed the Swedish nightingale's songs in different languages 'so instantaneously and correctly, as to both words and music, that it was difficult to distinguish the two voices. In order to test the powers of the somnambulist to the utmost, Mademoiselle Lind extemporised a long and elaborate chromatic exercise, which the girl imitated with no less precision, though in her waking state she durst not even attempt anything of the sort.'

The exaltation of the senses of hypnotised subjects is an equally wonderful phenomenon. Dr. Carpenter relates many very remarkable instances as occurring within his own experience. He has 'known a youth, in the hypnotised state,' he says, 'to find out, by the sense of smell, the owner of a glove which was placed in his hand, from amongst a party of more than sixty persons, scenting at each of them one after the other until he came to the right individual. In another case, the owner of a ring was unhesitatingly found out from amongst a company of twelve, the ring having been

withdrawn from the finger before the somnambule was introduced.' The sense of touch has, in other cases, been singularly intensified, insomuch that slight differences of heat,
which to ordinary feeling were quite inappreciable, would
be at once detected, while such differences as can be but
just perceived in the ordinary state would produce intense
distress.

In some respects, the increase of muscular power, or
rather of the power of special muscles, is even more striking,
because it is commonly supposed by most persons that the
muscular power depends entirely on the size and quality
of the muscles, the state of health, and like conditions,
not on the imagination. Of course every one knows that
the muscles are capable of greater efforts when the mind
is much excited by fear and other emotions. But the
general idea is, I think, that whatever the body is capable
of doing under circumstances of great excitement, it is in
reality capable of doing at all times if only a resolute effort
is made. Nor is it commonly supposed that a very wide
difference exists between the greatest efforts of the body
under excitement and those of which it is ordinarily capable.
Now, the condition of the hypnotised subject is certainly
not one of excitement. The attempts which he is directed
to make are influenced only by the idea that he *can* do what
he is told, not that he *must* do so. When a man pursued
by a bull leaps over a wall which under ordinary conditions
he would not even think of climbing, we can understand
that he only does, because he must, what if he liked he
could do at any time. But if a man who had been making
his best efforts in jumping, cleared only a height of four feet,
and presently being told to jump over an eight-feet wall,
cleared that height with apparent ease, we should be disposed
to regard the feat as savouring of the miraculous.

Now Dr. Carpenter saw one of Mr. Braid's hypnotised
subjects—a man so remarkable for the poverty of his physical development that he had not for many years ventured
to lift up a weight of twenty pounds in his ordinary state—

take up a quarter of a hundredweight upon his little finger, and swing it round his head with the utmost apparent ease, on being told that it was as light as a feather. 'On another occasion he lifted a half-hundredweight on the last joint of his fore-finger as high as his knee.' The personal character of the man placed him above all suspicion of deceit, in the opinion of those who best knew him ; and as Dr. Carpenter acutely remarks, ' the impossibility of any trickery in such a case would be evident to the educated eye, since, if he had practised such feats (which very few, even of the strongest men could accomplish without practice), the effect would have made itself visible in his muscular development.' 'Consequently,' he adds, ' when the same individual afterwards declared himself unable, with the greatest effort, to lift a handkerchief from the table, after having been assured that he could not possibly move it, there was no reason for questioning the truth of his conviction, based as this was upon the same kind of suggestion as that by which he had been just before prompted to what seemed an otherwise impossible action.'

The explanation of this and the preceding cases cannot be mistaken by physiologists, and is very important in its bearing on the phenomena of hypnotism generally, at once involving an interpretation of the whole series of phenomena, and suggesting other relations not as yet illustrated experimentally. It is well known that in our ordinary use of any muscles we employ but a small part of the muscle at any given moment. What the muscle is actually capable of is shown in convulsive contractions, in which far more force is put forth than the strongest effort of the will could call into play. We explain, then, the seeming increase of strength in any set of muscles during the hypnotic state as due to the concentration of the subject's will in an abnormal manner, or to an abnormal degree, on that set of muscles. In a similar way, the great increase of certain powers of perception may be explained as due to the concentration of the will upon the corresponding parts of the nervous system.

In like manner, the will may be directed so entirely to the operations necessary for the performances of difficult feats, that the hypnotised or somnambulistic subject may be able to accomplish what in his ordinary condition would be impossible or even utterly appalling to him. Thus sleep-walkers (whose condition precisely resembles that of the artificially hypnotised, except that the suggestions they experience come from contact with inanimate objects, instead of being aroused by the actions of another person) ' can clamber walls and roofs, traverse narrow planks, step firmly along high parapets, and perform other feats which they would shrink from attempting in their waking state.' This is simply, as Dr. Carpenter points out, because they are *not distracted* by the sense of danger which their vision would call up, from concentrating their exclusive attention on the guidance afforded by their muscular sense.'

But the most remarkable and suggestive of all the facts known respecting hypnotism is the influence which can by its means be brought to bear upon special parts or functions of the body. We know that imagination will hasten or retard certain processes commonly regarded as involuntary (indeed, the influence of imagination is itself in great degree involuntary). We know further that in some cases imagination will do much more than this, as in the familiar cases of the disappearance of warts under the supposed influence of charms, the cure of scrofula at a touch, and hundreds of well-attested cases of so-called miraculous cures. But although the actual cases of the curative influence obtained over hypnotised patients may not be in reality more striking than some of these, yet they are more suggestive at any rate to ordinary minds, because they are known not to be 'the result of any charm or miraculous interference, but to be due to simply natural processes initiated by natural though unfamiliar means.

Take, for instance, such a case as the following, related by Dr. Carpenter (who has himself witnessed many remarkable cases of hypnotic cure):—'A female relative of Mr.

Braid's was the subject of a severe rheumatic fever, during the course of which the left eye became seriously implicated, so that after the inflammatory action had passed away, there was an opacity over more than one half of the cornea, which not only prevented distinct vision, but occasioned an annoying disfigurement. Having placed herself under Mr. Braid's hypnotic treatment for the relief of violent pain in her arm and shoulder, she found, to the surprise alike of herself and Mr. Braid, that her sight began to improve very perceptibly. The operation was therefore continued daily; and in a very short time the cornea became so transparent that close inspection was required to discover any remains of the opacity.' On this, Carpenter remarks that he has known other cases in which secretions that had been morbidly suspended have been reinduced by this process; and is satisfied that, if applied with skill and discrimination, it would take rank as one of the most potent methods of treatment which the physician has at his command. He adds that 'the channel of influence is obviously the system of nerves which regulates the secretions—nerves which, though not under direct subjection to the will, are peculiarly affected by emotional states.'

I may remark, in passing, that nerves which are not ordinarily under the influence of the will, but whose office would be to direct muscular movements if only the will could influence them, may by persistent attention become obedient to the will. When I was last in New York, I met a gentleman who gave me a long and most interesting account of certain experiments which he had made on himself. The account was not forced on me, the reader must understand, but was elicited by questions suggested by one or two remarkable facts which he had casually mentioned as falling within his experience. I had only his own word for much that he told me, and some may perhaps consider that there was very little truth in the narrative. I may pause here to make some remarks by the way, on the traits of truthful and untruthful persons. I believe very slight powers of observation are necessary to detect want of veracity in any man, though absence of veracity in any particular story may not be easily detected or established. I am not one of those who believe every story they hear, and trust in every one they meet. But I have noticed one or two features by which the habitual teller of untruths may be detected very readily, as may also one who, without telling actual falsehoods, tries to heighten the effect of any story he may have to tell, by strengthening all the particulars. My experience in this respect is unlike Dickens's, who believed, and indeed found, that a man whom on first seeing he distrusted, and justly, could explain away the unfavourable impression. ' My first impression,' he says, ' about such people, founded on face and manner alone, was invariably true ; my mistake was in suffering them to come nearer to me and explain themselves away.' I have found it otherwise ; though of course Dickens was right about his own experience : the matter depends entirely on the idio-syncrasies of the observer. I have often been deceived by face and expression : never, to the best of my belief (and belief in this case is not mere opinion, but is based on results), by manner of speaking. One peculiarity I have never found wanting in habitually mendacious persons—a certain intona-tion which I cannot describe, but recognise in a moment, suggestive of the weighing of each sentence as it is being uttered, as though to consider how it would tell. Another, is a peculiarity of manner, but it only shows itself during speech ; it is a sort of watchfulness often disguised under a careless tone, but perfectly recognisable however disguised. Now, the gentleman who gave me the experience I am about to relate, conveyed to my mind, by every intonation of his voice and every peculiarity and change of manner, the idea of truthfulness. I cannot convey to others the impression thus conveyed to myself : nor do I expect that others will share my own confidence : I simply state the case as I know it, and as far as I know it. It will, however, be seen that a part of the evidence was confirmed on the spot.

The conversation turned on the curability of consumption. My informant, whom I will henceforth call A., said that, though he could not assert from experience that consumption was curable, he believed that in many cases where the tendency to consumption is inherited, and the consumptive constitution indicated so manifestly that under ordinary conditions the person would before long be hopelessly consumptive, an entire change may be made in the condition of the body, and the person become strong and healthy. He said : ' I belong myself to a family many of whose members have died of consumption. My father and mother both died of it, and all my brothers and sisters save one brother ; yet I do not look consumptive, do I ?' and certainly he did not. He then took from a pocket-book a portrait of his brother, showing a young man manifestly in very bad health, looking worn, weary, and emaciated. From the same pocket-book A. then took another portrait, asking if I recognised it. I saw here again a worn and emaciated face and figure. The picture was utterly unlike the hearty well-built man before me, yet it manifestly represented no other. If I had been at all doubtful, my doubts would have been removed by certain peculiarities to which A. called my attention. I asked how the change in his health had been brought about. He told me a very remarkable story of his treatment of himself, part of which I omit because I am satisfied he was mistaken in attributing to that portion of his self-treatment any part of the good result which he had obtained, and that if many consumptive patients adopted the remedy, a large proportion, if not all, would inevitably succumb very quickly. The other portion of his account is all that concerns us here, being all that illustrates our present subject. He said : ' I determined to exercise every muscle of my body ; I set myself in front of a mirror and concentrated my attention and all the power of my will on the muscle or set of muscles I proposed to bring into action. Then I exercised those muscles in every way I could think of, continuing the process till I had used in succession every muscle over which the will has control.

While carrying out this system, I noticed that gradually the will acquired power over muscles which before I had been quite unable to move. I may say, indeed, that every set of muscles recognised by anatomists, except those belonging to internal organs, gradually came under the control of my will.' Here I interrupted, asking (not by any means as doubting his veracity, for I did not) : 'Can you do what Dundreary said he thought some fellow might be able to do? can you waggle your left ear?' 'Why, certainly,' he replied ; and turning the left side of his head towards me, he moved his left ear about ; not, it is true, waggling it, but drawing it up and down in a singular way, which was, he said, the only exercise he ever gave it. He said, on this, that there are many other muscles over which the will has ordinarily no control, but may be made to obtain control ; and forthwith, drawing the cloth of his trousers rather tight round the right thigh (so that the movement he was about to show might be discernible) he made in succession the three muscles of the front and inner side of the thigh rise about half an inch along some nine or ten inches of their length. Now, though these muscles are among those which are governed by the will, for they are used in a variety of movements, yet not one in ten thousand, perhaps in a million, can move them in the way described.

How far A.'s system of exciting the muscles individually as well as in groups may have operated in improving his health, as he supposed, I am not now inquiring. What I wish specially to notice is the influence which the will may be made to obtain over muscles ordinarily beyond its control. It may be that under the exceptional influence of the imagination, in the hypnotic condition,. the will obtains a similar control for a while over even those parts of the nervous system which appertain to the so-called involuntary processes. In other words, the case I have cited may be regarded as occupying a sort of middle position between ordinary cases of muscular action and those perplexing cases in which the hypnotic subject seems able to influence pulsation, circulation, and processes of secretion in the various parts or organs of his body.

It must be noted, however, that the phenomena of hypnotism are due solely to the influence of the imagination. The quasi-scientific explanations which attributed them to magnetism, electricity, some subtle animal fluid, some occult force, and so forth, have been as completely negatived as the supernatural explanation. We have seen that painted wooden tractors were as effectual as the metal tractors of the earlier mesmerists ; a small disc of card or wood is as effective as the disc of zinc and copper used by the electro-biologists ; and now it appears that the mystical influence, or what was thought such, of the operator is no more essential to success than magnetic or electric apparatus.

Dr. Noble of Manchester made several experiments to determine this point. Some among them seem absolutely decisive.

Thus, a friend of Dr. Noble's had a female servant whom he had frequently thrown into the hypnotic state, trying a variety of experiments, many of which Dr. Noble had witnessed. Dr. Noble was at length told that his friend had succeeded in magnetising her from another room and without her knowledge, with some other stories even more marvellous, circumstantially related by eye-witnesses, 'amongst others by the medical attendant of the family, a most respectable and intelligent friend' of Dr. Noble's own. As he remained unsatisfied, Dr. Noble was invited to come and judge for himself, proposing whatever test he pleased. ' Now had we visited the house,' he says, ' we should have felt dissatisfied with any result,' knowing 'that the presence of a visitor or the occurrence of anything unusual was sure to excite expectation of some mesmeric process.' ' We therefore proposed,' he proceeds, ' that the experiment should be carried on at our own residence ; and it was made under the following circumstances :—The gentleman early one evening wrote a note as if on business, directing it to ourselves. He thereupon summoned the female servant (the mesmeric subject), requesting her to convey the note to its destination, and to wait for an answer. The gentleman himself, in her hearing, ordered a cab, stating that if anyone called he was going to a place named, but was expected to return by a certain hour. Whilst the female servant was dressing for her errand, the master placed himself in the vehicle and rapidly arrived at our dwelling. In about ten minutes after the note arrived, the gentleman in the meantime being secreted in an adjoining apartment, we requested the young woman who had been shown into our study, to take a seat whilst we wrote the answer ; at the same time placing the chair with its back to the door leading into the next room which was left ajar. It had been agreed that after the admission of the girl into the place where we were, the magnetiser, approaching the door in silence on the other side, should commence operations. There, then, was the patient or " subject" placed within two feet of her magnetiser, a door only intervening, and that but partially closed ; but she, all the while, perfectly free from all idea of what was going on. We were careful to avoid any unnecessary conversation with the girl, or even to look towards her, lest we should raise some suspicion in her own mind. We wrote our letter (as if in answer) for nearly a quarter of an hour, once or twice only making an indifferent remark, and on leaving the room for a light to seal the supposed letter, we beckoned the operator away. No effect whatever had been produced, although we had been told that two or three minutes were sufficient, even when mesmerising from the drawing-room, through walls and apartments, into the kitchen. In our own experiment the intervening distance had been very much less, and only one solid substance intervened, and that not completely ; but here we suspect was the difference—*the " subject" was unconscious of the magnetism and expected nothing.'*

In another case Dr. Noble tried the converse experiment with equally convincing results. Being in company one evening with a young lady said to be of high mesmeric susceptibility, he requested and received permission to test this quality in her.   In one of the usual ways he 'magnetised' her, and having so far satisfied himself, he 'demagnetised' her.   He next proceeded to 'hypnotise' her, adopting Mr. Braid's method of directing the stare at a fixed point.   'The result varied in no respect from that which had taken place in the foregoing experiment ; the duration of the process was the same, and its intensity of effect neither greater nor less.' 'De-hypnotisation' again restored the young lady to herself. 'And now,' says Dr. Noble, 'we requested our patient to rest quietly at the fire-place, to think of just what she liked, and to look where she pleased, excepting at ourselves, who retreated behind her chair, saying that a new mode was about to be tried, and that her turning round would disturb the process.   We very composedly took up a volume which lay upon a table, and amused ourselves with it for about five minutes, when on raising our eyes, we could see by the excited features of other members of the party that the young lady was once more *magnetised.*   We were informed by those who had attentively watched her during the progress of our little experiment, that all had been in every respect just as before.   The lady herself, before she was undeceived, expressed a distinct consciousness of having *felt our unseen passes streaming down the neck.'*

In a similar way, Mr. Bertrand, who was the first (Dr. Carpenter tells us) to undertake a really scientific investigation of the phenomena of mesmerism, proved that the supposed effect of a magnetised letter from him to a female somnambule was entirely the work of her own lively imagination.   He magnetised a letter first, which on receipt was placed at his suggestion upon the epigastrium of the patient, who was thrown into the magnetic sleep with all the customary phenomena.   He then wrote another letter, which he did not magnetise, and again the same effect was produced.   Lastly he set about an experiment which should determine the real state of the case.   'I asked one of my friends,' he says, 'to write a few lines in my place, and to strive to imitate my writing, so that those who should read the letter should mistake it for mine (I knew he could do so). He did this ; our stratagem succeeded, and the sleep was produced just as it would have been by one of my own letters.

It is hardly necessary to say, perhaps, that none of the phenomena of hypnotism require, as indeed none of them, rightly understood, suggest, the action of any such occult forces as spiritualists believe in. On the other hand, I believe that many of the phenomena recorded by spiritual ists as having occurred under their actual observation are very readily to be explained as phenomena of hypnotism. Of course I would not for a moment deny that in the great majority of cases much grosser forms of deception are employed. But in others, and especially in those where the concentration of the attention for some time is a necessary preliminary to the exhibition of the phenomena (which suitable 'subjects' only are privileged to see), I consider the resulting self-deception as hypnotic.

We may regard the phenomena of hypnotism in two aspects—first and chiefly as illustrating the influence of imagination on the functions of the body ; secondly, as showing under what conditions the imagination may be most readily brought to bear in producing such influence. These phenomena deserve far closer and at the same time far wider attention than they have yet received. Doubt has been thrown upon them because they have been associated with false theories, and in many cases with fraud and delusion. But, rightly viewed, they are at once instructive and valuable. On the one hand they throw light on some of the most interesting problems of mental physiology; on the other they promise to afford valuable means of curing certain ailments, and of influencing in useful ways certain powers and functions of the body. All that is necessary, it should seem, to give hypnotic researches their full value, is that all association of these purely mental phenomena with charlatanry and fraud should be abruptly and definitely broken off. Those who make practical application of the phenomena of hypnotism should not only divest their own minds of all idea that some occult and as it were extra-natural force is at work, but should encourage no belief in such force in those on whom the hypnotic method is employed. Their influence on the patient will not be lessened, I believe, by the fullest knowledge on the patient's part that all which is to happen to him is purely natural—that, in fact, advantage is simply to be taken of an observed property of the imagination to obtain an influence not otherwise attainable over the body as a whole (as when the so-called magnetic sleep is to be produced), or over special parts of the body. Whether advantage might not be taken of other than the curative influences of hypnotism is a question which will probably have occurred to some who may have followed the curious accounts given in the preceding pages. If special powers may be obtained, even for a short time, by the hypnotised subject, these powers might be systematically used for other purposes than mere experiment. If, again, the repetition of hypnotic curative processes eventually leads to a complete and lasting change in the condition of certain parts or organs of the body, the repetition of the exercise of special powers during the hypnotic state may after a while lead to the definite acquisition of such powers. As it now appears that the hypnotic control may be obtained without any effort on the part of the operator, the effort formerly supposed to be required being purely imaginary and the hypnotic state being in fact readily attainable without any operation whatever, we seem to recognise possibilities which, duly developed, might be found of extreme value to the human race. In fine, it would seem that man possesses a power which has hitherto lain almost entirely dormant, by which, under the influence of properly-guided imagination, the will can be so concentrated on special actions that feats of strength, dexterity, artistic (and even perhaps scientific) skill may be accomplished by persons who, in the ordinary state, are quite incapable of such achievements.

HEREDITARY TRAITS.

In Montaigne's well-known essay on the 'Resemblance of Children to their Fathers,' the philosopher of Périgord remarks that 'there is a certain sort of crafty humility that springs from presumption; as this, for example, that we confess our ignorance in many things, and are so courteous as to acknowledge that there are in works of nature some qualities and conditions that are imperceptible to us, and of which our understanding cannot discern the means and causes; by which honest declaration we hope to obtain that people shall also believe us of those that we say we do understand.' 'We need not trouble ourselves,' he goes on, 'to seek out miracles and strange difficulties; methinks there are such incomprehensible wonders amongst the things that we ordinarily see as surpass all difficulties of miracles.' He applies these remarks to inherited peculiarities of feature, figure, character, constitution, habits, and so forth. And certainly few of the phenomena of nature are more wonderful than these, in the sense of being less obviously referable to any cause which seems competent to produce them. Many of those natural phenomena which are regarded as most striking are in this respect not to be compared with the known phenomena of heredity. The motions of the planets can all be referred to regular laws; chemical changes are systematic, and their sequence at least is understood; the phenomena of heat, light, and electricity are gradually finding interpretation. It is true that all these phenomena become in a sense as miracles when we endeavour to ascertain their real cause. In their case we can ascertain the 'how,' but in no sense the 'why.' Gravity is a mystery of mysteries to the astronomer, and has almost compelled us to believe in that 'action at a distance' which Newton asserted to be unimaginable by anyone with a competent power of reasoning about things philosophical. The ultimate cause of chemical changes is as great a mystery now as it was when the four elements were believed in. And the nature of the ether itself in which the undulations of heat, light, and electricity are transmitted is utterly mysterious even to those students of science who have been most successful in determining the laws according to which those undulations proceed. But the phenomena themselves being at once referable (in our own time at least) to law, have no longer the mysterious and in a sense miraculous character recognised in them before the laws of motion, of chemical affinity, of light and heat and electricity, had been ascertained. It is quite otherwise with the phenomena of heredity. We know nothing even of the proximate cause of any single phenomenon ; far less of that ultimate cause in which all these phenomena had their origin. The inheritance of a trait of bodily figure, character, or manner is a mystery as great as that other and cognate mystery, the appearance of some seemingly sudden variation in a race which has for many generations presented an apparently unvarying succession of attributes, bodily, physical, or mental.

It need hardly be said that this would not be the place for the discussion of the problems of heredity and variation, even if in the present position of science we could hope for any profitable result from the investigation of either subject. But some of the curious facts which have been noted by various students of heredity will, I think, be found interesting ; and though not suggesting in the remotest degree any solution of the real difficulties of the subject, they may afford some indication of the laws according to which parental traits are inherited, or seemingly sudden variations introduced.

The commonest, and therefore the least interesting, though perhaps the most instructive of the phenomena of heredity, are those affecting the features and the outward configuration of the body. These have been recognised in all ages and among all nations. A portion of the Jewish system of legislature was based on a recognition of the law that children inherit the bodily qualities of the parents. The Greeks noted the same fact. Among the Spartans, indeed, a system of selection from among new-born children prevailed, which, though probably intended only to eliminate the weaker individuals, corresponded closely to what would be done by a nation having full belief in the efficacy of both natural and artificial selection, and not troubled with any strong scruples as to the method of applying their doctrines on such matters. Among the Romans we find certain families described by their physical characteristics, as the *Nasones* or Big-nosed, the *Labeones* or Thick-lipped, the *Capitones* or Big-headed, the *Buccones* or Swollen-cheeked. In more recent times similar traits have been recognised in various families. The Austrian lip and the Bourbon nose are well-known instances.[1]

Peculiarities of structure have a double interest, as illustrating both variation and persistence. We usually find them introduced without any apparent cause into a family, and afterwards they remain as hereditary traits, first inherited regularly, then intermittently, and eventually, in most cases, dying out or becoming so exceptional that their occurrence is not regarded as an hereditary peculiarity. Montaigne mentions that in the family of Lepidus, at Rome, there were three, not successively but by intervals, that were born with tne same eye covered with a cartilage. At Thebes there was a family almost every member of which had the crown of the head pointed like a lance-head; all whose heads were

---

[1] It is said by Ribot that of all the features the nose is the one which heredity preserves best.

not so formed being regarded as illegitimate. A better authenticated case is that of the Lambert family. The peculiarity affecting this family appeared first in the person of Edward Lambert, whose whole body, except the face, the palms of the hands, and the soles of the feet, was covered with a sort of shell consisting of horny excrescences. He was the father of six children, all of whom, so soon as they had reached the age of six weeks, presented the same peculiarity. Only one of them lived. He married, and transmitted the peculiarity to all his sons. For five generations all the male members of the Lambert family were distinguished by the horny excrescences which had adorned the body of Edward Lambert.

A remarkable instance of the transmission of anomalous characteristics is found in the case of Andrian Jeftichjew, who, three or four years ago, was exhibited with his son Fedor Jeftichjew in Berlin and Paris. They were called in Paris *les hommes-chiens*, or dog-men, the father's face being so covered with hair as to present a striking resemblance to the face of a Skye terrier. Andrian was thus described :—' He is about fifty-five years of age, and is said to have been the son of a Russian soldier. In order to escape the derision and the unkind usage of his fellow-villagers, Andrian in early life fled to the woods, where for some time he lived in a cave.

During this period of seclusion he was much given to drunkenness. His mental condition does not seem to have suffered, however, and he is on the whole of a kindly and affectionate disposition. It may be of interest to state that he is an orthodox member of the Russo-Greek Church, and that, degraded as he is intellectually, he has very definite notions about heaven and the hereafter. He hopes to introduce his frightful countenance into the court of heaven, and he devotes all the money he makes, over and above his outlay for creature comforts, to purchasing the prayers of a devout community of monks in his native village, Kostroma, after his mortal career is ended. He is of medium stature, but very strongly built. His excessive capillary development is not true hair, but simply an abnormal growth of the *down* or fine hairs which usually cover nearly the entire surface of the human body. Strictly speaking, he has neither head-hair, beard, moustache, eyebrows, nor eyelashes, their place being taken by this singular growth of long silky down. In colour this is of a dirty yellow ; it is about three inches in length all over the face, and feels like the hair of a Newfoundland dog. The very eyelids are covered with this long hair, while flowing locks come out of his nostrils and ears. On his body are isolated patches, strewed but not thickly with hairs one and a half to two inches long.' Dr. Bertillon, of Paris, compared a hair from Andrian's chin with a very fine hair from a man's beard, and found that the latter was three times as thick as the former ; and a hair from Andrian's head is only one-half as thick as an average human hair. Professor Virchow, of Berlin, made careful inquiry into the family history of Andrian Jeftichjew. So far as could be learned, Andrian was the first in whom this wonderful hirsuteness had been noticed. Neither his reputed father nor his mother presented any peculiarity of the kind, and a brother and sister of his, who are still living, are in no way remarkable for capillary development. The son Fedor, who was exhibited in company with Andrian, was illegitimate, and about three years of age. Andrian's legitimate children, a son and a daughter, both died young. Nothing is known of the former; but the daughter resembled the father. 'Fedor is a sprightly child,' said the account from which we have already quoted, 'and appears more intelligent than the father.' The growth of down on his face is not so heavy as to conceal his features, but there is no doubt that when the child comes to maturity he will be at least as hirsute as his parent. The hairs are as white and as soft as the fur of the Angora cat, and are longest at the outer angles of the eyes. There is a thick tuft between the eyes, and the nose is well covered. The moustache joins the whiskers on each side, after the English fashion, and this circumstance gives to accurate pictures of the child a ludicrous resemblance to a well-fed

Englishman of about fifty.   As in the father's case, the inside of Fedor's nostrils and ears has a thick crop of hair.'
' Both father and son are almost toothless, Andrian having only five teeth, one in the upper jaw and four in the lower, while the child has only four teeth, all in the lower jaw.   In both cases the four lower teeth are all incisors.   To the right of Andrian's one upper tooth there still remains the mark of another which has disappeared.   That beyond these six teeth the man never had any others is evident to anyone who feels the gums with the finger.'

The deficiency of teeth, accompanied as it is by what is in reality a deficiency not a redundancy of hair—for Andrian and his son have no real hair—accords well with Darwin's view, that a constant correlation exists between hair and teeth.   He mentions as an illustration the deficiency of teeth in hairless dogs.   The tusks of the boar, again, are greatly reduced under domestication, and the reduction is accompanied by a corresponding diminution of the bristles.   He mentions also the case of Julia Pastrana, a Spanish dancer or opera singer, who had a thick masculine beard and a hairy forehead, while her teeth were so redundant that her mouth projected, and her face had a gorilla-like appearance. It should rather be said that in general those creatures which present an abnormal development in the covering of their skin, whether in the way of redundancy or deficiency, present, generally, perhaps always, an abnormal dental development, as we see in sloths and armadilloes on the one hand, which have the front teeth deficient, and in some branches of the whale family on the other, in which the teeth are redundant either in number or in size.   In individual members of the human family it certainly is not always the case that the development of the hair and that of the teeth are directly correlated ; for some who are bald when quite young have excellent teeth, and some who have lost most of their teeth while still on the right side of forty have excellent hair to an advanced age.[1]

---

[1] Shakspeare, who was bald young (and, so far as one can judge

Another case, somewhat similar to that of Andrian and his son, is found in a Burmese family, living at Ava, and first described by Crawford in 1829. Shwe-Maong, the head of the family, was about thirty years old. His whole body was covered with silky hairs, which attained a length of nearly five inches on the shoulders and spine. He had four daughters, but only one of them resembled him. She was living at Ava in 1855, and, according to the account given by a British officer who saw her there, she had a son who was hairy like his grandfather, Shwe-Maong. The case of this family illustrates rather curiously the relation between the hair and teeth. For Shwe-Maong retained his milk-teeth till he was twenty years old (when he attained puberty), and they were replaced by nine teeth only, five in the upper and four in the lower jaw. Eight of these were incisors, the ninth (in the upper jaw) being a canine tooth.

Sex-digitism, or the possession of hands and feet with six digits each, has occurred in several families as a sudden variation from the normal formation, but after it has appeared has usually been transmitted for several generations. In the case of the Colburn family this peculiarity lasted for four generations without interruption, and still reappears occasionally. In a branch of a well-known Scotch family sex-digitism—after continuing for three or four generations—has apparently disappeared ; but it still frequently happens that the edge of the hands on the side of the little finger is partially deformed.

Hare-lip, albinism, halting, and other peculiarities, commonly reappear for four or five generations, and are seldom altogether eradicated in less than ten or twelve.

from his portraits, had a good set of teeth), suggests a correlation between hairiness and want of wit, which is at least likely to be regarded by those who 'wear his baldness while they're young' as a sound theory. 'Why,' asks Antipholus of Syracuse, 'is Time such a niggard of hair, being, as it is, so plentiful an excrement ?' 'Because,' says Dromio of Syracuse, 'it is a blessing that he bestows on beasts ; and what he hath scanted men in hair he hath given them in wit.'

The tendency to variation shown in the introduction of these peculiarities, even though they may have been eventually eradicated, is worth noticing in its bearing on cur views respecting the formation of new and persistent varieties of the human as of other races. It must be noticed that in the case of the human race the conditions not only do not favour the continuance of such varieties, but practically forbid their persistence. It is otherwise with some varieties, at least, of domestic animals, insomuch that varieties which present any noteworthy even though accidentally observed advantage have been made practically persistent; we say practically, because there seems little reason to doubt that in every case which has hitherto been observed the normal type would eventually be reverted to if special pains were not taken to separate the normal from the abnormal form.

An excellent illustration of the difference between the human race and a race of animals under domestication, in this particular respect, is found in the case of the Kelleia family on the one hand, and that of the Ancon or Otter sheep on the other.

The former case is described by Réaumur. A Maltese couple named Kelleia, whose hands and feet were of the ordinary type, had a son Gratio who had six movable fingers on each hand and six somewhat less perfect toes on each foot. Gratio Kelleia married a woman possessing only the ordinary number of fingers and toes. There were four children of this marriage—Salvator, George, André, and Marie. Salvator had six fingers and six toes like the father; George and André had each five fingers and five toes like the mother, but the hands and feet of George were slightly deformed; Marie had five fingers and five toes, but her thumbs were slightly deformed. All four children grew up, and married folk with the ordinary number of fingers and toes. The children of André alone (who were many) were without exception of the normal type, like their father. The children of Salvator, who alone was six-fingered and six-toed like Gratio the grandfather, were four in number; three of them resembled the father, while the other—the youngest—was of the normal type like his mother and grandmother. As these four children were the descendants of four grand parents of whom one only was hexadactylic, we see that the variety had been strong enough in their case to overcome the normal type in threefold greater strength. But the strangest part of the story is that relating to George and Marie. George, who was a pentadactyle, though somewhat deformed about the hands and feet, was the father of four children : first, two girls, both purely hexadactylic ; next, a girl hexadactylic on the right side of the body and penta-dactylic on the left side ; and lastly, a boy, purely penta-dactylic. Marie, a pentadactyle with deformed thumbs, gave birth to a boy with six toes, and three normally formed children. It will be seen, however, that the normal type showed itself in greater force than the variety in the third generation from Gratio ; for while one child of Salvator's, one of George's, three of Marie's, and all of André's (some seven or eight) were of the normal type—twelve or thirteen in all—only five, viz., three of Salvator's and two of George's, presented the variety purely. Three others were more or less abnormally formed in fingers and toes ; but even counting these, the influence of the variety was shown only in eight of the grandchildren of Gratio, whereas twelve or thirteen were of the normal type.

The story of the Ancon or Otter sheep, as narrated by Colonel David Humphreys in a letter to Sir Joseph Banks, published in the *Philosophical Transactions* for 1813, has been thus abridged by Huxley :—' It appears that one Seth Wright, the proprietor of a farm on the banks of the Charles River, in Massachusetts, possessed a flock of fifteen ewes and a ram of the ordinary kind. In the year 1791 one of the ewes presented her owner with a male lamb differing, for no assignable reason, from its parents by a disproportion-ately long body and short bandy legs ; whence it was unable to emulate its relatives in those sportive leaps over the neighbours' fences in which they were in the habit of

indulging, much to the good farmer's vexation. With the
" cuteness " characteristic of their nation, the neighbours of
the Massachusetts farmer imagined it would be an excellent
thing if all his sheep were imbued with the stay-at-home
tendencies enforced by Nature upon the newly-arrived ram ;
and they advised Wright to kill the old patriarch of his fold
and instal the new Ancon ram in his place. The result
justified their sagacious anticipations. . . . The young
lambs were almost always either pure Ancons or pure
ordinary sheep. But when sufficient Ancon sheep were
obtained to interbreed with one another, it was found that
the offspring were always pure Ancon. Colonel Humphreys,
in fact, states that he was acquainted with only " one questionable case of a contrary nature." By taking care to select
Ancons of both sexes for breeding from, it thus became easy
to establish an exceedingly well-marked race—so peculiar that
even when herded with other sheep, it was noted that the
Ancons kept together. And there is every reason to believe
that the existence of this breed might have been indefinitely
protracted : but the introduction of the Merino sheep—
which were not only very superior to the Ancons in wool and
meat, but quite as quiet and orderly—led to the complete
neglect of the new breed, so that in 1813 Colonel Humphreys
found it difficult to obtain the specimen whose skeleton was
presented to Sir Joseph Banks. We believe that for many
years no remnant of it has existed in the United States.'

It is easy, as Huxley remarks, to understand why,
whereas Gratio Kelleia did not become the ancestor of a
race of six-figured and six-toed men, Seth Wright's Ancon
ram became a nation of long-bodied, short-legged sheep.
If the purely hexadactylic descendants of Gratio Kelleia,
and all the purely hexadactylic members of the Colburn
family, in the third and fourth generations, had migrated
to some desert island, and had been careful not only to
exclude all visitors having the normal number of fingers
and toes, but to send away before the age of puberty all
children of their own which might depart in any degree

from the pure hexadactylic type, there can be no doubt that under favourable conditions the colony would have become a nation of six-fingered folk. Among such a nation the duodecimal system of notation would flourish, and some remarkable performers on the pianoforte, flute, and other instruments, might be looked for ; but we do not know that they would possess any other advantage over their penta-dactylic contemporaries. Seeing that the system of colonis-ing above described is antecedently unlikely, and that no special advantage could be derived from the persistence of any hitherto known abnormal variety of the human race, it is unlikely that for many generations yet to come we shall hear of six-fingered, hairy-faced, horny-skinned, or hare-lipped nations. The only peculiarities which have any chance of becoming permanent are such as, while not very uncommon, stand in the way of intermarriage with persons not similarly affected. A similar remark, as will presently appear, applies to mental and moral characteristics. The law according to which contrast is found attractive and similitude repugnant, though wide in its range, is not uni-versal ; and there are cases in which resemblance, if it has not the charm found (under ordinary circumstances) in con-trast, is yet a necessary element in matrimonial alliances.

The inheritance of constitutional traits comes next to be considered. It is probably not less frequently observed, and is in several respects more interesting than the inherit-ance of peculiarities of bodily configuration.

Longevity, which may be regarded as measuring the aggregate constitutional energy, is well known to be heredi-tary in certain families, as is short duration of life in other families. The best proof that this is the case is found in the action of insurance companies, in ascertaining through their agents the longevity of the ancestors of persons pro-posing to insure their lives. Instances of longevity during several successive generations are too common to be worth citing. Cases in which, for generation after generation, a certain age, far short of the threescore years and ten, has

not been passed, even when all the circumstances have
favoured longevity, are more interesting. One of the most
curious among these is the case of the Turgot family, in
which the age of fifty-nine had not been for generations
exceeded, to the time when Turgot made the name famous.
At the age of fifty, when he was in excellent health, and
apparently had promise of many years of life, he expressed
to his friends his conviction that the end of his life was
near at hand. From that time forward he held himself
prepared for death, and, as we know, he died before he had
completed his fifty-fourth year.

Fecundity is associated sometimes with longevity, but in
other cases it is as significantly associated with short duration
of life. Of families in which many children are born but few
survive, we naturally have less striking evidence than we
have of families in which many children of strong constitutions are born for several successive generations. What
may be called the fecundity of the short-lived is a quality
commonly leading in no long time to the disappearance of
the family in which it makes its appearance. It is the
reverse, of course, with fecundity in families whose members show individually great vigour of constitution and high
vital power. Ribot mentions several cases of this sort
among the families of the old French *noblesse.* Thus Anne
de Montmorency—who, despite his feminine name, was
certainly by no means feminine in character (at the Battle
of St. Denis, in his sixty-sixth year, he smashed with his
sword the teeth of the Scotch soldier who was giving him
his death-blow) was the father of twelve children. Three
of his ancestors, Matthew I., Matthew II., and Matthew III.,
had, in all, eighteen children, of whom fifteen were boys.
'The son and grandson of the great Condé had nineteen
between them, and their great-grandfather, who lost his life
at Jarnac, had ten. The first four Guises reckoned in all
forty-three children, of whom thirty were boys. Achille de
Harley had nine children, his father ten, and his great-
grandfather eighteen.' In the family of the Herschels in

Hanover and in England, a similar fecundity has been shown in two generations out of three. Sir W. Herschel was one of a family of twelve children, of whom five were sons. He himself did not marry till his fiftieth year, and had only one son. But Sir John Herschel was the father of eleven children.

Of constitutional peculiarities those affecting the nervous system are most frequently transmitted. We do not, however, consider them at this point, because they are viewed ordinarily rather as they relate to mental and moral characteristics than as affections of the body. The bodily affections most commonly transmitted are those depending on what is called diathesis—a general state or disposition of the constitution predisposing to some special disease. Such are scrofula, cancer, tubercular consumption, gout, arthritis, and some diseases specially affecting the skin. It would not be desirable to discuss here this particular part of our subject, interesting though it undoubtedly is. But it may be worth while to note that we have, in the variety of forms in which the same constitutional bad quality may present itself, evidence that what is actually transmitted is not a peculiarity affecting a particular organ, even though in several successive generations the disease may show itself in the same part of the body, but an affection of the constitution generally. We have here an answer to the question asked by Montaigne in the essay from which we have already quoted. The essay was written soon after he had for the first time experienced the pangs of renal calculus :—' 'Tis to be believed,' he says, ' that I derived this infirmity from my father, for he died wonderfully tormented ' with it ; he was ' never sensible of his disease till the sixty-seventh year of his age, and before that had never felt any grudging or symptom of it ' . . . . ' but lived till then in a happy vigorous state of health, little subject to infirmities, and continued seven years after in this disease, and dyed a very painful death. I was born about twenty-five years before his disease seized him, and in the time of his most flourishing and healthful state of body, his third child in order of birth : where could his propension to this malady lie lurking all that while?   And he being so far from the infirmity, how could that small part of his substance carry away so great an impression of its share?   And how so concealed that, till five-and-forty years after, I did not begin to be sensible of it? being the only one to this hour, amongst so many brothers and sisters, and all of one mother, that was ever troubled with it.   He that can satisfie me in this point, I will believe him in as many other miracles as he pleases, always provided that, as their manner is, he does not give me a doctrine much more intricate and fantastic than the thing itself, for current pay.'   When we note, however, that in many cases the children of persons affected like the elder Montaigne are not affected like the parents, but with other infirmities, as the tendency to gout, and *vice versâ* (a circumstance of which I myself have but too good reason to be cognisant, a parent's tendency to gout having in my case been transmit ed in the modified but even more troublesome form of the disease which occasioned Montaigne so much anguish), we perceive that it is not 'some small part of the substance' which transmits its condition to the child, but the general state of the constitution.   Moreover, it may be hoped in many cases (which would scarcely be the case if the condition or qualities of some part of the body only were transmitted) that the germs of disease, or rather the predisposition to disease, may be greatly diminished, or even entirely eradicated, by suitable precautions.   Thus persons inheriting a tendency to consumption have become, in many cases, vigorous and healthy by passing as much of their time as possible in the open air, by avoiding crowded and over-heated rooms, taking moderate but regular exercise, judicious diet, and so forth. We believe that the disease which troubled the last fifteen years of the life of Montaigne might readily have been prevented, and the tendency to it eradicated, during his youth.

Let us turn, however, from these considerations to others more interesting, though less important, and on the whole perhaps better suited to these pages.

The inheritance of tricks or habits is one of the most perplexing of all the phenomena of heredity. The less striking the habit, the more remarkable, perhaps, is its persistence as an inherited trait. Giron de Buzareingues states that he knew a man who, when he lay on his back, was wont to throw his right leg across the left ; one of this person's daughters had the same habit from her birth, constantly assuming that position in the cradle, notwithstanding the resistance offered by the swaddling bands.[1] Darwin mentions another case in his *Variation of Animals and Plants under Domestication* :—A child had the odd habit of setting its fingers in rapid motion whenever it was particularly pleased with anything. When greatly excited, the same child would raise the hand on both sides as high as the eyes, with the fingers in rapid motion as before. Even in old age he experienced a difficulty in refraining from these gestures. He had eight children, one of whom, a little girl, when four

[1] While penning the above lines I have been reminded of an experience of my own, which I had never before thought of as connected with the subject of heredity ; yet it seems not unlikely that it may be regarded as a case in point. During the infancy of my eldest son it so chanced that the question of rest at night, and consequently the question of finding some convenient way of keeping the child quiet, became one of considerable interest to me. Cradle-rocking was effective but carried on in the usual way prevented my own sleep, though causing the child to sleep. I devised, however, a way of rocking the cradle with the foot, which could be carried on in my sleep, after a few nights' practice. Now it is an odd coincidence (only, perhaps) that the writer's next child, a girl, had while still an infant a trick which I have noticed in no other case. She would rock herself in the cradle by throwing the right leg over the left at regular intervals, the swing of the cradle being steadily kept up for many minutes, and being quite as wide in range as a nurse could have given. It was often continued when the child was asleep.

Since writing the above, I have learned from my eldest daughter, the girl who as a child had the habit described, that a recent little brother of hers, one of twins, and remarkably like her, had the same habit, rocking his own cradle so vigorously as to disturb her in the next room with the noise. These two only of twelve children have had this curious habit ; but as this child is thirteen years younger than she is, the force of the coincidence in point of time is to some degree impaired.

years of age, used to set her fingers going, and to lift up her hands after the manner of her father. A still more remarkable case is described by Galton. A gentleman's wife noticed that when he lay fast asleep on his back in bed he had the curious trick of raising his right arm slowly in front of his face, up to his forehead, and then dropping it with a jerk, so that the wrist fell heavily on the bridge of his nose. The trick did not occur every night, but occasionally, and was independent of any ascertained cause. Sometimes it was repeated incessantly for an hour or more. The gentleman's nose was prominent, and its bridge often became sore from blows which it received. At one time an awkward sore was produced that was long in healing, on account of the recurrence, night after night, of the blows which first caused it. His wife had to remove the button from the wrist of his night-gown, as it made severe scratches, and some means were attempted of tying his arm. Many years after his death, his son married a lady who had never heard of the family incident. She, however, observed precisely the same peculiarity in her husband ; but his nose, from not being particularly prominent, has never as yet suffered from the blows. The trick does not occur when he is half asleep, as, for example, when he is dozing in his arm-chair ; but the moment he is fast asleep, he is apt to begin. It is, as with his father, intermittent ; sometimes ceasing for many nights, and sometimes almost incessant during a part of every night. It is performed, as it was with his father, with his right hand. One of his children, a girl, has inherited the same trick. She performs it, likewise, with the right hand, but in a slightly modified form ; for after raising the arm, she does not allow the wrist to drop upon the bridge of the nose, but the palm of her half-closed hand falls over and down the nose, striking it rather rapidly—a decided improvement on the father's and grandfather's method. The trick is intermittent in this girl's case also, sometimes not occurring for periods of several months but sometimes almost incessantly.

Strength in particular limbs or muscles is often transmitted hereditarily. So also is skill in special exercises. Thus in the north country there are families of famous wrestlers. Among professional oarsmen, again, we may note such cases as the Clasper family in the north, the Mackinneys in the south; while among amateur oarsmen we have the case of the Playford family, to which the present amateur champion sculler belongs. In cricket, the Walker family and the Grace family may be cited among amateurs, the Humphreys among professional players. Grace in dancing was transmitted for three generations in the Vestris family. It must, however, be noted that in some of these cases we may fairly consider that example and teaching have had much to do with the result. Take rowing for instance. A good oarsman will impart his style to a whole crew if he rows stroke for them ; and even if he only trains them (as Morrison, for instance, trained the Cambridge crew a few years ago), he will make good oarsmen of men suitably framed and possessing ordinary aptitude for rowing. I remember well how a famous stroke-oar at Cambridge (John Hall, of Magdalen,) imparted to one at least of the University crew (a fellow-collegian of his, and therefore rowing with him constantly also in his College boat) so exact an imitation of his style that one rather dusky evening, when the latter was ' stroking' a scratch four past a throng of University men, a dispute arose as to which of the two was really stroke of the four. Anyone who knows how characteristic commonly is the rowing of any first-class stroke, and still more anyone who chances to know how peculiar was the style of the University ' stroke-oar' referred to, will understand how closely his style must have been adopted, when experienced oarsmen, not many yards from the passing four, were unable to decide at once which of the two men were rowing,—even though the evening was dusky enough to prevent the features of the stroke (whose face was not fully in view at the moment) from being discerned. Seeing that a first-rate oarsman can thus communicate his style so perfectly to another, it cannot be regarded as demonstrably a case of hereditary transmission if the Claspers rowed in the same style as their father, or if the present champion amateur sculler (making allowances for the change introduced by the sliding seat) rows very much like his father and his uncle.

Some peculiarities, such as stammering, lisping, babbling, and the like, are not easily referable to any special class of hereditary traits, because it is not clear how far they are to be regarded as depending on bodily or how far on mental peculiarities. It might seem obvious that stammering was in most cases uncontrollable by the will, and babbling might seem as certainly controllable. Yet there are cases which throw doubt on either conclusion. Thus, Dr. Lucas tells us of a servant-maid whose loquacity was apparently quite uncontrollable. She would talk to people till they were ready to faint ; and if there were no human being to listen to her, she would talk to animals and inanimate objects, or would talk aloud to herself. She had to be discharged. 'But,' she said to her master, 'I am not to blame ; it all comes from my father. He had the same fault, and it drove my mother to distraction ; and his father was just the same.' Stammering has been transmitted through as many as five generations. The same has been noticed of peculiarities of vision. The Montmorency look, a sort of half squint, affected nearly all the members of the Montmorency family. The peculiarity called Daltonism, an inability to distinguish between certain colours of the spectrum, was not so named, as is often asserted, merely because the distinguished chemist Dalton was affected by it, but because three members of the same family were similarly affected. Deafness and blindness are not commonly hereditary where the parents have lost sight or hearing either by accident or through illness, even though the illness or accident occur during infancy ; but persons born either blind or deaf frequently if not commonly transmit the defect to some at least among their offspring. Similar remarks apply to deaf-mutism.

The senses of taste and smell must also be included in the list of those which are affected by transmitted peculiarities. If we include the craving for liquor among such peculiarities, we might at once cite a long list of cases ; but this craving must be regarded as nervo-psychical, the sense of taste having in reality very little to do with it. It is doubtful how the following hideous instance should be classed. It is related by Dr. Lucas. 'A man in Scotland had an irresistible desire to eat human flesh. He had a daughter ; although removed from her father and mother, who were both sent to the stake before she was a year old, and although brought up among respectable people, this girl, like her father, yielded to the horrible craving for human flesh.' He must be an ardent student of physiological science who regrets that at this stage circumstances intervened which prevented the world from ascertaining whether the peculiarity would have descended to the third and fourth generations.

Amongst the strangest cases of hereditary transmissions are those relating to handwriting. Darwin cites several curious instances in his *Variation of Plants and Animals under Domestication.* 'On what a curious combination of corporeal structure, mental character, and training,' he remarks, 'must handwriting depend. Yet everyone must have noted the occasional close similarity of the handwriting in father and son, even although the father had not taught the son. A great collector of franks assured me that in his collection there were several franks of father and son hardly distinguishable except by their dates.' Hofacker, in Germany, remarks on the inheritance of handwriting, and it has been even asserted that English boys when taught to write in France naturally cling to their English manner of writing. Dr. Carpenter mentions the following instance as having occurred in his own family, as showing that the character of the handwriting is independent of the special teaching which the right hand receives in this art :—'A gentleman who emigrated to the United States and settled in the back woods, before the end of last century, was accustomed from time to time to write long letters to his sister in England, giving an account of his family affairs. Having lost his right arm by an accident, the correspondence was temporarily kept up by one or other of his children ; but in the course of a few months he learned to write with his left hand, and before long, the handwriting of the letters thus written came to be indistinguishable from that of his former letters.'

I had occasion two or three years ago to consider in an article on ' Strange Mental Feats,' in my *Science Byeways*, the question of inherited mental qualities and artistic habits, and would refer the reader for some remarkable instances of transmitted powers to that article.[1] Galton in his work on *Hereditary Genius*, and Ribot in his treatise on *Heredity*, have collected many facts bearing on this interesting question. Both writers show a decided bias in favour of a view which would give to heredity a rather too important position among the factors of genius. Cases are cited which seem very little to the purpose, and multitudes of instances are omitted which oppose themselves, at a first view at any rate, to the belief that heredity plays the first part in the genesis of great minds. Nearly all the greatest names in philosophy, literature, and science, and a great number of the greatest names in art, stand absolutely alone. We know nothing achieved by the father or grandfather of Shakspeare, or of Goethe, or Schiller, or Evans (George Eliot), or Thackeray, or Dickens, or Huxley. None of Newton's family were in any way distinguished in mathematical or scientific work ; nor do we know of a distinguished Laplace, or Lagrange, or Lavoisier, or Harvey, or Dalton, or Volta, or Faraday, besides those who made these names illustrious. As to general literature, page after page might be filled with the mere names of those whose ancestry has been quite undistinguished. To say that among the ancestors of Goethe, Schiller, Byron, and so forth, certain qualities, virtues or vices, passions or insensibilities to passion, may be recognised ' among the ancestors of men of science, certain aptitudes for special subjects or methods of research,' among

---

[1] See my *Science Byeways*, p. 337 *et seq.*

the ancestors of philosophers and literary men certain qualities or capabilities, and that such ancestral peculiarities determined the poetic, scientific, or literary genius of the descendant, is in reality to little purpose, for there is probably not a single family possessing claims to culture in any civilised country among the members of which individuals might not be found with qualities thus emphasised so to speak. Such *à posteriori* reasoning is valueless. If instances could be so classified that after carefully studying them we could make even the roughest approach to a guess respecting the cases in which a family might be expected to produce men of any particular qualities, there would be some use in these attempts at generalisation; at present all that can be said is that some mental qualities and some artistic aptitudes have unquestionably in certain instances been transmitted, and that on the whole men of great distinction in philosophy, literature, science, and art, are rather more likely than others to have among their relations (more or less remote) persons somewhat above the average in mental or artistic qualities. But it is not altogether certain that this superiority is even quite so great as it might be expected to be if hereditary transmission played no part at all in the matter. For it cannot be denied that a great mathematician's son has rather a better chance than others of being a mathematician, a great author's son of being a writer, a great artist's son of being skilful in art, a great philosopher's son of taking philosophic views of things. Nearly every son looks forward while still young to the time when he shall be doing his father's work ; nearly every father hopes while his children are yet young that some at least among them will follow his pursuits. The fact that so few sons of great men do follow in their fathers' footsteps shows that, despite the strong ambition of the son and the anxious hope of the father, the son in the majority of instances has not had ability even to take a fairly good position in the work wherein the father has been perhaps pre-eminently distinguished.

I have said that certain mental qualities have certainly

been transmitted in some cases. Galton mentions one note-worthy instance relating to memory. In the family of Porson good memory was so notable a faculty as to give rise to the byword, ' the Porson memory.' Lady Hester Stanhope, says the late F. Papillon, ' she whose life was so full of adventure. gives, as one among many points of resemblance between herself and her grandfather, her retentive memory. " I have my grandfather's grey eyes," said she, " and his memory of places. If he saw a stone on the road, he remembered it ; it is the same with myself. His eye, which was ordinarily dull and lustreless, was lighted up, like my own, with a dull gleam whenever he was seized with passion." '

In endeavouring to form an opinion on the law of here-dity in its relation to genius, we must remember that a remark somewhat similar to one made by Huxley respecting the origin of new species applies to the origin of a man of genius. Be-fore such a man became celebrated no one cared particu-larly to inquire about his ancestry or relations ; when his fame was established, the time for making the inquiry had passed away. It is quite possible that, if we had exact and full information, in a great number of cases we might find the position taken up by Mr. Galton and M. Ribot greatly strengthened; it is, however, also possible that we might find it much weakened, not only by the recognition of a multitude of cases in which the approach of a great man was in no sort indicated by scintillations of brightness along the genealogical track, but by a yet greater number of cases in which families containing numbers of clever, witty, and learned folks have produced none who attained real distinction.

There is an excellent remark in a thoughtful but anony-mous paper on Heredity in the *Quarterly Journal of Science*, two years or so ago, which suggests some considerations well worth noting. ' If we look,' says the writer, ' on the in-tellect as not a single force but a complex of faculties, we shall find little to perplex us in the phenomenon of spon-taneity '—that is (in this case), in the appearance of a man of genius in a family not before remarkable in any way. ' Suppose a family who have possessed some of the attributes of greatness, but who, in virtue of a principle equally true in psychology and in mechanics, that " nothing is stronger than its weakest part," has remained in obscurity. Let a man of this family marry a woman whose faculties are the complement of his own. It is possible that a child of such a couple may combine the defects or weaknesses of both parents, and we have then the case of spontaneous imbecility or criminality. But it is also possible that he may combine the excellences of both, and burst upon the world as a spontaneous genius. . . . Again, we must remember that, even if we consider the intellect as " one and indivisible," it is far from being the only faculty needful for the attainment of excellence, even in the fields of pure science. Combined with it there must be the moral faculties of patience, perseverance, and concentration. The will must be strong enough to overcome all distracting temptations, whether in themselves good or evil. Lastly, there must be constitutional energy and endurance. Failing these, the man will merely leave among his friends the conviction that he might have achieved greatness, if——. We once knew a physician, resident in a small country town, who from time to time startled his associates by some profound and suggestive idea, some brilliant *aperçu*. But a constitutional languor prevented him from ever completing an investigation, or from leaving the world one written line.'

The effect of circumstances also must not be overlooked. It is certain that some of those who stand highest in the world's repute would have done nothing to make their names remembered but for circumstances which either aided their efforts or compelled them to exertion ; and it cannot be doubted, therefore, that many who have been by no means celebrated have required but favouring opportunities or the spur of adverse circumstances to have achieved distinction. We note the cases in which men who have been intended by their parents for the desk or routine work have fortunately been freed for nobler work, to which their powers have specially fitted them. But we are apt to forget that for each such case there must be many instances in which no fortunate chance has intervened. The theory that genius *will* make its way, despite all obstacles, is like the popular notion that 'murder will out,' and other such fancies. We note when events happen which favour such notions, but we not only do not note—in the very nature of things it is impossible that we should have the chance of noting—cases unfavourable to a notion which, after all, is but a part of the general and altogether erroneous idea that what we think ought to be, will be. That among millions of men in a civilised community, trained under multitudinous conditions, for diverse professions, trades, and so forth, exposed to many vicissitudes of fortune, good and bad, there should be men from time to time—

> Who break their birth's invidious bar,
> And grasp the skirts of happy chance,
> And breast the blows of circumstance,
> And grapple with their evil star,

is no truer proof of the general theory that genius will make its mark, despite circumstance, than is the occasional occurrence of strange instances in which murder has been detected despite seemingly perfect precautions.

It must, however, be in a general sense admitted that mental powers, like bodily powers, are inherited. If the ancestry of men of genius could be traced, we should in each case probably find enough, in the history of some line at least along which descent could be traced, to account for the possession of special powers, and enough in the history of that and other lines of descent to account for the other qualities or characteristics which, combined with those special powers, gave to the man's whole nature the capacity by which he was enabled to stand above the average level of his fellow-men. We might, with knowledge at once wider and deeper than we actually possess of the various families of each nation, and their relationships, predict in many cases, not that any given child would prove a genius, but that some one or other of a family would probably rise to distinction. To predict the advent of a man of great genius as we predict the approach of an eclipse or a transit, will doubtless never be in men's power ; but it is conceivable that at some perhaps not very remote epoch, anticipations may be formed somewhat like those which astronomers are able to make respecting the recurrence of meteoric showers at particular times and seasons, and visible in particular regions. Already we know so much as this, that in certain races of men only can special forms of mental energy, like special bodily characteristics, be expected to appear. It may well be that hereafter such anticipations may be limited to special groups of families.

When we pass from mental to moral qualities, we find ourselves in the presence of problems which could not be thoroughly dealt with in these pages. The general question, how far the moral characteristics of each person born into the world depends on those of the parents, or more generally of the ancestry, is one involving many considerations which, perhaps unfortunately, have been associated with religious questions. And apart from this, the answers to this question have been found to have a very wide range—from the opinion of those who (like Miss Martineau) consider that our characters, even where they seem to undergo changes resulting from the exercise of will, are entirely due to inheritance, to the view of those who consider, like Heinroth, that no moral characteristic can possibly be regarded as inherited in such sort as to modify either responsibility for evil-doing or credit for well-doing. Probably most will be content to accept a view between these extremes, without too nicely considering how far moral responsibility is affected by the influence of inherited tendencies.

There are, however, some illustrations relating to exceptional habits, which may be mentioned here without bringing in the general question.

I have not referred to insanity in speaking of inherited

mental qualities, because insanity must be regarded as a disease of the moral rather than of the mental nature.   Its origin may be in the mind, as the origin of mental diseases is in the brain, that is, is in the body ; but the principal manifestations of insanity, those which must guide us in determining its true position, are unquestionably those relating to moral habitudes.   Insanity is not always, or at least not always demonstrably hereditary.   Esquirol found among 1,375 lunatics 337 unquestionable cases of hereditary transmission.   Guislain and others regard hereditary lunacy as including, roughly, one-fourth of the cases of insanity. Moreau and others hold that the proportion is greater.   It appears, however, that mental alienation is not the only form in which the insanity of an ancestor may manifest itself. Dr. Morel gives the following instructive illustration of the 'varied and odd complications occurring in the hereditary transmission of nervous disease.'   He attended four brothers belonging to one family.   The grandfather of these children had died insane ; their father had never been able to continue long at anything ; their uncle, a man of great intellect and a distinguished physician, was noted for his eccentricities.   Now these four children, sprung from one stock, presented very different forms of physical disorder. One of them was a maniac, whose wild paroxysms occurred periodically.   The disorder of the second was melancholy madness ; he was reduced by his stupor to a merely automatic condition.   The third was characterised by an extreme irascibility and suicidal disposition.   The fourth manifested a strong liking for art ; but he was of a timorous and suspicious nature.   This story seems in some degree to give support to the theory that genius and mental aberration are not altogether alien ; that, in fact,

> Great wit to madness nearly is allied,
> And thin partitions do their bounds divide.

Of the hereditary transmission of idiotcy we naturally have not the same kind of evidence.   Madness often, if not generally, comes on or shows itself late in life, whereas idiotcy is not often developed in the adult. Insanity is the diseased or weakened condition of a mind possessing all the ordinary thinking faculties ; idiotcy implies that some of these faculties are altogether wanting. It has been asserted, by the way, that idiotcy is a product of civilisation. The civilised ' present, as peoples,' says Dr. Duncan, 'indications of defective vital force, which are not witnessed among those human beings that live in a state of nature. There must be something rotten in some parts of our boasted civilisation : and not only a something which has to do with our psychology, but a great deal more with our power of physical persistence. It is a fact that the type of the perfect minded, just above the highest idiots, or the simpletons, is more distinguishable amongst the most civilised of the civilised than among those who are the so-called children of nature. Dolts, boobies, stupids, *et hoc genus omne*, abound in young Saxondom ; but their representatives are rare amongst the tribes that are slowly disappearing before the white man.' But it seems barely possible that the difference may be due to the care with which civilised communities interfere to prevent the elimination of idiot infants by the summary process of destroying them. The writer from whom I have just quoted refers to the fact that, even under the Roman Empire, as during the Republic, idiots were looked upon as ' useless entities by the practical Roman.' They had no sanctity in his eyes, and hence their probable rarity ; doubtless the unfortunate children were neglected, and there is much reason for believing that they were ' exposed.' ' A congenital idiot soon begins to give trouble,' proceeds Dr. Duncan, 'and to excite unusual attention ; and, moreover, unless extra care is given to it, death is sure to ensue in early childhood.' May not idiot children in savage communities have an even worse chance of survival than under the Roman Empire? and may not dolts, boobies, and stupids, *et hoc genus omne*, among savages, have such inferior chances in the infantine and later in the adult struggle for existence, that we may explain thus the comparative rarity of these varieties in savage communities? It certainly does not seem to have been proved as yet that civilisation *per se* is favourable to the development of insanity.

The liking for strong drink, as is too well known, is often transmitted. It is remarked by Dr. Howe that 'the children of drunkards are deficient in bodily and vital energy, and are predisposed by their very organisation to have cravings for alcoholic stimulants. If they pursue the course of their fathers, which they have more temptation to follow and less power to avoid than the children of the temperate, they add to their hereditary weakness, and increase the tendency to idiotcy or insanity in their constitution ; and this they leave to their children after them.' Whatever opinion we may form on the general question of responsibility for offences of commission or of omission, on this special point all who are acquainted with the facts must agree, admitting that in some cases of inherited craving for alcoholic stimulants the responsibility of those who have failed and fallen in the strugg'e has been but small. 'The fathers have eaten sour grapes, and the children's teeth are set on edge.' Robert Collyer of Chicago, in his noble sermon ' The Thorn in the Flesh,' has well said, ' In the far-reaching influences that go to every life, and away backward as certainly as forward, children are sometimes born with appetites fatally strong in their nature. As they grow up the appetite grows with them, and speedily becomes a master, the master a tyrant ; and by the time he arrives at manhood, the man is a slave. I heard a man say that for eight-and-twenty years the soul within him had had to stand like an unsleeping sentinel, guarding his appetite for strong drink. To be a man at last under such a disadvantage, not to mention a saint, is as fine a piece of grace as can well be seen. There is no doctrine that demands a larger vision than this of the depravity of human nature. Old Dr. Mason used to say that "as much grace as would make John a saint, would hardly keep Peter from knocking a man down." '

There are some curious stories of special vices trans-mitted from parent to child, which, if true, are exceedingly significant, to say the least.[1] Gama Machado relates that a lady with whom he was acquainted, who possessed a large fortune, had a passion for gambling and passed whole nights at play. 'She died young,' he proceeds, 'of a pulmonary complaint. Her eldest son who was in appearance the image of his mother, had the same passion for play. He died of consumption like his mother, and at the same age ; his daughter who resembled him, inherited the same tastes, and died young.' Hereditary predisposition to theft, murder, and suicide, has been demonstrated in several cases. But the world at large is naturally indisposed to recognise con-genital tendency to crime as largely diminishing responsi-bility for offences or attempted offences of this kind. So far as the general interests of the community are concerned, the demonstrated fact that a thief or murderer has *inherited* his unpleasant tendency should be a *raison de plus* for prevent-ing the tendency from being transmitted any farther. In stamping out the hereditary ruffian or rascal by life imprison-ment, we not only get rid of the ' grown serpent ' but of the worm which

> Hath nature that in time would venom breed.

---

[1] The following statement from the researches of Brown-Sequard seems well worth noting in this connection :—' In the course of his masterly experimental investigations into the functions of the nervous system he discovered that, after a particular lesion of the spinal cord of guinea-pigs, a slight pinching of the skin of the face would throw the animal into a kind of epileptic convulsion. That this artificial epilepsy should be constantly producible in guinea-pigs, and not in any other animals experimented on, was in itself sufficiently singular ; and it was not less surprising that the tendency to it persisted after the lesion of the spinal cord seemed to have been. entirely recovered from. But it was far more wonderful that the offspring of these epileptic guinea-pigs showed the same predisposition, without having been themselves subjected to any lesion whatever ; whilst no such tendency showed itself in any of the large number of young bred by the same accurate observer from parents that had not thus been operated on.'

An illustration of the policy at least (we do not say the justice) of preventive measures in such cases, is shown in the case of a woman in America, of whom the world may fairly say what Father Paul remarked to gentle Alice Brown ; it 'never knew so criminal a family as hers.' A young woman of remarkably depraved character, infested, some seventy years since, the district of the Upper Hudson. At one stage of her youth she narrowly, and somewhat unfortunately, escaped death. Surviving, however, she bore many children, who in turn had large families, insomuch that there are now some eighty direct descendants, of whom one-fourth are convicted criminals, whilst the rest are drunkards, lunatics, paupers, and otherwise undesirable members of the community.

With facts such as these before us, we cannot doubt that in whatever degree variability may eliminate after awhile peculiar mental or moral tendencies, these are often transmitted for many generations before they die out. If it be unsafe to argue that the responsibility of those inheriting special characteristics is diminished, the duties of others towards them may justly be considered to be modified. Other duties than the mere personal control of tendencies which men may recognise in themselves are also introduced. If a man finds within himself an inherent tendency towards some sin, which yet he utterly detests, insomuch that while the spirit is willing the flesh is weak or perchance utterly powerless, he must recognise in his own life a struggle too painful and too hopeless to be handed down to others. As regards our relations to families in which criminal tendencies have been developed, either through the negligence of those around (as in certain dens in London where for centuries crime has swarmed and multiplied), or by unfortunate alliances, we may 'perceive here a divided duty.' It has been remarked that 'we do not set ourselves to train tigers and wolves into peaceful domestic animals ; we seek to extirpate them,' and the question has been asked, 'why should we act otherwise with beings, who, if human in form, are worse than wild beasts?' 'To educate the son of a garotter or a " corner-man " into an average Englishman,' may be 'about as promising a task as to train one of the latter into a Newton or a Milton.' But we must not too quickly despair of a task which may be regarded as a duty inherited from those who in past generations neglected it. There is no hope of the reversion of tiger or wolf to less savage types, for, far back as we can trace their ancestry, we find them savage of nature. With our criminal families the case is not so utterly hopeless. Extirpation being impossible (though easily talked of) without injustice which would be the parent of far greater troubles even than our criminal classes bring upon us, we should consider the elements of hope which the problem unquestionably affords. By making it the manifest interest of our criminal population to scatter, or, failing that, by leaving them no choice in the matter, the poison in their blood may before many generations be eradicated, not by wide-spreading merely, but because of the circumstance that only the better sort among them would have (when scattered) much chance of rearing families as well as of escaping imprisonment.

BODILY ILLNESS AS A MENTAL STIMULANT.

DURING special states of disease the mind sometimes develops faculties such as it does not possess when the body is in full health. Some of the abnormal qualities thus exhibited by the mind seem strikingly suggestive of the possible acquisition by the human race of similar powers under ordinary conditions. For this reason, though we fear there is no likelihood at present of any practical application of the knowledge we may obtain on this subject, it seems to me that there is considerable interest in examining the evidence afforded by the strange powers which the mind occasionally shows during diseases of the body, and especially during such diseases as are said, in unscientific but expressive language, to lower the tone of the nervous system.

We may begin by citing a case which seems exceedingly significant. Miss H. Martineau relates that a congenital idiot, who had lost his mother when he was less than two years old, when dying, 'suddenly turned his head, looked bright and sensible, and exclaimed, in a tone never heard from him before, "Oh my mother! how beautiful!" and sank down again—dead.' Dr. Carpenter cites this as a case of abnormal memory, illustrating his thesis that the basis of recollection 'may be laid at a very early period of life.' But the story seems to contain a deeper meaning. The poor idiot not only recalled a long-past time, a face that he had not seen for years except in dreams, but he gained for a moment a degree of intelligence which he had not possessed when in health. The quality of his brain was such, it appears, that with the ordinary activity of the circulation, the ordinary vitality of the organ, mental action was uncertain and feeble ; but when the circulation had all but ceased, when the nervous powers were all but prostrate, the feeble brain, though it may have become no stronger actually, became relatively stronger, in such sort that for the time specified, a mere moment before dissolution, the idiot became an intelligent being.

A somewhat similar case is on record in which an insane person, during that stage of typhus fever in which sane persons are apt to become delirious, became perfectly sane and reasonable, his insanity returning with returning health. Persons of strongest mind in health are often delirious for a short time before death. Since, then, the idiot in the same stage of approaching dissolution may become intelligent, while the insane may become sane under the conditions which make the sane become delirious, we recognise a relationship between the mental and bodily states which might be of considerable use in the treatment of mental diseases. It may well be that conditions of the nervous system which are to be avoided by persons of normal mental qualities may be advantageously superinduced in the case of those of abnormally weak or abnormally violent mind. It is noteworthy that different conditions would seem to be necessary for the idiotic and for the insane, if the cases cited sufficed to afford basis for generalisation. For the idiot of Miss Martineau's story became intelligent during the intense depression of the bodily powers immediately preceding dissolution, whereas the insane person became sane during that height of fever when delirium commonly makes its appearance.

Sir H. Holland mentions a case which shows that great bodily depression may affect a person of ordinary clear and powerful mind. 'I descended on one and the same day,' he says, 'two very deep mines in the Hartz Mountains, remaining some hours under ground in each. While in the second mine, and exhausted both from fatigue and inanition,

I felt the utter impossibility of talking longer with the German Inspector who accompanied me. Every German word and phrase deserted my recollection ; and it was not until I had taken food and wine, and been some time at rest, that I regained them again.'

A change in the mental condition is sometimes a sign of approaching serious illness, and is felt to be so by the person experiencing it. An American writer, Mr. Butterworth, quotes the following description given by a near relative of his who was suffering from extreme nervous debility. 'I am in constant fear of insanity,' she said, 'and I wish I could be moved to some retreat for the insane. I understand my condition perfectly ; my reason does not seem to be impaired; but I can think of *two things at the same time.* This is an indication of mental unsoundness, and is a terror to me. I do not seem to have slept at all for the last six months. If I sleep, it must be in a succession of vivid dreams that destroy all impression of somnolence. Since I have been in this condition I seem to have a very vivid impression of what happens to my children who are away from home, and I am often startled to hear that these impressions are correct. I seem to have also a certain power of anticipating what one is about to say, and to read the motives of others. I take no pleasure in this strange increase of mental power; it is all unnatural. I cannot live in this state long, and I often wish I were dead.'

It must, however, be remembered that persons who are in a state of extreme nervous debility, not only possess at times abnormal mental qualities, but are also affected morally. As Huxley has well remarked of some stories bearing on spiritualism, they come from persons who can hardly be trusted even according to their own account of themselves. Mr. Butterworth's relation described a mental condition which, even if quite correctly pictured as she understood it, may yet be explained without believing that any very marvellous increase had taken place in her mental powers. Among the vivid impressions which she constantly had of what might be happening to her children away from home, it would have been strange if some had not been correct. The power of anticipating what others were about to say is one which many imagine they have, mistaking the occasional coincidence between their guesses and what has been next said, for indications of a power which in reality they do not possess. And so also with regard to the motives of others. Many are apt, especially when out of health, to guess at others' motives, sometimes rightly, but oftener very wrongly, yet always rightly in their own belief, no matter what evidence may presently appear to the contrary.

The case cited by Mr. Butterworth affords evidence rather of the unhealthy condition of the patient's mind than of abnormal powers, except as regards the power of thinking of two things at the same time, which we may fairly assume was not ordinarily possessed by its relative. It is rather difficult to define such a power, however. Several persons have apparently possessed the power, showing it by doing two things at the same time which both appear to require thought, and even close attention. Julius Cæsar, for example, could write on one subject and dictate on another simultaneously. But in reality, even in cases such as these, the mind does not think of two things at once. It simply takes them in turn, doing enough with each, in a short time, a mere instant, perhaps, to give work to the pen or to the voice, as the case may be, for a longer time. When Cæsar was writing a sentence, he was not necessarily thinking of what he was writing. He had done the thinking part of the work before ; and was free, while continuing the mere mechanical process of writing, to think of matter for dictation to his secretary. So also while he was speaking he was free to think of matter for writing. If, indeed, the thought for each sentence of either kind had occupied an appreciable time, there would have been interruptions of his writing, if not of his dictation (dictation is not commonly a continuous process under any circumstances, even when shorthand writers take down the words). But a practised writer or speaker can in a moment form a sentence which shall occupy a minute in writing and several seconds in speaking.

I certainly do not myself claim the power of thinking of two things at once,—nay, I believe that no one ever had or could have such a power : yet I find it perfectly easy, when lecturing, to arrange the plan for the next ten minutes' exposition of a scientific subject, and to adopt the words themselves for the next twenty seconds or so, while continuing to speak without the least interruption. I can also work out a calculation on the black-board while con-tinuing to speak of matters outside the subject of the calcula-tion. It is more a matter of habit than an indication of any mental power, natural or acquired, to speak or write sentences, even of considerable length, after the mind has passed on to other matters. In a similar way some persons can write different words with the right and left hands, and this, too, while speaking of other matters. (I have seen this done by Professor Morse, the American naturalist, whose two hands added words to the diagrams he had drawn while his voice dealt with other parts of the drawing : to add to the wonder, too, he wrote the words indifferently from right to left or from left to right.) In reality the person who thus does two things at once is no more thinking of two things at once than a clock is, when the striking and the working machinery are both in action at the same time.[1]

[1] Since the above was written I have noticed a passage in Dr. Carpenter's *Mental Physiology*, p. 719, bearing on the matter I have been dealing with :—' The following statement recently made to me by a gentleman of high intelligence, the editor of a most important pro-vincial newspaper, would be almost incredible, if cases somewhat similar were not already familiar to us :—' I was formerly,' he said, ' a reporter in the House of Commons ; and it several times happened to me that, having fallen asleep from sheer fatigue towards the end of a debate, I had found, on awaking after a short interval of entire unconsciousness, that I had continued to note down correctly the speaker's words.' ' I believe,' he added, ' that this is not an uncom-mon experience among Parliamentary reporters.' The reading aloud with correct emphasis and intonation, or the performance of a piece of music, or (as in the case of Albert Smith) the recitation of a frequently-

As an illustration of special mental power shown in health, by a person whose mental condition in illness we shall consider afterwards, Sir Walter Scott may be mentioned. The account given by his amanuensis has seemed surprising to many, unfamiliar with the nature of literary composition (at least after long practice), but is in reality such as anyone who writes much can quite readily understand, or might even have known must necessarily be correct. ' His thoughts,' says the secretary to whom Scott dictated his *Life of Napoleon Buonaparte*, ' flowed easily and felicitously, without any difficulty to lay hold of them or to find appropriate language' (which, by the way, is more than all would say who had read Scott's *Life of Buonaparte*, and certainly more than can be said of his secretary, unless it really was a familiar experience with him to be unable to lay hold of his thoughts). ' This was evident by the absence of all solicitude (*miseria cogitandi*) from his countenance. He sat in

repeated composition, whilst the conscious mind is *entirely engrossed* in its own thoughts and feelings, may be thus accounted for without the supposition that the mind is actively engaged in two different operations at the same moment, which would seem tantamount to saying that there are two egos in the same organism.' An instance in my own experience seems even more remarkable than the reporter's work during sleep, for he had but to continue a mechanical process, whereas in my case there must have been thought. Late one evening at Cambridge I began a game of chess with a fellow-student (now a clergyman, and well known in chess circles). I was tired after a long day's rowing, but continued the game to the best of my ability, until at a certain stage I fell asleep, or rather fell into a waking dream. At any rate all remembrance of what passed after that part of the game had entirely escaped me when I awoke or returned to consciousness about three in the morning. The chessboard was there, but the men were not as when the last conscious move was made. The opponent's king was checkmated. I supposed my opponent had set the men in this position either as a joke or in trying over some end game. But I was assured that the game had continued to the end, and that I had won, apparently playing as if fully conscious ! Of course I cannot certify this of my own knowledge.

R

his chair, from which he rose now and then, took a volume from the book-case, consulted it, and restored it to the shelf —all without intermission in the current of ideas, which continued to be delivered with no less readiness than if his mind had been wholly occupied with the words he was uttering. It soon became apparent to me, however, that he was carrying on two distinct trains of thought, one of which was already arranged and in the act of being spoken, while at the same time he was in advance, considering what was afterwards to be said. 'This I discovered' (he should rather have said, ' this I was led to infer') ' by his sometimes introducing a word which was wholly out of place—*entertained* instead of *denied*, for example—but which I presently found to belong to the next sentence, perhaps four or five lines further on, which he had been preparing at the very moment when he gave me the words of the one that preceded it.' In the same way I have often unconsciously substituted one word for another in lecturing, the word used always belonging to a later sentence than the word intended to be used. I have noticed also this peculiarity, that when a substitution of this kind has been once made, an effort is required to avoid repeating the mistake, even if it be not repeated quite unconsciously to the end of the discourse. In this way, for example, I once throughout an entire lecture used the word 'heavens' for the word 'screen' (the screen on which lantern pictures were shown). A similar peculiarity may be noticed with written errors. Thus in my treatise on a scientific subject, in which the utmost care had been given to minute points of detail, I once wrote ' seconds ' for ' minutes ' throughout several pages—in fact, from the place where first the error was made, to the end of the chapter. (See the *first* edition of my *Transits of Venus*, pp. 131–136, noting as an additional peculiarity that the whole object of the chapter in which this mistake was made was to show how many minutes of difference existed between the occurrence of certain events.)

An even more curious instance of a mistake arising from doing one thing while thinking of another occurred to me fourteen years ago. I was correcting the proof-sheets of an astronomical treatise in which occurred these words : 'Calling the mean distance of the earth 1, Saturn's mean distance is 9·539 ; again, calling the earth's period 1, Saturn's mean period is 29·457 :—now what relation exists between these numbers 9·539 and 29·457 and their powers ? The first is less than the second, but the square of the first is plainly greater than the second ; we must therefore try higher powers, &c. &c.' The passage was quite correct as it stood, and if the two processes by which I was correcting verbal errors and following the sense of the passage had been really continuous processes of thought, unquestionably the passage would have been left alone. If the passage had been erroneous and had been simply left in that condition the case would have been one only too familiar to those who have had occasion to correct proofs. But what I actually did was deliberately to make nonsense of the passage while improving the sound of the· second sentence. I made it run, 'the first is less than the second, but the square of the first is plainly greater than the square of the second,' the absurdity of which statement a child would detect. If the first proof in its correct form, with the incorrect correction carefully written down in the margin, had not existed when, several months later, the error was pointed out in the *Quarterly Journal of Science,* I should have felt sure that I had written the words wrongly at the outset. For blunders such as this are common enough. But that I should deliberately have taken a correctly worded sentence and altered it into utter absurdity I could not, but for the evidence, have believed to be possible. The case plainly shows that not only may two things be done at once when the mind, nevertheless, is thinking only of one, but that something may be done which suggests deliberate reflection when in reality the mind is elsewhere or not occupied at all. For in this case both the processes on which

I was engaged were manifestly carried on without thought, one being purely mechanical and the other, though requiring thought if properly attended to, being so imperfectly effected as to show that no thought was given to it.

To return to Sir Walter Scott. It is known but too well that during the later years of his life there came with bodily prostration a great but not constant failure of his mental powers. Some of the phenomena presented during this part of his career are strikingly illustrative of abnormal mental action occurring even at times when the mental power is on the whole much weakened. *The Bride of Lammermoor*, though not one of the best of Scott's novels, is certainly far above such works as *Count Robert of Paris*, *The Betrothed*, and *Castle Dangerous*. Its popularity may perhaps be attributed chiefly to the deep interest of the ' ower true tale ' on which it is founded : but some of the characters are painted with exceeding skill. Lucy herself is almost a nonentity, and Edgar is little more than a gloomy, unpleasant man, made interesting only by the troubles which fall on him. But Caleb Balderstone and Ailsie Gourlay stand out from the canvas as if alive ; they are as lifelike and natural, yet as thoroughly individualised as Edie Ochiltree and Meg Merrilies. The novel neither suggested when it first appeared, nor has been regarded even after the facts became known, as suggesting that Scott, when he wrote it, was in bad health. Yet it was produced under pressure of severe illness, and when Scott was at least in this sense unconscious, that nothing of what he said and did in connection with the work was remembered when he recovered. ' The book,' says James Ballantyne, ' was not only written, but published, before Mr. Scott was able to rise from his bed ; and he assured me that when it was first put into his hands in a complete shape, *he did not recollect one single incident, character, or conversation it contained!* He did not desire me to understand, nor did I understand, that his illness had erased from his memory the original incidents of the story, with which he had been acquainted from his boyhood. These remained rooted where they had ever been ; or, to speak more explicitly, he remembered the general facts of the existence of the father and mother, of the son and daughter, of the rival lovers, of the compulsory marriage, and the attack made by the bride upon the hapless bridegroom, with the general catastrophe of the whole. *All these things he recollected*, just as he did before he took to his bed ; *but he literally recollected nothing else*—not a single character woven by the romancer, not one of the many scenes and points of humour, not *anything with which he was himself connected*, as the writer of the work.

Later, when Scott was breaking down under severe and long-continued labour, and first felt the approach of the illness which ultimately ended in death, he experienced strange mental phenomena. In his diary for February 17, 1829, he notes that on the preceding day, at dinner, though in company with two or three old friends, he was haunted by 'a sense of pre-existence,' a confused idea that nothing that passed was said for the first time ; that the same topics had been discussed, and that the same persons had expressed the same opinions before. 'There was a vile sense of a want of reality in all that I did or said.'

Dr. Reynolds related to Dr. Carpenter a case in which a Dissenting minister, who was in apparently sound health, was rendered apprehensive of brain-disease—though, as it seemed, without occasion—by a lapse of memory similar to that experienced by Sir Walter Scott. He 'went through an entire pulpit service on a certain Sunday morning with the most perfect consistency—his choice of hymns and lessons, and his *extempore* prayer being all related to the subject of his sermon. On the following Sunday morning he went through the introductory part of the service in precisely the same manner—giving out the same hymns, reading the same lessons, and directing the *extempore* prayer in the same channel. He then gave out the same text and preached the very same sermon as he had done on the previous Sunday. When he came down from the pulpit, it was found that he had not the smallest remembrance of having gone through precisely the same service on the previous Sunday ; and when he was assured of it, he felt considerable uneasiness lest his lapse of memory should indicate some impending attack of illness.   None such, however, supervened ; and no *rationale* can be given of this curious occurrence, the subject of it not being liable to fits of " absence of mind " and not having had his thoughts engrossed at the time by any other special pre-occupation.'   It is possible that the explanation here is the simple one of mere coincidence.   Whether this explanation is available or not would depend entirely on the question whether the preacher's memory was ordinarily trustworthy or not, whether in fact he would remember the arrangements, prayers, sermon, &c., he had given on any occasion.   These matters becoming, after long habit, almost automatic, it might very well happen that the person going through such duties would remember them no longer and no better than one who had been present when they were performed, and who had not paid special attention to them. That if he had thus unconsciously carried out his duties on one Sunday he should (being to this degree forgetful) con- duct them in precisely the same way on the next Sunday, would rather tend to show that his mental faculties were in excellent working order than the reverse.   Wendell Holmes tells a story which effectively illustrates my meaning ; and he tells it so pleasantly (as usual) that I shall quote it unaltered.   'Sometimes, but rarely,' he says, 'one may be caught making the same speech twice over, and yet be held blameless.   Thus a certain lecturer' (Holmes himself, doubt- less), 'after performing in an inland city, where dwells a *littératrice* of note, was invited to meet her and others over the social tea-cup.   She pleasantly referred to his many wanderings in his new occupation.   "Yes," he replied, "I am like the huma, the bird that never lights, being always in the cars, as he is always on the wing."   Years elapsed.   The lecturer visited the same place once more for the same purpose.   Another social cup after the lecture, and a second meeting with the distinguished lady. " You are constantly going from place to place," she said. " Yes," he answered, " I am like the huma," and finished the sentence as before. What horror when it flashed over him that he had made this fine speech, word for word, twice over ! Yet it was not true, as the lady might perhaps have fairly inferred, that he had embellished his conversation with the huma daily during that whole interval of years. On the contrary, he had never once thought of the odious fowl until the recurrence of precisely the same circumstances brought up precisely the same idea.' He was not in 'the slightest degree afraid of brain-disease. On the contrary, he considered the circumstance indicative of good order in the mental mechanism. 'He ought to have been proud,' says Holmes, speaking for him, and meaning no doubt that he *was* proud, ' of the accuracy of his mental adjustments. *Given certain factors, and a sound brain should always evolve the same fixed product with the certainty of Babbage's calculating machine.'*

Somewhat akin to the unconscious recurrence of mental processes after considerable intervals of time is the tendency to imitate the actions of others as though sharing in their thoughts, and according to many *because* mind acts upon mind. This tendency, though not always associated with disease, is usually a sign of bodily illness. Dr. Carpenter mentions the following singular case, but rather as illustrating generally the influence of suggestions derived from external sources in determining the current of thought, than as showing how prone the thoughts are to run in undesirable currents when the body is out of health :—' During an epidemic of fever, in which an active delirium had been a common symptom, it was observed that many of the patients of one particular physician were possessed by a strong tendency to throw themselves out of the window, whilst no such tendency presented itself in unusual frequency in the practice of others. The author's informant, Dr. C., himself a distinguished professor in the university, explained the tendency of what had occurred within his own knowledge ;

he having been himself attacked by the fever, and having
been under the care of this physician, his friend and col-
league, Dr. A.   Another of Dr. A.'s patients whom we shall
call Mr. B., seems to have been the first to make the attempt
in question; and impressed with the necessity of taking due
precautions, Dr. A. then visited Dr. C., *in whose hearing* he
gave directions to have the windows properly secured, as Mr.
B. had attempted to throw himself out. Now Dr. C. distinctly
remembers, that although he had not previously experienced
any such desire, it came upon him with great urgency as
soon as ever the idea was thus suggested to him ; his mind
being just in that state of incipient delirium which is marked
by the temporary dominance of some one idea, and by the
want of volitional power to withdraw the attention from it.
And he deemed it probable that, as Dr. A. went on to Mr.
D., Mr. E., &c., and gave similar directions, a like desire
would be excited in the minds of all those who might happen to be in the same impressible condition.' The case is
not only interesting as showing how the mind in disease
receives certain impressions more strongly than in health,
and in a sense may thus be said to possess for the time an
abnormal power, but it affords a useful hint to doctors and
nurses, who do not always (the latter indeed scarcely ever)
consider the necessity of extreme caution when speaking
about their patients and in their presence. It is probable
that a considerable proportion of the accidents, fatal and
otherwise, which have befallen delirious patients might be
traced to incautious remarks made in their hearing by foolish
nurses or forgetful doctors.

In some cases doctors have had to excite a strong antagonistic feeling against tendencies of this kind. Thus Zerffi
relates that an English physician was once consulted by the
mistress of a ladies' school where many girls had become
liable to fits of hysterics. He tried several remedies, but in
vain. At last, justly regarding the epidemic as arising from
the influence of imagination on the weaker girls (one hysterical girl having infected the others), he determined to exert

a stronger antagonistic influence on the weak minds of his patients. He therefore remarked casually to the mistress of the school, in the hearing of the girls, that he had now tried all methods but one, which he would try, as a last resource, when next he called—'the application of a red-hot iron to the spine of the patients so as to quiet their nervously-excited systems.' 'Strange to say,' remarks Zerffi—meaning, no doubt, ' it is hardly necessary to say that'—'the red-hot iron was never applied, for the hysterical attacks ceased as if by magic.'

In another case mentioned by Zerffi, a revival mania in a large school near Cologne was similarly brought to an abrupt end. The Government sent an inspector. He found that the boys had visions of Christ, the Virgin, and departed saints. He threatened to close the school if these visions continued, and thus to exclude the students from all the prospects which their studies afforded them. 'The effect was as magical as the red-hot iron remedy—the revivals ceased as if by magic.'

The following singular cases are related in Zimmermann's *Solitude :*—A nun, in a very large convent in France, began to mew like a cat. At last all the nuns began to mew together every day at a certain time, and continued mewing for several hours together. This daily cat-concert continued, until the nuns were informed that a company of soldiers was placed by the police before the entrance to the convent, and that the soldiers were provided with rods with which they would whip the nuns until they promised not to mew any more.' . . . 'In the fifteenth century, a nun in a German convent fell to biting her companions. In the course of a short time all the nuns of this convent began biting each other. The news of this infatuation among the nuns soon spread, and excited the same elsewhere ; the biting mania passing from convent to convent through a great part ot Germany. It afterwards visited the nunneries of Holland, and even spread as far as Rome.' No suggestion of bodily disease is made in either case. But anyone who considers

how utterly unnatural is the manner of life in monastic communities will not need the evidence derived from the spread
of such preposterous habits to be assured that in convents
the perfectly sane mind in a perfectly healthy body must be
the exception rather than the rule.

The dancing mania, which spread through a large part of
Europe in the fourteenth and fifteenth centuries, although it
eventually attacked persons who were seemingly in robust
health, yet had its origin in disease.   Dr. Hecker, who has
given the most complete account we have of this strange
mania, in his *Epidemics of the Middle Ages*, says that when
the disease was completely developed the attack commenced
with epileptic convulsions.   'Those affected fell to the
ground senseless, panting and labouring for breath.   They
foamed at the mouth, and suddenly springing up began their
dance amidst strange contortions.   They formed circles
hand in hand, and appearing to have lost all control over
their senses continued dancing, regardless of the bystanders,
for hours together, in wild delirium, until at length they fell to
the ground in a state of exhaustion.   They then complained
of extreme oppression, and groaned as if in the agonies of
death, until they were swathed in clothes bound tightly round
their waists ; upon which they again recovered, and remained free from complaint until the next attack. . . While
dancing they neither saw nor heard, being insensible to
external impressions through the senses ; but they were
haunted by visions, their fancies conjuring up spirits, whose
names they shrieked out ; and some of them afterwards
asserted that they felt as if they had been immersed in a
stream of blood, which obliged them to leap so high.
Others during the paroxysm saw the heavens open, and
the Saviour enthroned with the Virgin Mary, according as
the religious notions of the age were strangely and variously
reflected in their imaginations.'   The epidemic attacked
people of all stations, but especially those who led a seden-
tary life, such as shoemakers and tailors ; yet even the most
robust peasants finally yielded to it   They 'abandoned

their labours in the fields as if they were possessed by evil spirits, and those affected were seen assembling indiscriminately from time to time, at certain appointed places, and unless prevented by the lookers-on, continued to dance without intermission, until their very last breath was expended. Their fury and extravagance of demeanour so completely deprived them of their senses, that many of them dashed their brains out against the walls and corners of buildings, or rushed headlong in rapid rivers, where they found a watery grave. Roaring and foaming as they were, the bystanders could only succeed in restraining them by placing benches and chairs in their way, so that by the high leaps they were thus tempted to take, their strength might be exhausted. As soon as this was the case they fell, as it were, lifeless to the ground, and by very slow degrees recovered their strength. Many there were who even with all this exertion had not expended the violence of the tempest which raged within them ; but awoke with newly revived powers, and again and again mixed with the crowd of dancers ; until at length the violent excitement of their disordered nerves was allayed by the great involuntary exertion of their limbs, and the mental disorder was calmed by the exhaustion of the body. The cure effected by these stormy attacks was in many cases so perfect, that some patients returned to the factory or plough, as if nothing had happened. Others, on the contrary, paid the penalty of their folly by so total a loss of power, that they could not regain their former health, even by the employment of the most strengthening remedies.'

It may be doubted, perhaps, by some whether such instances as these illustrate so much the state to which the mind is reduced when the body is diseased, as the state to which the body is reduced when the mind is diseased, though, as we have seen, the dancing mania when fully developed followed always on bodily illness. In the cases we now have to deal with, the diseased condition of the body was unmistakable.

Mrs. Hemans on her deathbed said that it was impossible for imagination to picture or pen to describe the delightful visions which passed before her mind. They made her waking hours more delightful than those passed in sleep. It is evident that these visions had their origin in the processes of change affecting the substance of the brain as the disease of the body progressed. But it does not follow that the substance of the brain was undergoing changes necessarily tending to its ultimate decay and dissolution. Quite possibly the changes were such as might occur under the influence of suitable medicinal or stimulant substances, and without any subsequent ill effects. Dr. Richardson, in an interesting article on ether-drinking and extra-alcoholic intoxication (*Gentleman's Magazine* for October), makes a remark which suggests that the medical men of our day look forward to the discovery of means for obtaining some such influence over the action of the brain. After describing the action of methylic and ethylic ethers in his own case, he says : ' They who have felt this condition, who have lived as it were in another life, however transitorily, are easily led to declare with Davy that "nothing exists but thoughts ! the universe is composed of impressions, ideas, pleasures, and pains !" I believe it is so, and that we might by scientific art, and there is such an art, learn to live altogether in a new sphere of impressions, ideas, pleasures, and pains.' ' But stay,' he adds, as if he had said too much, ' I am anticipating, unconsciously, something else that is in my mind. The rest is silence ; I must return to the world in which we now live, and which all know.'

Mr. Butterworth mentions the case of the Rev. William Tennent, of Freehold, New Jersey, as illustrative of strange mental faculties possessed during disease. Tennent was supposed to be far gone in consumption. At last, after a protracted illness, he seemingly died, and preparations were made for his funeral. Not only were his friends deceived, but he was deceived himself, for he thought he was dead, and that his spirit had entered Paradise. ' His soul, as he thought, was borne aloft to celestial altitudes, and was enraptured by visions of God and all the hosts of Heaven.

He seemed to dwell in an enchanted region of limitless light and inconceivable splendour. At last an angel came to him and told him that he must go back. Darkness, like an overawing shadow, shut out the celestial glories; and, full of sudden horror, he uttered a deep groan. This dismal utterance was heard by those around him, and prevented him from being buried alive, after all the preparations had been made for the removal of the body.'

We must not fall into the mistake of supposing, however, as many seem to do, that the visions seen under such conditions, or by ecstatics, really present truths of which the usual mental faculties could not become cognisant. We have heard such cases as the deathbed visions of Mrs. Hemans, and the trance visions of Tennent, urged as evidence in favour of special forms of doctrine. We have no thought of attacking these, but assuredly they derive no support from evidence of this sort. The dying Hindoo has visions which the Christian would certainly not regard as heaven-born. The Mahomedan sees the plains of Paradise, peopled by the houris of his heaven, but we do not on that account accept the Koran as the sole guide to religious truth. The fact is, that the visions pictured by the mind during the disease of the body, or in the ecstatic condition, have their birth in the mind itself, and take their form from the teachings with which that mind has been imbued. They may, indeed, seem utterly unlike those we should expect from the known character of the visionary, just as the thoughts of a dying man may be, and often are, very far removed from the objects which had occupied all his attention during the later years of his life. But if the history of the childhood and youth of an ecstatic could be fully known, or if (which is exceed-ingly unlikely) we could obtain a strictly truthful account of such matters from himself, we should find nearly every circumstance of his visions explained, or at least an explanation suggested. For, after all, much which would be necessary to exactly show the origin of all he saw, would be lost, since the brain retains impressions of many things of which the conscious memory has entirely passed away.

The vivid picturing of forgotten events of life is a familiar experience of the opium-eater. Thus De Quincey says : ' The minutest incidents of childhood or forgotten scenes of later years, were often revived. I could not be said to recollect them, for if I had been told of them when waking, I should not have been able to acknowledge them as part of my past experience. But placed as they were before me in dreams like intuitions, and clothed in all their evanescent circumstances and accompanying feelings, I recognised them instantaneously.' A similar return of long-forgotten scenes and incidents to the mind may be noticed, though not to the same degree, when wine has been taken in moderate quantity after a long fast.

The effects of hachisch are specially interesting in this connection, because, unless a very powerful dose has been taken, the hachischin does not wholly lose the power of introspection, so that he is able afterwards to recall what has passed through his mind when he was under the influence of the drug. Now Moreau, in his interesting *Etudes Psychologiques* (*Du Hachich et d'Aliénation Mentale*), says that the first result of a dose sufficient to produce the *hachisch fantasia* is a feeling of intense happiness. 'It is really *happiness* which is produced by the hachisch ; and by this simply an enjoyment entirely moral, and by no means sensual as we might be induced to suppose. This is surely a very curious circumstance ; and some remarkable inferences might be drawn from it ; this, for instance, among others—that every feeling of joy and gladness, even when the cause of it is exclusively moral—that those enjoyments which are least connected with material objects, the most spiritual, the most ideal, may be nothing else than sensations purely physical, developed in the interior of the system, as are those procured by hachisch. At least so far as relates to that of which we are internally conscious, there is no distinction between these two orders of sensations, in spite of the diversity in the causes to which they are due; for the hachisch-eater is happy, not like the gourmand or the famished man when satisfying his appetite, or the voluptuary in gratifying his amative desires, but like him who hears idings which fill him with joy, like the miser counting his treasures, the gambler who is successful at play, or the ambitious man who is intoxicated with success.'

My special object, however, in noting the effects of opium and hachisch, is rather to note how the mental processes or faculties observed during certain states of disease may be produced artificially, than to enter into the considerations discussed by Dr. Moreau. It is singular that while the Mohamedan order of Hachischin (or Assassins) bring about by the use of their favourite drug such visions as accompany the progress of certain forms of disease, the Hindoo devotees called the Yogi are able to produce artificially the state of mind and body recognised in cataleptic patients. The less-advanced Yogi can only enter the state of abstraction called reverie; but the higher orders can simulate absolute inanition, the heart apparently ceasing to beat, the lungs to act, and the nerves to convey impressions to the brain, even though the body be subjected to processes which would cause extreme torture under ordinary conditions. 'When in this state,' says Carpenter, 'the Yogi are supposed to be completely possessed by Brahma, "the supreme soul," and to be incapable of sin in thought, word, or deed.' It has been supposed that this was the state into which those entered who in old times were resorted to as oracles. But it has happened that in certain stages of disease the power of assuming the death-like state has been possessed for a time. Thus Colonel Townsend, who died in 1797, we read, had in his last sickness the extraordinary power of apparently dying and returning to life again at will. ' I found his pulse sink gradually,' says Dr. Cheyne, who attended him, ' so that I could not feel it by the most exact or nice touch. Dr. Raymond could not detect the least motion of the heart, nor Dr. Skrine the least soil of the breath upon the bright mirror held to the mouth. We began to fear he was actually dead. He then began to breathe softly.' Colonel Townsend repeated the experiment several times during his illness, and could always render himself insensible at will.

Lastly, I may mention a case, which, however, though illustrating in some degree the influence of bodily illness on the mind, shows still more strikingly how the mind may influence the body—that of Louise Lateau, the Belgian peasant. This girl had been prostrated by a long and exhausting illness, from which she recovered rapidly after receiving the sacrament. This circumstance made a strong impression on her mind. Her thoughts dwelt constantly on the circumstances attending the death of Christ. At length she noticed that, on every Friday, blood came from a spot in her left side. 'In the course of a few months similar bleeding spots established themselves on the front and back of each hand, and on the upper surface of each foot, while a circle of small spots formed in the forehead, and the hæmorrhage from these recurred every Friday, sometimes to a considerable amount. About the same time, fits of ecstasy began to occur, commencing every Friday between eight and nine in the morning, and ending about six in the evening ; interrupting her in conversation, in prayer, or in manual occupations. This state,' says Dr. Carpenter, 'appears to have been intermediate between that of the biologised and that of the hypnotised subject ; for whilst as unconscious as the latter of all sense-impressions, she retained, like the former, a recollection of all that had passed through her mind during the ecstasy. She described herself as suddenly plunged into a vast flood of bright light, from which more or less distinct forms began to evolve themselves ; and she then witnessed the several scenes of the Passion successively passing before her. She minutely described the cross and the vestments, the wounds, the crown of thorns about the head of the Saviour, and gave various details regarding the persons about the cross, the disciples, holy women, Jews and Roman soldiers. And the progress of her vision might be traced by the succession of actions she performed at various stages of it : most of these movements were expressive of her own emotions, whilst regularly about three in the afternoon she extended her limbs in the form of a cross. The fit terminated with a state of extreme physical prostration ; the pulse being scarcely perceptible, the breathing slow and feeble, and the whole surface bedewed with a cold perspiration. After this state had continued for about ten minutes, a return to the normal condition rapidly took place.'

There seems no reason for supposing that there was any deceit on the part of Louise Lateau herself, though that she was self-deceived no one can reasonably doubt. Of course many in Belgium, especially the more ignorant and superstitious (including large numbers of the clergy and of religious orders of men and women), believed that her ecstasies were miraculous, and no doubt she believed so herself. But none of the circumstances observed in her case, or related by her, were such as the physiologist would find any difficulty in accepting or explaining. Her visions were such as might have been expected in a person of her peculiar nervous organisation, weakened as her body had been by long illness, and her mind affected by what she regarded as her miraculous recovery. As to the transudation of blood from the skin, Dr. Tuke, in his 'Illustrations of the Influence of the Mind upon the Body in Health and Disease' (p. 267), shows the phenomenon to be explicable naturally. It is a well-authenticated fact, that under strong emotional excitement blood escapes through the perspiratory ducts, apparently through the rupture of the walls of the capillary passages of the skin.

We see, then, in Louise Lateau's case, how the mind affected by disease may acquire faculties not possessed during health, and how in turn the mind thus affected may influence the body so strangely as to suggest to ignorant or foolish persons the operation of supernatural agencies.

s

The general conclusion to which we seem led by the observed peculiarities in the mental faculties during disease is, that the mind depends greatly on the state of the body for the co-ordination of its various powers.   In health, these are related in what may be called the normal manner. Faculties capable of great development under other conditions exist in moderate degree only, while probably, either consciously or unconsciously, certain faculties are held in control by others.   But during illness, faculties not ordinarily used suddenly or very rapidly acquire undue predominance, and controlling faculties usually effective are greatly weakened.   Then for a while the mental capacity seems entirely changed.   Powers supposed not to exist at all (for of mental faculties, as of certain other qualities, *de non existentibus et de non apparentibus eadem est ratio*) seem suddenly created, as if by a miracle.   Faculties ordinarily so strong as to be considered characteristic seem suddenly destroyed, since they no longer produce any perceptible effect.   Or, as Brown-Sequard says, summing up the results of a number of illustrative cases described in a course of lectures delivered in Boston : 'It would seem that the mind is largely dependent on physical conditions for the exercise of its faculties, and that its strength and most remarkable powers, as well as its apparent weakness, are often most clearly shown and recognised by some inequality of action in periods of disturbed and greatly impaired health.'

DUAL CONSCIOUSNESS.

RATHER more than two years ago I considered in the pages of 'Science Byways' the theory originally propounded by Sir Henry Holland, but then recently advocated by Dr. Brown-Sequard, of New York, that we have two brains, each perfectly sufficient for the full performance of mental functions. I did not for my own part either advocate or oppose that theory, but simply considered the facts which had been urged in support of it, or which then occurred to me as bearing upon it, whether for or against. I showed, however, that some classes of phenomena which had been quoted in support of the theory seemed in reality opposed to it, when all the circumstances were considered. For example, Brown-Sequard had referred to some of those well-known cases in which during severe illness a language forgotten in the patient's ordinary condition had been recalled, the recollection of the language enduring only while the illness lasted. I pointed to a case in which there had not been two mental conditions only, as indicated by the language of the patient, but three; the person in question having in the beginning of his illness spoken English only, in the middle of his illness French only, and on the day of his death Italian only (the language of his childhood). The interpretation of that case, and of others of a similar kind, must, I remarked, be very different from that which Brown-Sequard assigned, perhaps correctly, 'to cases of twofold mental life.' A case of the last-named kind has recently been discussed in scientific circles, which seems to me to bear very forcibly on the question whether Holland's theory of a dual brain is correct.   I propose briefly to describe and examine this case, and some others belonging to the same class, two of which were touched upon in my former essay, but slightly only, as forming but a small part of the evidence dealt with by Brown-Sequard, whose arguments I was then considering.   I wish now to deal, not with the question of the duality of the brain, but with the more general question of dual or intermittent consciousness.

Among the cases dealt with by Brown-Sequard was that of a boy at Notting Hill, who had two mental lives. Neither life presented anything specially remarkable in itself.   The boy was a well-mannered lad in his abnormal as well as in his normal condition,—or one might almost say (as will appear more clearly after other cases have been considered) that the *two* boys were quiet and well-behaved.   But the two mental lives were entirely distinct.   In his normal condition the boy remembered nothing which had happened in his abnormal condition ; and *vice versâ*, in his abnormal condition he remembered nothing which had happened in his normal condition.   He changed from either condition to the other in the same manner.   'The head was seen to fall suddenly, and his eyes closed, but he remained erect if standing at the time, or if sitting he remained in that position (if talking, he stopped for a while, and if moving, he stopped moving) ; and after a minute or two his head rose, he started up, opened his eyes, and was wide awake again.' While the head was drooped he appeared as if either sleeping or falling asleep.   He remained in the abnormal state for a period which varied between one hour and three hours ; it appears that every day, or nearly every day, he fell once into his abnormal condition.

This case need not detain us long ; but there are some points in it which deserve more attention than they seem to have received from Dr. Brown-Sequard.   It is clear that if the normal and abnormal mental lives of this boy had been entirely distinct, then in the abnormal condition he would have been ignorant and—in those points in which manners depend on training—ill-mannered. He would have known only, in this condition, what he had learned in this condition; and as only about a tenth part of his life was passed in the abnormal condition, and presumably that portion of his life not usually selected as a suitable time for teaching him, the abnormal boy would of necessity have been much more backward in all things which the young are taught than the normal boy. As nothing of this kind was noted, it would appear probable that the boy's earlier years were common to both lives, and that his unconsciousness of his ordinary life during the abnormal condition extended only to those parts of his ordinary life which had passed since these seizures began. Unfortunately, Brown-Sequard's account does not mention when this had happened.

It does not appear that the dual brain theory is required so far as this case is concerned. The phenomena seem rather to suggest a peculiarity in the circulation of the brain corresponding in some degree to the condition probably prevailing during somnambulism or hypnotism, though with characteristic differences. It may at least be said that no more valid reason exists for regarding this boy's case as illustrating the distinctive duality of the brain than for so regarding some of the more remarkable cases of somnambulism ; for though these differ in certain respects from the boy's case, they resemble it in the circumstances on which Brown Sequard's argument is founded. Speaking generally of hypnotism,—that is, of somnambulism artificially produced,—Dr. Carpenter says, 'In hypnotism, as in ordinary somnambulism, no remembrance whatever is preserved, in the waking state, of anything that may have occurred during its continuance ; although the previous train of thought may be taken up and continued uninterruptedly on the next occasion when hypnotism is induced.' In these respects the phenomena of hypnotism precisely resemble those of dual consciousness as observed in the boy's case. In what follows, we observe features of divergence. Thus ' when the mind is not excited to activity by the stimulus of external impressions, the hypnotised subject appears to be profoundly asleep ; a state of complete torpor, in fact, being usually the first result of the process just described, and any subsequent manifestation of activity being procurable only by the prompting of the operator. The hypnotised subject, too, rarely opens his eyes ; his bodily movements are usually slow ; his mental operations require a considerable time for their performance ; and there is altogether an appearance of heaviness about him which contrasts strongly with the comparatively wide-awake air of him who has not passed beyond the ordinary biological state.'

It would not be easy to find an exact parallel to the case of the two-lived boy in any recorded instance of somnambulism. In fact, it is to be remembered that recorded instances of mental phenomena are all selected for the very reason that they are exceptional, so that it would be unreasonable to expect them closely to resemble each other. One case, however, may be cited, which in certain points resembles the case of Dr. Brown-Sequard's patient. It occurred within Dr. Carpenter's own experience. A young lady of highly nervous temperament suffered from a long and severe illness, characterised by all the most marked forms of hysterical disorder. In the course of this illness came a time when she had a succession of somnambulistic seizures. 'The state of somnambulism usually supervened in this case in the waking state, instead of arising, as it more commonly does, out of the conditions of ordinary sleep. In this condition her ideas were at first entirely fixed upon one subject—the death of her only brother, which had occurred some years previously. To this brother she had been very strongly attached ; she had nursed him in his last illness ; and it was perhaps the return of the anniversary of his death, about the time when the somnambulism first occurred, that gave to her thoughts that particular direction. She talked constantly of him, retraced all the circumstances of his illness, and was unconscious of anything that was said to her which had not reference to this subject. . . . Although her eyes were open, she recognised no one in this state,—not even her own sister, who, it should be mentioned, had not been at home at the time of her brother's last illness.' (It will presently appear, however, that she was able to recognise those who were about her during these attacks, since she retained ill-feeling against one of them ; moreover, the sentences which immediately follow suggest that the sense of sight was not dormant.) 'It happened on one occasion, that when she passed into this condition, her sister, who was present, was wearing a locket containing some of their deceased brother's hair. As soon as she perceived this locket she made a violent snatch at it, and would not be satisfied until she had got it into her possession, when she began to talk to it in the most endearing and even extravagant terms. Her feelings were so strongly excited on this subject, that it was deemed prudent to check them ; and as she was inaccessible to all entreaties for the relinquishment of the locket, force was employed to obtain it from her. She was so determined, however, not to give it up, and was so angry at the gentle violence used, that it was found necessary to abandon the attempt, and having become calmer after a time, she passed off into ordinary sleep. Before going to sleep, however, she placed the locket under her pillow, remarking, " Now I have hid it safely, and they shall not take it from me." On awaking in the morning she had not the slightest consciousness of what had passed ; but the impression of the excited feelings still remained, for she remarked to her sister, ' I cannot tell what it is that makes me feel so, but every time that S. comes near me I have a kind of shuddering sensation ;' the individual named being a servant, whose constant attention to her had given rise to a feeling of strong attachment on the side of the invalid, but who had been the chief actor in the scene of the previous evening. This feeling wore off in the course of a day or two. A few days afterwards the somnambulism again returned ; and the patient being upon her bed at the time, immediately began to search for the locket under her pillow.' As it had been removed in the interval, ' she was unable to find it, at which she expressed great disappointment, and continued searching for it, with the remark, " It *must* be there—I put it there myself a few minutes ago, and no one can have taken it away." In this state the presence of S. renewed her previous feelings of anger ; and it was only by sending S. out of the room that she could be calmed and induced to sleep. The patient was the subject of many subsequent attacks, in every one of which the anger against S. revived, until the current of thought changed, no longer running exclusively upon what related to her brother, but becoming capable of direction by *suggestions* of various kinds presented to her mind, either in conversation, or, more directly, through the several organs of sense.'

I have been particular in quoting the above account, because it appears to me to illustrate well, not only the relation between the phenomena of dual consciousness and somnambulism, but the dependence of either class of phenomena on the physical condition. If it should appear that dual consciousness is invariably associated with some disorder either of the nervous system or of the circulation, it would be impossible, or at least very difficult, to maintain Brown-Sequard's explanation of the boy's case. For one can hardly imagine it possible that a disorder of the sort should be localised so far as the brain is concerned, while in other respects affecting the body generally. It so chances that the remarkable case recently dealt with by French men of science forms a sort of connecting link between the boy's case and the case just cited. It closely resembles the former in certain characteristic features, while it resembles the latter in the evidence which it affords of the influence of the physical condition on the phenomena of double consciousness. The original narrative by M. Azam is exceedingly prolix ; but it has been skilfully condensed by Mr. H. J. Slack, in the pages of a quarterly journal of science. I follow his version in the main.

The subject of the disorder, Felida X., was born in Bordeaux in 1843. Until the age of thirteen she differed in no respect from other girls. But about that time symptoms of hysterical disorder presented themselves, and although she was free from lung-disease, she was troubled with frequent spitting of blood. After this had continued ab ut a year, she for the first time manifested the phenomena of double consciousness. Sharp pains attacked both temples, and in a few moments she became unconscious. This lasted ten minutes, after which she opened her eyes, and entered into what M. Azam calls her second state, in which she remained for an hour or two, after which the pains and unconsciousness came on again, and she retuined to her ordinary condition. At intervals of about five or six days, such attacks were repeated ; and her relations noticed that her character and conduct during her abnormal state were changed. Finding also that in her usual conditi n she remembered nothing which had passed when she was in the other state, they thought she was becoming idiotic ; and preser.tly called in M. Azam, who was connected with a lunatic asylum. Fortunately, he was not so enthusiastic a student of mental aberration as to recognise a case for the lunatic asylum in every instance of phenomenal mental action. He found Felida intelligent, but melancholy, morose, and taciturn, very indu-trious, and with a strong will. She was very anxious about her bodily health. At this time the mental charges occurred more frequently than before. Nearly every day, as she sat with her work on her knees, a violent pain shot suddenly through her temples, her head dropped upon her breast, her arms fell by her side, and she passed into a sort of sleep, from which neither noises, pinches, nor pricks could awaken her. This condition lasted now only two or three minutes. 'She woke up in quite another state, smiling gaily. speaking briskly, and trilling (*fredonnant*) over her work, which she recommenced at the point where she left it. She would get up, walk actively, and scarcely complained of any of the pains she had suffered from so severely a few minutes before. She busied herself about the house, paid calls, and behaved like a healthy young girl of her age. In this state she remembered perfectly all that had happened in her two conditions.' (In this respect her case is distinct from both the former, and is quite exceptional. In fact, the inclusion of the consciousness of both conditions during the continuance of one condition only, renders her case not, strictly speaking, one of double consciousness, the two conditions not being perfectly distinct from each other.) 'In this second life, as in the other, her moral and intellectual faculties, though different, were incontestably sound. After a time (which in 1858 lasted three or four hours), her gaiety disappeared, the torpor suddenly ensued, and in two or three minutes she opened her eyes and re-entered her ordinary life, resuming any work she was engaged in just where she left off. In this state she bemoaned her condition, and was quite unconscious of what had passed in the previous state. If asked to continue a ballad she had been singing, she knew nothing about it, and if she had received a visitor, she believed she had seen no one. The forgetfulness extended to everything which happened during her second state, and not to any ideas or information acquired before her illness.' Thus her early life was held in remembrance during both her conditions, her consciousness in these two conditions being in this respect single ; in her second or less usual condition she remembered also all the events of her life, including what had passed since these seizures began ; and it was only in her more usual condition that a portion of her life was lost to her—that, namely, which had passed during her second condition. In 1858 a new phenomenon was noticed as occasionally occurring—she would sometimes wake from her second condition in a fit of terror, recognising no one but her husband. The terror did not last long, however ; and during sixteen years of her married life, her husband only noticed this terror on thirty occasions.

A painful circumstance preceding her marriage somewhat

forcibly exhibited the distinction between her two states of consciousness. Rigid in morality during her usual condition, she was shocked by the insults of a brutal neighbour, who told her of a confession made to M. Azam during her second condition, and accused her of shamming innocence. The attack—unfortunately, but too well founded as far as facts were concerned—brought on violent convulsions, which required medical attendance during two or three hours. It is important to notice the difference thus indicated between the character of the personalities corresponding to her two conditions. 'Her moral faculties,' says M. Azam, 'were incontestably sound in her second life, though different,'—by which, be it understood, he means simply that her sense of right and wrong was just during her second condition, not, of course, that her conduct was irreproachable. She was in this condition, as in the other, altogether responsible for her actions. But her power of self-control, or rather perhaps the relative power of her will as compared with tendencies to wrong-doing, was manifestly weaker during her second condition. In fact, in one condition she was oppressed and saddened by pain and anxiety, whereas in the other she was almost free from pain, gay, light-hearted, and hopeful. Now I cannot altogether agree with Mr. Slack's remark, that if, during her second state, 'she had committed a robbery or an assassination, no moral responsibility could have been assumed to rest upon her with any certainty, by any one acquainted with her history,' for her moral faculties in her second condition being incontestably sound, she was clearly responsible for her actions while in that condition. But certainly, the question of punishment for such an offence would be not a little complicated by her twofold personality. To the woman in her ordinary condition, remembering nothing of the crime committed (on the supposition we are dealing with), in her abnormal condition, punishment for that crime would certainly seem unjust, seeing that her liability to enter into that condition had not in any degree depended on her own will. The drunkard who, waking in the morning with no recollection of the events of the past night, finds himself in gaol for some crime committed during that time, although he may think the punishment he has to endure severe measure for a crime of which in his ordinary condition he is incapable, knows at least that he is responsible for placing himself under that influence which made the crime possible. Supposing even he had not had sufficient experience of his own character when under the influence of liquor, to have reason to fear he might be guilty of the offence, he yet perceives that to make intoxication under any circumstances an excuse for crime would be most dangerous to the community, and that he suffers punishment justly. But the case of dual consciousness is altogether different, and certainly where responsibility exists under both conditions, while yet impulse and the restraining power of will are differently related in one and the other condition, the problem of satisfying justice is a most perplexing one. Here are in effect two different persons residing in one body, and it is impossible to punish one without punishing the other also. Supposing justice waited until the abnormal condition was resumed, then the offender would probably recognise the justice of punishment ; but if the effects of the punishment continued until the usual condition returned, a person would suffer who was conscious of no crime. If the offence were murder, and if capital punishment were inflicted, the ordinary individuality, innocent entirely of murder, would be extinguished along with the first, a manifest injustice. As Huxley says of a similar case, ' the problem of responsibility is here as complicated as that of the prince-bishop, who swore as a prince and not as a bishop. 'But, your highness, if the prince is damned, what will become of the bishop ? ' said the peasant.'[1]

---

[1] Should any doubt whether these conditions of dual existence are a reality (a doubt, however, which the next case dealt with in the text should remove), we would remind them that a similar difficulty unmistakably existed in the case of Eng and Chang, the Siamese twins. It would have been almost impossible to inflict any punishment on one

It does not appear to me that there is in the case of Felida X. any valid reason for regarding the theory of two brains as the only available explanation. It is a noteworthy circumstance, that the pains preceding each change of condition affected both sides of the head. Some modification of the circulation seems suggested as the true explanation of the changes in condition, though the precise nature of such modification, or how it may have been brought about, would probably be very difficult to determine. The state of health, however, on which the attacks depended seems to have affected the whole body of the patient, and the case presents no features suggesting any lateral localisation of the cerebral changes.

On the other hand, the case of Sergeant F. (a few of the circumstances of which were mentioned in my essay entitled ' Have we two Brains ? '), seems to correspond with Dr. Holland's theory, though that theory is far from explaining all the circumstances. The man was wounded by a bullet which fractured his *left* parietal bone, and his *right* arm and leg were almost immediately paralysed. When he recovered consciousness three weeks later, the *right* side of the body was completely paralysed, and remained so for a year. These circumstances indicate that the cause of the mischief still existing lay in the shock which the left side of the brain received when the man was wounded. The right side may have learned (as it were) to exercise the functions formerly belonging to the left side, and thus the paralysis affecting the right side until this had happened may have passed away. These points are discussed in the essay above named, however, and need not here detain us. Others which were not then dealt with may now be noted with advantage. We would specially note some which render it doubtful whether in the abnormal condition the man's brain acts at all, whether in fact his condition, so far as consciousness was concerned, is not similar to that of a frog deprived of its

by which the other would not have suffered, and capital punishment inflicted on one would have involved the death of the other.

biain in a certain well-known experiment. (This appears to be the opinion to which Professor Huxley inclines, though, with proper scientific caution, he seems disposed to suspend his judgment.) The facts are very singular, whatever the explanation may be.

In the normal condition, the man is what he was before he was wounded—an intelligent, kindly fellow, performing satisfactorily the duties of a hospital attendant. The abnormal state is ushered in by pains in the forehead, as if caused by the constriction of a band of iron. In this state the eyes are open and the pupils dilated. (The reader will remember Charles Reade's description of David Dodd's eyes, 'like those of a seal.') The eyeballs work incessantly, and the jaws maintain a chewing motion. If the man is *en pays de connaissance*, he walks about as usual; but in a new place, or if obstacles are set in his way, he stumbles, feels about with his hands, and so finds his way. He offers no resistance to any forces which may act upon him, and shows no signs of pain if pins are thrust into his body by kindly experimenters. No noise affects him. He eats and drinks apparently without tasting or smelling his food, accepting assafœtida or vinegar as readily as the finest claret. He is sensible to light only under certain conditions. But the sense of touch is strangely exalted (in all respects apparently except as to sensations of pain or pleasure), taking in fact the place of all the other senses. I say the sense of touch, but it is not clear whether there is any real sensation at all. The man appears in the abnormal condition to be a mere machine. This is strikingly exemplified in the following case, which I translate directly from Dr. Mesnet's account:—'He was walking in the garden under a group of trees, and his stick, which he had dropped a few minutes before, was placed in his hands. He feels it, moves his hand several times along the bent handle of the stick, becomes watchful, seems to listen, suddenly he calls out, "Henry!" then, "There they are! there are at least a score of them! join us two, we shall manage it." And then putting his hand behind his back as if to take a cart-ridge, he goes through the movement of loading his weapon, lays himself flat on the grass, his head concealed by a tree, in the posture of a sharpshooter, and with shouldered weapon follows all the movements of the enemy whom he fancies he sees at a short distance.' This, however, is an assumption: the man cannot in this state *fancy* he sees, unless he has at least a recollection of the sensation of sight, and this would imply cerebral activity. Huxley, more cautious, says justly that the question arises 'whether the series of actions constituting this singular pantomime was accompanied by the ordinary states of consciousness or not? Did the man dream that he was skirmishing? or was he in the condition of one of Vaucanson's automata—a mechanism worked by molecular changes in his nervous system? The analogy of the frog shows that the latter assumption is perfectly justifiable.'

The pantomimic actions just related corresponded to what probably happened a few moments before the man was wounded ; but this human automaton (so to call him, without theorising as to his actual condition) goes through other performances. He has a good voice, and was at one time a singer in a *café*. 'In one of his abnormal states he was observed to begin humming a tune. He then went to his room, dressed himself carefully, and took up some parts of a periodical novel which lay on his bed, as if he were trying to find something. Dr. Mesnet, suspecting that he was seeking his music, made up one of these into a roll and put it into his hand. He appeared satisfied, took up his cane and went downstairs to the door. Here Dr. Mesnet, turned him round, and he walked quite contentedly in the opposite direction, towards the room of the *concierge*. The light of the sun shining through a window now happened to fall upon him, and seemed to suggest the footlights of the stage on which he was accustomed to make his appearance. He stopped, opened his roll of imaginary music, put himself into the attitude of a singer, and sung, with perfect execution, three songs, one after the other. After which he wiped his face with his handkerchief and drank, without a grimace, a tumbler of strong vinegar and water which was put into his hand.'

But the most remarkable part of the whole story is that which follows. 'Sitting at a table in one of his abnormal states, Sergeant F. took up a pen, felt for paper and ink, and began to write a letter to his general. in which he recommended himself for a medal on account of his good conduct and courage.' (Rather a strange thing, by the way, for a mere automaton to do.) 'It occurred to Dr. Mesnet to ascertain experimentally how far vision was concerned in this act of writing. He therefore interposed a screen between the man's eyes and his hands ; under these circumstances, F. went on writing for a short time, but the words became illegible, and he finally stopped, without manifesting. any discontent. On the withdrawal of the screen, he began to write again where he had left off. The substitution of water for ink in the inkstand had a similar result. He stopped, looked at his pen, wiped it on his coat, dipped it in the water, and began again with a similar result. On another occasion, he began to write upon the topmost of ten superimposed sheets of paper. After he had written a line or two, this sheet was suddenly drawn away. There was a slight expression of surprise, but he continued his letter on the second sheet exactly as if it had b en the first. This operation was repeated five times, so that the fifth sheet contained nothing but the writer's signature at the bottom of the page. Nevertheless, when the signature was finished, his eyes turned to the top of the blank sheet, and he went through the form of reading what he had written— a movement of the lips accompanying each word ; moreover, with his pen, he put in such corrections as were needed, in that part of the blank page which corresponded with the position of the words which required correction in the sheets which had been taken away. If the five sheets had been transparent, therefore, they would, when superposed, have formed a properly written and corrected letter. Immediately after he had written his letter, F. got up, walked down to the garden, made himself a cigarette, lighted and smoked it. He was about to prepare another, but sought in vain for his tobacco-pouch, which had been purposely taken away. The pouch was now thrust before his eyes and put under his nose, but he neither saw nor smelt it ; when, however, it was placed in his hand, he at once seized it, made a fresh cigarette, and ignited a match to light the latter. The match was blown out, and another lighted match placed close before his eyes, but he made no attempt to take it ; and if his cigarette was lighted for him, he made no attempt to smoke. All this time his eyes were vacant, and neither winked nor exhibited any contraction of the pupil.'

These and other similar experiments are explained by Dr. Mesnet (and Professor Huxley appears to agree with him) by the theory that F. 'sees some things and not others ; that the sense of sight is accessible to all things which are brought into relation with him by the sense of touch, and, on the contrary, insensible to all things which lie outside this relation.' It seems to me that the evidence scarcely supports this conclusion. In every case where F. appears to see, it is quite possible that in reality he is guided entirely by the sense of touch. All the circumstances accord much better with this explanation than with the theory that the sense of sight was in any way affected. Thus the sunlight shining through the window must have affected the sense of touch, and in a manner similar to what F. had experienced when before the foot-lights of the stage, where he was accustomed to appear as a singer. 'In this respect there was a much closer resemblance between the effect of sunlight and that of the light from footlights, than in the circumstances under which both sources of light affect the sense of sight. For in one case the light came from above, in the other from below ; the heat would in neither case be sensibly localised. Again, when a screen was interposed

T

between his eyes and the paper on which he was writing, he probably became conscious of its presence in the same way that a blind man is conscious of the presence of objects near him, even (in some cases) of objects quite remote, by some subtle effects discernible by the sense of touch excited to abnormal relative activity in the absence of impressions derived from the sense of sight. It is true that one might have expected him to continue writing legibly, notwithstanding the interposed screen; but the consciousness of the existence of what in his normal condition would effectually have prevented his writing legibly, would be sufficient to explain his failure. If, while in full possession of all our senses, the expectation of failure quite commonly causes failure, how much more likely would this be to happen to a man in F.'s unfortunate abnormal condition. The sense of touch again would suffice to indicate the presence of water instead of ink in his pen when he was writing. I question whether the difference might not be recognised by any person of sensitive touch after a little practice; but certainly a blind man, whose sense of touch was abnormally developed, would recognise the difference, as we know from experiments which have indicated even greater delicacy of perception than would be required for this purpose. The experiment with superposed sheets of paper is more remarkable than any of the others, but certainly does not suggest that light makes any impression upon Sergeant F. It proves, in fact, so far as any experiment could prove such a point, that the sense of touch alone regulates the man's movements. Unconscious of any change (because, after the momentary surprise produced by the withdrawal of the paper, he still found he had paper to write on), he continued writing. He certainly did not in this case, as Dr. Mesnet suggests, see all things which are brought into relation with him by the sense of touch; for if he had, he would not have continued to write when he found the words already written no longer discernible.

On the whole, it appears reasonable to conclude, as Professor Huxley does, that though F. may be conscious in his abnormal state, he may also be a mere automaton for the time being. The only circumstance which seems to oppose itself very markedly to the latter view is the letter-writing. Everything else that this man did was what he had already done prior to the accident. If it could be shown that the letters written in his abnormal state were transcripts, not merely *verbatim et literatim*, but exact in every point, of some which he had written before he was wounded, then a strong case would be made out for the automaton theory. Certainly, few instances have come under the experience of scientific men where a human being has so closely resembled a mere machine as this man appears to do in his abnormal condition.

The moral nature of F. in his abnormal condition is for this reason a matter of less interest than it would be, did he show more of the semblance of conscious humanity. Still it is worthy of notice, that, whereas in his normal condition he is a perfectly honest man, in his abnormal state 'he is an inveterate thief, stealing and hiding away whatever he can lay hands on with much dexterity, and with an absolutely absurd indifference as to whether the property is his own or not.'

It will be observed that the cases of dual consciousness thus far considered, though alike in some respects, present characteristic divergences. In that of the boy at Norwood, the two characters were very similar, so far as can be judged, and each life was distinct from the other. The next case was only introduced to illustrate the resemblance in certain respects between the phenomena of somnambulism and those of double or rather alternating consciousness. The woman Felida X. changed markedly in character when she passed from one state to the other. Her case was also distinguished from that of the boy by the circumstance that in one state she was conscious of what had passed in the other, but while in this other state was unconscious of what had passed in the former. Lastly, in Sergeant F.'s case we have to deal with the effect of an injury to the brain, and find a much greater difference between the two conditions than in the other cases. Not only does the man change in character, but it may justly be said that he is little more than an animal, even if he can be regarded as more than a mere automaton while in the abnormal condition. We find that a similar variety characterises other stories of double consciousness. Not only are no two cases closely alike, but no case has been noted which has not been distinguished by some very marked feature from all others.

Thus, although in certain respects the case we have next to consider resembles very significantly the case of Sergeant F., it also has a special significance of its own, and may help us to interpret the general problem presented to us by the phenomena of dual consciousness. I abridge, and in some respects simplify, the account given by Dr. Carpenter in his interesting treatise on *Mental Physiology.* Comments of my own are distinguished from the abridged narrative by being placed within brackets :—

A young woman of robust constitution had narrowly escaped drowning. She was insensible for six hours, and continued unwell after being restored to animation. Ten days later she was seized with a fit of complete stupor, which lasted four hours ; when she opened her eyes she seemed to recognise no one, and appeared to be utterly deprived of the senses of hearing, taste, and smell, as well as of the power of speech. Sight and touch remained, but though movements were excited and controlled by these senses, they seemed to arouse no ideas in her mind. In fact, her mental faculties seemed entirely suspended. Her vision at short distances was quick, and the least touch startled her ; but unless she was touched or an object were placed where she could not help seeing it, she took no notice of what was passing around her. [It does not appear to me certain that at this stage of her illness she *saw* in the ordinary sense of the word ; the sense of touch may alone have been affected, as it certainly is affected to some degree by any object so placed that *it could not but be seen by a short-sighted person.* But it is clear that later the sense of sight was restored, supposing, which is not perhaps probable, that it was ever lost in the early stage.] She did not even know her own mother, who attended constantly upon her. Wherever she was placed she remained. Her appetite was good, but [like F.] she ate indifferently whatever she was fed with, and took nauseous medicines as readily as agreeable food. Her movements were solely of the automatic kind. Thus, she swallowed food put into her mouth, but made no effort to feed herself. Yet when her mother had conveyed the spoon [in the patient's hand] a few times to her mouth, the patient continued the operation. It was necessary, however, to repeat this lesson every time she was fed, showing the complete absence of memory. ' The very limited nature of her faculties, and the automatic life she was leading, appear further evident from the following particulars. One of her first acts on recovering from the fit had been to busy herself in picking the bedclothes ; and as soon as she was able to sit up and be dressed, she continued the habit by incessantly picking some portion of her dress. She seemed to want an occupation for her fingers, and accordingly part of an old straw bonnet was given to her, which she pulled into pieces with great minuteness ; she was afterwards bountifully supplied with roses : she picked off the leaves, and then tore them up into the smallest particles imaginable. A few days subsequently, she began forming upon the table, out of those minute particles, rude figures of roses, and other common garden flowers ; she had never received any instructions in drawing. Roses not being so plentiful in London, waste paper and a pair of scissors were put into her hand, and for some days she found an occupation in cutting the paper into shreds ; after a time these cuttings assumed rude shapes and figures, and more particularly the shapes used in patchwork. At length she was supplied with proper materials for patchwork, and after some initiatory instruction, she took to her needle and to this employment in good earnest. She now laboured incessantly at patchwork from morning till night, and on Sundays and week-days, for she knew no difference of days ; nor could she be made to comprehend the difference. She had no remembrance from day to day of what she had been doing on the previous day, and so every morning commenced *de novo.* Whatever she began, that she continued to work at while daylight lasted ; manifesting no uneasiness for anything to eat or drink, taking not the slightest heed of anything which was going on around her, but intent only on her patchwork.' From this time she began to improve, learning like a child to register ideas. She presently learned worsted-work, and showed delight in the harmony of colours and considerable taste in selecting between good and bad patterns. After a while she began to devise patterns of her own. But she still had no memory from day to day of what she had done, and unless the unfinished work of one day was set before her on the next, she would begin something new.

And now, for the first time, ideas derived from her life before her illness seemed to be awakened within her. When pictures of flowers, trees, and animals were shown her, she was pleased ; but when she was shown a landscape in which there was a river or a troubled sea, she became violently agitated, and a fit of spasmodic rigidity and insensibility immediately followed. The mere sight of water in motion made her shudder. Again, from an early stage of her illness she had derived pleasure from the proximity of a young man to whom she had been attached. At a time when she did not remember from one hour to another what she was doing, she would anxiously await his evening visit, and be fretful if he failed to pay it. When, during her removal to the country, she lost sight of him, she became unhappy and suffered from frequent fits ; on the other hand, when he remained constantly near her, she improved in health, and early associations were gradually awakened.

At length a day came when she uttered her first words in this her second life. She had learned to take heed of objects and persons around her ; and on one occasion, seeing her mother excessively agitated, she became excited herself, and suddenly, yet hesitatingly, exclaimed, 'What's the matter?' After this she began to articulate a few words. For a time she called every object and person 'this,' then gave their right names to wild flowers (of which she had been passionately fond when a child), and this 'at a time when she exhibited not the least recollection of the "old familiar friends and places" of her childhood.' The gradual expansion of her intellect was manifested chiefly at this time in signs of emotional excitement, frequently followed by attacks of spasmodic rigidity and insensibility.

It was through the emotions that the patient was restored to the consciousness of her former self. She became aware that her lover was paying attention to another woman, and the emotion of jealousy was so strongly excited, that she had a fit of insensibility which resembled her first attack in duration and severity. But it restored her to herself. 'When the insensibility passed off, she was no longer spell-bound. The veil of oblivion was withdrawn ; and, as if awakening from a sleep of twelve months' duration, she found herself surrounded by her grandfather, grandmother, and their familiar friends and acquaintances. She awoke in the possession of her natural faculties and former knowledge; but without the slightest remembrance of anything which had taken place in the year's interval, from the invasion of the first fit to the [then] present time. She spoke, but she heard not ; she was still deaf, but being able to read and write as formerly, she was no longer cut off from communication with others. From this time she rapidly improved, but for some time continued deaf. She soon perfectly understood by the motion of her lips what her mother said ; they conversed with facility and quickness together, but she did not understand the language of the lips of a stranger. She was completely unaware of the change

in her lover's affections which had taken place in her state
of second consciousness ; and a painful explanation was
necessary. This, however, she bore very well ; and she
has since recovered her previous bodily and mental health.

There is little in this interesting narrative to suggest that
the duality of consciousness in this case was in any way
dependent on the duality of the brain. During the patient's
abnormal condition, the functions of the brain [proper]
would seem to have been for a time in complete abeyance,
and then to have been gradually restored. One can perceive
no reason for supposing that the shock she had sustained
would affect one side rather than the other side of the brain,
nor why her recovery should restore one side to activity and
cause the side which (on the dual brain hypothesis) had
been active during her second condition to resume its
original activity. The phenomena appear to suggest that in
some way the molecular arrangement of the brain matter
became modified during her second condition ; and that
when the original arrangement was restored all recognisable
traces of impressions received while the abnormal arrangement lasted were obliterated. As Mr. Slack presents one
form of this idea, 'the grey matter of the brain may have its
molecules arranged in patterns somewhat analogous to those
of steel filings under the influence of a magnet, but in some
way the direction of the forces—or vibrations—may be
changed in them. The pattern will then be different.' We
know certainly that thought and sensation depend on
material processes,—chemical reactions between the blood
and the muscular tissues. Without the free circulation of
blood in the brain, there can be neither clear thought nor
ready sensation. With changes in the nature of the circulation come changes in the quality of thought and the nature
of sensation, and with them the emotions are changed also.
Such changes affect all of us to some degree. It may well
be that such cases as we have been dealing with are simply
instances of the exaggerated operation of causes with which
we are all familiar ; and it may also be that in the exaggera-

tion itself of these causes of change lies the explanation of the characteristic peculiarity of cases of dual consciousness,— the circumstances, namely, that either the two states of consciousness are absolutely distinct one from the other, or that in one state only are events remembered which happened in the other, no recollection whatever remaining in this latter state of what happened in the other, or, lastly, that only faint impressions excited by some intense emotion experienced in one state remain in the other state.

It seems possible, also, that some cases of another kind may find their explanation in this direction, as, for instance, cases in which, through some strange sympathy, the brain of one person so responds to the thoughts of another that for the time being the personality of the person thus influenced may be regarded as in effect changed into that of the person producing the influence. Thus, in one singular case cited by Dr. Carpenter, a lady was 'metamorphosed into the worthy clergyman on whose ministry she attended, and with whom she was personally intimate. I shall never forget,' he says, 'the intensity of the lackadai-ical tone in which she replied to the matrimonial counsels of the physician to whom he (she) had been led to give a long detail of his (her) hypochondriacal symptoms : "A wife for a dying man, doctor." No *intentional* simulation could have approached the exactness of the imitation alike in tone, manners, and language, which spontaneously proceeded from the idea with which the fair subject was possessed, that she herself experienced all the discomforts whose detail she had doubtless frequently heard from the real sufferer.' The same lady, at Dr. Carpenter's request, mentally 'ascended in a balloon and proceded to the North Pole in search of Sir John Franklin, whom she found alive , and her description of his appearance and that of his companions was given with an inimitable expression of sorrow and pity.'

It appears to us that very great interest attaches to the researches made by Prof. Barrett into cases of this kind, and that it is in this direction we are to look for the explanation of many mysterious phenomena formerly regarded as supernatural, but probably all admitting (at least all that have been properly authenticated) of being interpreted so soon as the circumstances on which consciousness depends shall have been determined. Thus the following account of experiments made at the village school in Westmeath seem especially suggestive : 'Selecting some of the village children, and placing them in a quiet room, giving each some small object to look at steadily, he found one amongst the number who readily passed into a state of reverie. In that state the subject could be made to believe the most extravagant statements, such as that the table was a mountain, a chair a pony, a mark on the floor, an insuperable obstacle. The girl thus mesmerised passed on the second occasion into a state of deeper sleep or trance, wherein no sensation whatever was experienced, unless accompanied by pressure on the eyebrows of the subject. When the pressure of the fingers was removed, the girl fell back in her chair utterly unconscious of all around, and had lost all control over her voluntary muscles. On reapplying the pressure, though her eyes remained closed, she sat up and answered questions readily, but the manner in which she answered them, her acts and expressions, were capable of wonderful diversity, by merely altering the place on the head where the pressure was applied. So sudden and marked were the changes produced by a movement of the fingers, that the operation seemed very like playing on some musical instrument. On a third occasion the subject, after passing through these, which have been termed the biological and phrenological states, became at length keenly and wonderfully sensitive to the voice and acts of the operator. It was impossible for the latter to call the girl by her name, however faintly and inaudibly to those around, without at once eliciting a prompt response. If the operator tasted, smelt, or touched anything, or experienced any sudden sensation of warmth or cold, a corresponding effect was produced on

the subject, though nothing was said, nor could the subject
have seen what had occurred to the operator. To be
assured of this he bandaged the girl's eyes with great care,
and the operator having gone behind the girl to the other
end of the room, he watched him and the girl, and repeatedly assured himself of this fact.' Thus far, Professor
Barrett's observations, depending in part on what the
operator experienced, may be open to just so much doubt
as may affect our opinion of the veracity of a person unknown ; but in what follows we have his own experience
alone to consider. 'Having mesmerised the girl himself,
he took a card at random from a pack which was in a
drawer in another room. Glancing at the card to see what
it was, he placed it within a book, and in that state brought
it to the girl. Giving her the closed book, he asked her to
tell him what he had put within its leaves. She held the book
close to the side of her head, and said, 'I see something
inside with red spots on it ; and she afterwards said there
were five red spots on it. The card was the five of
diamonds. The same result occurred with another card ;
and when an Irish bank-note was substituted for the card,
she said, 'Oh, now I see a number of heads—so many that
I cannot count them.' He found that she sometimes failed
to guess correctly, asserting that the things were dim ; and she
could give no information of what was within the book unless he had previously known what it was himself. More
remarkable still, he asked her to go in imagination to
Regent Street, in London, and tell him what shops she had
seen. The girl had never been out of her remote village,
but she correctly described to him Mr. Ladd's shop, of
which he happened to be thinking, and mentioned the large
cloc: that overhangs the entrance to Beak Street. In many
other cases he convinced himself that the existence of a
distinct idea in his own mind gave rise to an image of the
idea (that is, to a corresponding image) on the mind of the
subject ; not always a clear image, but one that could not
fail to be recognised as a more or less distorted reflection of

his own thought.' It is important to notice the limit which a scientific observer thus recognised in the range of the subjects' perception. It has been stated that subjects in this condition have been able to describe occurrences not known to any person, which yet have been subsequently verified. Although some narratives of the kind have come from persons not likely to relate what they *knew* to be untrue, the possibility of error outweighs the probability that such narratives can really be true. There is a form of unconscious cerebration by which untruthful narratives come to be concocted in the mind. For instance, Dr. Carpenter heard a scrupulously conscientious lady asseverate that a table 'rapped' when nobody was within a yard of it; but the story was disproved by the lady herself, who found from her note-book, recording what really took p'ace, that the hands of six persons rested on the table when it rapped. And apart from the unconscious fiction-producing power of the mind, there is always the possibility, nay, often the extreme probability, that the facts of a case may be misunderstood. Persons may be supposed to know nothing about an event who have been conscious of its every detail; nay, a person may himself be unconscious of his having known, and in fact of his really knowing, of a particular event. Dual consciousness in this particular sense is a quite common experience, as, for instance, when a story is told us which we receive at first as new, until gradually the recollection dawns upon us and becomes momentarily clearer and clearer, not only that we have heard it before, but of the circumstances under which we heard it, and even of details which the narrator from whom a few moments before we receive it as a new story has omitted to mention.[1]

[1] An instance of the sort turns up in Pope's correspondence with Addison, and serves to explain a discrepancy between Tickell's edition of the *Spectator* and the original. In No. 253, Addison had remarked that none of the critics had taken notice of a peculiarity in the description of Sisyphus lifting his stone up the hill, which is no sooner carried to the top of it but it immediately tumbles to the bottom.

The most important of all the questions depending on dual consciousness is one into which I could not properly enter at any length in these pages—the question, namely, of the relation between the condition of the brain and responsibility, whether such responsibility be considered with reference to human laws or to a higher and all-knowing tribunal. But there are some points not wanting in interest which may be here more properly considered.

In the first place it is to be noticed that a person who has passed into a state of abnormal consciousness, or who is in the habit of doing so, can have no knowledge of the fact in his normal condition except from the information of others. The boy at Norwood might be told of what he had said and done while in his less usual condition, but so far as any experience of his own was concerned, he might during all that time have been in a profound sleep. Similarly of all the other cases. So that we have here the singular circumstance to consider, that a person may have to depend on the information of others respecting his own behaviour— not during sleep or mental aberration or ordinary absence of mind—but (in some cases at least) while in possession of all his faculties and unquestionably responsible for his actions. Not only might a person find himself thus held responsible for actions of which he had no knowledge, and perhaps undeservedly blamed or condemned, but he might find himself regarded as untruthful because of his perfectly

---

'This double motion,' says Addison, 'is admirably described in the numbers of those verses. In the four first it is heaved up by several spondees intermixed with proper breathing places, and at last trundles down in a continual line of dactyls.' On this Pope remarks : 'I happened to find the same in Dionysius of Halicarnassus's Treatise, who treats very largely upon these verses. I know you will think fit to soften your expression, when you see the passage, which you must needs have read, though it be since slipt out of your memory.' These words, by the way, were the last (except 'I am, with the utmost esteem, &c.') ever addressed by Pope to Addison. It was in this letter that Pope with sly malice asked Addison to look over the first two books of his (Pope's) translation of Homer.

honest denial of all knowledge of the conduct attributed to him. If such cases were common, again, it would not improbably happen that the simulation of dual consciousness would become a frequent means of attempting to evade responsibility.

Another curious point to be noticed is this. Supposing one subject to alternations of consciousness were told that in his abnormal condition he suffered intense pain or mental anguish in consequence of particular actions during his normal state, how far would he be influenced to refrain from such actions by the fear of causing pain or sorrow to his 'double,' a being of whose pains and sorrows, nay, of whose very existence, he was unconscious? In ordinary life a man refrains from particular actions which have been followed by unpleasant consequences, reasoning, in some cases, ' I will not do so-and-so, because I suffered on such and such occasions when I did so' (we set religious considerations entirely on one side by assuming that the particular actions are not contrary to any moral law), in others, ' I will not do so-and-so because my so doing on former occasions has caused trouble to my friend A or B :' but it is strange to imagine any one reasoning, ' I will not do so-and-so because my so doing on former occasions has caused my second self to experience pain and anguish, of which I myself have not the slightest recollection.' A man may care for his own well-being, or be unwilling to bring trouble on his friends, but who is that second self that his troubles should excite the sympathy of his fellow-consciousness? The considerations here touched on are not so entirely beyond ordinary experience as might be supposed. It may happen to any man to have occasion to enter into an apparently unconscious condition during which in reality severe pains may be suffered by another self, though on his return to his ordinary condition no recollection of those pains may remain, and though to all appearance he has been all the time in a state of absolute stupor ; and it may be a reasonable question, not perhaps whether he or his double shall suffer such pains, but whether the body which both inhabit will suffer while he is unconscious, or while that other consciousness comes into existence. That this is no imaginary supposition is shown by several cases in Abercrombie's treatise on the 'Intellectual Powers.' Take, for instance, the following narrative :—'A boy,' he tells us, 'at the age of four suffered fracture of the skull, for which he underwent the operation of the trepan He was at the time in a state of perfect stupor, and after his recovery retained no recollection either of the accident or of the operation. At the age of fifteen, however, during the delirium of fever, he gave his mother an account of the operation, and the persons who were present at it, with a correct description of their dress, and other minute particulars. He had never been observed to allude to it before ; and no means were known by which he could have acquired the circumstances which he mentioned.' Suppose one day a person in the delirium of fever or under some other exciting cause should describe the tortures experienced during some operation, when, under the influence of anæsthetics, he had appeared to all around to be totally unconscious, dwelling in a special manner perhaps on the horror of pains accompanied by utter powerlessness to shriek or groan, or even to move ; how far would the possibilities suggested by such a narrative influence one who had a painful operation to undergo, knowing as he would quite certainly, that whatever pains his *alter ego* might have to suffer, not the slightest recollection of them would remain in his ordinary condition?

There is indeed almost as strange a mystery in unconsciousness as there is in the phenomena of dual consciousness. The man who has passed for a time into unconsciousness through a blow, or fall, or fit, cannot help asking himself like Bernard Langdon in that weird tale, Elsie Venner, 'Where was the mind, the soul, the thinking principle all that time?' It is irresistibly borne in upon him that he has been dead for a time. As Holmes reasons, 'a man is stunned by a blow and becomes unconscious,

another gets a harder blow and it kills him. Does he
become unconscious too? If so, *when*, and *how does he
come to his consciousness?* The man who has had a slight
and moderate blow comes to himself when the immediate
shock passes off and the organs begin to work again, or
when a bit of the skull is "pried" up, if that happens to be
broken. Suppose the blow is hard enough to spoil the
brain and stop the play of the organs, what happens then?'
So far as physical science is concerned, there is no answer to
this question ; but physical science does not as yet comprehend all the knowable, and the knowable comprehends not
all that has been, is, and will be. What we know and can
know is nothing, the unknown and the unknowable are alike
infinite.

ELECTRIC LIGHTING.

ALTHOUGH we certainly have no reason to complain of the infrequency of attempts in newspapers, &c., as well as in scientific journals, to explain the principles on which electric lighting depends, it does not seem that very clear ideas are entertained on this subject by unscientific persons. Nor is this, perhaps, to be wondered at, when we observe that in nearly all the explanations which have appeared, technical expressions are quite freely used, while those matters about which the general reader especially desires information are passed over as points with which every one is familiar. Now, without going quite so far as to say that there is no exaggeration in the picture presented some time back in *Punch*, of one who asked whether the electric fluid was 'anything like beer, for instance,' I may confidently assert that the very vaguest notions are entertained by nine-tenths of those who hear about the electric light, respecting the nature of electricity. Of course, I am not here referring to the doubts and difficulties of electricians on this subject. It is well known that Faraday, after a life of research into electrical phenomena, said that when he had studied electricity for a few years he thought he understood much, but when he had nearly finished his observational work he found he knew nothing. In the sense in which Faraday spoke, the most advanced students of science must admit that they know nothing about electricity. But the greater number of those who read about the electric light are not familiar even with electrical phenomena, as distinguished. from the inter-

U

pietation of such phenomena. I am satisfied that there is no exaggeration in a passage which appeared recently in the 'Table Talk' of the *Gentleman's Magazine*, describing an account of the electric light as obtained from some new kind of gas, carried in pipes from central reservoirs, and chiefly differing from common gas in this, that the heat resulting from its consumption melted ordinary burners, so that only burners of carbon or platinum could be safely employed.

I do not propose here to discuss, or even to describe (in the proper sense of the word) the various methods of electric lighting which have been either used or suggested. What I wish to do is to give a simple explanation of the general principles on which illumination by electricity depends, and to consider the advantages which this method of illumination appears to promise or possess.

Novel as the idea of using electricity for illuminating large spaces may appear to many, we have all of us been long familiar with the fact that electricity is capable of replacing the darkness of night by the light of broad day over areas far larger than those which our electricians hope to illuminate. The lightning flash makes in an instant every object visible on the darkest night, not only in the open air, but in the interior of carefully darkened rooms. Nay, even if the shutters of a room are carefully closed and the room strongly illuminated, the lightning flash can yet be clearly recognised. And it must be remembered that though the suddenness of the flash makes us the more readily perceive it (under such circumstances, for instance), yet its short duration diminishes its apparent intensity. This may appear a contradiction in terms, but is not so in reality. The perception that there has been a sudden lighting up of the sky or of a room, is distinct from the recognition of the actual intensity of the illumination thus momentarily produced. Now it is quite certain that the eye cannot assign less than a twenty-fifth of a second or so to the duration of the lightning flash, for, as Newton long since showed, the retina retains the sensation of light for at least this interval after the light has disappeared. It is equally certain, from Wheatstone's experiments, that the lightning flash does not actually endure for the 100,000th part of a second. Adopting this last number, though it falls far short of the truth—the actual duration being probably less than 1,000,000th of a second— we see that so far as the eye is concerned, an amount of light which was really emitted during the 100,000th part of a second is by the eye judged to have been emitted during an interval 4,000 times as long. It is certain, then, that the eye's estimate of the intensity of the illumination resulting from a lightning flash is far short of the truth. This is equally true even in those cases where lightning is said to be for awhile continuous. If the flashes for a time succeed each other at less intervals than a twenty-fifth of a second, the illumination will appear continuous. But it is not really so. To be so, the flashes should succeed each other at the rate of at least 100,000, and probably of more than 1,000,000 per second.

While the lightning flash shows the brilliancy which the electric illumination can attain, it shows also the intense heat resulting from the electric discharge. This might, indeed, be inferred simply from the brilliancy of the light, since we know that this brilliancy can only be due to the intense heat to which the particles along the track of the electric flash have been raised. But it is shown in a more convincing manner to ordinary apprehension by the effects which the lightning flash produces where—in the common way of speaking—it strikes. The least fusible substances are melted. Effects are produced also which, though at first not seemingly attributable to intense heat, yet in reality can be no otherwise explained. Thus, when the trunk of a tree is torn into fragments by the lightning stroke, though the tree is scorched and blackened, a small amount of heat would account for that particular effect, while the destruction of the tree seems attributable to mechanical causes. It is, indeed, from effects such as these that the idea of the any error arise from the use of the ordinary method of expression, so long as we carefully hold in remembrance that it is only employed for convenience, and must not be regarded as scientifically precise.

Electricity may be excited, as I have said, in many ways. With the ordinary electrical machine it is excited by the friction of a glass disc or cylinder against suitable rubbers of leather and silk. The galvanic battery developes electricity by the chemical action of acid solutions on metal plates. We may speak of the electricity generated by a machine as frictional electricity, and of that generated by a galvanic battery as voltaic electricity ; in reality, however, these are not different kinds of electricity, but one and the same property developed in different ways. The same also is the case with magnetic electricity, of which I shall presently have much to say : it is electricity produced by means of magnets, but is in no respect different from frictional or voltaic electricity. Of course, however, it will be understood that for special purposes one method of producing electricity may be more advantageously used than another. Just as heat produced by burning coal is more convenient for a number of purposes than heat produced by burning wood, though there is no scientific distinction between coal-produced heat and wood-produced heat, so for some purposes voltaic electricity is more convenient than frictional electricity, though there is no real distinction between them.

Every one knows that when by means of an ordinary electrical machine electricity has been generated in sufficient quantity and under suitable conditions to prevent its dispersion, a spark of intense brilliancy and greater or less length, according to the amount of electricity thus collected, can be obtained when some body, not similarly electrified, is brought near to what is called the conductor of the machine. The old-fashioned explanation, still repeated in many of our books, ran somewhat as follows :—'The positive electricity of the conductor decomposes the neutral or mixed fluid of the body, attracting the negative fluid and repelling the positive. When the tension of the opposite electricities is great enough to overcome the resistance of the air, they re-combine, the spark resulting from the heat generated in the process of their combination.' This explanation is all very well ; but it assumes much that is in reality by no means certain, or even likely. All we *know* is, that whereas before the spark is seen the electrical conditions of the conductor and the object presented to it were different, they are no longer different after the flashing forth of the spark. It is as though a certain line (straight, crooked, or branched) in the air had formed a channel of communication by which electricity had passed, either from the conductor to the object or from the object to the conductor,— or *possibly* in both directions, two different kinds of electricity existing (before the flash) in the conductor and the object, as the old-fashioned explanation assumes.[1] Again, we know that the passage of electricity along the air-track, supposing there really is such a passage, but in any case the observed change in the relative electrical conditions of the conductor and the object, is accompanied by the generation

---

[1] It is supposed by many, that when the spark is long enough we can note the direction in which it travels ; and observations of the motion of lightning from the earth to the cloud have been collected, as showing that the usually observed direction of the flash is sometimes reversed. In reality, no one has ever seen a lightning flash travel either one way or the other. If the attention is fixed on the storm cloud, as usual when a lightning storm is watched, every flash appears to pass from the cloud to the earth. If, on the contrary, at the moment when the attention is fixed on some terrestrial object the lightning flashes near that particular object, the flash will seem to pass from the object to the cloud. In either case the motion is apparent only. If there is motion at all, the passage of the electric spark occupies less than the 100,000th part of a second, and of course it is utterly impossible that any eye could tell at which end of its track the flash first appeared. In every case the flash seems to travel from the end to which attention was more nearly directed. The apparent motion corresponds to the chance direction of the eye.

of an intense heat along the aërial track where the spark is seen.

In the case of electricity generated by means of a galvanic battery, we do not note the same phenomena unless the battery is a strong one. We have in such a battery a steady source of electricity, but unless the battery is powerful, the electricity is of low intensity, and not competent to produce the most striking phenomena of frictional electricity. For instance, voltaic electricity, as used in telegraphic communication, is far weaker than that obtained from even a small electrical machine. What is called the positive extremity of the battery neither gives a spark, nor attracts light bodies. The same is true of the other, or negative extremity. The difference of the condition of these extremities can only be ascertained by delicate tests— the deflections of the needle, in fact, by which telegraphic communications are made, may in reality be regarded as the indications of a very delicate electroscope.

But when the strength of a galvanic battery is sufficiently great, or, in other words, when the total amount of chemical action brought into play to generate electricity is sufficient, we obtain voltaic electricity not only surpassing in intensity what can be obtained from electrical machines, but capable of producing spark after spark in a succession so exceedingly rapid that the light is to all intents and purposes continuous.

Without considering the details of the construction of a galvanic battery, which would occupy more space than can here be spared, and even with fullest explanation would scarcely be intelligible (except to those already familiar with the subject), unless illustrations unsuited to these pages were employed, let us consider what we have in the case of every powerful galvanic battery, on whatever system arranged. We have a series of simple batteries, each consisting of two plates of different metal placed in dilute acid. Whereas, in the case of a simple battery, however, the two different metals are connected together by wires to let the electric current pass (the current ceasing to pass when the wires are disconnected), in a compound battery, in which (let us say) the metals are zinc and copper, the zinc of one battery is connected with the copper of the next, the zinc of this with the copper of another, and so on, the wire *to* the copper of the first battery and the wire *from* the zinc of the last battery being free, and forming what are called the poles of the compound battery — the former the positive pole, the later the negative pole.[1] When these free wires are connected, the current of electricity passes, when they are disconnected the current ceases to pass, unless the break between them is such only that the electricity can, as it were, force its way across the gap. When the wires are connected, so that the current flows, it is as though there were a channel for some fluid which flowed readily and easily along the channel. When the circuit is absolutely broken, it is as though such a cha nel were dammed completely across. If, however, while the poles are not connected by copper wires or by other freely conducting substances, yet the gap is such as the electricity can pass over, the case may be compared to the partial interruption of a channel at some spot where, though the fluid which passes freely along the channel is not able to move so freely, it can yet force its way along, with much disturbance and resistance. Just as at such a part of the course of a liquid stream—say, a river—we find, instead of the quiet flow observed elsewhere, a great noise and tumult, so, where the current of electricity is not able to pass readily we perceive evidence of resistance in the generation of much heat and light (if the resistance is great enough).

It will be observed that I have spoken in the preceding paragraph of the passage of a current along the wire connecting the two poles of a powerful electric battery, or along

---

[1] The extremity of the wire connected with the metal least affected by the acid solution is called the positive pole, that of the wire connected with the metal most affected by the solution is called the negative pole.

any substance connecting those poles which possesses the property of being what is called a good conductor of electricity. But the reader is not to assume that there is such a current, or that it is known to flow either from the positive to the negative pole, or from negative to positive pole ; or, again, that, as some have suggested, there are two currents which flow simultaneously in opposite directions. We speak conventionally of the current, and for convenience we speak as though some fluid really made its way (when the circuit is complete) from the positive to the negative pole of the compound battery. But the existence of such a current, or of any current at all, is purely hypothetical. I should be disposed, for my own part, to believe that the motion is of the nature of wave-motion, with no actual transference of matter, at least when the circuit is complete. According to this view, where resistance takes place we might conceive that the waves are converted into rollers or breakers, according to the nature of the resistance – actual transference of matter taking place through the action of these changed waves, just as waves which have traversed the free surface of ocean without carrying onward whatever matter may be floating on the surface, cast such matter ashore when, by the resistance of the shoaling bottom or of rocks, they become converted either into rollers or into breakers.

I may also notice, with regard to good conductors and bad conductors of electricity, that they may be compared to substances respectively transparent and opaque for light-waves, or again, to substances which allow heat to pass freely or the reverse. Just as light-waves fail to illuminate a transparent body, and heat-waves fail to warm a body which allows them free passage, so electricity-waves (if electricity really is undulatory, as I imagine) fail to affect any substance along which they travel freely. But as light-waves illuminate an opaque substance, and heat-waves raise the temperature of a substance which impedes their progress, so waves of electricity, when their course is impeded, produce effects which are indicated to us by the resulting heat and light.

A powerful galvanic battery is capable of producing light of intense brilliancy. For this purpose, instead of taking sparks between the two metallic poles, each of these is connected with. a piece of carbon (which is nearly as good a conductor as the metal), and the sparks are taken between these two pieces of carbon, usually set so that the one connected with the negative pole is virtually above the one connected with the positive pole, and at a distance of a tenth of an inch from each other or more, according to the strength of the battery. Across this gap between the carbons an arc of light is seen, which in reality results from a series of electric sparks following each other in rapid succession. This arc, called the voltaic arc, is brilliant, but it is not from this arc that the chief part of the light comes. The ends of the carbon become intensely bright, being raised to a white heat. Both the positive and negative carbons are fiercely heated, but the positive is heated most. As (ordinarily) both carbons are thus heated in the open air, combustion necessarily takes place, though it is to be noticed that the lustre of the carbons is not due to combustion, and would remain undiminished if combustion were prevented. The carbons are thus gradually consumed, the positive nearly twice as fast as the negative. If they are left untouched, this process of combustion soon increases the distance between them till it exceeds that which the electricity can pass over. Then the light disappears, the current ceasing to flow. But by bringing the carbon points near to each other (they must, indeed, be made to touch for an instant), the current is made to flow again, and the light is restored.

The following remarks by M. H. Fontaine (translated by Dr. Higgs) may help to explain the nature of the voltaic arc : —' In truth, the voltaic arc is a portion of the electric circuit possessing the properties of all other parts of the same circuit. The molecules swept away from point to point (that is, from one carbon end to the other) ' constitute between these points a mobile chain, more or less conductive, and more or less heated, according to the intensity of the current and the nature and separation of the electrodes' (that is, the quality and distance apart of the carbon or other substances between which the arc is formed). 'These things happen exactly as if the electrodes were united by a metallic wire or carbon rod of small section' (so as to make the resistance to the current great), 'which is but saying that the light produced by the voltaic arc and that obtained by incandescence arise from the same cause—that is, the heating of a resisting substance interposed in the circuit.'

The intensity of the light from the voltaic arc and the carbon points varies with circumstances, but depends chiefly on the amount of electricity generated by the battery. A fair idea of its brilliancy, as compared with all other lights, will be gained from the following statements :—If we represent the brightness of the sun at noon on a clear day as 1,000, the brightness of lime glowing under the intense heat of the oxy-hydrogen flame is about 7 ; that of the electric light obtained with a battery of 46 elements (Bunsen's), 235. With a battery of 80 elements the brightness is only 238. (These results were obtained in experiments by Fizeau and Foucault.) The intensity does not therefore increase much with the number of the component elements after a certain number is passed. But it increases greatly with the surface, for the experimenters found that with a battery of 46 elements, each composed of 3, with their zinc and copper respectively united to form one element of triple surface, the brightness became 385, or more than one-third of the midday brightness of the sun (that is, the apparent intrinsic lustre of his disc's surface), and 55 times the brightness of the oxy-hydrogen lime-light.

Another way of obtaining an intense heat and light from the electric current generated by a strong battery is to introduce into the electric circuit a substance of small conducting power, and capable of sustaining an intense heat without disintegration, combustion, or melting. Platinum has been used for this purpose.   If the conductive power of copper be represented by 100, that of platinum will be represented by 18 only.   Thus the resistance experienced by a current in passing through platinum is relatively so great, that if the current is strong the platinum becomes intensely heated, and shines with a brilliant light.   A difficulty arises in using this light practically, from the circumstance that when the strength of the current reaches a certain point, the platinum melts, and, the circuit being thus broken, the light immediately goes out.

The use of galvanic batteries to generate an electric current strong enough for the production of a brilliant light, is open to several objections, especially on the score of expense.   It may, indeed, be safely said that if no other way of obtaining currents of sufficient intensity had ever been devised, the electric light would scarcely have been thought of for purposes of general illumination, however useful in special cases.   (In the electric lighting of the New Opera House at Paris, batteries are used.)   The discovery by Orsted that an electric current can make iron magnetic, and the series of discoveries by Faraday, in which the relation between magnetism and electricity was explained, made electric lighting practically possible.   One of these shows that if a properly insulated wire coil is rapidly rotated in front of a fixed permanent magnet (or of a set of such magnets), currents will be induced in the coil, which may be made to produce either alternating currents or currents in one direction only, in wire conductors.   An instrument for generating electric currents in this way, by rapidly rotating a coil in front of a series of powerful permanent magnets fixed symmetrically around it, is called a magneto-electric machine. Another method, now generally preferred, depends on the rotation of a coil in front of an electro-magnet ; that is, of a bar of soft iron (bent in horseshoe form), which can be rendered magnetic by the passage of an electric current through a coil surrounding it.   The rapid rotation of the coil in front of the soft iron generates a weak current, because iron always has some traces of magnetism in it, especially if it has once been magnetised. This weak current being caused to traverse the coil surrounding the soft iron increases its magnetism, so that somewhat stronger currents are produced in the revolving coiL These carried round the soft iron still further increase its magnetism, and so still further strengthen the current. In this way coil and magnet act and react on each other, until from the small effects due to the initial slight magnetism of the iron, both coil and the magnet become, so to speak, saturated. Machines constructed on this principle are called dynamo-electric machines, because the generation of electricity depends on the dynamical force employed in rapidly rotating the coils.

We need not consider here the various forms which magneto-electric and dynamo-electric machines have received. It is sufficient that the reader should recognise how we obtain an electric current of great intensity in one case from mechanical action and permanent magnetism,[1] and in the other from mechanical action and the mere residue of magnetism always present in iron.

In the cases here considered it is in reality the sudden presentation of the coil (twice at each rotation) before the positive and negative poles of the magnet, which induces a momentary but intense current of electricity. The rotation being exceedingly rapid, these currents succeed each other with sufficient rapidity to be appreciably continuous. A similar principle is involved in the use of what is called the inductive coil, except that in this case the sudden beginning and ceasing of a current in one coil (and not magnetic action) induces a momentary but strong current: matters are so arranged that the current induced by the starting of the inducing current, immediately causes this to cease; while the current induced by the cessation of the inducing current immediately causes this current to begin again : so that by a self-acting process we have a constant series of in-

---

[1] So called, though in reality the best magnets gradually lose force.

tense induced currents, succeeding each other with great rapidity, so as to be practically continuous, as with those produced by magneto-electric and dynamo-electric machines.

All that I have said about the voltaic arc, the incandescence resulting from resistance to the current's flow, and so forth, in relation to electricity generated by galvanic batteries, applies to electricity generated by induction coils, or by magneto-electric and by dynamo-electric machines. Only it is to be noticed that in some of these machines the currents alternate in direction with each revolution of the swiftly turning coil, in others the currents are always in the same direction, and in yet others the currents may be made to alternate or not, as may be most convenient.

We have now to consider how light suitable for purposes of illumination may be obtained from the electric current. Hitherto we have considered only light such as might be used for special purposes, where a bright and very intense light was required, where expense and complexity of construction might not be open to special objections, and where in general the absolute steadiness of the light was not an essential point. But those who have seen the electric light used even by the most experienced manipulators for the illustration of lectures will know that the light as so obtained, though of intense brilliancy, is altogether unsuited for purposes of ordinary illumination.

If we consider a few of the methods which have been devised for overcoming the difficulties inherent in the problem of electric lighting, the reader will recognise at once the nature of these difficulties, and the probability of their being effectually overcome in the future, for though much has been done, much yet remains to be done in mastering them.

Let us consider first the Jablochkoff candle, the invention of which brought about, in July 1877, the first great fall in the value of gas property.

The Jablochkoff candle consists of two carbons placed side by side (instead of one above the other in a vertical line). Thus placed, with a slight interval between them, the carbon rods would allow the passage of the electric current at the place of nearest approach, and therefore of least resistance to its passage. A variable and imperfect illumination would result. M. Jablochkoff, however, interposes between the separate carbon rods a slip of plaster of Paris, which is a non-conducting material. The upper points of the carbon rods are thus the only parts at which the current can cross. They are connected by a little bridge of carbon, which is necessary for the starting of the light—just as in the case of the ordinary electric light, the two carbons must, in order to start the light, be brought into contact. When the current flows, the small bridge of carbon connecting the two points is presently consumed, but the arc between the points is still maintained: for the plaster becomes vitrified by the intense heat of the two carbon points on each side, and melts down as the carbons are consumed. If the light is in any way put out, however, a small piece of carbon must be set again, to form a bridge between the carbon points. Throughout the burning of the Jablochkoff candle the fused portion of the insulating layer forms a conducting bridge between the carbon points ; and hence there is a considerable loss of electric force (probably about thirty per cent.), which in the ordinary arrangement would increase the intensity of the light. The great advantage of the candle consists in the circumstance that throughout its consumption the carbon ends are at a constant distance from each other without any mechanical or other arrangement being necessary to maintain them in due position.

One point should be noticed here. In the ordinary arrangement of carbon points, the positive carbon, as we have already said, is much more intensely heated, and consumes twice as fast as the negative carbon. Now, if one carbon of the Jablochkoff candle were connected with the positive, and the other with the negative pole of the battery or of a machine, the former side would consume twice as fast as the latter, and the two points would no longer remain at the same horizontal level, which is essential to the proper burning of the Jablochkoff candle. By using a machine which produces alternating currents, M. Jablochkoff obviates this difficulty, the carbons being alternately positive and negative (in extremely rapid succession), and therefore consuming at the same rate.

The Jablochkoff candle lasts only about an hour and a half. But four, six, or more candles may be used in the same globe or lantern, and automatic arrangements adopted to cause a fresh candle to be ignited at the moment when its predecessor is burnt out.

In Paris and elsewhere (as in Holborn, for instance), each Jablochkoff lamp is enclosed in an opal glass globe. Mr. Hepworth remarks on this, that in his opinion the use of the opal globe is a mistake, as it shuts off quite 50 per cent. of the light without any corresponding advantage, except the correction of the glare. ' This wasteful disadvantage will no doubt be remedied in the future,' he says, by the use of some less dense medium. ' Mr. Shoolbred states that from a series of careful photometric experiments carried out by the municipal authorities with the Jablochkoff lights, each naked light is found to possess a maximum intensity of 300 candles. With the opal globe this was reduced to 180 candles, showing a loss of 40 per cent., while during the darker periods through which the light passed the light was as low as 90 candles. It may be mentioned here that Mr. Van der Weyde, who has long used the electric light for photographic purposes, has given much attention to the important problem of rendering the electric light available as an illuminator without wasting it, and yet without throwing the rays directly upon the object to be illuminated. The rays are intercepted by an opal disc about four inches in diameter, and the whole body of the rays is gathered up by a concave reflector (lined with a white material), and thrown out in a flood of pure white light, in which the most delicate shades of tint are discernible. He can use any form of electric candle in this way. Only it should be noticed, before the employment of his method is advocated for street illumination, that there is a difference between the problems which the photographer and the street-lighter have to solve. The Jablochkoff candle, for instance, must be screened on all sides, and even above, when used to illuminate the streets. If its direct light is allowed to escape in any direction, there will be a mischievous and unsightly beam, and from every point along the path of the beam, the intensely bright light of the candle will be directly visible. Again : it is essential that whatever substance is used to screen the light should be dense enough to cause the whole globe to seem uniformly bright or nearly so. The only modification which seems available (when these essential points have been secured) is that the tint of the globe should be such as to correct any colour which the light may be found to have in injurious excess. We may, however, remark that the objection which has been often raised against the colour of the electric light can hardly be just—the injury to the eyes in certain cases arising probably from the strong contrast between the light and the background on which it is projected. For, as to colour, the electric light derived either from the glowing carbon or from incandescent metal is appreciably the same as sunlight.

The Rapieff burner, employed in the 'Times' office, consists of four carbon pencils, arranged thus $\stackrel{\vee}{\wedge}$ (except that the two v's are not in the same plane, but in planes at right angles to each other). The spark crosses the space between the points of the v's, and arrangements are made for keeping the two points at the right distance from each other, and also for keeping the ends of the two pencils which form each point in their proper position. If the current is from any cause interrupted, an automatic arrangement is adopted to allow the current to pass to the other lamps in the same circuit. There are six lamps in circuit at the 'Times' office ; and M. Rapieff has exhibited as many as ten. The advantages claimed for this light are the following :—' First, its production by any description of dynamo-electric machine with either alternating or continuous currents ; secondly, great diversibility and complete independence of the several lights, and long duration without change of carbons ; and lastly, the extreme facility with which any ordinary workman or servant can renew the carbons when necessary, without extinguishing the lights.'   The last-named advantage results, it need hardly perhaps be said, from the use of two carbons to form each point.   One can be removed, the other remaining to keep the voltaic arc intact until a new carbon has been substituted for its fellow ; then it in turn can be replaced by a new carbon, the new carbon already inserted keeping the voltaic arc intact.

The six lamps at the ' Times ' office thoroughly illuminate the room, and give light for working the eight Walter presses used in printing the paper.   The light has been thus used since the middle of last October, and it is said that other rooms in the building are shortly to be illuminated in the same manner.   ' Each lamp is enclosed in an opal globe of about four inches in diameter, and so little heat is given off, that the hand can be placed on the globe without inconvenience, even after the light has been burning for some time.'

In the Wallace lamp there are two horizontal plates of carbon, about nine inches in diameter, instead of mere carbon points.   When the current is passing, these carbon plates are separated by a suitable small distance which remains unchanged.   The electric arc, being started at the point along the edge of the carbons where there is least resistance to the passage of the current, gradually passes along the edge of the carbons as combustion goes on, changing the position of the place of nearest approach and consequently of least resistance.   The light will thus burn for many hours (even for a hundred with large carbon plates), and any number of lights up to ten can be worked from the machine.   The objection to the Wallace lamp is, that the light does not remain at one point, but travels along the whole extent of the carbons.   It will not be easy to design a glass shade which will be suitable for a light thus changing in position.

The Werdermann regulator is on an entirely new plan ; but it has not yet been submitted to the test of practical working outside the laboratory. The positive carbon, which is lowest, ends in a sharp point, which strangely enough retains its figure, while the carbon burns away at the rate of about two inches per hour. The negative carbon is a block having its under side, against which the positive carbon presses, slightly convex. The positive carbon is pressed steadily against the negative by the action of a weight. The increased resistance to the passage of the current, at the sharp point of the positive carbon, generates sufficient heat to produce a powerful light. The light resembles a steadily radiant star, but 'with all its softness and purity of tint, it is so intense, that adjacent gas-flames are thrown on the wall as transparent shadows.' The light will last for fifteen hours without attention, the positive carbon rod being used in lengths of three feet. The carbon block hardly undergoes any change. When the lamp has been burning a long time, a slight depression can be seen at the place where the positive carbon touches it, but by shifting the carbon in its holder this is easily remedied. Mr. Werdermann lately exhibited a row of ten small lamps burning side by side at the same time. 'The two wires from the machine,' says Mr. Hepworth, 'were carried one on either side of this row of lamps, branch wires being led from them for the service of each lamp. Mr. Werdermann says that his perfected lamps will be furnished with keys, by which the current can be turned on or off, as in the case of gas. We may say in fact, that in the nature of its connections and various arrangements, it ("the Werdermann lamp") most nearly comes up in convenience to the use of gas.'

We do not yet know certainly what arrangement Mr. Edison employs to obtain the light of which so much has been heard. It is asserted that his light is obtained from the incandescence of an alloy of iridium and platinum,

which will bear without fusion a heat [1] of 5,000 degrees
Fahrenheit It would be unsafe, however, to assume that
this account is trustworthy, or to infer (as we might in the
case of almost any other inventor), that such being the
nature of his plan, it could lead to no result of practical
value. As has been well remarked by a contemporary
writer, whatever Edison's invention may be, 'it is certain to
be something to command respect, even if it does not quite
come up to the glowing accounts which have reached us in
advance.'

The following passage from one of these accounts, which
appeared in the 'New York Herald,' will be read with interest,
and may be accepted as trustworthy so far as it goes.'
'The writer last night saw the invention in operation in
Mr. Edison's laboratory. The inventor was deep in experimental researches. What he called the apparatus consisted of a small metal stand placed on the table. Surrounding the light was a small glass globe. Near by was
a gas jet burning low. The Professor looked up from his

---

[1] My occasional use of the word 'heat' where in scientific writing
'temperature' would be the word used, has exposed me to peevish, not
to say petulant comments from Professor P. G. Tait, who has denounced
half the mathematical world for using the word 'force,' in the sense
in which Newton used it, and has spoken of an eminent physicist as
one deserving universal execration and opprobrium for not explaining,
when speaking of work done against gravity, that terrestrial gravity
was meant, and not gravity on the sun, or Jupiter, or Mars, or anywhere
in the heavens above or in the earth beneath, but only at the earth's
surface. Where there is no risk of confusion, the word 'heat' may
be used either to signify temperature, as when in ordinary speech and
writing we talk of blood-heat, fever-heat, summer-heat, and so forth.
Science, indeed, very properly forbids the use of the word in any sense
save one. But outside the pages of scientific treatises, there is no
inaccuracy in using a word in a sense popularly attributed to it, when
no mistake can possibly arise. No one can suppose, when I speak
of a heat of so many degrees Fahrenheit or Centigrade, that I mean
anything but such and such a degree of heat, any more than if I
spoke of the intense heat of that *savant entêté*, Professor P. G. Tait, any
one would imagine that I referred to his calorific condition.

work, to greet the reporter, and in reply to a request to view the invention, waved his hand towards the light, with the exclamation, "There she is!" The illumination was such as would come from a brilliant gas jet surrounded with ground glass, only that the light was clearer and more brilliant. "Now I extinguish it and light the gas, and you can see the difference," said Mr. Edison, and he touched the spring. Instantly all was darkness. Then he turned on the gas. The difference was quite perceptible. The light from the gas appeared in comparison tinted with yellow. In a moment, however, the eye · had become accustomed to it, and the yellowish tint disappeared. Then the Professor turned on the electric light, giving the writer the opportunity of seeing both, side by side. The electric light seemed much softer ; a continuous view of it for three minutes did not pain the eye ; whereas looking at the gas for the same length of time caused some little pain and confusion of sight. One of the noticeable features of the light, when fully turned on, was that all the colours could be distinguished as readily as by sunlight. "When do you expect to have the invention completed, Mr. Edison ? " asked the reporter. "The substance of it is all right now," he answered, putting the apparatus away and turning on the gas. "But there are the usual little details that must be attended to before it goes to the people. For instance, we have got to devise some arrangement for registering a sort of meter, and again, there are several different forms that we are experimenting on now, in order to select the best." "Are the lights to be all of the same degree of brilliancy ? " asked the reporter. "All the same ! " "Have you come across any serious difficulties in it as yet ? " "Well, no," replied the inventor, "and that's what worries me, for in the telephone I found about a thousand ;[1] and so in the

[1] The comments made by one of Mr. Edison's assistants on this point are interesting and instructive. 'Mr. Batchelor, the Professor's assistant, who here joined in the conversation,' proceeds the report of the *Herald,* 'said, "Many a time Mr. Edison sat down almost on the

quadruplex. I worked on both over two years before I overcame them." '

Other methods, as the Sawyer-Man system, and the Brush system, need not at present detain us, as little is certainly known respecting them. In the former it is said that the light is obtained from an incandescent carbon pencil, within a space containing nitrogen and no oxygen, so that there is no combustion. In the latter the carbon points are placed as in the ordinary electric lamp, but are so suspended in the clasp of a regulator, that they burn 14 inches of carbon without adjustment, the carbons lasting eight hours, and producing a flood of intense white light, estimated as equivalent to 3,000 candles.

I have little space to consider the cost of electric lighting, even if the question were one which could be suitably dealt with in these pages. Opinions are very much divided as to the relative cost of lighting by gas and by electricity ; but the balance of opinion seem to be in favour of the belief that in America and France certainly, and probably in this country, where gas is cheap, electric lighting will on the whole be as cheap as lighting by gas. It should be noticed, in making a comparison between this country and others in which coal is dearer, that the cheapness of coal here, though favourable in the main to gas illumination, is also favourable, though in less degree (relatively) to electric lighting. Machines for generating electricity can be worked

point of giving up the telephone as a lost job ; but at the last moment, he would see light." "Of all things that we have discovered, this is about the simplest," continued Mr. Edison, "and the public will say so when it is explained. We have got it pretty well advanced now, but there are some few improvements I have in my mind. You see, it has got to be so fixed that it cannot get out of order. Suppose when one light only is employed it got out of order once a year, where two were used it would get out of order twice a year, and where a thousand were used you can see there would be much trouble in looking after them. Therefore, when the light leaves the laboratory, I want it to be in such a shape that it cannot get out of order at all, except of course by some accident." '

more cheaply here than in America. Nay, it has even been found advantageous in some cases to use a gas engine to generate electricity. Thus Mr. Van der Weyde used an Otto gas engine driven at the cost of 6*d.* an hour for gas, to produce the light which he exhibited publicly on the night of November 9. So that the cheapness of gas may make the electric light cheaper. Then it is to be remembered that important though the question of cost is, it is far from being all-important. The advantages of electric lighting for many purposes, as in public libraries, in cases where many persons work together under conditions rendering the vitiation of the air by gas lighting exceedingly mischievous, and in cases where the recognition of delicate differences of tint or texture is essential, must far more than compensate for some slight difference in cost. The possibility (shown by actual experience to be real) of employing natural sources of power to drive machines for generating electricity, is another interesting element of the subject, but could not be properly dealt with save in greater space than this here available.

www.ingramcontent.com/pod-product-compliance
Lightning Source LLC
Chambersburg PA
CBHW031028120726
47905CB00007B/2090